AMANDA LESTER

AND THE PURPLE RAINBOW PUZZLE

Also by Paula Berinstein

Amanda Lester and the Pink Sugar Conspiracy

Amanda Lester and the Orange Crystal Crisis

Amanda Lester and the Purple Rainbow Puzzle

PAULA BERINSTEIN

The Writing Show
P.O. Box 2970
Agoura Hills, CA 91376-2970

www.amandalester.net
www.writingshow.com

ISBN: 978-1942361-02-2 (softcover)
ISBN-10: 1942361025 (softcover)
ISBN: 978-1-942361-03-9 (ebook)
ISBN-10: 1942361033 (ebook)

Cover design: Anna Mogileva
Text set in Garamond Premier Pro
Printed in the United States of America

For Cole, Ella, Alex, Kennedy, Keenan, Alyssa, and Auguste

TABLE OF CONTENTS

Acknowledgements   i

Chapter 1	A Plethora of Problems	1
Chapter 2	In Search of Blixus	20
Chapter 3	Jackie Lumpenstein and His Annotated Meat Cookbook	39
Chapter 4	Manny Companion	49
Chapter 5	All Together Again	56
Chapter 6	The Key to the Key	66
Chapter 7	A Big Blowup	75
Chapter 8	Bickering	82
Chapter 9	Simon Binkle, Ladies' Man	89
Chapter 10	Blixus's Trail Goes Cold	95
Chapter 11	Crocodile's Flat	102
Chapter 12	Saving the World	114
Chapter 13	To Bee or Not to Bee	124
Chapter 14	Leprechauns	134
Chapter 15	Enter Inspector Lestrade	142
Chapter 16	Amphora's Hidden Talent	148
Chapter 17	Gordon, I Could Kiss You	155
Chapter 18	Penrith	165
Chapter 19	Through the Sarcophagus	178
Chapter 20	In the Tunnels	189
Chapter 21	Angry Bees	195
Chapter 22	Gordon Bramble to the Rescue	204

Chapter 23	The Lockbox	211
Chapter 24	All Eyes on David Wiffle	217
Chapter 25	Stinky Locks	222
Chapter 26	A Third Way	230
Chapter 27	Revolting Parents	242
Chapter 28	The Silver Coin	248
Chapter 29	At the Zoo	256
Chapter 30	There's Something About Mavis	264
Chapter 31	Chasing Rainbows	274
Chapter 32	Holmes vs. Hacker, Round One	280
Chapter 33	Metadata in Danger	287
Chapter 34	Breaking Up Is Hard to Do	297
Chapter 35	Now You Tell Me	304
Chapter 36	Back to the Tunnels	311
Chapter 37	Like a Myth Come True	321
Chapter 38	Prisoners!	328
Chapter 39	So That's How He Got the Coins	337
Chapter 40	Holmes vs. Moriarty	343
Chapter 41	Insight	354
Chapter 42	Unhappy Endings	366
Discussion Questions for Your Reading Group		381
Q and A with Author Paula Berinstein		383
About the Author		386

ACKNOWLEDGEMENTS

There are two kinds of series. Both involve recurring characters, but in one case the episodes are more or less self-contained. Amanda Lester, Detective, is the other sort: the story is ongoing, and each installment owes much to those that have preceded it.

Finding test readers for any book past the first can be tough. Sure, you can ask people who haven't read the others, but even though each title should stand on its own, you can miss continuity errors. That's why you have to ask much of your beta readers: you want them to stick with you from book to book so they'll spot those problems.

That is why I am so grateful to the people who made it through to this third Amanda Lester book: Alex Hetzler, Alyssa Spillar, Keenan Spillar, and Barbara Wong, as well as my husband, Alan Chaney. You guys are the best!

My cover designer, Anna Mogileva, continues to produce amazing work. She spoils me. I don't know what I'd do without her.

And of course, there's Alan. I honestly don't think I could do any of this without his love and support. Thank you, sweetie, for everything!

1
A PLETHORA OF PROBLEMS

Who would have thought a little twerp like David Wiffle could bring an entire detective school to its knees? After all, he was just a little prig with the maturity level of a toddler. Which, come to think of it, was exactly why he'd been able to mess everything up. Toddlers have way too much power, with their "No, this" and "No that," thought his classmate Amanda Lester. But at least they don't normally have access to priceless artifacts. Unfortunately David did, and he had destroyed it. *The Detective's Bible!* On purpose. The fact that he was crazy with grief at the time only partly excused him, or at least that was how Amanda saw the situation.

So it was no wonder that when his mother, Celerie, descended on Headmaster Thrillkill's office screaming her head off, Amanda, who just happened to be there, found it hard to be sympathetic. Yes, her son was missing, and yes, Amanda's friend Editta Sweetgum was also missing, and—oh no! Here came *her* mother too, waving her arms and screaming even louder than Mrs. Wiffle. The noise coming out of her mouth was even more jarring than the earthquake repair work in the hall, and those guys seemed to be competing for the title of Loudest Hammer Man Ever.

"I demand an investigation at *once*," Mrs. Wiffle spat before she'd even made it through the door. *Bang!*

"I said it first," yelled Mrs. Sweetgum, practically stepping on the other parent's well-shod heel. *Bang, bang, clang!* "After all, Editta went missing before David did."

Despite her loyalty to the headmaster, Amanda had to admit that this sounded juicy. She wondered if he would kick her out of his office and she'd miss all the excitement. Parent-teacher conferences were supposed to be private. But the headmaster did nothing, which in itself was rather strange. Normally he was so strict. Still, considering all the terrible things that had been going on lately, she could see how he might be distracted.

"How dare you involve my son in such a sordid business," said Mrs. Wiffle, who could have been a model if she'd been taller. Her pale red hair was exactly the same shade as her son's, her eyes the same cornflower blue, and she had a look that screamed "designer." She was rail thin, which might have explained why she was wearing a sweater in summer. Amanda thought it odd that she'd say such a thing considering that detective work involved sordid business by definition. Surely David's mother knew that. Her own husband, David's father, Wink, a private detective descended from Sir Bailiwick Wiffle, had been killed because of it. *Clang, clatter.*

"How dare you lose my daughter," said Mrs. Sweetgum, which made more sense, since Editta had shocked everyone by purposely running off with the notorious criminals Blixus, Mavis, and Nick Moriarty a couple of weeks before. Of course the teachers and the local police had scoured the area, but they hadn't found a trace of her or the Moriartys.

"I want that librarian fired," said Mrs. Wiffle, "If it hadn't been for her, my son wouldn't have had to destroy that book." *Bang, bang, bang.*

Amanda sighed. It wasn't Mrs. Bipthrottle's fault that David had taken the *Bible*, and it certainly wasn't her fault that his roommates had stolen it from him. If anything, Headmaster Thrillkill was to blame. *He* had been responsible for keeping the *Bible* safe. How it had ended up lost in the school's basement, then stashed in an obscure corner of the library by an overzealous maid, only to be secretly removed to David's room, had nothing to do with the librarian. Well, maybe a little, but only about a tenth of a millionth of a percent. It was Thrillkill who had kept the *Bible's* disappearance secret rather than enlisting the students' help in finding it, and now he was paying the price.

"I want to know who brainwashed my daughter," said Mrs. Sweetgum, changing the subject entirely. She was almost a dead ringer for Editta, or perhaps Editta was a dead ringer for her. The woman had the same beaky nose, brown eyes, and limp hair as her daughter. The main difference was that the mother dyed her hair black, as opposed to Editta's natural brown. It didn't become her. "Editta would never have associated herself with those *people* on her own. It had to be the influence of that Amanda Lester, the one descended from that incompetent Inspector Lestrade. I wouldn't put anything past that family." *Crash.*

Uh oh. This was getting personal. Amanda had been criticized before for being related to Lestrade, the inept Scotland Yard detective who sometimes worked with Sherlock Holmes. Fortunately she had finally come to terms with her ancestry and decided that Lestrade was Lestrade and she wasn't and that was that. What did matter, though, was that she was being accused of something she hadn't done and would never even think of. And by the mother of a friend she had tried to help—a mother who didn't seem to recognize her.

Editta's story was certainly an odd one. When she had returned to the Legatum Continuatum Enduring School for Detectives from spring break despondent and uncommunicative, Amanda had tried to talk her out of whatever had been bothering her. That her friend had ignored her and run off to be with the Moriartys' thirteen-year-old son, Nick, Amanda's ex-best friend and sort of ex-boyfriend, wasn't her fault. In fact, Amanda had been horrified and had been trying to find Editta ever since. How could her mother say such things?

"Ms. Sweetgum is right," said Mrs. Wiffle. "You need to do something about that Lestrade girl." Amanda's father had changed the family name to Lester, but people who wanted to insult them called them Lestrade. Fortunately, she was getting used to that too. "Ever since David came to Legatum, she's gone out of her way to make trouble for him. Why, she even hit him over the head with a drawing pad last term and wasn't punished. What kind of a school are you running, Gaston?" *Clunk.*

"I second that," said Mrs. Sweetgum. "That Lestrade girl encouraged the Moriarty boy to corrupt my daughter. If he hadn't played those tricks on her, she'd be home where she belongs and he'd be in custody now instead of causing grief all over the UK." *Blunk!*

Actually, Nick Moriarty, aka Nick Muffet, *was* causing grief all over the UK, or at least parts of it. Since he'd betrayed Amanda and the detectives, he and his parents had contaminated the domestic sugar supply, invented new types of deadly weapons, and nearly caused the extinction of a freshly discovered species of living crystal before disappearing into thin air. However, if the Moriartys indeed possessed the *Bible*, they would do a lot worse than that.

Amanda was beginning to wonder why Headmaster Thrillkill still wasn't saying anything. It wasn't like Mr. Gruff not to hold his own, especially with two hysterical women. Perhaps it was because he felt guilty. Wink Wiffle had been his best friend and he hadn't been able to prevent his murder. In fact, he hadn't even realized that Wink was dead. And he should have been able to keep Editta from running off with the country's most notorious criminal, a man he'd tangled with again and again.

"We demand that you expel the Lestrade girl," said Mrs. Wiffle. *Clash, clang, clatter, thunk.*

"And find my daughter at once!" said Mrs. Sweetgum. *Thud.*

"And furthermore, I hold you personally responsible for the death of my husband," said Mrs. Wiffle. "I don't care what the two of you were to each other. I've instructed my solicitor to file a suit for wrongful death." *Glunk*.

Wink Wiffle's body had been discovered a few weeks previously when a powerful earthquake had struck the Lake District and exposed the remains. The detectives suspected that Mavis Moriarty had killed him but they hadn't been able to establish proof. They had, however, found Wink's wedding ring in Mavis's quarters—quarters she'd occupied when she infiltrated the school in the role of cook's assistant during spring term.

Finally, after what seemed like minutes, Thrillkill spoke. Amanda had never been so relieved to hear his voice, which was much gentler than usual.

"Ladies, let me say how sorry I am for everything that's happened," he said. *Sklunk*.

"Sorry isn't good enough," interrupted Mrs. Sweetgum.

"Sorry won't bring back my Wink," said Mrs. Wiffle.

"You are correct," said Thrillkill. "Wink's death and Editta's disappearance occurred on my watch and I take full responsibility." He seemed to think of something, turned around to the shelves behind him, and grabbed the hair dryer sitting there. He opened a desk drawer and threw it inside. Amanda didn't know why he'd left the thing out. He used it to melt icicles. Winter was months away.

"So what?" said Mrs. Sweetgum. "My daughter—" *BANG!* "What's going on out there? It sounds as though Beelzebub and his legions have invaded."

"It's just construction," said Mrs. Wiffle, inclining her head toward the other parent. "Ignore it." She turned back to Thrillkill. "My son is devastated. He'll never be the same." *BANG*.

"I demand your resignation," said Mrs. Sweetgum, scowling at the headmaster.

"Yes, your resignation," said Mrs. Wiffle. "And restitution, starting with the expulsion of—" *CRASH!*

"I'm afraid it isn't our policy—" said Thrillkill.

"Policy!" yelled Mrs. Sweetgum. "My daughter is being held prisoner by the most evil criminals in the world and you talk to me about policy?" *Bang, bang, thud.*

"You should be ashamed, Gaston," said Mrs. Wiffle, looking for something in her purse. "I thought you were Wink's friend."

"I was Wink's friend," said Thrillkill. "You know very well that we were like brothers, Celerie. Of course I understand how you feel—both of you—and I can assure you that we're going to make this right. Whatever it takes." *Rap, rap, rap.* "Oh, blast that noise." He stood up and peered out into the hall.

Surely he didn't mean he was going to make things right by expelling Amanda? How would that help? She couldn't believe he would do such a thing, especially after having asked her to stay for the summer to make a film that would, in his words, "save the world." She'd planned to go to Los Angeles and work with her idol, action film director Darius Plover, who'd offered her the opportunity to help him with his movie "Sand" for a couple of months. However, when Thrillkill had appealed to her sense of duty, she'd agreed to stay, even though it meant missing out on the chance of a lifetime—and having to work side by side with Scapulus Holmes.

Poor Holmes. She'd discovered only recently how crazy he was about her. At first she was horrified, since she had never wanted anything to do with Sherlock Holmes or his descendants. The famous detective was an arrogant jerk. If it hadn't been for him, no one would have heard of Lestrade and she wouldn't have had to suffer the eternal embarrassment of being related to him. But against all odds, she'd found herself head over heels about Scapulus and they'd finally gotten together...until Nick Moriarty had turned up. As soon as Holmes had seen the tender way Amanda looked at him, he'd clammed up and had barely spoken to her since.

She felt terrible. Yes, she had been shocked to see that Nick wasn't dead after the explosion at the Moriartys' sugar factory. She must have had some weird expression on her face when he'd popped up at the quarry outside Windermere with the living crystals she'd tried so hard to save. And yes, she had once had feelings for him, which might have leaked out onto her face for just a teensy moment. But those were long gone. Once she discovered who he really was—not Nick Muffet, her best friend, but Nick Moriarty, criminal—those feelings had died.

Still, Holmes had seen something on her face that had spooked him. Was he right? Did she still care about Nick? No, it was impossible. Just because she'd momentarily pictured him holding out a welcoming arm for her, as he'd once done, didn't mean anything. It was a slip. She knew that the real Nick was a heartless boy who had laughed at her for trying to save her father, not the gallant friend who'd tried to protect her from David Wiffle or broken a clock just because she didn't like the noise it made.

She should tell Holmes how she really felt and make everything right. He was a wonderful boy and she was mad about him. It wouldn't take much. She'd explain everything and the hurt would melt away. But if it was that easy, why did she balk every time she felt the urge to approach him?

"So you're going to resign then?" said Mrs. Wiffle, breaking into Amanda's thoughts. "And expel that girl?"

"I didn't say that," said Thrillkill. "What I meant was that we're going to find Editta and bring Wink's murderer to justice." He riffled the pages of a book that was sitting on his desk: *School Administration for Dummies.* Celerie Wiffle eyed it. He pulled the volume toward himself and onto his lap. She made a tsk tsk face.

"I don't believe you," said Mrs. Sweetgum. "If you intended to fix things, we wouldn't be having this conversation. Do you realize my daughter might be dead?"

"Ms. Sweetgum," said Thrillkill. Amanda could tell that he was losing his patience but trying not to look like it. "If we don't bring Editta back safe and sound, and if we don't find Wink Wiffle's murderer, I promise you I will resign. But not yet. Let me do my job. If you do that, I can assure you you won't be disappointed." *Glump.*

"We are already disappointed," said Mrs. Sweetgum. "I wish you had been more accommodating because now I'm afraid I'm going to have to add your effigy to my collection." She pulled out her phone and tapped in a note.

"Effigy?" said Mrs. Wiffle. *Squeak.*

"Yes," said Mrs. Sweetgum. "I'm already sticking pins into effigies of those Moriarty people. It will be a trivial matter to include Mr. Thrillkill."

"You're not serious," said Celerie Wiffle with a look of horror on her face. "That's crazy talk."

"I'll show you what's crazy," said Mrs. Sweetgum. "If you insult me like that, I'll add you too. You'll be hearing from me, Mr. Thrillkill. And you," she said looking at David's mother, "will be feeling a few twinges, as will that Lestrade girl. Come to think of it, I'll bet that spoiled son of yours had something to do with my daughter's disappearance."

"Spoiled?" cried Mrs. Wiffle. "You have the nerve to call my David spoiled? I'll have you know that David has had a very strict upbringing. My husband and I—"

"Your husband is dead," said Mrs. Sweetgum. Amanda gasped. She couldn't believe Editta's mother would be so cruel. "And my daughter may be as well. If she's still alive, she will not be coming back to this miserable excuse for a school. Good day, Headmaster. Ms. Wiffle."

As she blasted out of the headmaster's office, Andalusia Sweetgum stepped on Amanda's foot. When she felt the foot she screeched to a halt, looked right through Amanda, and swished out into the hall. Then Celerie Wiffle rose and practically flew out of the office, prancing even faster than Editta's mother, heels clicking loudly. She didn't look at Amanda either.

Amanda was torn. Thrillkill was a strong man. With the exception of his icicle phobia, nothing got to him. Well, nothing *used* to get to him. He had been acting a bit peculiar lately, behaving as though nothing was wrong when the sky was falling. Obviously he was feeling pressured. But Amanda still had complete confidence in him. You didn't face down the likes of Belarus Mafioso Jumbo Pinchuk, serial killer Potato Skootch, and arch criminal Blixus Moriarty and live to tell the tale unless you were Superman. Thrillkill was facing many challenges, but he would come through as he always did.

Suddenly a well-dressed young man blew by Amanda and stopped in front of the headmaster's desk.

"It's polite to knock," said Thrillkill.

"You Gaston Thrillkill?" said the visitor.

"I am."

"Here you are, then," said the man, coughing all over them. "You've been served." Out he went, bashing into Amanda in his hurry. Thrillkill threw the paper across the desk and onto the floor.

"Blast," he said. "That was all we needed." He sat back in his chair, then swiveled around and faced his bookcase. The book on his lap fell to the floor. He picked it up and threw it in the trash.

"I take it that's the lawsuit," said Amanda. "The paper, not the book."

"Correct," said Thrillkill, still facing the bookcase. "Never mind the book. It was a discard from the library." Amanda didn't know if she believed him. Suddenly he slued around and said, "Your father."

"My father?" said Amanda. "What about him?"

"Is he available?"

Amanda was confused. Herb Lester, a former prosecuting attorney for the City of Los Angeles and then a barrister at the Crown Prosecution Office in London, had recently freaked out following his kidnapping and near death at the hands of the Moriartys. Suffering from PTSD, he'd gone off to find himself and was now devoting his life to yoga, a development Amanda's mother, Lila, couldn't cope with. As a result they were getting a divorce. So what did Thrillkill mean, "Is he available?"

"I don't understand the question, sir," said Amanda.

"To represent the school," said Thrillkill. "We're going to need a barrister. Celerie Wiffle has filed a wrongful death suit." He picked up the legal document from the floor and skimmed it. "Bad news."

"That was fast," said Amanda.

"Yes," said Thrillkill. "She's a well-organized woman. I see she's hired Dapple Payslip as her attorney. This is no laughing matter." He made as if to tear up the papers, then crumpled them into a ball instead.

"Dapple Payslip? Who is that?" Amanda knew a few names of UK lawyers, but not many. She'd only been in the country a few months and had been rather tied up during that time. Obviously she'd need to brush up.

"Mmm," said Thrillkill. "Not someone you want to fool with. She's only the most cutthroat barrister in London. She could ruin us." He tossed the paper into the corner.

Amanda didn't want to say that they were well on their way to ruination for reasons other than Dapple Payslip. "And you want my father to be opposing counsel?" she said.

"Yes," said Thrillkill. "There's none better."

Amanda had never thought of her father as a superstar. She knew he was good, but otherwise he was just her father. Now it seemed that he had built quite a reputation, although not a good enough one to make him District Attorney of Los Angeles, a position he'd run for and lost.

"The thing is…" said Amanda. She wasn't sure how to tell him. She understood her father, but she didn't think Thrillkill would. He'd think Herb was weak.

"Don't tell me he's booked up," said Thrillkill.

"Er, not exactly," said Amanda. It was probably better just to come out with it. She steeled herself for his reaction. "He, uh, quit."

"Quit the Crown Prosecution Service?" said Thrillkill. "That's good, then. Now he's a free agent." He looked delighted, if you could be delighted under the circumstances.

"A little too free," said Amanda. Boy, this was difficult.

"Miss Lester, would you please get to the point? We don't have time for dilly-dallying."

"Sorry, sir. He's, uh, he's quit working altogether. He's, uh, he's practicing yoga."

"You what?" roared Thrillkill. Amanda could never get used to that Britishism. It sounded like the speaker was blaming the listener for something when in fact it just meant "What?"

"Yes, sir. It seems that he's had some trouble adjusting since his kidnapping. He and my mother have split up."

"Sorry to hear that," said Thrillkill, who seemed to be performing mental calculations. "But that doesn't mean he can't work. I know how devoted he is to Lila, but—"

"It isn't that, sir," said Amanda. She really didn't want to have to explain, but he was giving her no choice. "He's just, uh, different now. I don't think he wants to be a lawyer anymore."

"Nonsense," said Thrillkill. "Herb Lester is the best lawyer in the Legatum family, and that's going some. He lives and breathes the law. He'll do this for us."

"You can try," said Amanda. Let him experience her father's transformation for himself. Then he'd see. "Would you like me to phone him?"

"Let's do that now, shall we?" said Thrillkill.

"All right," said Amanda, pulling out her phone. She pressed her father's icon and waited a moment. When the outgoing message came on, her jaw dropped. Her father had begun it with one long toneless "OM."

She looked at Thrillkill. His face had twisted into geometrical shapes. "I can hear that," he said.

Then Herb Lester's recorded voice gently pushed aside the mantra. Amanda didn't think she'd ever heard him use that tone before. "Namaste. You have reached a place of peace. I am on a spiritual journey and may not return your call for some time. Blessings."

Amanda held the phone away from her ear, stared at it, and sighed. She left a halting message, ended the call, and looked down at her lap. "You see what I mean, Professor."

"Well I'll be," said Thrillkill. "I never would have expected that. Shall we come up with another name, then?"

"I think we'd better," said Amanda.

After Thrillkill had left half a dozen messages for various attorneys, he turned to Amanda and said, "Here is a list of critical problems that need our attention. Please prioritize them. Take five minutes, but no longer. Go."

He passed her a hand-written list scrawled on a piece of scrap paper, then grabbed it away and added an item at the bottom before shoving it back at her. It read:

Find the *Detective's Bible*.
Solve Wink Wiffle's murder.
Find out what Wink's key goes to.
Rescue Editta Sweetgum.
Find Philip Puppybreath and Gavin Niven.
Monitor Professor Redleaf's computer.
Make film about our options without the *Bible*.
Speak to David Wiffle.
Find attorney and prepare for wrongful death lawsuit.

It was quite a list. Everything on it was critical, but did she have to do this now? She glanced at him. He was absolutely serious.

She twirled a strand of her thick brown hair around her finger and studied the list. Her hair had got so much longer since she'd come to Legatum that now it curled around her finger at least four times. Maybe there was something in the damp climate that made it grow faster.

Holmes loved her hair. During their short time together he'd told her how beautiful it was at least once an hour—how beautiful *she* was, which she still didn't believe. Not that he was lying. It was just that she thought her face was okay but nothing special, although truth be told, she didn't worry much about that kind of stuff. She always had too many other things on her mind, like making films, solving mysteries, and now, prioritizing tasks.

She contemplated the first item, Find the *Detective's Bible*. As long as the *Bible* was missing, the teachers would remain fractious and distracted, and some might even leave. The fate of the school was at stake. It was hard to see what could be more important.

As for Wink Wiffle's murder, the trail was growing colder by the day. They had to find the killer soon. Also, finding the murderer might mollify Celerie Wiffle and get her to drop the lawsuit against the school. That was pretty important as well.

The key had been discovered with Wink's remains. The teachers seemed to agree that it belonged to a lockbox or chest of some kind. However, no one could find such an object, and because Wink seemed to have swallowed the key to keep it safe, they knew it was critical and might even reveal the murderer's identity. The sooner they found the lock that went with it the better.

It went without saying that they had to rescue Editta from the Moriartys' clutches. She might be dead already. If she was alive she was in great danger. The more quickly they could bring her back, the faster she could be deprogrammed and return to normal, her obsession with Nick Moriarty all but forgotten.

Philip Puppybreath and Gavin Niven had been Nick's roommates, but when he left Legatum they transferred to David Wiffle's room. These same roommates had stolen the *Bible* from David with the intention of selling it to Blixus Moriarty. When

Amanda and her friends had fought the Moriartys and David's roommates at the Windermere quarry, the roommates had run off and hadn't been seen since. If they had joined up with Moriarty or been captured, they were in as much danger as Editta. If not, there was no telling what might happen to them as runaways. They had to be found ASAP.

The problem with Professor Redleaf's computer was an open secret. Before she was killed in the earthquake the previous term, the cyberforensics teacher had noticed something on her screen that had shocked her. The entire class had seen the look on her face, but the teachers wouldn't discuss the incident, and Holmes, the computer whiz who had been assigned to look into the situation, had remained closed-mouthed as well. That the headmaster would even acknowledge that something weird was going on surprised Amanda. Maybe now that he had, she'd find out what the big deal was. It was hard to say how important the item was without knowing more about the situation though.

Making the film about the school's options without the *Bible* had been Thrillkill's idea. Amanda couldn't tell how valuable such a film might be. All she knew was that he'd thought the project critical enough to interfere with her fulfilling her heart's desire. It had to be important.

The task involving David Wiffle confused her. Was there something special the headmaster wanted to ask him? Did he plan to expel the boy for what he'd done? Was he going to hold him back and make him repeat last term? Or did he plan to try to help David, who'd been through so much in such a short time? She wished she could abstain on that one.

As far as the attorney was concerned, Thrillkill had already begun the search, so Amanda didn't think the task belonged on the list. He'd obviously given it a high priority. What would be the point of assigning it a number?

It seemed that Professor Thrillkill wanted Amanda to go with her gut on these items or he would have given her more time. She closed her eyes, thought a moment, and wrote a big number one next to the task involving Editta's recovery. This was really a life or death matter. Nothing could be more important.

She took a deep breath and wrote a large number two next to the names Puppybreath and Niven. Their situation was comparable to Editta's. In fact, the two items should probably both be number one. Just because she didn't care for the two boys didn't make them less important. She crossed out the two and replaced it with a one.

While the *Bible* was obviously going to determine what happened to the entire school, figuring out what that key went to might accomplish multiple purposes: help bring Wink Wiffle's murderer to justice, provide closure to David Wiffle and his mother, and potentially lead to Blixus Moriarty. No one knew what Wink had been working on when he was murdered. He might have had an inside line on the Moriartys, or some other criminal endeavor of major importance. He'd probably been killed for what he knew, so finding out what that was should be given a high priority. Amanda wrote a big two next to the key task.

She couldn't believe that she was assigning a priority of three to the *Bible*. This was the issue that was tearing the school apart, yet she didn't think it was the most important one. Thrillkill would probably make *her* repeat last term for that, but she didn't care. The other tasks were more time-sensitive.

Number four was finding Wink Wiffle's murderer, which might or might not actually be a subset of the number two task, the key. She was pretty sure that solving one of the two mysteries would resolve the other, and she was tempted to make them both number two, but the five minutes were almost up so she hurried along to number five, which she assigned to Professor Redleaf's computer.

That left David Wiffle, the attorney, and the film. She felt that she didn't have enough information to rank them properly. She assigned a six to the lawsuit, a seven to the film, and an eight to poor David, not because she disliked him, which she did, but because she was pretty sure Thrillkill would find a way to talk to him soon no matter what else was going on.

There. She'd done it. She passed the list to Thrillkill, who took it gently and peered at it over his glasses.

"Very well," he said cryptically. "Miss Lester, I want you to get on the horn and get hold of your friends Miss Halpin, Miss Kapoor, Mr. Binkle, and Mr. Ng. Please invite them to return to Legatum for the summer. Oh, and invite Mr. Bramble as well." Gordon Bramble was David Wiffle's best friend, or former best friend. Amanda wasn't sure. He was a pleasant-faced, freckled kid whose favorite expression was, "Yeah." Thrillkill handed her the list and said, "With the exception of the David Wiffle talk and the attorney, I want the six of you to tackle these items, along with Mr. Holmes, who of course is already here. In the order you specified, which I happen to agree with. Chop, chop, Miss Lester. Critical tasks."

Amanda realized that her mouth was hanging open just in time to stop a drop of saliva from dribbling. She'd never expected the list to be anything but an academic exercise, and she certainly didn't anticipate having to execute it. The responsibility was overwhelming. But as she considered what Thrillkill had asked of her, she realized that she'd have help from the best and most capable friends in the world—except for Gordon Bramble, whom she could have done without. What did Thrillkill want with *him*? The kid was a big fat zero. Oh well. He would probably keep out of their way.

"Um, sir, what about the teachers?" she said, realizing that Thrillkill hadn't mentioned them.

"What about them, Miss Lester?" said Thrillkill.

"Can I ask them for help as well?"

"You may always ask the teachers, me, and any of the staff for help. That's what we're here for. Now off you go."

Amanda was so excited, both in a good and bad way, that she could barely catch her breath. She felt a great urgency to accomplish the tasks, but the responsibility and time constraints were overwhelming. Still, it was a huge honor that Thrillkill had assigned them to her, a mere first-year student.

She thought the best way to start would be to plop herself down in the Holmes House common room and contact her friends. As she was dodging various construction workers, piles of debris, and yellow emergency tape, she noticed one of the older students, Harry Sheriff, who was considered a heartthrob by many of the girls, walking down the hall. She was surprised to see him, since she thought she and Holmes were the only students who had stayed for the summer. As they passed each other, Harry broke into an enormous grin. Amanda nodded and smiled at him and continued on her way. It was a bit odd that he had seemed so jovial since they'd never spoken. Perhaps he felt compelled to acknowledge her because there were so few students around, although "acknowledge" was too mild a word. He'd looked as if she'd just told him a joke or something. Oh well. Whatever.

Nick had been a *real* heartthrob, at least in her eyes, and obviously Editta's. The poor girl had been so lovesick that she had given up everything to be with him. Amanda wondered how that was going. She couldn't imagine the two of them together. Sure, Nick had flirted with Editta, which was probably what had got her going, but he hadn't meant it. He did that with everyone. The problem was that Editta had taken him seriously. No, wait a minute. That wasn't true. The problem was that Amanda had taken him seriously. She'd thought he was her best friend, that he *got* her and she him, only to find out he'd been using her all along—using her as a way to stay at Legatum so he could help his mother and the cook run their nefarious sugar enterprise right under the detectives' noses. She had no right to judge Editta. None at all.

When Nick had died, or at least when everyone had thought he'd died in the sugar factory explosion he'd set off, she'd believed he was out of her life. But he hadn't died, as they'd discovered when he showed up at the quarry with his parents, trying to create living crystals to use as weapons. What was it with those Moriartys anyway, always turning everything into weapons? Why were they so violent? Was it something genetic? With parents like Blixus and Mavis, it seemed that Nick didn't have a chance. But that didn't excuse him. Just because you had a gene didn't mean you *had* to act a certain way. He should know better. He'd certainly acted like he knew better when he was her friend. But of course he was a good actor. He'd even told her so. She just hadn't understood what he really meant.

And then, just when Amanda was beginning to get used to the idea that Nick was dead—enough to form a new relationship with Scapulus Holmes, a boy she'd never expected to like, let alone love— Nick had turned up alive. How dare he play with her like that? He'd enjoyed seeing the look on her face that day at the quarry. He'd taunted her and called her Lestrade and broken her heart all over again. How could he be so cruel?

Of course she was glad he wasn't dead, and not just because now she might be able to resolve her issues with him. But when he reappeared, everything else *dis*appeared. How dare he do that to her? How dare he do that to Holmes, who had never even known him, let alone hurt him?

Scapulus. What should she do about him? Should she try to convince him she hated Nick and loved *him*? Or should she leave things alone, let him go without a word? If she tried to get him back she'd be committing herself, and she didn't feel ready for that. But if she let him walk away, she'd lose him forever, and she couldn't bear the thought of that either. She felt as if wild horses were tearing her apart. It was best not to think about any of it.

Except that there Holmes was right in front of her, his beautiful mocha skin thick with construction dust. She looked down at her own body. She was all dusty too. She was so preoccupied she hadn't even noticed. What she did notice was that he suddenly seemed taller. He must have shot up overnight.

As soon as Holmes saw her, a look of pain came over his face. Then, catching himself, he walked right up to her and said, "Has Thrillkill said anything about the film?"

After everything that had happened, *this* was what he had to say? Now it was Amanda's turn to wince. She felt an urge to turn her back on him and walk away, but that wouldn't do. Instead she said, "No, nothing yet, but he's asked me to call some of the kids back to campus. He's given me a list of stuff he wants us all to do."

"Me too?"

"Yes," she said. "Do you want to see it?"

"Of course," he said, attempting to look nonchalant. It wasn't working.

He set the laptop he was carrying down on a bench and took the list from Amanda. It was Professor Redleaf's computer—the same one the teacher had been using that day in front of her class. As he was reading the list, Amanda sat down and glanced at the screen.

"Don't look at that!" he cried, but it was too late. As she watched in horror, the screen deformed and, like a kid with chewing gum, blew a bubble at her. After a moment the bubble retracted back into the screen, only to be replaced by the words, "Hello, Amanda. It's about time we met, don't you think?"

Holmes went limp. She knew this was what he'd been trying to keep from her, and no wonder.

"What in the world was that?" she said.

He sighed. "I'm afraid you know as much as I do. I've been trying to figure this out for months and I'm no further along than when I started."

2

IN SEARCH OF BLIXUS

At last Amanda knew what Professor Redleaf had seen right before she died, and it was beyond weird. A screen that seemed alive!

However, when she thought about it, the bubble might be easily explained.

"Scapulus," she said trying to keep her voice neutral, "do you think there might be a flaw in the computer's materials?"

"I wish," Holmes said. He sounded unbelievably frustrated. "I wondered if perhaps the screen was heating unevenly, and I spent a fair amount of time looking into the possibility, but the problem is that every time it contorts itself into shapes, a personalized message appears. That, of course, signifies intention."

"Yes," said Amanda. "My explanation would have been too easy."

"I'm afraid so." He met her eyes and quickly turned away. She felt a twinge, as though Editta's mother were already stabbing her effigy.

"Who is that on the other end?" she said.

"I don't know. I've tried to figure that out too. He or she is too clever. I haven't been able to trace the signal to its origin. It's being routed dynamically and I can't keep up with it."

"Have you tried profiling the hacker?" said Amanda. Understanding people's motivations often helped identify them and make it possible to predict what they were going to do next. Amanda was used to doing that when making films. That way she could write complex characters and theoretically direct actors more effectively, although she'd had trouble with the latter. Until she'd come to the UK a few months before, everyone who worked with her had left in a huff, no doubt due to her control freak attempts to boss them. She'd gotten much better about that, though. You couldn't boss detectives, and Amanda had learned to tone it down.

"I have, but I've come up empty-handed." He sighed.

"The obvious question is, is it Moriarty?" The criminal was certainly the most likely prospect.

"I can't tell," said Holmes. "It could be."

"Who else would do such a thing?" She tried to imagine who it might be, but all she could think of was Moriarty, Moriarty, Moriarty.

Holmes sat down on the bench, then seemed to remember that he should invite her to do so as well. She'd never seen him so distracted. He motioned to the space next to him. "As far as we know, the overlap between those who want to hurt us and those who are technically capable of something like this is rather small. There could be more of them out there that we aren't aware of, of course."

She eyed the spot for a little too long, then tentatively lowered herself onto it. Now the computer was between them. "How long does it take to become this proficient?"

"It depends on several factors: where you start from, who you learn from, your intelligence, and your motivation."

"Could I do it?" she asked. She knew it was a dumb question. Her technical expertise lay in working with video and 3D software, not systems stuff. She was learning, though. After Holmes had taken over Professor Redleaf's class last term, she'd advanced exponentially.

"Not today you couldn't," he said. "Put it this way: *I* couldn't do this right now. If I could replicate the process, I could find the hacker."

"You can't do this?" she said, aghast. She thought Holmes could do anything, or at least anything related to computing. His filmmaking skills could definitely use some work.

"Not at the moment, no. I could eventually, but it would take a while. I don't have the physics at my command." He absently stroked the keyboard with a finger, then leaned forward and blew the dust away.

"Is there anyone at Legatum who could do this right now?" she said.

"Not that I know of."

"Not even Simon?" Simon Binkle, one of Amanda's best friends and a total geek, had one of those technical minds Amanda couldn't begin to comprehend. He was at least as smart as Holmes, and better at building things.

"Not even Simon. I think he has the capacity, but he doesn't have the knowledge right now, no."

Suddenly she got an idea. She didn't know why it popped into her head, but she thought she might as well ask.

"Could Harry Sheriff do it?" She didn't trust that guy. Maybe he was the hacker.

"Harry Sheriff?" Holmes was aghast. "That fifth-year bloke all the girls are crazy about? Not a chance."

She turned and looked at him. "How do you know?"

He seemed to feel her gaze on him. It took him a moment to meet it. She felt as if she were torturing him. "I've observed him. He's frivolous. Unless he's putting on an act, he doesn't have it in him."

She turned to the front again. Out of the corner of her eye she could see Holmes relax. "What about the teachers?"

He thought for a moment. "Professor Redleaf could have done it in time."

"Yes. I thought so. Unfortunately..."

"I know," he said sadly. "I miss her too." Amanda didn't exactly miss the cyberforensics teacher. She'd barely known her. But that didn't matter. What mattered was that *he* missed her. "Other than that, let me think. Professor Ducey has the right kind of mind, but I don't think he has the background." Professor Ducey was the logic teacher, and he was so intelligent he was scary. "Actually, you're going to laugh, but Sidebotham could do it. She's the smartest teacher at the school."

"You're kidding. That old lady?" Amanda had a hard time imagining the old prune as the school's pride and joy.

"Yup. That old lady, as you say, is easily as intelligent as Professor Redleaf was. But she doesn't have the background either."

"And the Moriartys do?"

Holmes looked upset again. Amanda wondered if Nick was capable of this kind of hacking and Holmes knew it. She wished she hadn't asked.

"I think they do, yes."

She let that sit. She didn't want to get into a discussion of which Moriarty could do what.

"What do we do now?" she said.

"I guess continue as I have been. Unless the hacker does something different that gives me more insight."

She wondered if he realized what he'd said. The idea was brilliant. "Do you think we could goad them into doing that?"

He sat up and looked at her. "Now there's a strategy. I like that. What do you have in mind?"

"I don't know," she said, trying to smile, "but I'll see what I can come up with."

"Good thinking, Amanda." He looked so happy it was almost as if the last few days hadn't happened. He opened his mouth to say something, then apparently thought better of whatever it was and clamped it shut.

"About the film," she said.

"Yes, the film. You don't really want to do that, do you?"

"Not particularly. Do you?" He shook his head. If it hadn't been for the hacker, he might not even be on campus now. What would he be doing instead? Probably getting another patent. When she'd found out that he'd got one, she'd gone nuts, thought he was a know-it-all.

But that was before. Now she admired him beyond just about anyone else, even Darius Plover.

She snapped to. He was waiting for her to tell him about the film. "I'll set something up with Thrillkill, shall I? We need to understand what he wants."

"Thanks," he said looking at her just a little too long. He picked up the computer, turned away, and walked toward the boys' dorm. Amanda had to stop herself from running after him.

When Amanda got to the common room, she saw that the school's two décor specialists, Alexei Dropoff and Noel Updown, whom the kids called the décor gremlins because they always changed the scenery when the kids weren't looking, hadn't altered the decoration since the last day of school. The room was still set up to look like Downton Abbey. Normally the men concocted a new look each day so the students could practice their observing skills, because Professor Sidebotham, the school's observation teacher, gave them daily pop quizzes based on what they had seen, heard, and touched. Sometimes Amanda enjoyed the constant change, but often it just got wearying, and by the end of each term she was so sick of the quizzes that she hoped never to see a new lamp or chair again. She guessed that because there were so few students around now, the gremlins had eased up and given themselves a bit of a rest in preparation for the fall term—if there actually ended up being one, the way things were going.

As she sat down on a red leather sofa, Amanda looked out the huge picture windows that faced the east side of the campus. She loved gazing out at that view, even when the trees were bare and the landscape brown. It had been raining heavily and the ground was muddy. She hated this weather. It was warm enough that you could wear T-shirts, but you still had to act like it was winter because of all the mess.

Los Angeles, her hometown, wasn't like that. In L.A. it almost never rained and the temperature rarely dropped below the mid-fifties. If anything the place was too hot and dry. That was why so many brush fires broke out each year. Fires or no, she missed her home. England was beautiful, but it was so much work to live there. In L.A. life was breezy. No snow to shovel, no icicles to dodge, no freezing temperatures that required wearing a jacket indoors. But there was also no Legatum, and in L.A. she hadn't had friends. England was definitely better despite the weather.

The view out the windows was stunning. Amanda could see a beautiful rainbow shining against a cloud-studded blue-gray sky. She thought it was the loveliest thing she had ever seen, shimmering there in the vapor. The colors were so bright you almost had to wear sunglasses. She smiled in spite of herself and snapped a picture to savor. It was a good thing she'd captured the scene because within a couple of seconds, the rainbow had vanished.

Now that she had time to think away from Holmes, she turned her attention to the question of the hacker's identity. Blixus Moriarty was brilliant. There was no doubt of that. Whether he could be the hacker, however, she didn't know. When Professor Redleaf had seen whatever she had, Moriarty had been in prison. Were inmates allowed access to computers? If not, it was always possible that someone had sneaked a tablet or phone in for him to use. She was sure he'd have found a way if he'd wanted to. As far as she was concerned, he was the prime suspect.

Mavis Moriarty was a different matter. Amanda knew little about her. She'd posed as the Legatum cook's assistant, and Amanda and her friends had discovered that she had actually cooked all the meals herself and let the cook take the credit. Everyone said that the cook was blackmailing Mavis, but no one knew why. She'd obviously learned how to cook for large groups somewhere, but that didn't mean she wasn't a hacker as well. Nick had lied so much about himself and his parents that she didn't really know anything about Mavis. Amanda mentally filed her in the "possible" category.

Nick himself was super smart. He was a whiz with his computer. She'd seen him root around under the hood many times. But whether his expertise exceeded what she'd seen him do she didn't know. If he did have the knowledge necessary to hack Professor Redleaf, when and where did he practice? In his dorm room? Some vacant classroom? Or had he been holding off while at Legatum, only to return to his real work after his disappearance?

Nick certainly had the motivation. Like his father he would stop at nothing to further their criminal enterprise, but something told Amanda that he couldn't have pulled off a stunt of this magnitude. She mentally filed him in the "unlikely" category. But wait a moment. The message she'd seen, directed to her personally, had Nick written all over it. Yes, the hacker had called her Amanda rather than Lestrade, but that was probably to hide his identity. Calling her by her ancestor's name would be a dead giveaway, and Nick was way more clever than that. No, he wasn't an unlikely suspect at all. Too bad. She desperately wished it weren't him but she knew better. She changed his designation to "prime suspect." It was okay to have two prime suspects, wasn't it?

Of course Blixus Moriarty knew all kinds of criminals who could have helped him. Aside from the few she'd seen at the sugar factory, she had no idea who these people were or what they could do. She and Holmes would have to find out. Amanda and Holmes again. Well, Thrillkill *had* assigned her all the tasks on the list, and Professor Redleaf's computer was one of them, so yes, this was her project as well as his. Fortunately her friends would be back on campus soon, and they would be better suited to work on the question than she was, plus less likely to upset Holmes.

Her friends! She'd better get in touch with them at once, before they became involved in something they couldn't get out of. What had each of them said they were going to do over the summer? Amphora Kapoor, one of her two roommates, had declared that she was going to spend all of June, July, and August designing and making clothes. Surely she could leave that. Simon had planned to work on his skateboard designs and his Earth-tilting project. Amanda had to laugh. Simon actually thought he might be able to reverse global warming via some scheme to alter the tilt of the earth. Ivy Halpin, Amanda's other roommate, who was blind, had mentioned that she was going to work on her sensory observation seminars for Professor Sidebotham and also write some music. She could put those things off for a while. And Clive Ng, a geology enthusiast and recent addition to their little group, had informed them that he was going rock hunting all summer, again something that could wait. Good. They were all available.

She decided to start with Ivy. Ivy was her best friend, a joy to be around, and the caretaker of a gorgeous golden retriever who was the best dog on the planet. Nigel was technically a guide dog, but he was so much more. He was sweet, protective, and wicked smart. Everyone loved him, even Amphora, who had balked when she'd learned she would be sharing a dorm room with him. Ivy and Nigel had left Legatum only a couple of days before, but already Amanda couldn't wait to see them again.

She pressed Ivy's icon. The phone rang and rang and finally went to voice mail. Behind her outgoing message, Ivy had recorded one of her original compositions. The girl had talent coming out of her fingertips. If she weren't going to be a detective, she could easily be a successful musician. Amanda left a message and went on to Amphora.

Amphora was a good friend, but where Ivy was easygoing and fun to be around, Amphora was prickly and a lot of work. Not that she couldn't be good company, and she was smart, creative, and talented, but unfortunately she was rather used to getting her own way and had definite ideas about what that way should be. She was also a complainer, which didn't endear her to the other students, especially Simon, who often found it difficult to be in the same room with her.

And she was afraid of everything: germs, murderers, even the beautiful living crystals she'd discovered the previous term, which she'd erroneously thought were poisonous.

Amanda called Amphora. After two rings, her friend picked up.

"Amanda!" said Amphora breathlessly. Either she was unbelievably happy to hear from Amanda or she'd been in the middle of who knew what. "Miss me already?"

"I do!" exclaimed Amanda. "But someone else misses you more."

"You mean Scapulus?" said Amphora. "I knew it. It was just a matter of time." Obviously she didn't realize that Holmes and Amanda were an item. If she did, she never would have said something so hurtful.

"No, not Scapulus," said Amanda.

"Harry Sheriff then?" said Amphora.

"Harry Sheriff? Since when do you know him?"

"I know all the cute guys," said Amphora. Right. Of course. Amphora was boy crazy. She *would* know them all.

"Actually, it's someone even cuter," said Amanda. She knew Amphora wouldn't like the joke but it was too tempting an opportunity to pass up.

"Go on then," said Amphora. "Which of my admirers is it?"

"Thrillkill," said Amanda.

"What? No, who is it really?"

"I'm serious," said Amanda. "It really is Thrillkill. He wants you to come back to campus. You and Ivy and Simon and Clive."

"Why? Did we do something wrong? Oh no! He isn't going to expel us, is he? Do you really think he minds that we went after the Moriartys? We didn't know Editta was going to run off with them like that. She would have found another way to do it anyway, you know." Typical Amphora. Always leaping to the worst possible conclusion.

"No," said Amanda. "It isn't that. And yes, I do think Editta would have run off with them sooner or later." If she'd been able to find them, of course—never an easy prospect.

"Well, what does he want then?" said Amphora impatiently. She was getting so worked up that Amanda wasn't sure how she'd take the real reason for her call.

"He wants us to work on some critical tasks. Really important stuff, like the *Bible* and Wink Wiffle's murder."

"He does? That's brilliant!" Amanda breathed a sigh of relief. Amphora wasn't going to make a scene. "Oh, wait a minute. I don't think my parents are going to like this. They think I need a rest."

Amanda laughed. "Tell them you'll spend lots of time lying by the pool."

"Pool? What pool? Oh, I get it. You're pulling my leg. Very funny."

"Just tell them how important this stuff is. Don't scare them, though, or they might come up here and yell at Thrillkill like David and Editta's mothers did this morning."

Amphora gasped. "You're kidding me. They actually came to the school and yelled at Thrillkill?"

"Yes, and it was terrible. I was in his office talking to him and I heard everything. Celerie Wiffle has even filed a wrongful death lawsuit against the school because Wink's body was found here. So he needs us—quite badly. Please come, Amphora." By now she wasn't sure she wanted her to, but it was too late to backpedal.

"Goodness, I have to, don't I? I'll tell my parents something or other. I'll be on the train as soon as I can make it. Oh, is Simon coming?"

Amanda wasn't looking forward to Simon and Amphora's bickering. She hoped the fact that they'd won Professor Tumble's bruises and scars design challenge together might have improved their relationship.

"Thrillkill wants him," she said. "I don't know if he'll be able to make it, though. I haven't talked to him yet."

"I hope he can't. He's probably too busy creating Frankenstein's monster." So much for an improved relationship. Amanda wondered if those two would ever get along. Maybe when they were fifty. "Is Ivy coming too?"

"I'm not sure. I'll let you know."

"I can't wait. I'll text you."

"Fab! Bye."

Next Amanda tried Simon. He picked up on the first ring.

"Hullo, Amanda," he said. "What's shakin'?"

Amanda went through her spiel again and Simon said that he too would be on the next train, although he'd be coming from Cambridge rather than London like Amphora. His parents would support him completely. He'd see her in a few hours.

When Clive answered, he was out looking for rocks near his home in Cornwall. He said it would take him a while to get back, but he'd be there as soon as possible. Excellent. Now she just had to wait for Ivy to phone. Then she remembered Gordon. She still had his contact details from the time when she and Nick played a trick on his buddy David. She pressed his icon.

"Hullo," he said after the third ring.

"Gordon, it's Amanda Lester," she said. "From school."

"What do you want?"

Of course he was hostile. He and David had practically made a career out of hating Amanda and her friends. Once they'd met, it hadn't taken long for all-out war to break out between the two groups, but lately things had changed. Gordon had started to rebel against David's bossiness and had been lurking around Amanda's little circle. How he felt now was uncertain, although from his tone it seemed that he still didn't like her.

"Thrillkill asked me to call you."

"Thrillkill? Why? He's not blaming me for what David did, is he?"

"No, Gordon, he isn't. He needs your help."

Gordon's voice changed. He seemed to have exhaled. "Thrillkill needs *my* help? Really?"

"Yes. He wants you to come back to Legatum for the summer and help a group of us attack some critical problems."

"Which problems? I don't know how to fix walls." He sounded defensive.

"Not the earthquake stuff. Things having to do with Mr. Wiffle's murder and Editta and the Moriartys."

"Really, wow." She could hear his excitement leap out of the phone. "This is bitchen! Hey, you're not making this up, are you?"

"If you don't believe me, call Thrillkill. He'll tell you."

"I will, right now." He hung up. What manners.

While she was waiting to hear back from Ivy, Amanda decided to go over the other items on the list. The highest priorities were Editta, Philip, and Gavin, all of whom were probably with the Moriartys. Therefore, the best way to proceed was to locate Blixus and his family.

She'd faced this problem before. The last time, Holmes had been able to hack Philip's phone and deduce that the Moriartys had returned to Lake Windermere. However, the phones had no doubt been ditched and were now untraceable.

Was it possible, though, that Editta still had *her* phone? Her friends had been trying to contact her ever since she'd run away, but she hadn't answered. That was probably by choice. When Editta had failed to turn up for school last term, they'd tried everything they could think of—to no avail—even patterns of three messages in quick succession, which Editta would consider lucky. When she'd finally showed up on the third day of classes, she'd apologized but had never mentioned whether she'd received their messages. Everyone had assumed she'd ignored them.

If the same *was* true now, Editta would be reading her messages but not responding to them. Maybe there was a way to incentivize her, unless, of course, Blixus had taken her phone away. He might have trashed it for security purposes, but it was worth a try. The only question was, what should they say?

They certainly didn't want to say something like "Your parents are dead," which of course wasn't true. That would get her attention, but it might scare her so much that who knew what she might do. Anyway, if her parents were sending her messages she'd know they were alive. Amanda figured they might try that strategy as a last resort, but there was no point blowing everything now. She had to come up with something safer and more reliable.

What if they were to tell Editta she'd won a lot of money? No, that was ridiculous. How about that she was getting a free pass to attend Legatum for the next five years? No, what did she care about that anymore? Wait—what about an omen or curse? Editta was as superstitious as her mother. That could work. Still, it would be better to try to hack her location first and not involve her directly. That way there would be nothing for her to tell Nick or Blixus—assuming she was still with them.

The problem with that idea was that Amanda would have to get Holmes to do it, and she didn't want to talk to him any more than necessary. Maybe Simon could do it. That would be better. She'd wait for him. She made a note: the Editta task was now in progress.

As for finding Blixus, there were other options. They might be able to locate him through his associates. Weren't some of Blixus's henchmen from the sugar factory still in prison? She was sure they were. She could talk to them and see if they'd give up the Moriartys' whereabouts. It wouldn't be easy, but it could probably be done. Her dad had wormed information out of prisoners hundreds of times. All she'd need to do is come up with a good reason for them to talk. Hm. What would that be?

Amanda certainly couldn't make any promises regarding parole or conditions of their incarceration. For that she'd need the help of someone like her dad. It was too bad he'd quit being an attorney. He could undoubtedly come up with some carrot that might get the thugs to talk—better accommodations, more conjugal visits, nicer food. He might know someone who could do that for her, though. It would certainly be a feather in any prosecutor's cap if they were to locate the Moriartys, who after all were fugitives from the law. Yes, that was it. She'd phone her dad and see what he could do, except she'd left a message for him not forty minutes before and he hadn't answered. Well, she'd try again. It couldn't hurt.

After leaving yet another voice mail, she thought maybe her mother might be able to help. Lila Lester was a successful mystery novelist who knew everyone in the law enforcement business. She and Herb had been throwing dinner parties for his associates at the Crown Prosecution Service. Lila probably knew all of them intimately by now, not to mention their families, friends, schoolmates, and nannies. But her mother was even more difficult a personality than Amphora, and Amanda didn't relish the idea of opening that can of worms.

There might be another way though. Amanda had recently become friends with her dad's Liverpool relatives, Despina and Hillary Lester. They were a little overbearing, but they were first-rate detectives and hardier than they appeared. Despina was a poster child for obesity, and Herb was a bit of a nebbish, but they'd both fought the Moriartys alongside Amanda and her friends, and they'd more than held their own. Sure, Despina could be a bit much, but her heart was in the right place, and Hill had major connections at a Liverpool magistrates' court. They would definitely know someone who could help, and she'd rather talk to them than her mother.

Amanda pressed Despina's icon. As usual, her cousin picked up halfway through the first ring.

"Amanda, darling!" cried Despina. "I was just thinking about you. I want to tell you about your cousin Jeffrey."

As much as Amanda appreciated Despina's enthusiasm, she had no desire to meet her son, Jeffrey, a newly minted Scotland Yard detective inspector. From everything she'd heard he was a typical Lestrade. Actually, he really was a Lestrade, being the only one in the Lester family to use the original surname. That made him the second Inspector Lestrade of Scotland Yard, a designation he thought gave him cachet. Amanda wasn't sure the world was ready for another one. G. Lestrade had been quite enough. Still, she thought she'd better listen.

"How is he, Despina?" she said, attempting patience.

"Fabulous!" said Despina. "He's been spending all his time trying to find that awful Blixus Moriarty. He's been looking all over London."

"You mean Blixus and Mavis are there?" said Amanda. This could be a valuable lead.

"Actually, he doesn't know that for sure," said Despina. "But it's the logical place, isn't it? It's much easier to remain anonymous when you're in a big city."

"I suppose so," said Amanda. "They were wearing disguises when we saw them, though. That could help them anywhere."

"Those old things?" said Despina. "Junk and more junk. Not like the kinds of things you and that lovely Indian girl come up with, are they?"

Despina was referring to Amphora, who was actually English, but of Indian descent, and very tall and elegant. And yes, she and Amanda were much more talented at creating effective disguises than the Moriartys, despite Nick's alleged theater background. Amanda had been making costumes and applying theatrical makeup all her life, and Amphora was a natural designer.

"That's nice of you to say," said Amanda. "So Jeffrey has located the Moriartys?" She thought if she pushed the matter, Despina would get to the point faster.

"Not exactly. But he has plenty of leads. He's been out knocking on doors non-stop. It's been so exciting. One tip took him to an old folks home where a gangster who was once associated with Blixus was living. Unfortunately the man had moved to Malibu and wasn't available for questioning. He followed another lead to an off-track betting parlor, but the bookie told him he had no idea where the Moriartys were, and anyhow he was quitting to pursue his lifelong dream of doing movie stunts and wouldn't be following them anymore. That was most unfortunate as he seemed so very promising. Then Jeffrey was told that someone saw Blixus at the British Museum, but the place is so humongous that he got lost in the Roman antiquities section and had to call for help finding his way back. But you see what I mean. Very, very hopeful. He'll locate those crooks any day now."

"I'm sure he will, Despina," said Amanda, almost choking on her lie.

"Ready to get together again, dear?" said Despina. "I've got gajillions of ideas for outings." Amanda didn't doubt it. The woman was a whirlwind of social activity—a bit too much of a whirlwind.

"Almost," said Amanda, trying to humor her. "I was just wondering if I might ask you for a favor first."

This request seemed to flatter Despina so much that for a moment she could barely speak, but the silence didn't last.

"Anything, anything," she said even more breathlessly. "Would you like to see the pictures of Windermere we took? We've got oodles of inspiring views. How about if I send you that family history I told you about? No, I know. You'd love to see my seashell collection. I did promise you—"

This was going to be more difficult than Amanda had thought. "Actually, I was looking for a referral."

"Name it," said Despina cheerfully. "We know plumbers, roofers, babysitters—oh, and there's a lovely woman who translates from German into Spanish. You don't need a tutor, do you? No, of course you wouldn't. I know. You're looking for a birthday party clown. We know the nicest little man—"

"No, it's none of those," said Amanda. "I'm looking for a prosecutor."

"A prosecutor? You mean like your father? Why don't you ask him whatever it is? Is it juicy, dear?"

Oh dear. Despina didn't know about Herb quitting. Amanda didn't even want to think about what she'd say, but she had to tell her. She prepared herself for a barrage.

"You know he quit the Crown Prosecution Service, right?"

"NO!" Despina stopped talking at once. So that was what it took to get her to shut up: a shock. Amanda didn't want to have to resort to such extreme tactics, but it was good to know that *something* worked. For two seconds anyway. "You have got to be joking. Why would he do a thing like that?"

Amanda sighed. "It's complicated."

"Nonsense," said Despina. "Your father isn't a complicated person. He's as simple as I am."

Despina obviously didn't realize how that statement sounded. Amanda didn't think tipping her off was a good idea. "He didn't used to be. He is now."

"Have you two been arguing?" said Despina. "Having trouble getting along?"

"For once, no," Amanda said without thinking. "I mean, no, of course not." She paused. "The truth is that he's suffering from PTSD and isn't himself."

"Oh, well, that makes sense," said Despina. "Being kidnapped is a very traumatic experience. Did you know that Jeffrey was almost kidnapped once?"

"No, I didn't. Perhaps you can tell me about that another time. I need to find this lawyer pretty quickly."

"All right, dear. We'll have lunch next Saturday and catch up." Maybe, maybe not. Despina was always trying to dictate her schedule, but this wasn't the time to protest. "Now, what kind of solicitor do you need?"

"I don't need a solicitor. I need a barrister." In England, a solicitor was a lawyer who did deskwork. A barrister was what Americans refer to as a litigator, or trial lawyer.

"Oh my," said Despina. "That sounds serious. Out with it, young lady."

Amanda sighed. This was taking much longer than she'd hoped, but not longer than she'd feared.

"It's for Headmaster Thrillkill," she said.

"I'm all ears."

Suddenly Amanda's phone beeped. She'd received a text. She pulled the phone away from her ear and saw that it was from Ivy, telling her that her parents were going to drive her and Nigel up from Dorset at once. Thank goodness. The news was so welcome that she might be able to put up with Despina a few minutes longer.

"This is completely confidential, Despina. You can tell Hill, but no one else. Not even Jeffrey." She hoped Despina could keep a secret. She was pretty sure she could, despite her ebullience. She took being a detective very seriously, even though she didn't actually practice as one.

"Of course, dear. Always."

"I need someone who can arrange for us to talk to Blixus Moriarty's associates in prison."

"You what?" shrieked Despina. "Why would you want to do that? That's too dangerous for you, dear. You should let Jeffrey do it. Ah, but he's tied up, isn't he? You say this is for Gaston, is it?"

"Yes. We need to find Blixus as soon as possible. We've got to get Editta back."

"Oh yes, Editta. Foolish girl. What could she possibly want with that Moriarty boy? Although he is kind of dreamy, isn't he?" Amanda suddenly had the most ridiculous image of Despina flirting with Nick. Yeah, that would go well.

"I'll tell you what," said Despina. "Hill knows someone who can fix you right up, don't you, Hill?" She turned away from the phone and yelled the last part, practically deafening Amanda, who could hear Hill in the background saying, "Say what?"

"Momentito, dear," said Despina. "Back in a jif." Now Amanda could hear the two of them talking, although she could only make out a few words, like "disaster," "bad haircut," and "shame on her." Then Despina returned and said, "Yes. Just as I thought. The person you want is Balthazar Onion. He's outstanding. Tell him Hill sent you. He'll bend over backwards to help you. He's based in Edinburgh, but he travels."

"Fantastic. Thank you so much, Despina. Please thank Hill for me too. I've got to run, but I'll call you later."

"Toodles, kiss, kiss," she said, and was gone.

She had a name! Amanda fervently hoped that Mr. Onion was as good an attorney as Hill claimed. She punched in his number.

3

JACKIE LUMPENSTEIN AND HIS ANNOTATED MEAT COOKBOOK

Amanda had considered talking to prisoners before but hadn't actually done it. When Blixus and Mavis Moriarty were captured at their sugar factory and sent to Strangeways Prison in Manchester, she'd thought of speaking to Blixus about Nick. She wanted to understand how he could have treated her the way he did. But time and events had gotten away from her and she'd never followed through. Despite the fact that she knew both of them personally—Mavis from her position at Legatum and Blixus from the time he'd tied her up and told Nick to leave her for dead—the thought of meeting them again freaked her out, as did the prospect of entering one of the most dangerous prisons in the UK.

Now, however, she had no choice. Of course it wasn't the Moriartys she was trying to see, but there was still the issue of that awful place—a place with such a horrible reputation that it was constantly in the news. She knew, though, that dealing with criminals wherever they were was part of a detective's job, so she attempted to put the creepy thoughts out of her mind.

When the receptionist at Onion, Bearbite, Sklippy, and Capfizzle put her through to Balthazar Onion, she talked so fast that her mouth practically outpaced her brain.

"Mr. Onion, my name is Amanda Lester and I was referred to you by my cousin Hillary Lester at the magistrates' court and I was wondering if you can help me, I need to talk to some prisoners at Manchester Prison and Hill told me you were the one to see, this is very important because Gaston Thrillkill—you know him, right?— needs to find Blixus and Mavis Moriarty urgently and we thought that interviewing some of their associates might give us leads, and oh, by the way, my father is Herb Lester, he used to work for the Crown Prosecution Service, do you know him?"

Once she stopped speaking, she realized that she'd babbled incoherently, but Mr. Onion shocked her by matching her thought for thought. In his heavy Scottish brogue he said, "Aye, good plan, I know a couple of the fellas, and I know Gaston well, and yer father and yer cousin—excellent people—and I can help you but only if you meet me in Manchester today, can you get there this afternoon, Miss Lester?"

This afternoon! That was fast. Could she make it? She hadn't attacked the rest of the list, she needed to meet with Holmes and Thrillkill about the film, and she had to get her assignment from Darius Plover, but yes, if she left at once she could get to Manchester in time.

"I can, Mr. Onion. Thank you so much for your help. I can't tell you—"

"Thank me later, Miss Lester," he said. "I will meet you at the warden's office at half past one sharp."

"Goodbye Mr.—" she said, but he was already gone.

This time she couldn't leave campus without telling Thrillkill. If she failed to show up for their meeting he'd be furious. Would he let her do something so dangerous, though? Maybe she should make up some other reason for being away. No, that wouldn't do. If anything went wrong he'd find out anyway, and besides, he'd told her to pursue

Blixus and Mavis. She was doing exactly what he wanted. As far as danger was concerned, she'd already been involved in treacherous situations and he'd never admonished her. Legatum took a sink or swim approach to learning, and as the headmaster had told them on their first day, the students would not be coddled. No, he wouldn't mind. He might even be glad.

She didn't usually phone Thrillkill—it was better to text so she wouldn't interrupt him—but this news required real-time interaction. When he answered her call, she started to deliver her breathless spiel again, but he stopped her with one word: "Go."

Amanda grabbed her bag and skateboard and rushed out the front entrance of the school. It would take her about twenty minutes to get to the train station on her skateboard. Then two hours or so on the train and she'd be there.

Fortunately she was too preoccupied to worry about the ride. Amanda did not have a happy history with trains. During spring term when she'd ridden to London to find her father, she'd encountered a cheeky monkey who'd peed on her. Then last term when she and Simon had traveled to London again to search for crystals in the sugar factory ruins, they'd run into a couple of nasty clowns in full costume, and two young toughs who had punched Simon in the nose. Editta would have said that bad things come in threes (although how could that be if the number three was lucky?) and would have warned her that this was the third time riding the train, but not being superstitious Amanda wasn't worried. She should have been, however, because something happened this time too. Well, two somethings. No, actually three.

As she was making her way through town, she caught a glimpse of a boy and a girl kissing. She thought nothing of it until she realized the boy was Harry Sheriff. Typical, she thought, and wondered which girl he had mesmerized now. For some reason she just had to know, so she maneuvered herself into a position where she could see better.

The girl, who was older than Amanda, had long blond hair and a stunningly beautiful face. She was wearing turquoise shorts and a red T-shirt—a rather bold but aesthetically pleasing combination. Harry had changed from the T-shirt and jeans he'd been wearing earlier into a tank top and shorts that showed off his muscles. His golden hair was all messed up from the girl running her hands through it.

Big deal, Amanda thought. He sure was full of himself. Then he came up for air for a second, caught a glimpse of Amanda, and winked. Terrific. Flirting with one girl while you're in the midst of kissing another. He *would* do something like that. How could Amphora like him?

Seeing Harry like that was a little weird, but not that bad. What *was* weird was that she could have sworn she saw something that looked like a zombie sneak into an alley. The person—she couldn't tell if it was male or female—looked almost exactly like one of those ghouls from a horror movie: discolored skin, wild-eyed, slovenly, with torn clothing. She almost ran after it but stopped herself when she remembered that she might miss her train. Once she'd boarded she realized she'd been acting silly, that she'd probably seen a homeless person and had let her imagination run away with her. Obviously the pressure of all the critical tasks she was responsible for was getting to her. Zombie indeed.

The third thing that happened was much more serious. When Amanda got to the station she thought she saw Nick getting on a train. Not the train she was supposed to board, but another one. He, if it was he, was by himself, wearing a black turtleneck and a dark gray backpack. The idea of sweltering in a turtleneck on such a warm day was ludicrous, and it made Amanda wonder if it was supposed to be part of a disguise. But the boy was gone so quickly that she couldn't be sure it actually was Nick.

She picked up her skateboard and ran toward the train, but the doors shut in her face and it moved out of the station. She looked at the schedule board to see where it was headed: Oxenholme Station, the first stop on the way to London. Had the Moriartys returned there? If so, she was going the wrong way: Manchester lay in the opposite direction.

Should she hop the next train to Oxenholme or meet Mr. Onion as planned? If it wasn't Nick, she would have blown her opportunity to interview Blixus's associates. If it was, wouldn't it make sense to follow him? But could she catch up with him? By the time he'd have got to Oxenholme, he'd be too far ahead of her. She'd never be able to tell where he'd got off. She concluded, sadly, that there was no way to follow him. She'd been so close. Unless, of course, it hadn't been Nick at all, which she supposed was possible.

The whole way to Manchester she couldn't get Nick out of her mind. Had he been hiding out near Legatum this whole time? If so, what was he doing? Where was Editta? What had his parents done with the white van in which they'd left the quarry? Did any of them have the *Detective's Bible*?

By the time she got to Strangeways Prison, Amanda had got herself all in a tizzy. She was certain they wouldn't let her in and she'd have to go back empty-handed. However her fears proved groundless and soon she was standing outside the warden's office, waiting for Mr. Onion to conclude his business.

"Miss Lester, I presume," he said when Amanda walked in. He was a large middle-aged man with a florid complexion and a receding hairline. He could have stood to lose a few pounds, which might have improved the fit of his rather rumpled suit.

"Yes, sir," said Amanda, reaching out to shake his hand. His grip was so strong she thought he might break one of her bones.

"Warden Doodle," said the little man behind the desk. He was so short than when he stood up to shake hands, he was no taller than Amanda, who was all of five feet. His face was so nondescript that Amanda couldn't remember what it looked like when she was actually looking at him. He head-motioned to her purse. "Bag stays here. No phones, writing implements, or paper. No bobby pins, jewelry, or hearing aids. You got any hidden piercings you take the studs out, okay?"

Amanda nodded. Only her ears were pierced, and she wasn't wearing earrings. She did wonder about the fillings in her teeth, though. Was she allowed to bring those in?

"Ten minutes with each prisoner," said the warden. "Starting... now."

Balthazar Onion grabbed Amanda's hand and pulled her out of the warden's office to the security station, where they were frisked, x-rayed, and given a stern lecture. Then the guard let them into the visiting room, which was outfitted with bulletproof glass separating inmate from visitor. However, unlike in the movies you didn't have to speak by phone. You could actually hear each other.

Amanda and Balthazar Onion sat down in front of an empty pane of glass and watched as a prisoner in chains was brought out from the cell area by two burly guards. Mr. Onion leaned over to Amanda and said, "Jackie Lumpenstein. Caught in the sugar factory raid last March."

Amanda did indeed recognize the man. She'd seen him briefly when she'd hidden from him and another Moriarty associate when she'd come looking for her father. He did look like a lump, probably as a result of eating all those burgers and onions and drinking all that beer he seemed to consume. Come to think of it, he still smelled like onions, even through the thick glass.

"What do you want, Onion?" he said as he sat down.

"Where's Moriarty?" said Balthazar Onion.

"Never heard of the guy," said Lumpenstein. He eyed Amanda suspiciously. "Who's the kid?"

"My daughter," said Mr. Onion without missing a beat. "Don't get cute with me unless you want to end up in solitary. There are no onions there. Know what I mean?"

"Don't know what you're talking about," said Lumpenstein smugly. "Why'd you bring her here? I ain't interested in children."

"I don't care what you're interested in," said Mr. Onion, leaning forward in a menacing way. "I just want to know where Blixus is. That's nae such a tough question, is it?"

Jackie looked at the ceiling. Amanda wondered if he was going to start whistling. She'd seen characters do that in the movies when they were trying to be cool. "Wouldn't be if I knew the guy. Your wife must be quite a looker. The girl ain't half bad."

"Shut up," said Mr. Onion. "She's on work-study and I'm her supervisor. Now, about Moriarty..."

"Work-study at eleven?" said Lumpenstein.

"I'm thirteen," said Amanda. Realizing that he'd successfully baited her she clamped her hand over her mouth.

"Gotcha," said Lumpenstein, grinning. A silver upper tooth sparkled.

Then Amanda got an idea. "I'm actually looking for Nick Moriarty," she said. "I'm his girlfriend. I've got something of his."

"I'll bet you do, sweetie," said Lumpenstein, showing that awful tooth.

Mr. Onion opened his mouth to say something but Amanda pinched his arm so tightly that he shut it.

"I need to give him a key," said Amanda.

"Key to what?" said Lumpenstein with interest.

"It's private," said Amanda.

"Ha ha, I'll bet it is," said Lumpenstein lasciviously.

"Shut up, Jackie," said Mr. Onion.

"No, he's right, *Dad*," said Amanda, playing along with the cover story. "It is quite something. Now, wouldn't you like to see Nick happy?"

"I wouldn't like to see that kid at all," said Lumpenstein, failing to realize that he'd just admitted to knowing the Moriartys after all, which of course he did since he worked in their factory. "All full of himself, he is." He wasn't the first person to say that. Ivy and Amphora felt the same way. Amanda still didn't see what they were talking about.

"It's important for Blixus too," she said hoping he didn't feel that way about Nick's father too.

"Look, girlie," said Lumpenstein. "I ain't fallin' for that. You ain't got no key, and there ain't nothin' special that Moriarty kid needs that goes with a key, so forget it."

"It's for his boat," Amanda blurted out.

"Boat?" said Lumpenstein. "You mean that old fishing boat, The Falls?"

Aha. So Jackie knew about the boat. "That's the one."

"Bah," said Lumpenstein. "They left that at Windermere. They ain't going to use it again."

Amanda and Mr. Onion looked at each other. Jackie Lumpenstein obviously knew exactly where the Moriartys were. She got an idea.

"They will when Nick realizes that he left his *Explosions!* game there," said Amanda. "He loves that. And don't say he can get a new one because that one has all his saved games on it." That was actually true.

"And the key is for what?" said Lumpenstein.

"He put the game in a lockbox and left it there accidentally," said Amanda, continuing to invent. "Look, I know you think we have ulterior motives, and maybe we do," Mr. Onion gave her a sharp look, "but I love Nick more than anything, and no matter what else he might have done I want him to have his game. It's the only way I can show him how much I care. Someday he'll be caught and he'll want it when he's in prison. Don't you miss any of your possessions?"

"Yeah, I miss my twenty million pounds," said Lumpenstein. "And my Cambridge University class ring." He chuckled.

It seemed that Lumpenstein was a real joker. He certainly had the name for it. Gazillions of comedians were named Jackie, or used to be in the old days anyway.

"I can see that you don't appreciate the relationship between a boy and his game," said Amanda. "Fair enough. But surely there's something in this world you love. Isn't there? Whatever it is, wouldn't you love to have it right now?"

Lumpenstein looked at her for a moment. "Well, there is my annotated meat cookbook," he said hesitantly.

It wasn't what she'd expected him to say, but if he wanted a meat cookbook, she could work with that.

"What if I could get that for you?" said Amanda. Mr. Onion kicked her softly under the counter. She kicked him back.

"Tell you what," said Lumpenstein. "You get me that cookbook and I'll find a way to get that key to Nick. Okay?"

"It's a deal," said Amanda before Mr. Onion could say anything.

Lumpenstein gave Mr. Onion a look of triumph, blew Amanda a kiss, and asked the guard to return him to his cell. As he walked through the door to the prisoners' area, he did a little dance, causing his chains to rattle.

"What was that?" said Mr. Onion when Lumpenstein had gone. "You realize he can't take your key."

"I know that," said Amanda. "But since I don't actually have one, it doesn't matter. Now we know he knows where they are, right? So all we need to do is send in an undercover agent to watch him and we'll find out."

"Is that what you think?" said Mr. Onion. "Miss Lester, this is nae television. We canna just grab an MI-5 agent, send him in there, and sit back and wait. And you do realize that he's going to tip the Moriartys off, do you not?"

"I understand, but consider this. I don't have a key, but I do have Nick's game. Well, I don't have it, but Headmaster Thrillkill does. Nick would want that game. I think he'll come looking for it."

"Don't be naïve," said Mr. Onion. "The boy is as ruthless as his da. He would never take a chance like that."

Apparently he didn't know Nick the way she did. "He would," said Amanda. "He thinks he can get away with anything. He'll come after it. He may not have thought about the game for a while, but once Jackie mentions it, he'll remember."

"And you're going to watch for him, is that it? Of all the harebrained, crazy schemes—"

"I'll admit there's a chance it won't work," said Amanda. "So just in case, shall we speak to the other Moriarty associate?"

"Guard," said Mr. Onion, turning around and motioning as if calling a waiter. "We're ready for Manny Companion."

4

MANNY COMPANION

Manny Companion was an albino, and one of the best-looking men Amanda had ever seen. His long white hair, which reminded Amanda of a palomino's mane, fell down below his shoulders and framed his chiseled face perfectly. Why a guy like that had turned to crime when he could easily have been a movie star she couldn't imagine, although come to think of it, Blixus Moriarty was pretty handsome as well. Oh well. There was no accounting for taste.

Manny looked Amanda and the lawyer up and down, turned to the guard, and said, "We're done here."

This wasn't good. He wasn't even going to sit down. Amanda blurted out, "You look like Johnny Winter." She knew about the great blues guitarist because her great-aunt Euphoria liked him.

Manny turned around and said, "Yeah, I do, and I'm a better guitarist than he ever was."

Amanda seriously doubted that, but she thought he might have given her an in.

"I don't know," she said. "He was the man." Mr. Onion flashed her a look.

Manny strode over to the chair opposite Amanda and Mr. Onion and sat down. "Who are you?" he said.

"A fan," said Amanda.

"You wish," said Manny.

"I do wish," said Amanda. "Show me." Mr. Onion looked at her again and a shadow of a smile rippled across his face.

"I ain't got a guitar," said Manny.

"Air guitar then," said Amanda. If he really knew his stuff, he'd want to show off however he could.

Manny looked at her slyly, picked up an imaginary guitar, and started to rock his fingers off. Finding that he couldn't play sitting down, he stood up and banged on the phantom instrument, making all kinds of swirls in the air as he moved his fingers up and down its invisible neck.

"Siddown," said the guard. "You ain't Johnny Winter, Companion."

"I told you I was better," said Manny.

"I can see that you're very good," said Amanda. "I'd like to hear you play the real thing."

"Tell you what," said Manny. "I don't know why you're here, but if you get me a guitar I might tell you something. Assuming I have the info you want, of course."

Mr. Onion knocked Amanda's knee with his own. She knocked back.

"I don't have one with me," she said.

"Obviously," said Manny. "You're going to have to sweet-talk the warden. They don't let people bring stuff in here."

As if. All kinds of things were smuggled into prisons every day, although guitars were rather difficult to conceal.

Manny put his hand up to the glass and nodded to Amanda to do the same. She placed her hand opposite his. It was about half the size.

"Dealio," he said.

"Deal," she said.

Manny gave her a big smile and left her with an air riff.

50

"Miss Lester," said Mr. Onion when he'd left, "you're going to make quite a detective. You've got the gift of gab."

"Actually, Mr. Onion, I didn't realize that until just this moment," said Amanda. "I made everything up as I went along."

"I'm impressed," he said. "I wonder if I can get you to write some of my closing arguments." He pulled his head back and looked at her. "I can see your father in you."

"Do you know him well?"

"Well enough," said Mr. Onion. "He's a brilliant barrister. I heard he quit the Crown Prosecution Service, though. Where's he gone?"

Not this again. She hoped the lawyer wouldn't be judgmental. She'd see if she could get away with a half-truth.

"I think he's trying to make up his mind. Nothing firm yet."

"You tell him we'd be lucky to have him up in Edinburgh. I'll make him an offer he can't refuse. In fact, I think I'll phone him when I get back today."

He could try, thought Amanda, but he probably wouldn't get anywhere.

"Mr. Onion," said Amanda, "do you think you could convince the warden to let Manny play the guitar for us?"

"I think we might be able to make a deal," said Mr. Onion. "However, he'd have to tell us what we want to know first."

"So if he doesn't tell us where the Moriartys are, no guitar."

"Something like that."

"Mr. Doodle must think it's important to find out, right?" said Amanda.

"He appreciates the situation. They did escape on his watch. Guard!" There was that waiter thing again. "We're ready. Please take us back to Mr. Doodle."

The guard gave Mr. Onion a look, unlocked the door to the hall, and ushered the two visitors out. But when they made their proposal to the warden, he gave them a flat out no.

51

"Uh uh," he said. "No can do."

"But—" said Amanda.

"You don't think he knows where Moriarty is, do you?" said Mr. Onion.

"Not a chance," said Mr. Doodle. "Anyhow, I don't want to set any precedents. I do this for him, they're all going to want something. And no meat cookbook either. Sorry."

Amanda thought the warden was not only being unreasonable, but foolish. If either Manny or Jackie were to open up in exchange for a small favor—even to give them a clue—they might actually find the Moriartys. Wouldn't that go a long way toward restoring the man's reputation? What a dork.

"Do you think we could sneak that cookbook in at least?" she asked Balthazar Onion.

"Not the entire book," he said. "Maybe some pages."

Amanda thought for a moment. She wasn't sure the prisoner would be happy with that. "What if I were to scan it, or take pictures of the pages?"

"As long as Jackie gets his beloved annotations, I think that could work," he said.

"So now all I have to do is get hold of it. Uh, I forgot to ask where it is. Can we go back in?"

But Mr. Doodle told them no—they'd had their time for today. They could come back next week.

Now Amanda had two options: wait a week, which would leave Editta with the Moriartys even longer, or try to find the cookbook on her own.

"Do you know where Jackie lives?" she asked Mr. Onion.

"That was my next thought," he said. "Unfortunately he lives in London."

Not London again. Getting there and back was a project. Maybe Mr. Onion would go with her, though, and help her through any rough spots they might encounter.

"His wife and kids might not give up the book," he said.

"I guess we'd have some explaining to do," said Amanda. "This sounds complicated." She thought for a moment. "You don't suppose Manny would make do with a harmonica?"

"Wouldn't that be convenient?" said Mr. Onion. "Let's think this through. We can't simply buy a copy of the book because Jackie wants his annotations. We don't even know the name of the book, for that matter. We can't get a guitar into the prison. I wonder, though, if something else could get them to talk."

"Like what?"

"A visit from a celebrity chef?" said Mr. Onion.

"Like Jamie Oliver, you mean?" said Amanda. "Do you think he'd do it?" The idea of getting the celebrity chef to do them a favor seemed ludicrous. But she seemed to remember that someone she knew had a connection with him. Who was it again? Oh, right—another of Amphora's crushes. "Wait a minute. I have an idea. It's a longshot, but it might work."

"Go," said Mr. Onion. For a tough guy, he was pretty patient.

"The cook we had at Legatum last term—and of course, this is confidential so you can't say a thing."

"My lips are sealed," said Mr. Onion. "We in law enforcement have a special arrangement with the school. We would never give away its existence. I think you know that."

"I do," said Amanda. "I just wanted to stress how important it is that no one ever find out."

Mr. Onion nodded.

"Anyway," she continued, "the cook we had last term studied with Jamie Oliver. Maybe he could put in a word. Oh, except he left and I don't know where he's gone."

"That's a shame," said Mr. Onion.

"He knows a lot about candy," said Amanda.

That he did. Rupert Thwack had kept a huge stash of the stuff hidden in a disused compartment in an old classroom and had accidentally left it behind. Not that that would help with the current problem.

"Wait a minute," she said. "I think I can find Rupert, the cook."

Amphora probably knew where he was. She'd been warned not to bug him, but she'd no doubt ignored the directive. Anyway, he didn't work for Legatum anymore, so what did it matter now? Amanda had to talk to her.

The problem with all of these potential solutions to the problem of the Moriartys' location was the amount of time they would take. Get on a train to London, find Jackie Lumpenstein's flat, make sure his wife was at home, and somehow persuade her to part with his precious meat cookbook. Or, find out where Rupert Thwack was, contact him, and convince him to speak to Jamie Oliver, who may or may not help them and whose visit to the prison may or may not convince Jackie to give up Blixus's whereabouts. Or, figure out how to smuggle in a guitar and listen to Jackie play it without the warden finding out. Longshots all.

"This is getting too complicated," said Amanda. "There has to be another way." She wracked her brain. "Mr. Doodle is causing a lot of trouble. Maybe we could get him transferred or something. Although not fast enough." She sighed.

"I'm not ready to give up," said Mr. Onion, "but you're right. There has to be a better way. We just need to find it. Your father really could help here. He's got the influence to get Doodle moved. What do you think?"

Amanda didn't want to tell him how spaced out Herb was. If he snapped out of it one day, people would always wonder about his suitability for practicing law.

"I'm sure he'd want to help," she said. "Unfortunately he's in the U.S. right now. The City of Los Angeles called him in to consult on an important case." It was a plausible lie. She was getting a little too good at deceiving people, but she'd worry about that some other time.

"Pity," said Mr. Onion. "I'm sure he could have persuaded Doodle."

"I need to think about this," said Amanda. "I'll phone you when I've come up with something."

"Better make it quick," said Mr. Onion. "I'm leaving for Mongolia next week."

5

ALL TOGETHER AGAIN

When Amanda returned to Legatum after her trip to Manchester, she found that her friends had arrived and were having a confab in the Holmes House common room. When they saw her they peppered her with questions.

Simon was so disappointed that he hadn't been able to see the inside of a prison that he made her promise to take him next time. Ivy felt that Manny was bluffing about his ability to play guitar and was exploiting his resemblance to Johnny Winter. Amphora said she might be able to get hold of Rupert Thwack except that he was off doing a motorcycle tour of South America and was incommunicado. Clive, whose straight black hair seemed to have grown about a foot since she'd last seen him, offered up his own annotations on meat cookery if they would be helpful (who knew?), and Gordon, who wasn't actually in Holmes House and wandered in late, said he'd be happy to provide a distraction by creating some glitter explosions. Unfortunately none of these contributions would help the situation. Neither did the kids' reactions when they found out about the lawsuit.

"I can kind of see why Editta's mum is upset," said Simon, who seemed unhappy to be sitting on a Victorian fainting couch. Amanda couldn't blame him. It was a sissy piece of furniture.

"Kind of?" said Amphora, wrapping the drapes around herself and adjusting the fit. They made her look like a fine fin de siècle lady. "If I were her I'd hire a hit man to kill Thrillkill."

"You wish," said Simon.

"You don't think I would?" said Amphora.

"Shut up, you two," said Ivy, who had ensconced herself on the piano bench with Nigel settled underneath. "I'm still fining you for arguing."

Ivy had gotten so sick of Simon and Amphora's bickering that she'd begun to charge them 20p every time they made a nasty remark. In American money that was about thirty-five cents, depending on the exchange rate—not exactly a deterrent. Still, she had quite a bit of money saved up as a result. Amanda had suggested they all go out to dinner with the proceeds, but Ivy had protested that that would just reward the two for their bad behavior. She'd find a use for the funds later.

"We certainly didn't need this," said Amanda, who had returned to the red leather couch. The material was a bit warm for summer temperatures, but she liked how shiny it was. "But believe it or not, the lawsuit is way down on my priorities list. Look."

She showed them the list of tasks she'd made.

"You have two number ones," said Simon. She just knew he was going to say that. Simon was so precise about everything.

"I know," she said. "They both lead us to Blixus so I made them the same."

"He isn't making you speak to Wiffle, is he?" said Simon. He made a gagging gesture.

"No," said Amanda. "That's his task."

"Has Scapulus made any progress with Professor Redleaf's computer?" said Ivy, accidentally pressing on a couple of high piano keys. The tinkling sound was not unpleasant.

"No, but I have," said Amanda. Everyone but Ivy looked at her. *She* sat up even straighter. "Well, I have and I haven't."

"Out with it," said Amphora, emerging from the drapes and joining Amanda on the couch.

Amanda sat quietly for a moment. How could she tell the others what she'd seen? They'd think she was hallucinating. Although Holmes had seen it too. He'd back her up.

"You're not going to believe this," said Amanda, preparing herself for adverse reactions.

"Say it anyway," said Simon. "We'll decide what to believe."

"The screen made a bubble while I was looking at it, and then it sent me a personal message," she said.

No one said a word. Her friends didn't laugh or protest or tell her she must be crazy. Even Gordon kept his mouth shut.

"Blixus," said Ivy at last.

"Maybe," said Simon.

"You don't think it was Nick?" said Amphora, just as Holmes entered the room. He stopped as soon as he heard his rival's name.

"Don't say his name," Ivy whispered rather loudly. She was sitting too far from Amphora to speak softly.

"It's not like I'm talking about Voldemort," said Amphora in a stage whisper.

Holmes surveyed the scene, then said, "We don't know who it is, but they've been at it for a while. I wasn't going to say anything, but since the cat is out of the bag—"

"I had to tell them," said Amanda. So she'd told. Big deal. Why should he keep important information like this to himself?

"I suppose it was time," said Holmes, leaning against the doorway and looking for a place to sit. Amanda was certain he'd take a seat as far away from her as he could. "I thought maybe I could find him and no one would have to know."

Now he was sounding like his famous ancestor: arrogant and superior. Who was he not to tell them? Amanda felt her temper rise. Maybe he wasn't so great after all. Maybe he was revealing his true colors. If that was the case, it was better to find out now and avoid a big mess later.

"I'm sorry," said Holmes. "That was misguided of me. It won't happen again."

Amanda wished he hadn't apologized. It would have been so easy not to have to worry about him. Now she was stuck all over again.

"I don't understand," said Gordon, who hadn't figured out where to sit either. It wasn't his common room and he seemed uneasy. "How can a computer screen make a bubble? You mean it was exposed to heat or something?"

"No," said Holmes, selecting a gold-brocaded Queen Anne chair that had been placed next to the fainting couch. Hm, not as far away from her as her might have sat. Amanda wondered what that meant. "It forms and deforms, leaving the screen exactly as it was before. I've seen it happen dozens of times now. And there's always a personal message afterwards. Someone is doing this on purpose."

"What do the messages say?" said Clive.

"The one I saw said, 'Hello, Amanda. It's about time we met, don't you think?'" said Amanda.

"Hoo boy," said Simon. "That implies it's someone you don't know."

"You expect a person like that to tell the truth?" said Amphora.

"Don't say it," said Ivy. "I've got a nice 20p fine waiting for you if you do."

"I'm not saying anything," said Amphora. "I just meant that—oh, never mind." She absent-mindedly inspected an antique porcelain lamp.

"She's right," said Gordon, taking a seat across from Amanda and Amphora. The chair matched the one Holmes had selected. "I wouldn't trust someone like that."

Amanda was gobsmacked. Not only was Gordon participating in their conversation, but he was actually making sense. Maybe he really had changed since he and David were no longer best friends. She'd have to watch him more closely.

"Do you have any idea who it is?" said Ivy.

"Not really," said Holmes. "I certainly haven't been able to identify his location. If Blixus is behind this, it could be any of many possibilities. He subcontracts his tech work all over the place. It could even be someone in China or Antarctica for all we know."

No wonder he'd been having so much trouble tracing the hacker. If that were the case, he might as well be on Mars.

"But I don't understand how the guy can make the screen move," said Amphora.

"I don't either," said Holmes. "It's pretty scary."

"All the more important to find Blixus," said Amanda. "It seems that all roads are leading to him."

Blixus Moriarty: the spider at the center of the web. He really had become the focus of their lives. She resented that. He had no right, no right at all. If only that earthquake had never occurred, he'd still be in prison and they wouldn't be jumping through all these hoops. Of course Nick would still be out there, somewhere, doing who knew what. And she'd still think he was dead.

"Have you tried Editta lately?" said Ivy, interrupting Amanda's reverie.

"I try her once every few hours," said Amanda. "You?"

"Same," said Ivy. "No reply."

"Me too," said Amphora. "I even told her that Thrillkill wanted her to teach a special forensic accounting seminar. She'd eat that up. But nothing." That was bad. Editta loved numbers more than anything, except maybe Nick. If that didn't get her attention, nothing would.

"Maybe her phone is dead, or even gone," said Clive from a leather armchair in the same seating group.

"Scapulus?" Amanda looked at Holmes.

"It must be dead or off," he said. "I've tried pinging it."

"You don't think she's dead?" blurted Gordon. Everyone froze.

"Be quiet, Gordon," said Amphora after a few seconds. "It isn't nice to talk like that."

"But we have to—" Gordon wanted to speak, but Simon shook his head. "But I just—" Another head shake. Gordon looked down at his shoes.

"Say," said Clive, brightening. "Has anyone tried to track that van the Moriartys were driving at the quarry?"

"They found it abandoned in Windermere," said Simon. "No prints or anything."

"How did you know that?" said Amanda.

"Professor Kindseth told me," said Simon.

That wasn't surprising. Simon and Professor Kindseth had really hit it off using the school's 3D printer to make lab gadgets. Not that the teacher played favorites. Legatum frowned on that. But he probably imparted a lot of information while they were working together, giving Simon a bit of an inside line.

"What about the boat?" said Clive.

"Nothing there either," said Simon. "There's no sign that they ever came back to it after they left the quarry. The teachers searched it thoroughly."

"So now we're not just looking for the Moriartys," said Ivy. "We also need to find this hacker. Amanda, do you think you can profile him?"

"I can tell you right now that he enjoys playing games with us," said Amanda. "Either that or he's conveying Blixus's messages. That means he's either a troll or a yes man. Yes woman, maybe."

"In that case," said Ivy, "maybe we can try to follow the money. If he's a yes man, he'll probably stop working if he isn't paid. Unless Blixus is threatening him."

"Good idea," said Clive, "but won't it be hard to hack his pay? How are we going to figure out where Blixus's money is?" He was always so logical. Amanda was glad they'd become friends.

"Editta could do it," said Amphora. Everyone looked at her. "I know. Kind of a circular argument."

"Say," said Gordon. "Do you think anyone in Editta's family could do it?"

"That's not a bad idea," said Ivy. Amanda agreed, but the idea of such impeccable logic coming from Gordon made her wonder if she was missing something. "You mean that someone else in her family is also good at accounting, or even an accountant?"

"Maybe," said Gordon.

"Would they talk to us?" said Amphora. "Obviously her mother is furious with the school."

"Her mother is a lunatic," said Simon. Ivy lifted up her sunglasses and gave him what would have been quite a look if she could see. "You know she is," said Simon.

"Her mother is a bit strange," said Amanda. "She actually does believe in voodoo. I heard her threaten to stick pins in an effigy of Thrillkill. And one of me, by the way." She still wondered if that twinge she'd been feeling had come from Andalusia Sweetgum. Not that she really believed it possible, but the timing was quite a coincidence.

"That's terrible," said Amphora. "She's not a nice person."

"Maybe if she thought it would help Editta she'd talk to us," said Ivy.

"Doubt it," said Simon, resting his foot on the fainting couch. He was obviously having trouble getting comfortable. "She's not rational, especially right now."

"What about her dad?" said Clive.

"She doesn't have one," said Amanda.

"Oh, sorry," said Clive.

"He died," said Amanda.

"How did I not know that?" said Amphora.

"I don't know," said Amanda. Editta was funny. Sometimes she was completely relaxed with her friends and sometimes she got all solitary. It was possible she hadn't opened up to Amphora. "She does have a stepfather, though."

"Oh, right," said Clive. "Maybe him then?"

"What does he do again?" said Simon.

"He's a tree surgeon," said Amanda.

"Not too helpful, unfortunately," said Clive. "Not that operating on trees isn't a noble profession." Amanda looked out the window, where the trees were healthy and well-trimmed. They looked lovingly cared for. She wondered if Editta's stepfather had worked on them. "Siblings?"

"I'm afraid not," said Amanda. "She's an only child like me."

"So what does her mother actually do then?" said Gordon. "Is she the detective in the family?"

"It was her father," said Amanda. Blumkin Sweetgum had been descended from a line of detectives in Wales. Amanda couldn't remember which one. "But I think she does something administrative. Ivy, what was it?"

"She's a secretary at a police station," said Ivy. "In Brixworth."

"Where's that?" said Amanda.

"It's a village near Northampton," said Simon.

"Near Birmingham?" said Amanda. She still didn't have her UK geography straight.

"Not exactly close, but in that direction," he said. "Between there and where I live in Cambridge."

"So she's sympathetic to law enforcement," said Amanda.

"Have to be, wouldn't she?" said Simon. "To send her daughter here."

"I suppose so," said Amanda. Somehow voodoo and detecting didn't seem to go together. No wonder Editta had trouble fitting in. "What I meant was, maybe she'll talk to us if we have a good idea." It was an extreme longshot, but the situation called for crazy ideas.

"What are we going to say to her?" said Amphora. "Hi, Mrs. Sweetgum. We're friends of your daughter and we'd like your help catching a hacker who can move stuff remotely, and—"

"That's exactly it!" said Amanda. "She'll love that. It's kind of like magic."

"I suppose it is," said Amphora. "You do it, Amanda."

"Okay, I'll—"

"Wait a minute," said Gordon. "Why does she always get to do everything?"

Whose idea was it to bring Gordon back for the summer again? Amanda could see that he was going to be a royal pain as usual.

"First of all, she doesn't," said Ivy. "And second, do you want to talk to Mrs. Sweetgum?" Silence. "Just as I thought. Amanda is Editta's friend and—"

"No, he's right, Ivy," said Amanda. "She hates me right now. You should have heard her threaten to stick pins in me. I mean my effigy. Gordon should do it."

Gordon broke into a huge smile. "Radical," he said. "I'll do it right now. What's her number?"

All this time Holmes had sat there without saying a word. Now he spoke.

"This is a waste of time. Do you have any idea how long it would take to find Blixus's money and figure out where it goes?"

Amanda was taken aback. "What do you mean?"

"If Blixus can hire a hacker as sophisticated as this, don't you think he's made sure his money can't be found?"

The air seemed to go out of the room. Simon said, "Good point, man."

Ivy sighed. "You're right, Scapulus," she said. "We got carried away."

"So I don't get to phone Editta's mother after all?" said Gordon. He looked so disappointed.

"Sorry," said Amanda. "Next time."

"You guys are no fun," said Gordon. "I'm out of here." He got up rather gracelessly and left the room.

"Don't be like that, Gordon," said Amanda, surprising herself. What did she care whether Gordon participated or not?

"Let him go," said Simon.

"Boy, he's sensitive," said Amphora when Gordon had left. Simon gave her a look. "What? I'm not like that."

"Don't even think it, Simon," said Ivy.

6

THE KEY TO THE KEY

When the meeting had broken up, Amanda motioned to Simon. She didn't feel comfortable about what she was about to say and wasn't looking forward to his response. She wished there were another way but she couldn't think of one. "I have a huge favor to ask you," she said.

"Uh oh."

"What do you mean 'uh oh'?" This wasn't going to go well.

"I know what you're going to say," he said. Was that a smug look on his face or was he just squinting?

"You do not."

"Yep, I do. I know you."

"Okay, if you're so smart, what is it?" she said.

"It's about Scapulus."

"Nuts!" said Amanda. "How did you know?"

"It's written all over your face. You want to know what he knows about Professor Redleaf's computer, but you don't want to ask him."

Amanda scrunched up her face and looked at him closely. "How did you know that?"

"Look, I'm not some wizard or something. I'm just good at observing. Want to hear more?" She couldn't tell if he was being smug.

"No!" she said. This was spooky. She knew Professor Sidebotham's observing class was going to turn them all into freaks, and here was evidence already.

"Want me to ask him then?" said Simon.

"Would you? It's for the good of the school." Ouch. That was laying it on a bit thick.

"You don't have to snow me," said Simon without missing a beat. "You should do it yourself but I'll let you off this one time. You can owe me."

Wonderful. Owing Simon a favor would be like being indebted to a Mafioso. She'd end up paying a huge price. Maybe she should just talk to Holmes herself.

"Look, if it helps, I want to know too," said Simon. "And I understand why you don't want to talk to him, although you do have to make that film together, so you'll have to eventually."

He was right. She was being a coward. At the moment, however, she didn't care. "So you'll do it?"

"I'll do it."

"Thanks, Simon. I'll make it up to you."

"Yes, you will," he said.

But when he came back from talking to Holmes, he shook his head. "He won't tell me."

"But it's for Thrillkill," said Amanda.

"I told him that. He said he'd tell Thrillkill and the teachers but no one else."

This made Amanda's blood boil. What was the big secret? "But he just told me he'd kept the whole thing to himself for too long."

"Apparently he's changed his mind," said Simon.

"What is wrong with him?"

"He thinks you love Nick."

Amanda stared at him. Simon's facade was deceptive. Everyone thought he was a geek but in fact he knew everything that was going on around him and could read signs she sometimes missed.

"I suppose you think I love Nick too," she said.

"I do."

"I don't see how you can say that, Simon. You know what he did to me."

"Doesn't matter," he said. "He's your true love."

Amanda certainly didn't expect to hear Simon talk like that. The only way you could put him and the words "true love" in the same sentence was when you were talking about his inventions.

"I wish I could fine you for that," she said. "Look, for the last time, he was never my boyfriend. I will admit that he was my best friend for a while, but that was just an illusion. And now I'm going to tell you something you don't know."

"I'm all ears," said Simon moving in close.

"If you breathe a word of this I'll deny it," she said. She was not going to have the whole school gossiping about her again.

"I'm discreet. You know that."

"Fine. Okay, here goes: I love Scapulus." There. For better or worse, it was out.

"I know," he said.

She wanted to pop him. Here she was spilling her guts and he was telling her it was no big deal.

"What do you mean you know?" she said. "You just said that Nick was my true love." She wished he'd pick a point of view and stick with it.

"He is," said Simon.

"What are you talking about?"

"It's easy," said Simon. "Nick was your first love. You'll have feelings for him all your life. You love Scapulus but Nick is imprinted on you, like a duck with her ducklings."

"Oh great. Now I'm a duck."

"I said *like* a duck. Trust me. You will never be free of Nick. You may end up hating him but you'll always love him, even if he really does die. But Scapulus is better for you and you know it."

She was getting angry. It was as if Simon were sentencing her to a terrible future. "That's depressing," she said. "How can you say such a thing?"

"I'm just telling the truth like I always do," said Simon.

She'd had just about enough of that. "If you're so smart, then who's your first love?" she said.

"Dunno. It hasn't happened yet."

"I think it's Amphora," said Amanda. "You guys fight to cover up your true feelings for each other."

"Don't even try that stuff with me," said Simon. She hated it when he got like that. He was supposed to take the bait and he never would. "Anyway, the point is that now that you know what's really going on, you can fix things and move on. Make up your mind to be happy. Tell Scapulus how you feel."

"Can't," she said stubbornly. "Won't."

"Fine," he said. "Stay stuck."

Amanda wanted to hit him. He treated feelings as if they were some kind of lab chemicals.

"I can't wait until you fall in love," she said. "You'll see how easy it is. And by the way, I'm going to tease the heck out of you, so you'd better prepare."

"I don't care," said Simon. "If it works it works. If it doesn't I'll move on."

"You wish," she said. "Remember this day because I'm going to be telling you I told you so."

"Fine. Now that that's straightened out, what are we going to do about Professor Redleaf's computer?"

She laced her hands behind her back for a moment, then gave him a sidelong look.

"No," he said. "I won't do it."

"Please," she said. She didn't know why she was saying that. If he thought it was the right thing to do, he'd do it. If not, he wouldn't.

"It isn't right," said Simon.

"Come on, Simon," she said. "We have to find out. The more we know, the faster we can find the hacker and stop them from stealing our data."

"All right, but if this ever gets out *I'll* deny it," he said.

"Thank you," she said. "I know how much you hate spying on people." As if.

After her talk with Simon, Amanda was even more depressed. He was obviously crazy. The very idea that Nick was her true love was disgusting. If that was the case, what did it say about her? And even if it were true, which it wasn't, what if she wasn't Nick's true love? What if it was some other girl, like the one she saw him with at Schola Sceleratorum, or Editta? She'd be doomed to a life of unrequited love for a criminal. How mean Simon could be sometimes. Just when you thought he had finally gotten a clue, he'd come up with something like this. What was wrong with him?

As if the prospect of that weren't bad enough, she'd been working incredibly hard at her tasks and had nothing to show for her efforts. The visit to Strangeways had got her nowhere and the brainstorming session with her friends had been a total bust. She'd failed to make any progress with either of the item ones on the list, or item five. Maybe she should go on to number two, the key.

When Wink Wiffle's body was originally discovered, no one had noticed the small key lying in the dirt nearby. It had taken a bit of digging and Amphora's keen eyesight for it to come to light. Apparently Wink had swallowed the key, but after he was murdered his body had deteriorated so quickly that the little silver thing had fallen into the dirt. When the teachers had moved the body, they'd disturbed the soil surrounding the area so much that the key had been inadvertently buried.

Amanda didn't know much about keys, but it sure didn't look like it went to a door. By the time Professor Stegelmeyer had declared that it belonged to a lockbox or chest, she'd just about reached that conclusion on her own. The problem was that no one had been able to find such an item among Wink's possessions, and his wife had never seen him use one. The detectives scoured both Wink's house and his office to no avail. They had also tried to trace his movements, not only for the sake of the key, but also to look for his murderer.

Wink and his family had lived hundreds of miles away in Cornwall, so it would be difficult, although not impossible, for Amanda to go through his belongings again. Not that Celerie Wiffle would allow such a thing. She was so negative about the school and anyone connected with it that Amanda didn't dare approach her. However the teachers had taken many pictures and even some video of Wink's office and parts of his house, and Amanda and her friends could easily go through those. If they did that, perhaps they'd see something that would give them a hint as to where the lockbox or chest might be.

There was also a minuscule chance that the key had something to do with the secrets trove under the school. The kids had discovered this astonishing place while exploring Legatum's basements. It was filled with compartments not unlike safety deposit boxes, each with two locks. The earthquake had damaged parts of the trove and left some of the compartments open, but most were still intact and locked tight.

From the open drawers the kids could see that each one contained paper snippets with a few words scribbled on them. They had concluded that these were Legatum's secrets, separated and obscured so that anyone who found them couldn't decipher what they meant. They suspected that there was metadata somewhere that made sense of everything, but they didn't know where it was. Since Professor

Snaffle was the secrets teacher, they speculated that she had both the metadata and the keys to the drawers, although where she kept them wasn't apparent.

And then Ivy had made a startling announcement: she had managed to get into some of the compartments by picking the locks. With her excellent hearing, she could tell just how far to push the pins. This was great news, but the problem was that each of the right-hand locks in the pairs was different from all the others and it would have taken her forever to crack them all. Still, the left-hand locks appeared to have been fashioned from one master, so it was possible that one key would fit every one. Was this that key?

If the key did in fact go to the trove, why would Wink Wiffle have it? Would one of the teachers have given it to him, and if so, why? Had he stolen it? As far as Amanda knew, Wink had never taught at Legatum, so he wouldn't have had access to the trove. This whole line of inquiry deserved careful thought, although she had a sinking suspicion that she was engaging in wishful thinking. If this key was the master for the trove, why were the teachers still trying to figure out what it went to? Unless they were trying to misdirect the students, but that seemed unlikely. They knew the kids were aware of the trove by now. They'd been in the basements too often not to know. There was no need for a cover-up.

No, the key to the key was Wink Wiffle himself. And that idea led right back to dear old Blixus again, or at least to his wife. Everyone knew by know that Mavis had hidden Wink's wedding ring in her room, but no one knew why. Although they couldn't prove that she had killed him she was the prime suspect, and many believed that the ring was a trophy.

As logical a conclusion as that was, people were still wondering if Mavis and Wink had known each other. No one was aware of a connection, but Wink did know Blixus so it was possible he knew Mavis too. But a wedding ring was personal, and the fact that Mavis had taken that implied that she'd harbored a grudge against Wink—

or perhaps against his wife, Celerie. Still, no one had been able to find any evidence linking Mavis to either of the Wiffles.

It was true, of course, that Mavis had had contact with their son, David, but when he claimed he'd never spoken to her, that line of inquiry had fallen by the wayside. There was, however, the issue of Mavis's son, Nick, who had squabbled with David and even tried to beat him up. But would Mavis have murdered Wink because of that? It seemed unlikely, and even less likely that she'd have taken Wink's ring if so. No, they were back to the prospect of examining the pictures of Wink's belongings to see what other possibilities they might reveal.

As she was making her way to Thrillkill's office to ask him for access to the pictures, Amanda saw the headmaster in the hall talking to Professor Browning, the sketching teacher. He was looking at her in the oddest way. "OMG," she thought: "Headmaster Thrillkill has a crush on Julia Browning!" How sad. She wondered if Professor Browning knew. Forget that—she wondered if Thrillkill's feelings were returned. Professor Browning was married and had small children, or so Amanda thought. That would be terrible! Boy, love was difficult. She hoped Thrillkill would get over the woman soon. Otherwise he was headed for a world of hurt.

"Ah, Miss Lester," said Thrillkill when he saw her. He'd broken his leg in the quake and was still using crutches. The whole school had signed his cast but it was getting so beat up that you couldn't make out the names anymore.

"Hello, Professor," said Amanda. "Professor Browning."

"Good evening, Miss Lester," said Professor Browning. "This is one talented artist we have here, Professor Thrillkill."

"So I'm told," said Thrillkill. "Good skill for making storyboards, eh? How's that film coming?"

Storyboards? What did Thrillkill know about storyboards? "I'll have news for you soon, sir," said Amanda. She had no intention of telling him that she hadn't yet started work on his number seven task, the film. He seemed to think she could handle everything at once.

"Excuse me, but would it be possible to look at those pictures of Mr. Wiffle's belongings?" she said.

"Yes, of course," said Thrillkill. "Ask Ms. Canoodle for a link."

Drusilla Canoodle was the school's dean of admissions, but she helped Thrillkill with other tasks as well. She was a nice woman, if a bit mysterious.

"Thank you, sir," said Amanda. At least that was easy.

As Amanda and Amphora were examining the pictures the next morning, Amphora noticed something.

"Look at those paintings," she said, pointing to an image of Wink's office. "You see that one on the end? What is that?"

Amanda appraised the painting. "I don't know. It looks like a nice place though."

The painting had been executed in an impressionistic style and depicted an idyllic-looking village. Whoever had created it was talented.

"It looks familiar somehow. Can we zoom in?" said Amphora.

"Sure," said Amanda. "Let me just—"

"OMG," said Amphora. "Look at the signature. Mr. Wiffle painted that picture himself."

"I had no idea he was so creative," said Amanda. She hadn't known Wink, but it was hard to picture him doing something artistic.

"Hang on," said Simon. "She's right. There's something about it. That could be a real place."

"That's just what I was thinking," said Amphora. "We need to find out where it is. It might give us a clue."

7

A BIG BLOWUP

When the girls told Simon about the painting, he said he was sure he could match the place Wink had depicted with a satellite view of the area as long as the rendition was accurate. Whether it was, or whether the view Wink had painted was even contemporary, no one knew. Of course it was also unclear whether it had anything to do with the key or Wink's death, but all felt the idea worth a try. They had so little to go on that they had to follow even the slimmest of leads.

But before they could say "Bacon and eggs," Gordon came running up breathlessly and said, "There are zombies in Windermere!"

Amphora sniffed. "What are you talking about?" Amanda didn't know if her disapproval had to do with Gordon or his message.

"I saw them," said Gordon. He looked incredibly proud of himself. He was obviously one of those people who loved to be the one to deliver news.

"Cool!" said Clive. "Let's go see."

"Hang on a minute," said Simon. "There's no such thing as zombies. Someone must be making a film or something."

Amanda wondered how many film shoots Simon had seen. They certainly weren't common in Windermere like they were in L.A. Maybe where he lived in Cambridge they were, though. She hadn't been there, but she'd seen pictures. With all those beautiful college buildings it looked like a perfect location.

"Nope, they're real," said Gordon. "There weren't any cameras around. I saw one of them go into a newsagent's and one was crossing the street."

"Can't be," said Simon. "What did they look like?"

"They were all pasty-looking," said Gordon. "With ragged clothes and kind of dirty."

"Were they walking funny?" said Clive.

"Yeah," said Gordon. "All slow-like."

"But not eating any brains?" said Ivy, giggling.

"Well, no," said Gordon as if he wished they had been.

"That's because there's no such thing as zombies," said Simon. "They were homeless people."

Gordon dug his heels in. "Nuh uh. They didn't look like homeless people. Their faces were kind of purple and scabby. I forgot to mention that."

"Did you take any pictures?" said Amphora.

"No," said Gordon. He looked beaten. "Didn't have my phone."

Normally Amanda would have been skeptical too, but she knew better. "I saw one too," she said. Everyone turned to look at her. "What—you think I'm delusional too?"

"I'm not delusional," Gordon protested.

"Film shoot then," said Simon.

"I don't think so," said Amanda. She knew what a film shoot looked like and it wasn't that.

"Rubbish," said Simon. "They were in costume. The shoot was somewhere nearby and they just came into town to get supplies."

Amanda had to admit that this explanation made sense. She'd seen actors do that. They wouldn't even take off their costumes, just go running errands as Klingons or cowboys or whatever. Seeing that was a cool aspect of living in L.A.

"Sorry, Gordon," said Ivy. "The idea is lovely, but I think Simon is right."

"Isn't," said Gordon. "You'll see."

"Gosh, I hope they're real," said Clive, looking defeated.

"We've got more important things to do," said Simon. "Come on, Clive. Let's check out this painting."

Clive sighed and obediently followed Simon out of the room.

Number three on Thrillkill's list was the *Bible*. This particular task seemed hopeless. Everyone had seen David Wiffle run over the book with an earthmover, then throw it in that watery pit at the quarry. The teachers had dragged the pit and divers had searched it repeatedly, but they had found no *Bible*, crushed or otherwise. They hadn't come up with so much as one page, which was weird because even if the thing was waterlogged, you'd have expected some kind of detritus to be present. That made everyone think that somehow Moriarty had managed to retrieve it. But when? The avalanche Clive had created had filled the pit with boulders. There was no way Blixus or even Nick could have slipped in there and got hold of the thing. Maybe the book was magic after all.

"Perhaps it wasn't real in the first place," said Ivy. "Maybe there really are copies and the original is still out there."

"Yes," said Amphora. "Maybe the teachers know exactly where it is and are trying to throw Moriarty off."

That didn't make sense. The teachers did some weird things, but that sounded counterproductive.

"If so, they're making a pretty good show of it, with all that arguing and panic," said Amanda. "Would they really go to all that trouble? If they did it for Blixus's benefit, how would he even know it was happening?"

"If there's another mole at Legatum he would," said Amphora.

"If that's the case," said Ivy, "who is it?"

"Surely not one of the teachers," said Amanda, who didn't like the idea at all. They'd been fooled enough. Being infiltrated wasn't just dangerous, it was embarrassing. "Although that Professor Snool is pretty shifty." Samuel Snool taught the weapons class, and he looked like a criminal himself. Not Jackie Lumpenstein or Manny Companion criminal. They were cocky. He was paranoid.

"And Professor Pargeter," said Amphora. Honoria Pargeter was the school's poisons expert and a real nut job.

"They're all weird," said Amanda. "But are there telltale signs?"

"What, like being caught in the act?" said Amphora.

"That would make it easy, wouldn't it?" said Ivy.

"I don't think they'd be so stupid as to be obvious," said Amanda. "They're highly trained and very experienced."

"Probably true," said Ivy. She hesitated. Amanda knew what was coming next. "The moles so far haven't been teachers."

"What do you mean 'so far'?" said Amphora. "You mean there are going to be more?"

"You never know in this business," said Ivy.

"Oh great," said Amphora. "Just what we need. Like we have nothing else to worry about."

"Look," said Amanda, trying to nip that topic in the bud, "the problem is that we can't watch all of them, even with our listening devices, and even with Gordon's help. There are just too many of them."

"Not to mention too many students," said Amphora. "Although not now, during the summer."

Actually, what would be the point of infiltrating during the summer? With very few people around, there wasn't much to infiltrate. However, there was one person present whom Amanda didn't trust under any circumstances.

"Speaking of students," said Amanda, "you know that Harry Sheriff?"

"Boy, do I," said Amphora. "He's so cool."

"He most certainly is not," said Amanda. "He keeps grinning and winking at me."

"Oooooh," said Amphora. "You're lucky. He's noticed you. I'm jealous."

"Don't get too excited," said Amanda. "I saw him kissing some girl in Windermere."

"Really?" said Amphora. This topic was way more exciting to her than zombies or secret books. "Who was she? Details, please."

"She had long blond hair. She was beautiful."

"Does he look like he's a good kisser?" said Amphora.

"Oh for heaven's sake," said Amanda. "First of all, who cares, and second, how should I know? What does a good kisser look like?"

"I'll bet Professor Scribbish is a good kisser," said Amphora. Christopher Scribbish was the best-looking of all the male teachers. His curly black hair was legendary among the students.

"He sounds like he would be," said Ivy.

Only she knew what that meant. Amanda had no idea how you could sound like a good kisser. "You'll have to enlighten us another time," she said. They didn't have time for this folderol. Ivy should know better.

"You know what you need, Amanda?" said Amphora. "A boyfriend who knows how to kiss."

Amanda was getting tired of Amphora's frivolous remarks. She wished she'd concentrate on important matters instead of oohing and aaahing over guys all the time.

"Would you forget about this? We need to figure out what happened to the *Bible*."

"I don't think Simon is a good kisser," said Amphora.

That did it. Amanda stood up, stuck her hands on her hips, and said, "And you wonder why people don't take you seriously."

As soon as the words left her mouth, she knew she had done something terrible. Amphora's ego was already so fragile. The last thing she needed was insults from her friends. Plus now there would be even more tension between them.

Amphora stared daggers at Amanda, then got up and faced her.

"I'm transferring," she said. "I don't want to be your roommate anymore. In fact, I don't want to have anything to do with you."

And with that, she left the room, presumably to file her transfer request.

~◊◊◊~

"Oh, Ivy," said Amanda when Amphora had gone. "Why did I say that?" She wanted to slap herself. What she'd done was unforgiveable. Why did she keep opening her big mouth?

"That was bad," said Ivy.

"I know! Do you think she'd sit still for an apology?"

"Not right now. You could try a bit later."

"She'll never forgive me," said Amanda. "Why do I do things like that?"

"You're a doer," said Ivy. "You become impatient when people get in the way of things you think are important."

It was true. That was why she used to lose all her actors when she was directing a film, and why she'd lost Jill and Laurie, the only friends she'd had back in L.A. But that couldn't be the only explanation. Ivy was being kind.

"Right, like I insulted Scapulus because I wanted to get things done."

"That was just surprise," said Ivy. "You didn't expect him to be preppy." She was referring to the day when Amanda had seen Holmes for the first time. She'd taken one look at him and blurted out, "What a dork." She'd never been so embarrassed in her life, even when people

80

teased her about being descended from G. Lestrade, the man who was such a nothing that he didn't even have a first name.

"You know, Ivy," said Amanda, thinking of Holmes's incredible eyes, "the funny thing is that he isn't preppy at all. When you get to know him, he's actually kind of unconventional. I don't know why he dresses that way."

"He's eccentric," said Ivy.

"Exactly. That's just what he is, but not like Sherlock Holmes. Scapulus is eccentric in a good way."

"Sherlock was the greatest detective of all time," said Ivy.

"How about if we work at becoming the greatest detectives of all time and find that *Bible*?" said Amanda. She was getting tired of discussing unpleasant things.

"That's an excellent idea," said Ivy. "Here's what I think. It has to be in the pit. I wonder if there's a way to test the water to see if it has paper residue in it."

"Good thinking! If it doesn't, then Blixus has to have it. And if it does, it just disintegrated."

"We should be able to do the tests ourselves. That won't be difficult like doing that DNA sequencing on the crystals."

Last term when Ivy had suggested the crystals on Wink Wiffle's skull might have absorbed his DNA, the kids had tried to extract the stuff but had given up because the procedure was too complicated. That was when Professor Stegelmeyer had stepped in and done the work for them and they'd discovered that the skeleton was David's father. Testing water samples was child's play by comparison.

But before the girls could figure out how to get hold of some water from the quarry, Simon and Clive came running back into the common room, and their news wasn't good.

"They've found a dead body in a flat in Ulverston," said Simon. "And Wink Wiffle's fingerprints are all over the place."

8

BICKERING

The news that the police had found another body provided yet another distraction from Amanda's list. Events were moving too quickly for her to keep up.

"A dead body?" she said. "Who is it? Not someone we know?" The idea of losing another member of the Legatum family was almost too much to bear. Not that any dead body was a good thing.

"It's a criminal," said Simon matter-of-factly.

"Blixus?" said Ivy. She sounded almost gleeful at the prospect.

"No," said Clive. "But get this: he worked for Blixus."

"Whoa!" said Amanda. "This is huge." Then a nasty thought popped into her head. "Wait a minute. You don't suppose Mr. Wiffle murdered him, do you? It was a he, right?"

"How old is the body?" said Ivy.

"Dunno yet, and yes, it was a he," said Simon.

"Did you see it?" said Amanda.

"Me?" said Simon. "No. How could I have seen it?"

"No, of course you didn't," said Amanda. "I'm starting to get everything mixed up. Too many things happening at once." Maybe she should implement a project management system. Nah, too time-consuming.

"What else do you know about it?" said Ivy.

"Guy's name was Leon Pleth," said Simon. "Went by the nickname Crocodile."

"Crocodile?" said Amanda. "Whatever for? This isn't Florida. Why do criminals always have nicknames?" She ran through half a dozen of them in her mind: Jumbo Pinchuk, Maps Glappsy, Bugsy Siegel, Sweetums Bickie, Vixen Amado, Oil Blade. She had to admit that they were kind of evocative.

"Maybe he had big teeth," said Clive. He laughed at his own joke.

"How did he die?" said Amanda.

"Shot," said Simon.

"Okay, so the guy worked for Blixus and was shot, and Wink Wiffle's fingerprints were found in his flat in Ulverston," said Amanda. "That doesn't mean Wink killed him."

"Uh oh," said Simon, staring off into the distance.

"What?" said Clive. He looked at Simon expectantly.

"I'll bet that painting is of Ulverston," said Simon.

"Aren't you jumping to conclusions?" said Amanda.

"Yup," said Simon. "But I'll bet I'm right."

"What makes you think that?" said Ivy.

"Because I remember now," said Simon. "I've seen that place before, and Ulverston is where it is."

The next thing that happened was that David Wiffle himself stuck his head into the common room and said, "Where's Gordon?" Normally this wouldn't have been at all remarkable except that David was supposed to be at home in Cornwall.

"What are you doing here?" Amanda blurted out.

"Oh brother," said Simon under his breath.

"None of your beeswax," said David, using one of his favorite expressions, a cliché as usual. Poor David. He didn't have a creative bone in his body. "Where's Gordon?"

"How should we know?" said Amanda, forgetting all the terrible stuff David had been through. He pushed her buttons so easily.

"Never mind," said David, and left. Amanda breathed a sigh of relief. David was such hard work.

"Why do you suppose he's here?" said Ivy.

"Actually, he's on my list," said Amanda.

"What's on your list?" said Simon.

"Thrillkill wants to talk to him," said Amanda.

"Then why is he on *your* list?" said Clive.

"I don't know," said Amanda. She had wondered about that. What was she supposed to do, take notes? "Actually, it makes no sense."

"What do you think is going to happen to him?" said Ivy.

"I have no idea," said Amanda.

"Do you think he'll be expelled?" said Clive.

"Not if Thrillkill wants to win that lawsuit," said Simon. "All he needs to do is make Mrs. Wiffle even madder."

He had a point. Thrillkill was skating on very thin ice.

"What a mess," said Ivy. "Her husband is dead, he might have murdered a criminal who works for the Moriartys, and her son destroyed the most important thing the school owns, which he stole. I feel sorry for her."

"So do I," said Amanda, "but that doesn't mean she should sue the school." There must have been something in the Wiffle genes, or maybe the family culture. All of them were a pain in the neck. It was a good thing David was an only child. She couldn't bear the thought of having to deal with yet another Wiffle.

"What would you do?" said Simon.

That shut them up. No one had an answer.

"I think Thrillkill will try to help David," said Ivy after about thirty seconds. "It's the only thing that makes sense. Yes, he destroyed the *Bible*, which is like committing treason. But he took it because he was trying to protect it and when he destroyed it he was temporarily insane. He'd lost his father, he'd done something that could ruin the school, and he went berserk. So he can't really be blamed."

"Do you think he's fixable?" said Amanda. Wouldn't that be something? She'd heard of people who'd been train wrecks as children becoming amazing adults. How they'd pulled off such metamorphoses she had no idea.

"I don't," said Simon.

"Simon!" said Ivy. "That's mean."

"Just being realistic." Boy, he could be a downer. Not that he was often wrong.

"Clive, what do you think?" said Ivy.

"I think if we're nicer to him he might have a chance."

"Be nice to David Wiffle?" said Amanda. That was too hard. Wouldn't it be better to send him to a therapist or something?

"Sure, why not?" said Clive. "What can it hurt?"

"It can't hurt anything," said Simon, "but it can't help either. He's too far gone."

A smile spread across Clive's face. "Care to test your theory?"

"Go on."

"Cut it out, you two," said Ivy. "You don't turn someone's misery into a game."

"Oh, I don't know," said Simon. "You've turned Amphora's unhappiness into a profit center."

Ivy lifted up her sunglasses and did that withering look thing.

"Simon," she said, "you have a lot to learn. People have feelings. It's nice to consider them. Amphora's right. You probably are a bad kisser."

"Hey," said Amanda. "How did you know about that?"

"How do I know about anything?" said Ivy. "I hear things."

She got up, gave Nigel's lead a little yank, and walked out the door, leaving the three friends to their own thoughts. She must have been really mad at Simon to do that. Amanda couldn't recall another time when she'd actually stormed out of a room. Not that she was exactly storming. More like drizzling.

"We have to figure out what Wink Wiffle was doing in Crocodile Pleth's flat," said Amanda.

"I am too a good kisser," said Simon. "Wanna see?"

"Absolutely not," said Amanda. "You can kiss Clive."

"Not me," said Clive, wrinkling up his face.

"Come here, Amanda," said Simon. He patted the seat next to him.

"Nope," she said. "I'm not going to kiss you. Anyway, we need to figure this out."

Simon got up, moved next to Amanda, put his arms around her, and puckered up.

"Get away from me!" she said, pushing him back.

"You don't know what you're missing," said Simon calmly, leaning away again. She was glad he'd backed off. This kind of behavior from Simon of all people made her nervous.

"Hey, cool rainbow," said Clive, pointing out the window.

"What?" said Amanda. She didn't want to look, but she couldn't help noticing the colors out of the corner of her eye. "Who cares? We have to figure out what happened to the *Bible*. I mean Crocodile. I mean both."

Just then her phone rang. It was Darius Plover. She'd forgotten all about him.

"Hello, Mr. Plover," she said tentatively.

"Amanda!" said Darius, all smiles in his voice. "Ready to get started?"

Amanda looked at the two boys, who were listening eagerly. They didn't know about Darius Plover or Amanda's summer gig with him. Nick had known she was corresponding with him, but that was all.

"Uh, yes, absolutely" she said, watching Simon mouth the words, "Is that *Darius Plover*?"

"Excellent," said Darius. "I'm sending you a link and a project plan. Can you get back to me later today? Oh, wait a minute. The time difference. How about early tomorrow? That will be my wee hours of the morning. I'll be up."

"Yes, I will," she said. "First thing tomorrow."

"Super," he said. "Talk to you then."

Amanda could feel the two boys' eyes boring into her. "Tell me you weren't just talking to Darius Plover," said Simon.

"Okay," said Amanda. "I wasn't just talking to Darius Plover."

"You were," said Simon indignantly. "How could you not tell us?"

"Oh, I don't know," said Amanda. "Maybe a little thing called *privacy!*"

"You have a personal relationship with the world's coolest action film director and *you didn't tell us?*" He actually looked hurt. She couldn't remember another time when that had happened.

"It isn't your business," said Amanda.

"You don't want to be a detective after all," said Simon.

"Why?" said Amanda. "Because I'm working with Darius Plover?"

"You're *working* with him?" said Clive.

"I am," said Amanda. "I'm a consultant." Suddenly it dawned on her that neither Simon nor Clive thought she was making the whole thing up. She had to give them credit. Most people would have thought she was faking.

"You're leaving us," said Simon. He seemed genuinely concerned.

"I am not!" yelled Amanda.

"I would," said Simon.

"Me too," said Clive.

"What is wrong with you two?" said Amanda. "The world is ending and you would run off and make movies instead of trying to fix it?"

"Have to think about that," said Simon.

She couldn't believe he'd say a thing like that. He'd been beside himself when Thrillkill had questioned his lineage and he'd thought he might have to leave Legatum. "You're nuts."

"Ha ha!" said Simon in a rare moment of levity. "Gotcha."

So that was what he was up to. Amanda gave Simon the dirtiest look she could muster. "You...don't...deserve...me," she said, and made herself the fourth person to stomp out of the common room in less than an hour.

9

SIMON BINKLE, LADIES' MAN

Great. They hadn't been there a day and already everyone was fighting. Maybe they should all turn around and go home. Maybe Amanda should get on that plane, fly to L.A., and work with Darius Plover in person after all. Who needed all this trouble?

She thought about going to her room but feared that Ivy or Amphora would be there, and she didn't want to see them. She couldn't go back to the common room after she'd just made a dramatic exit. She needed to find a quiet place to regroup. The Disguise classroom on the top floor!

But getting there wasn't so easy. The construction workers had blocked so much of the school that the place had become an obstacle course. Furthermore it was incredibly dusty. It might not have been the worst idea to grab a few brooms and engage in a little sportsmanlike cleanup, as the kids had done when they'd invented the game of bumper brooms right after the earthquake. That had been fun, if you forgot about the terror and the danger. This was different, though. Amanda felt that the workers had invaded her space, and she didn't want to spend more time around them than she had to.

Suddenly she heard Simon's voice behind her. She didn't want to talk to him and she certainly didn't want to kiss him, so she ducked into a supply closet.

"How bad is it?" he was saying to a construction worker.

"This part?" said the guy. "Not too bad. But those classrooms down there, not so good."

Amanda had no idea where "down there" was, but she resolved to avoid it.

"But this could have been prevented, right?" said Simon.

"Oh yeah," said the guy. "The codes around here aren't strict enough."

"I'll bet you could design the school to withstand an 8.0 quake," said Simon. "All you'd need to do is build it on rollers."

"Sure," said the guy. "When you're starting from scratch."

"Not now?" said Simon.

"Nah," said the guy. "Not practical."

"But it could be done in theory, right?" said Simon.

"Sure," said the guy. "In theory you could build the whole country on rollers." He laughed.

"Hey," said Clive, who was obviously with him. "He was just asking."

"Look, kids," said the guy, "I've got work to do. Why don't you app boys run along and find something else to do?"

That remark made Amanda mad. Simon and Clive might be technically inclined, but they weren't "app boys." They were serious engineers. She burst out of the closet and said, "Shut up, bozo," then grabbed the two boys and pulled them down the hall, leaving the construction worker rolled over laughing.

"I thought you were mad at me," said Simon.

"I was," said Amanda. "Now I'm not, okay?"

"Don't toy with our hearts," said Clive.

Amanda stopped pulling and faced the two boys. "Now you look here, funnymen," she said. "There's some serious stuff going down here. Are you comedians or are you detectives?"

"Can't we be both?" said Clive, mock pleading.

"Only when the things on this list have been taken care of," said Amanda. "Now let's figure out this Wink Wiffle thing. Or the *Bible* thing. Or where Blixus is. Or something."

"All right," said Simon. "Let's figure out where that view in the painting is."

They decided that the best place to work on the problem was the lab. Not that there were any chemicals or machinery involved. It was just that the labs were quiet during the summer and they weren't likely to be disturbed.

On the way, Simon said, "I've been watching Scapulus like I told you I would. I saw something come out of Professor Redleaf's computer."

"He didn't know you saw, did he?" said Amanda. "What was it?"

"Nope," said Simon. "When that guy gets involved in something, he's dead to the world. I'm surprised he felt the earthquake."

That he had. Right after the quake he'd sent Amanda several texts to ask if she was okay. They'd come so fast it seemed as if he'd merely thought them. They'd annoyed her at the time. What she wouldn't give for that kind of attention from him now.

"You're going to think I'm crazy," said Simon.

"No, I won't," said Amanda. If he was crazy so was she. "I saw that bubble myself."

"All right, then," said Simon. "I saw what looked like a gold coin. I kid you not."

That was definitely crazier than a bubble. Although if the light had hit the screen in just the right way...

"A real one?" said Clive eagerly.

"No," said Simon. "I don't think so. It looked 3D and all, but it absorbed back into the screen again."

"Just like the bubble," said Amanda.

"Just like the bubble."

"Wow," said Clive. "That's a mean trick. Are you sure it wasn't a hologram or something?"

"I suppose it's a possibility," said Simon.

"Well, it wasn't a hologram when that bubble shot out of the screen," said Amanda. "And it wasn't a 3D effect like when you wear those red and green glasses."

"How do you know?" said Clive.

"I was close to it," said Amanda. "It was absolutely real."

"You didn't touch it, did you?" said Clive.

"No. Why?" What did he mean? He couldn't really believe the bubble would bite her or something.

"Because holograms can look real," he said. "That's a much more likely explanation than the hacker being able to manipulate matter."

That made sense. Still, it would be a good idea to confirm Clive's theory. "Scapulus will know," she said.

"Okay, you ask him," said Simon.

"You know he won't talk to me."

"If you can help solve the problem he will," said Simon.

"How can I solve the problem?" said Amanda. "I'm not even that good at computing yet."

"You'll think of something."

It didn't take Simon long to match the pattern in the painting with a location in Ulverston, which was about fifteen miles from Windermere. Now they had two proof points that Wink had been there: his fingerprints at Crocodile's flat and the painting. The fingerprints might have been made just the one time he'd been there, or they might have been deposited over time, but the painting had to have taken longer to create. That meant that Wink had spent many days in the place, if not longer. It also meant that there may have been a strong link between him and Crocodile, which implied another connection between him and Blixus, since Crocodile had worked for the criminal.

What would one of Blixus's henchman have been doing living in such an out-of-the-way place? And what would Wink have been doing there? He lived in Cornwall, for heaven's sake. It was hundreds of miles away. Would Thrillkill tell Mrs. Wiffle what they'd discovered? With the lawsuit pending, they weren't supposed to speak to each other. Of course he could inform her through his attorney—when he found one. But the idea of her having one more reason to hate Legatum and everyone associated with it was extremely unpleasant.

Obviously they needed to connect quite a few dots, some of which they didn't even have yet. They'd have to determine the times of the two men's deaths, find whatever the key belonged with to figure out what the relationship between Wink and Crocodile was, come up with a motive for murder, and deduce what Blixus and possibly Mavis had to do with all of this. Such an investigation could take months all by itself. With the *Bible*, Editta and the roommates, the lawsuit, the film, and whatever else was also in play, the chances of something falling by the wayside were huge, especially since everyone was feuding. If they were to work together they could cover just about everything on the list. If they were squabbling, not so much. Therefore Amanda decided that the first order of business was to make up and start getting along again.

Since Simon and Clive were right there, she thought she'd start with them. Not that she was feuding with Clive. She couldn't imagine that happening. He was way too laid back. She turned her attention to Simon. She had just the offer to make him come round.

"I'm sorry about earlier," she said. "Would you like to kiss me now?"

Simon gave her a quizzical look. "What are you talking about?"

"You wanted to kiss me," she said. "I wasn't ready. I am now."

He grinned, put down his tablet, threw his arms around her, and kissed her softly on the mouth. It was an amazing kiss, or at least it seemed to be—she'd never kissed a boy before—and for a moment she saw Nick's face in her mind.

"Well?" said Simon.

"I uh, er," said Amanda. She could feel her face going red.

Simon broke into a huge grin and gently slid the back of his hand down her cheek. He must have seen that in the movies. No way was that a Simon thing. Even so, his touch gave her the shivers.

"Told ya."

When Amanda's phone rang a few seconds later, she jumped. She couldn't get that kiss out of her mind.

She was surprised to hear Mr. Onion's voice. She'd completely forgotten about the lawyer.

"I have news," said Mr. Onion. "Your Gaston Thrillkill has asked me to defend Legatum in the Celerie Wiffle lawsuit."

Amanda didn't know what to say. She'd had so little to do with the man that she didn't even know if he was a good lawyer. She'd hoped to hear something about Mr. Doodle relenting and letting Manny have his guitar, or Jackie his cookbook.

"That's, uh, great, Mr. Onion," she said. "Can I help?"

"You surely can," said Mr. Onion. "I'm going to need a timeline and a boatload of facts. You'll be hearing from Mr. Thrillkill, but I wanted to give you a heads up. I hope you're not busy."

10

BLIXUS'S TRAIL GOES COLD

If she didn't figure out how to slow down, Amanda was sure she'd get nothing done. The most important tasks were those two item ones on the list, plus Darius Plover. Period. Not the key, not David Wiffle, not the *Bible*, and not Thrillkill's lawsuit. She had to locate Blixus, and she had to look at Darius Plover's project plan and write up a response. Now.

Ivy and Amphora might be in their room, but she had to get her computer and that was where it was. On the way she passed Mrs. Scarper in her tiny office. The matron waved as Amanda walked by. Poor woman. *She'd* hate to have to keep track of a bunch of teenage girls. Surely there were more fulfilling occupations.

When Amanda got to her door it was closed. She put her ear to it and listened. Amphora was saying, "I'm sorry, Ivy, but I can't stay here. If you want to come with me, fine, but I'm not rooming with Amanda anymore."

"She's just stressed," said Ivy. "She didn't mean it."

"She's so bossy," said Amphora.

That stung. Amanda thought she had conquered her tendency to tell people what to do. She opened the door and barged in.

"I am not bossy," she said, trying not to cry.

"Were you listening at the door?" said Amphora. She was sitting cross-legged on her bed. Ivy was lying on her stomach on hers.

"No," said Amanda. "Of course not. I was just about to come in."

95

"I thought you were listening, but then again, I'm just a dilettante," said Amphora. "Who would take me seriously?"

"I'm sorry," said Amanda. "You know I didn't mean that."

"I do, do I? The great Amanda Lester has decreed what I do and don't know."

"Amphora," said Ivy, sitting up.

"No, she needs to hear this," said Amphora. "I've had just about enough of you, Amanda. You prance around as if you're some kind of celebrity. Just because you like making movies does not entitle you to boss people. You're not really a director and we're not your actors. And I meant what I said about transferring. I'm going to move in with Prudence and Owla."

Amanda felt like screaming at her. Who was Amphora to tell her that she was an elitist? This was the girl who'd told David Wiffle she was more of an aristocrat than he was. But things would never get back to normal if she mentioned that.

"I'm sorry you feel that way," Amanda said. "However you're right. I am bossy. I've been trying to fix myself but I haven't succeeded yet. I have no excuse."

Amphora's mouth dropped open. She had obviously expected an argument and Amanda's conciliatory remarks had thrown her for a loop. She burst into tears.

"Oh, Amanda, I'm so sorry," she said, falling into her friend's arms. "I didn't mean it. I don't know why I said such terrible things."

Now both girls were crying. "Me either," sobbed Amanda. "I'm so sorry. You guys are my best friends. Please don't be mad at me."

Now Ivy had joined them in their group hug. Nigel seemed confused. He wasn't sure where to nose in and was everywhere at once, licking first one and then another of the girls.

"I have to tell you something," Amanda blubbered. And then she told them all about Darius Plover. Amazingly, this was one thing that Ivy had not figured out and the two of them were astonished. They'd known about Amanda's obsession with film, but they'd never dreamed she knew anyone so famous, let alone worked for him.

"I have to say something too," said Ivy. "Unfortunately it isn't something fun like Darius Plover."

"Go on," said Amphora.

"The secrets trove," said Ivy. "We have to figure out what's going on with it. With the teachers fighting and threatening to close the school, it could be in danger. No one is keeping track."

"That's right," said Amanda. "But I don't have any time."

"We'll handle it," said Ivy. "All we have to do is figure out where the metadata is. Then we can make sense of the whole thing."

"Any ideas?" said Amanda.

"Not a one," said Ivy.

Darius Plover's project plan was clear and concise. He'd identified scenes in the film that needed more oomph and asked Amanda to come up with as many ideas as possible. She wasn't to censor herself or worry about budgets, just brainstorm. Then, when she was finished, she was to go back and list pros and cons for each alternative. That was it. Easy peasey.

Except that it wasn't easy. Each scene required careful analysis. Amanda had to reread the script, think about what each segment needed to accomplish, and tweak it enough to make it a killer, but not in a way that would completely change the story.

The assignment was tough and she spent several hours on it. Still, she was pleased with the results. She'd come up with some ideas for making the villains more complex. They weren't just thugs. They felt threatened and were attempting to stabilize their world. That would add more texture to the scenes. She'd phone Darius first thing in the morning and see what he thought. For now, though, it was back to Blixus.

She needed to approach the problem systematically, go through each option for locating the criminal logically and thoroughly. First up, the two prisoners, Jackie and Manny.

Were they really the answer? Did they even know where Blixus was? They'd been arrested during the raid on the sugar factory and had been in Strangeways ever since. They had not seen Blixus since he and Mavis had escaped, so what were the chances they actually knew where the Moriartys were?

If they did, they'd have to have heard through the prison grapevine or from a visitor—unless there was a way they were in touch with Moriarty directly via phone or computer. What were the odds of that? Even if they had communicated with him, he probably hadn't told them where he was. The fewer the people who knew, the less the chance he'd be caught. No, Amanda doubted that they knew. Their requests for cookbooks and guitars were just trying it on, not legitimate offers. Scratch the prison, although she would have loved to see if Manny could actually play.

Perhaps the Crocodile connection would reveal something about Blixus's whereabouts. Amanda had no idea how, but they did have sort of a lead. If Crocodile worked for Blixus, he'd have to have kept in touch. Maybe his phone would yield a clue. It was possible that Blixus had even visited him. The police had said they'd discovered Wink's fingerprints in Crocodile's flat, but what about Blixus's? That was easy enough to find out. She'd just ask Thrillkill.

Unfortunately, Thrillkill told her that the only prints found at Crocodile's flat were the man's own and Wink's. No Blixus. And by the way, no murder weapon or phone.

What other clues did they have to Blixus's whereabouts? None, really. The detectives had checked all his known hiding places, as had Scotland Yard, although from what Amanda had seen of Jeffrey Lestrade, she wasn't holding her breath. Were there other Moriarty associates who might know, and if so, was there a way to get them to talk? Again, even if she could track them down, she doubted that they knew anything.

Wait a minute. What about hacking their phones? Holmes had done that before, although now that she thought about it, he'd hacked the roommates' phones, not the Moriartys'. Still, maybe he could figure out something. But that meant talking to him and she really didn't want to do that. He'd already have looked into that possibility anyway.

Had Blixus left a trail? How about Philip and Gavin, or Editta? They wouldn't have done so purposely, but perhaps accidentally. If so, what would that trail look like? She decided to make a list of clues to look for:

- Crystals. Maybe, but hadn't the kids taken all the crystals out of the van the Moriartys had been using at the quarry? Perhaps they'd had some in their pockets when they'd left, although there was no reason they should have left them for her to find. Still, an errant crystal might indicate which way they'd gone.

- Clothing. Perhaps they'd left an item behind somewhere— maybe parts of those disguises they'd been using. Not that the disguises were much to write home about, but there should be some hats and facial appliances such as eyebrows and maybe a mustache for Blixus.

- Phones. Had they been using disposable phones that might have fingerprints on them? That didn't seem like much of a lead. Trash doesn't sit around in bins as long as that.

- Fibers. Perhaps, but those were so small that they were worse than needles in haystacks, and where would she look?

- Pink sugar. That was an interesting idea. The stuff stuck to everything and was extremely difficult to get rid of. But when the police had found the van abandoned in Windermere, there had been no sugar nearby. If the Moriartys or Editta had got it on their feet, they would have tracked it only a short way. Another dead end.

- The gun that had killed Crocodile. Amanda wasn't even sure Blixus had committed the murder, but if they were to find the gun, they might be able to trace it. Not that Blixus would have left it lying around.

Therein lay the rub. Blixus Moriarty was not a sloppy man. His wife and son, on the other hand, had made plenty of mistakes. Perhaps they had left something that could lead the detectives to them. And surely the kids—Editta and the two roommates—didn't know what they were doing, assuming they were still with the group.

Amanda felt like pulling her hair out. None of these ideas seemed the least bit sound. Maybe it was time to take another tack.

What about profiling them? She was good at that. If she could figure out their thinking, she might be able to predict where they'd gone with some accuracy.

If she were a criminal trying to escape the notice of the law, where would she go? Not to relatives or friends. That would be too obvious. She wouldn't go to any property she was known to own or rent. The boat had already been searched, although there was no reason for Blixus not to use another one.

And then she realized what he must have done. It was so obvious. She and Simon had thought of it before, when they'd seen Blixus sail away on the Thames. If she were Blixus (an awful thought), she'd leave the country. And if that was what he'd done, they were out of luck. They'd have to trust the problem to Interpol or the local authorities in some place like Belgium or Norway and turn their attention to other things. No doubt Blixus was laughing himself silly by now. Some days being a detective was just so depressing.

11

CROCODILE'S FLAT

Amanda had so much trouble sleeping that night that she got up at 4:00 A.M. and phoned Darius Plover. It was only 8:00 the previous night in L.A. and he was surprised to hear from her. He took a quick peek at her work and gave her a virtual pat on the back, saying he'd phone to discuss next steps.

The police had scheduled Crocodile's autopsy for that morning, but Amanda couldn't stand the idea of waiting around, so at 6:00 she phoned Eustace Plantagenet and asked him if he'd take her to Crocodile's place in Ulverston. Of course she had woken him up.

"'Manda, is that you?" said the English surfer dude who gave tours of Windermere. He'd been invaluable at the quarry and had kept in touch, despite Amphora's continual attempts to flirt with him, which he took with good humor and then ignored. "Oh no, am I late for work?"

Amanda explained that no, he wasn't late, but if he'd do her this one favor she'd introduce him to some L.A. surfers. That got his attention and he agreed at once. He could drive her to the flat before work, but wasn't it a crime scene and therefore off limits?

"Not at all," she told him blithely.

Within a half hour he appeared at the front gate and they were off. Fortunately he had left his tram in Windermere and had brought his old Vauxhall, which was far less conspicuous and much faster.

"I'm glad you called," he said. "There's something I want to talk to you about."

"Oh, right, the surfer thing. I'll do that later today. I promise."

"No, not that," he said. "I don't know if you know this, but I've spoken to Mr. Thrillkill."

"Sure," she said. "I saw you with him after the quarry thing."

"Yes," he said, "but I don't think you know what I told him." Uh oh. She hoped he hadn't tattled on her and her friends. Not that she could think of anything specific they'd done wrong. They were always breaking rules these days, though, and there had to be something.

Eustace continued. "After fighting the Moriartys with you guys, I realized that being a detective was the coolest thing ever and I want to become one. He said that this was a bad time—too chaotic or something—but if I'm serious I should be prepared to prove myself, even though I'm not related to any famous detectives. Of course he swore me to secrecy, but that's no problem. I'd never tell a soul about Legatum."

Amanda was gobsmacked. Not only was she unaware of this conversation, but she couldn't believe Thrillkill would have encouraged the young man. He had been so strict with Simon, whose detective connection was a bit tenuous. Now he was considering training someone who had none? On the other hand, Eustace might make an excellent detective and Thrillkill might have recognized his potential. He was conscientious, dogged, and flexible. She'd watch to see if he also had the nose for sleuthing.

"That's great news, Eustace," she said. "Let me know if there's anything I can do to help."

"You bet I will," he said. He seemed so excited. Who knew?

When they arrived at Crocodile's first-floor flat, they could see that the door was blocked with yellow crime scene tape. However upon looking in a couple of windows, they concluded that no one was there to stop them entering. It would have been weird to post a guard around the clock anyway, with manpower so squeezed and all. The local police didn't exactly have the budget for that kind of thing.

"What are we going to do?" said Eustace, eyeing the tape.

"As I see it we have two choices," said Amanda, mentally weighing the options. "Go in the door or crawl through a window."

"But aren't they locked?" said Eustace.

"Let's take a look."

But before they could try the locks, Amanda saw something out of the corner of her eye—a person moving between buildings, but not an ordinary person. He was pale and scruffy, with old, tattered clothes. He—or she—looked like a zombie!

"Come on," she said as quietly as she could, grabbing Eustace's hand and pulling him along with her.

"Hey, what are we doing?" said Eustace. "We can't get in by running away."

"I saw something," said Amanda.

"What?" whispered Eustace, taking a cue from Amanda's hushed tone.

"Just come on," she said.

But when they got to where she had seen the zombie, it had disappeared. These zombies, or whatever they were, certainly were elusive.

"Nuts," she said. "Lost 'em."

"Lost what?" said Eustace.

"The zombie."

"What? Are you kidding?"

"I'm not kidding, but it might have been a homeless person. Or an actor. The thing is, we keep seeing these zombies but no one can get close enough to see what's going on. Of course that was in Windermere. Not here."

Eustace gave her a sidelong look. "If there were zombies, it would be the coolest thing ever, but come on, Amanda. You know it was just a homeless person. There are tons of them around. Not just in Windermere either."

"Maybe," she said. "But there's something about these guys. I'm not the only one who's noticed."

"Like what?" he said.

"They're not just rumpled. Their coloring…" What was their coloring anyway? It was so nondescript that she couldn't picture it. Professor Sidebotham would not be pleased.

"Have you got a picture?" he said.

"Unfortunately no. That would help, wouldn't it?"

"Next time you see one of these guys, don't worry about following them. Just take the picture."

"You're right," she said. "From now on, I'm keeping my camera at the ready."

"Good," he said. "Let's get back to the crime scene." She could hear him giggling. Obviously he thought she was crazy.

When they returned to Crocodile's flat they discovered that everything was locked up tight as expected. Amanda desperately wished Clive had come with them and brought his acoustic levitator, which would probably have got them in in about thirty seconds, but unfortunately she hadn't thought of that. The device, which allowed Clive to lift things without touching them, had come in handy on more than one occasion.

"Wait a minute," she said, suddenly getting an idea. "What kinds of locks are on the windows?"

"They're pretty basic," said Eustace. "All you do is turn the handle and the little bar goes up and down into and out of the latch."

"Perfect!" cried Amanda, and whipped out her phone. She pressed an icon and waited a moment. While this mysterious behavior was occurring, Eustace peered into the flat.

"It's pretty messy in there," he said.

"Clive," said Amanda into the phone. "Oh, sorry. I forgot how early it is. But please can I talk to you for a second? Thanks. Listen, do you think your acoustic levitator would work over the phone? Yes, I know you have to put that foil behind the thing but...a window lock. Yes, I know it's breaking and entering but...take pictures through the windows and enlarge them? I don't think that will work. I'm not sure what we're looking for. Just information about Crocodile's connection with Blixus or Wink. We're trying to find Blixus. I think Crocodile's computer is still there. Eustace, is there a computer inside?"

"Yup," said Eustace. "You don't think we can read it from outside, do you?"

"Scapulus?" said Amanda, turning back to Clive. "I don't think even he could do that with the power off. You could ask him. Oh, sorry. *I* could ask him. Do you think if you were here in person you could get the acoustic levitator to open the window lock? We could come back and get you. Yes, Eustace." She turned to Eustace. "Clive says hi."

"Hi, Clive," said Eustace. "How's that head?"

"He says it's almost completely better," said Amanda. Clive had been hit by a rock at the quarry, but the nurse had seen to him and he was doing well. "Hang on a minute. What if we could turn the computer on remotely? Remember when Simon charged up Scapulus's tablet with the crystals at the quarry? Why couldn't we use a beam of energy to do that? The password. Oh, right, *that*. Scapulus could do that, though, couldn't he? Yes, I suppose I should call him. Or would you like us to come get you and your acoustic levitator? Yes, we'd still have the password problem—unless the thing is actually on and signed in. The crime scene people wouldn't leave it like that, though, would they? Didn't think so. Okay, I'll call Scapulus."

"I got the gist of that," said Eustace when Amanda had hung up.

She didn't want to call Holmes in the worst way, especially so early in the morning. Was there anything else? "Wait a minute. Maybe that key Wink had opens this door."

"What key?" said Eustace.

"Oh, but I don't have it. I could ask Simon to send me a picture and we could get a duplicate made, though."

"I don't think any locksmiths are open yet," said Eustace. "What key?"

"The key Wink Wiffle swallowed before he died."

"Oh, tasty," said Eustace. "What does it look like?"

"It's small and—hang on. I'll draw you a picture."

She took her Kangaroo Egg Film Society membership card out of her bag, turned it over, and made a quick sketch.

"Nope," said Eustace. "That isn't for this door. It's not for a door at all."

"You know about keys?"

"Oh yeah. My dad's an ironmonger."

"A what?"

"You guys call it a hardware store, I think. He's got one. I know all about that stuff."

Amanda grabbed him and planted a big kiss on his forehead. "Eustace, you're a gem," she said. "We can get into this place easily. Why didn't you say?"

"I thought you had a plan," said Eustace.

"Unfortunately no," said Amanda. "So what do we do?"

Eustace looked around. There was no one nearby. "Pick the lock," he said, grinning.

Amanda was beginning to see that Eustace would make a great detective. He knew gadgets better than Simon did. Different types of gadgets to be sure, but incredibly useful ones. After checking again to make sure they weren't being watched, he got them into Crocodile's flat in about a minute. Amanda pulled him inside and slammed the door.

Eustace was right. Crocodile was a slob. He didn't own much, but what he did possess was thrown about so carelessly that it was a wonder he could find anything. For all she knew, he couldn't.

The computer seemed the obvious place to start. The problem, of course, was that she couldn't get in without Holmes's help—unless the thing wasn't password-protected, which was a remote possibility. She pulled on a pair of latex gloves so as not to leave fingerprints and switched it on. It sputtered a bit, and for a moment the screen was completely dark. Then it started painting Crocodile's desktop! There was no logon screen. Boy, the guy was dumb. Or maybe he didn't keep anything worthwhile on his computer. If that was the case they'd be disappointed.

They were. There was very little on the computer at all. In fact, it seemed disused except for the Web browser. In the history Amanda found that Crocodile had been particularly interested in bees and King Arthur, two topics she never would have associated with him. Whether these might have anything to do with Blixus she didn't know. It was difficult to see how, but she made a few notes so she could follow up.

She shut off the computer and made her way to Crocodile's card table, which seemed to do double duty as a dining area and workbench. A thin accordion file lay there with its corner off the table. Crocodile didn't seem to go in much for information, either in digital form or hard copy. Inside were a few sheets of rumpled paper. One of them had a bunch of numbers on it, some of which had been crossed out and corrected. Another showed a list of UK addresses, and a third contained a phone number. That was it. Amanda snapped pictures of each sheet and put them back carefully.

"What do you suppose all that is?" said Eustace.

"I don't know," she said, "but you can check that phone number right now."

Eustace pulled out his phone and thumbed a search.

"I don't know what this means," he said, "but it's a number for a truck rental place in Birmingham."

"I wonder what he wanted with that," she said. "We'll check that out later. The numbers don't make any sense as far as I can tell, but we can look up the addresses. Want to do that while I nose around some more?"

"Sure," said Eustace, who seemed beyond happy to be contributing. He took Amanda's phone and looked at the picture of the list she'd made, then thumbed away.

In one of the closets, Amanda found a safe. It had been left open, presumably by the crime scene investigators, and was empty. She extracted a swab from her evidence kit and took a sample swipe, although she didn't expect to find anything. Whatever had been there was probably cash or jewels or something of that nature and wouldn't have left residue. Still, it didn't hurt to try.

"This is weird," called out Eustace. "These addresses all seem to be farms. They're all over the Midlands."

"Farms?" said Amanda. "What would he want with those?"

"There might be something they have in common," said Eustace. "Can't tell from the addresses or the images."

"We'll look at it back at Legatum," said Amanda. "Maybe we can find a pattern."

"I'd be glad to take a gander," said Eustace, who really did seem to want to become a detective. He was getting keener by the moment.

"The safe is empty, the refrigerator's full of beer, and there isn't much else," said Amanda. "A few items of clothing, some paper cups, that kind of thing. What a life this guy must have had."

"Ready to go?" said Eustace. "I have to get to work."

"Yup," she said. "Let's roll."

When Eustace dropped Amanda off at Legatum, the first thing she saw was a bunch of teachers arguing heatedly. She caught the words "Moriarty," "Earful," and "Jarndyce" before the teachers saw her and shut up abruptly. She wondered if Earful referred to the school's founder, Lovelace Earful, but she knew exactly what Jarndyce was: the horrendous lawsuit in Charles Dickens's book *Bleak House*, which dragged on so long no one could remember what it was about. The teachers were obviously upset about Celerie Wiffle's suit and the threat of another one from Andalusia Sweetgum. As they should be, she thought. This was serious stuff.

"Good morning, Miss Lester," said Professor Feeney. "May I have a word?"

Uh oh. Amanda had never taken a class from the criminals and their methods teacher, so whatever she wanted had to be about something bad—the *Bible*, most likely, but maybe Wink Wiffle's murder. She steeled herself and stopped in front of the professor.

"I'm going to be giving a summer seminar on brainstorming techniques," said the teacher. "There are enough students on campus to make it worthwhile." Actually, the school had filled up with quite a few students who had returned to work on the murder mystery and a variety of other issues. It wasn't a bad idea. "I would like to invite you and your friends to attend. We start Friday morning at 9:00. We'll be covering topics like how to think your way out of a tight spot, what to do when you've run out of leads, that sort of thing."

This wasn't what Amanda had been expecting and she was overjoyed. Not that she had the time to attend a class, but it was an excellent idea. She could have used that very knowledge earlier when she and Eustace had faced Crocodile's locked flat.

"Yes," she said. "That sounds great. I'll tell them."

Professor Feeney smiled—the first time Amanda had ever seen her do so. She had bad teeth. "Brilliant," she said. "See you then."

As Amanda continued down the hall to the dining room (she'd forgotten to eat breakfast and was dying for a cup of tea), she felt a sense of relief. At least something normal was going on around the school. Maybe there was hope after all. If Professor Feeney was planning on teaching when no one usually did, that must mean that she and the other Punitori—the militant group of teachers who wanted to hunt down whoever had stolen the *Bible* and "neutralize" them—weren't planning on dissolving the school anytime soon.

But before she could get her cuppa, Amanda ran into Professor McTavish, the police procedures teacher, whom she also didn't know well.

"Oh, Miss Lester," he said in his Scottish brogue. She loved hearing him talk and could even understand much of what he said. "A word?"

"Certainly, Professor." She wasn't quite as nervous now that Professor Feeney had been so nice.

"I'm going to be giving a seminar on Mondays at 4:00 p.m.," he said. "Topics we don't always have time for during the year, such as how to use public records, chat up witnesses, and turn observations into action. I call it Companion to Procedures. I would like to see you there. It's informal—no uniforms—and you may bring a snack if you wish. But please do attend, and alert the other first-years."

Another seminar? Wow. Things really were looking up. Amanda breathed a sigh of relief. "Pleasure, Professor," she said. "See you then."

Then she ran into Professor Kindseth. Figuring that he too would be teaching a summer class she said, "What time shall I be there, Professor?"

"Be where, Miss Lester?" said the teacher.

"Your summer seminar," she said.

"What summer seminar?"

"You're not teaching a special class?" said Amanda.

"I wasn't planning to," said Professor Kindseth. "Would you like me to?"

"Well, uh, I thought—"

Professor Kindseth burst into such hearty laughter that Amanda took a step back to avoid being spit on. "I see what's happening here," he said. "Since you're here anyway you thought you might as well get your money's worth. Nice idea."

"No, it wasn't that," she said. "I don't care about the money—I mean, I would never do such a thing. That is, unless you wanted to, but even then I would never—I mean, sorry, Professor."

"Not a bad idea, though," he said, looking thoughtful. "A special class in 3D printing perhaps?"

This was definitely tempting. Simon and Professor Kindseth had cooked up a variety of useful gadgets on the 3D printer. Why not go for it?

"Sign me up," she said before he could protest.

"Very well, then," he said. "Shall we say Thursdays at noon?"

"We shall," she said. "I'll tell the others."

"Yes," he said, walking away. "Brilliant idea."

Wow. This was great! Amanda would have liked a class on secrets, but apparently Professor Snaffle wasn't in the mood or was otherwise occupied. Not that she was sure what a class in secrets might consist of, but it sounded extremely interesting, and considering that Ivy had made progress with the trove, useful. Oh well. You couldn't have everything.

But when she got to the dining room, Amanda received two nasty surprises. First Harry Sheriff was helping himself to a cup of tea with about twelve spoonfuls of sugar in it, and when he saw her he looked up brightly and grinned at her again. Then he did something even worse: he made a kissing gesture. This so unnerved her that she dropped her empty cup on the floor, which sent him into guffaws.

Now she was mad. She turned to him and said, "What is the matter with you?"

He just kept grinning and said, "You're quite a lovely specimen, you know that?" Then he poured his tea into a paper cup and walked off, leaving the dirty china for someone else to bus.

The second surprise was that Amanda caught sight of Scapulus Holmes sitting at "their" table at the far end of the room. It was the place they'd settled on for working on their films and other projects.

Amanda thought it strange that he would still sit there, considering how he seemed to have gone off her. She didn't know whether to smile, go over, or ignore him, but when she saw him looking indignant, she decided she'd better talk to him.

"That guy is a boor," said Holmes. "If he does that again I'm going to deck him."

This didn't sound like the Holmes she knew. It was more the kind of thing Nick would say.

"I'll deck him myself," she said. "I don't understand why he's acting this way. He seems to have developed a weird thing about me."

Holmes was silent, although Amanda got the distinct feeling that he was debating what to say. At last he said, "We need to get started."

"Yes," she said. "Sorry I've been so busy. Thrillkill gave me a list of tasks and they all seem to be urgent."

"No worries," he said. "When are you free?"

"Any time."

"Now?"

Being with Holmes at that moment was just about the last thing she wanted, but she didn't have a good reason to postpone. "Sure."

But just then Simon ran into the dining room and said, "Hey, you two, can you come here for a minute? I want you to see something."

Amanda and Holmes got up and followed Simon into the Holmes House common room next door.

"There," said Simon, pointing outside. "Does that rainbow look weird to you?"

"The colors are out of order," said Holmes.

"Yes," said Simon. "That's exactly what I thought."

12

SAVING THE WORLD

Amanda had never paid that much attention to rainbows. Not scientifically, anyway. She loved to look at them, but that was about it. She wasn't sure she'd have realized the colors were out of order if Simon hadn't said something.

"I don't understand," she said. "What does it mean?"

"Dunno," said Simon. "But it isn't right."

"What's it supposed to look like?" said Amanda.

"The colors go from one end of the visible spectrum to the other," said Holmes. "Red on the outer part, then orange, yellow, green, blue, indigo, and violet. In a double rainbow the order is reversed because the light is reflected twice. But I've never heard of a rainbow where the colors weren't in spectrum order."

Amanda looked closely. The boys were right. This one had yellow on the outside, then purple, green, red, blue, orange, and indigo. How odd.

"It's physically impossible," said Simon.

"Obviously not," said Amanda.

"What are you looking at?" said Amphora, who had just entered the common room. "Ooooh, pretty."

"It's wrong," said Amanda.

"What do you mean wrong?" said Amphora. "How can a rainbow be wrong?"

"Actually," said Holmes, "it isn't necessarily. There are variations such as supernumerary rainbows in which the light pattern is unusual. There are series of faint rainbows on the inside of the primary rainbow. The colors can vary because of the interference."

"I've never heard of that," said Simon.

"They're rare," said Holmes. "There are a number of other variations as well. This is quite a treat."

Amphora snapped a picture and said, "I'm going to design some clothes based on this rainbow. It's gorgeous."

"I'll say," said Amanda.

"Hey, what are you all doing?" said Gordon out of the blue. He sure was losing his inhibitions around the Holmes House group.

"Look at that," said Amphora. "Isn't it luscious?"

"The colors are all mixed up," said Gordon.

"What are you looking at?" said David, on his heels. Amanda couldn't tell if they were together or their simultaneous appearance was a coincidence.

"A rainbow," said Holmes. "A very unusual one."

"That's stupid," said David. "Who cares?"

Amanda had never felt more sorry for him.

As Amanda and Holmes were walking back to the dining room to start their film project, they simultaneously received a text from Thrillkill. The local police had just completed Crocodile's autopsy. The criminal had been killed *after* Wink's murder, so there was no chance Wink was responsible—unless he'd hired someone to do the dirty work for him. This was good news of a sort. At least David and his mother wouldn't have that issue to contend with. Wink was off the hook.

Amanda and Holmes were not, however. If they didn't come up with a plan to show Thrillkill soon, he'd bug them night and day. The problem was that they didn't know exactly what they were supposed to do.

"He told me he wanted a film that would explore Legatum's options without the *Bible*," said Amanda.

"That's a first step, but it's a bit vague," said Holmes.

"He said he wanted it to save the world."

"Options, save the world," said Holmes, mulling over what she'd told him. "A reconstruction plan, then. For life afterwards."

"That's an interesting way to put it," she said as tactfully as she could. She wasn't sure that was what she wanted. It was too technical. Reconstruction sounded like some kind of huge document with diagrams and equations, but she wasn't going to say so. It did have another meaning and she focused on that instead. "I've kind of been thinking of Thrillkill as Abraham Lincoln, so the term is apt."

"Hm, good point," he said. "We can use that. Although I hope we're not going to go through a civil war like America did."

"Sometimes I think we're already in one," she said. "The way the teachers have been fighting."

That was exactly what was happening. The teachers were at war. It was a horrifying thought.

"We need to bring them together," said Holmes. Yes! Now he was getting it.

"Right. That's exactly what we need. A sort of rah rah thing, but practical."

He laughed. "That's a pretty tall order."

"I know," she sighed.

"You know what?" he said. "We're starting in the wrong place."

She hoped he wasn't going to suggest some kind of deep research. They didn't have time for that. "What do you mean?"

"We're working top down, saying, 'This is our prescription.' We can't do that. We don't know enough about the problem."

Uh oh. That was exactly what he was doing. He was going to take his usual methodical approach and it would take them ten years to make a film they were supposed to create in just a few weeks.

"We know that the *Bible* is gone, probably forever," she said.

"Yes, but we don't know what that means. We have no idea what's in it."

"They're not going to tell us."

"Maybe not," said Holmes, "but we can make some educated guesses."

That was more like it. Guessing wouldn't take any time at all. "Well, sure. I've already thought about what might be in there."

"No, I mean by using evidence."

Not that. There wasn't time. "What evidence?" she said.

"Interviews," he said. "We'll talk to them. Get their opinions, ideas, learn their fears and concerns. Then we'll deduce what's in the *Bible* from what they do and don't say."

Yes! They could do that quickly. He'd got the message. Amanda wanted to kiss him, but she didn't dare. He might get the wrong idea and things would blow up completely. They seemed stable at the moment, although that was probably an illusion. Anyhow, there had been quite enough kissing for one summer. There would be plenty of time for that later, after they'd saved the world.

"Great idea!" she said instead. "Let's get started."

Despite the fact that Professor Also was a member of the militant Punitori faction, Amanda wanted to start with her. The history of detectives teacher had become a kind of confessor to her and she felt great affection for the woman. Plus she was less scary than some of the other teachers. Holmes decided that his target should be Professor

Mukherjee, the legal issues teacher, who was a member of the Realist group. That way he and Amanda could compare the two sides' positions.

When Amanda arrived at Professor Also's office, the teacher was uncharacteristically reticent.

"You know I can't tell you what's in the book," she said.

"I understand," said Amanda. She hadn't expected anyone to give up those secrets. They were too big a deal. "But I still think you can be helpful."

"To tell you the truth," said Professor Also, "I'm not sure this film is a good idea. The way forward is clear. We just need to get on with it." She crossed her arms. Amanda could tell she wasn't happy about being interviewed.

"Why do you say that, Professor?" said Amanda.

"Look, Miss Lester," said the teacher. "The Realists want to throw up their hands and surrender. Detectives don't do that. We fight. Blixus Moriarty has plagued us long enough. We need to find him and neutralize him. I'm sorry to have to say that. I know you were friends with that boy, but it's the only way." She fiddled with a pencil. You didn't see those much anymore. Using one in the digital age said something about a person. They were either of a practical mind or completely clueless about technology. Professor Also was the former.

"When you say 'neutralize,' what do you mean?" The word sounded terrible.

"I think you know," said Professor Also.

"You mean kill him?" Amanda was astonished that one of the teachers would openly advocate murder.

"You will never hear me say that," said the teacher.

"But that's what you mean," said Amanda.

"I didn't say that," said Professor Also.

It was obvious that Amanda wasn't going to pin her down. "Okay, let's say for the sake of argument that you did find the Moriartys and neutralize them. What about the *Bible?*"

"We take it back," said Professor Also, as if doing so would be easy.

"You're sure they have it?" said Amanda.

"There is no doubt in my mind," said the teacher. "It may not be easy to find, but they have it and we'll get it." She was confident in an edgy way. Amanda hadn't seen this side of her before.

"So you think it's legible despite the fact that it was crushed and soaked?" said Amanda. She didn't see how that was possible. She'd seen the water in the pit. It was so gritty it looked like it could dissolve the Statue of Liberty.

"I do," said Professor Also.

"Why is that?" said Amanda.

"Miss Lester, I am about to tell you something in confidence," said the teacher. "This information is not to leave this room."

"Of course."

Professor Also eyed Amanda as if she was about to divulge a great secret. "*The Detective's Bible* is virtually indestructible."

This was new. How could such a thing be possible?

"How do you mean?" said Amanda.

"Lovelace Earful was no dummy," said Professor Also. "He was a brilliant technologist. He created that book out of special materials so it would last a thousand years."

That sounded like a stretch. Amanda wasn't sure she believed it. Back in 1887 when the *Bible* was created, technology was a lot less advanced than now. Still, the detectives had their secrets. But if that was true, a lot of other things didn't make sense.

"If that's the case, why is everyone so upset? If it can't be destroyed, I mean."

"Well, of course it can be burned," said Professor Also. "That would destroy it. I'm sure there are other ways as well—acid perhaps. But the main problem now is that we don't know where it is and it might have fallen into the hands of people who will use it against us. Do you see?"

"Yes," said Amanda. This new fact had broad implications. If the *Bible* was so hardy, why all the fuss? And if it could be burned, then it couldn't be made of metal. What else could last so long? She'd seen the *Bible* and it was a book, not a stone tablet. Things were getting curiouser and curiouser. "So all the teachers know about the special materials?"

"Indeed they do," said Professor Also.

"Does David Wiffle know?"

"No. Nor do the parents."

"But if he did know, he might not feel quite as bad, right?" said Amanda.

"You're not proposing that we tell him?"

"I don't know," said Amanda. "Has anyone considered it?"

"Not that I know of," said the teacher. "It would be a mistake." She was not reacting well. Amanda didn't like Professor Also's behavior when she was upset. She seemed like a different person.

"Because?"

"Word might get out," said Professor Also. "You can't be too careful."

"So if the *Bible* is indestructible—"

"*Virtually* indestructible," said Professor Also.

"Right," said Amanda. "If it's as hardy as that, we should be able to find it sooner or later."

"One would hope so," said Professor Also, "but not necessarily. Blixus Moriarty might have hid it anywhere. If it's in an abandoned building or a hole in the ground, we might never know. Of course we have our ways of tracking both him and objects—"

This was also new. "What did you just say?" said Amanda.

"I said we can track Moriarty and also things," said the teacher.

"Do you know where he is?" said Amanda.

"Sadly, no. But we'll find him. It's just a matter of time."

"How do you know where to look?"

The teacher eyed Amanda as if assessing whether she ought to answer. For a moment she looked as if she was going to stonewall, but something seemed to click and she opened up.

"Physical evidence, satellite photography, witnesses, informants, cyberinvestigation, that sort of thing."

The list seemed logical, but Amanda was surprised. The teachers hadn't shared their personal methods with the students. Obviously a lot more went on at Legatum than the kids knew.

"Informants?" said Amanda. "You're not saying that Editta Sweetgum is a mole, are you? Or Philip Puppybreath and Gavin Niven?" If that were the case, she really would be surprised. She'd never thought of the kids who'd run off to be with the Moriartys as good actors. You couldn't do that without being able to fool an awful lot of people.

"I wish," said Professor Also. She looked dreamy for a moment, then caught herself. "No, none of them. At least not now. It's possible that they'll regret their actions and try to contact us though."

"But you're not counting on that."

"Not that specifically, no. But there are other ways."

"Such as Crocodile Pleth?" said Amanda.

"If he were still alive, yes," said the teacher. "Actually, that's not true. There's much we can learn from tracing his movements."

"So where do we go from here?"

"We find the Moriartys," said Professor Also. "One way or another that will get us the book."

"And the Realists?" said Amanda.

"If we have to, we'll split from them," said the professor.

"What does that mean?" said Amanda.

"It means, Miss Lester, that we'll form our own school."

After Amanda left Professor Also's office she found herself chuckling. The teacher had not warmed to the idea of the film, but through skillful questioning Amanda had got her answers anyway. She was chuffed.

When she met Holmes back at their table, he said that he too had completed a successful interview. Professor Mukherjee had told him in no uncertain terms that they were doomed. He wouldn't say what was in the *Bible* either, but he had explained that it was gone, kaput, finito, and they would have to give up. He said he planned to leave at the end of the summer after cleaning up a few loose ends.

Amanda desperately wanted to tell Holmes about Professor Also's claim that the book was indestructible, but she had promised not to say anything. It was important to find out what Professor Mukherjee thought about the matter, though, because if he were to realize that the book hadn't been destroyed, he might be more optimistic.

"What does Professor Mukherjee think happened to the *Bible*?" she said, hoping that Holmes might reveal something important.

"He doesn't know," said Holmes. "He says it doesn't matter, though. It's gone."

"So if the Moriartys have it it's of no use to them because of what David did?" she said hopefully.

"I guess," said Holmes. "Why are you asking?"

"Think about it," said Amanda, gazing into Holmes's eyes. He seemed to have forgotten himself because he gazed right back. "If the book was destroyed, why would Blixus have taken the remnants? Surely he wouldn't think he could put them back together."

"I guess he wouldn't have," said Holmes looking confused.

"Exactly," she said. "I think it's intact. And he has it."

"I'm still not following you."

"I think the Realists are up to something," she said.

"You're not making sense."

"Scapulus," she said. "Please just trust me."

That was rich. Asking him to trust her after everything that had happened. He'd never go for it.

"You know something," he said. "What is it?"

"I can't tell you."

"But you do know something. What's going on?"

"I'd tell you if I could. I swear." He searched her face. His look was so intense that she flinched. "Please don't do that," she said.

The air between them crackled but he didn't pursue the feeling. She was grateful. Whatever his faults, Holmes knew when to hold back.

"All right," he said. "Let's continue with the interviews. Then we'll see what we've got."

13

TO BEE OR NOT TO BEE

As soon as Amanda left Holmes, Darius Plover called. "Bingo!" he said before she could even say hello.

"Hi, Mr. Plover."

"No need to be so formal. Darius is fine."

"Darius then," she said. She didn't mind calling him by his first name. Everyone used first names in L.A. "You like my ideas?"

"I think they're spot on," he said. "I'm going to use every one of them."

This was too good to be true. There had to be a catch.

"You're kidding," she said. "I mean, that's wonderful."

"Don't think you're off the hook, though," he said. "The devil is in the details. Now we're going to dig in. Are you ready?"

"I'm ready. What's next?"

"I want you to rewrite the scenes."

She must have misheard him. There was no way Darius Plover would ask *her* to write part of his film.

"Excuse me?" she said.

"What, you don't want to?" he said, teasing.

"Of course I want to. But are you—I mean would you—I mean, sure!"

"You get more time for this," he said. "One week. Think you can make it?"

In her copious free time. But she'd find a way. He was offering her the chance of a lifetime.

"Absolutely," she said. "I'm on it."

No sooner had Amanda ended the call with Darius than Despina phoned. While she had grown to respect her cousin's abilities, the woman could drone on and on. Now was not a good time for a long chat.

"Amanda, darling!" gushed Despina.

"Hi, Despina," said Amanda.

"Hill and I are taking an archaeology tour of Cumbria. Did you know that there are gobs of stone circles around here? Mini Stonehenges within reach! Your cousin Jeffrey will be meeting us. It's the perfect opportunity for you two to get together."

Oh great. Cousin Jeffrey again.

"I'd love to, Despina, but—"

"Tomorrow good?"

"Not really. I—"

"We'll see you at 10:00, dear. You'll love Jeffrey. Did I tell you he's a detective inspector now?"

"Yes, you told me," said Amanda as patiently as she could. About a thousand times.

"We're so excited," said Despina. "He's going to be famous, you know."

Like the other Inspector Lestrade? Ha!

"I'm sure he will," said Amanda, gagging.

"Anyway, you'll see when you meet him," said Despina. "You're going to be fast friends. I can feel it. See you domani, dear. Bye now."

Amanda had been through this kind of thing with Despina before. The woman didn't listen. She simply decided that you were going to do something and that was that. How could someone who was such a good detective—for Despina was, in her own way—be so tone deaf? Amanda knew that there was no way she was going to escape the visit, so she steeled herself for what would befall her the following morning and went off to interview more teachers.

While she was talking to Professor Pargeter, the intimidating toxicology teacher she didn't know at all, Amanda received a text from Amphora: "Got something!!!!!" She was so curious to know what Amphora had found that she had trouble completing the interview and more than once said Kill Bill instead of Thrillkill and Harbinger instead of Pargeter. The teacher had stared right through her in the most disconcerting way, but each time she'd managed to regain her composure and soldier on—ish.

As soon as she'd completed the interview, in which Professor Pargeter had told her that everything in the world was toxic, you just had to know where to look, she texted Amphora back and asked her to meet in the common room. When she got there she found the décor gremlins in the middle of a heated argument, as usual.

"If you weren't so fat," Alexei was saying, "you wouldn't have trouble getting through those aisles in Room 27."

"I am not fat," said Noel. "The aisles are only fifteen inches wide. How do you expect a normal human being to fit? We need to install movable library shelves."

"Nonsense," said Alexei. "Stop eating candy."

"I don't eat candy," said Noel. "Just because you have a natural swimmer's body doesn't make me fat, and why am I arguing with a philistine like you? You twist everything I say."

Alexei humphed. "Russians do not twist."

"Oh really? Ever heard of Baba Yaga?"

"Baba Yaga is a sacred figure in Russian literature. The idea that you would denigrate her—"

Amanda could see where this train was headed. "Hello, gentlemen," she said, hoping that they'd forget what they were talking about.

"Amanda, dahlink," said Alexei. Sometimes Amanda thought he sounded like Despina with all the dears and darlings that came out of his mouth.

"Hello, Amanda," said Noel. "Do you think I'm fat?"

Uh oh. She most definitely did not want to get in the middle of this. If she said yes, she'd annoy Noel. If she said no, Alexei would get all huffy.

"I think you're as fat as I am," she said, hoping she was being sufficiently diplomatic.

"There, you see?" said Alexei.

What? She wasn't fat. How could he think she was fat?

"I see nothing," said Noel. "Amanda is not fat. She's not even pleasantly plump anymore."

That she had been when she'd entered Legatum, but now that the school's cuisine had changed she'd slimmed down.

"I propose a test then," said Alexei. "Amanda, see if you can get through the aisles in Basement Room 27. If you can, you're not fat. If you can't, you and Noel must go on diets."

Amanda felt her dander rise. She was not fat and she did not have to prove it.

"I'm sorry, Mr. Dropoff," she said. "I'm meeting Amphora and we have to do something."

"I didn't mean now," he said.

"Don't listen to him," said Noel. "You don't have to do it. He's being patently ridiculous. You meet your friend and run along."

"Do what?" said Amphora, entering the common room.

"Nothing," said Amanda, trying not to look at either gremlin. If she didn't encourage them, maybe they'd stop.

Amphora gave her a look like, "This again?" Amanda nodded. "Oh," mouthed Amphora.

"Hello, you two," said Amphora.

"Miss Kapoor," said Alexei.

"Ditto," said Noel.

"Amanda, I need to show you something," said Amphora, getting the message.

"Sorry," said Amanda, but the two gremlins had already turned their attention to some blue glass vases with bubbles in them and were arguing over the skill of the artist.

Amphora pulled her out of the common room. "At it again?"

"Yup. What's so important?" said Amanda.

"Just this," said Amphora. "I found out what Mr. Wiffle was doing before he died."

At last they were getting somewhere! Amanda couldn't wait to hear more.

"Well?" she said.

"He had Crocodile under surveillance," said Amphora.

That wasn't exactly a surprise. Couldn't she get on with it already?

"And?" said Amanda.

"Bees," said Amphora proudly.

"Bees?"

"Bees."

"Oh well, the case is solved then," said Amanda sarcastically.

"Stop it," said Amphora. "You already know this?"

"No, of course I don't know this," said Amanda. "You're going so slow. Can you please hurry up?"

"Oh, sorry," said Amphora. "I've been learning these little dramatic tricks from someone in the film business and they just leak into my speech." She grinned. She had a beautiful smile.

"Cut it out," said Amanda. "Just get to the point."

"Wink Wiffle received a tip that there had been a rash of bee thefts in the countryside," said Amphora eagerly. "His informant said that Crocodile was involved."

"Bee thefts, you say?" said Amanda. Who stole bees?

"Bee thefts."

It made sense. Those lists of farms… "Well, that explains that," said Amanda.

"You did know about this. Why didn't you tell me?"

"I didn't know anything," said Amanda. "I mean I knew something, but not anything, really."

"Now who isn't getting to the point?"

"Oh, my turn to be sorry," said Amanda. "Eustace and I—"

"Eustace?" said Amphora suspiciously. "You saw Eustace?"

Why did she have to make everything so difficult? She didn't own the guy. "Yes," said Amanda. "And—"

"And you didn't invite me?" said Amphora.

"You should be glad," said Amanda. She leaned in close and whispered. "We broke the law." That should put her off. Amphora would worry half to death that she'd go to prison for life if she so much as littered.

"So what else is new?"

Amanda was taken aback. Was that the reputation she'd built? "I don't break the law."

"Oh, really?" said Amphora. "How about the time you stole that truck, and the time you broke into the factory, and the time—"

When Amanda had been trying to get to London to save her father, she'd accidentally ended up in Edinburgh and had managed to escape from an angry truck driver by stealing his vehicle. It wasn't one of her prouder moments.

"Those were necessities."

"So?" said Amphora. "I'm sure this was too. What did you do?"

"We broke into Crocodile's flat," whispered Amanda, "but if you tell anyone—"

"Of course I'm not going to tell anyone!" screamed Amphora.

"Tell anyone what?" said David Wiffle, sticking his head into the common room.

"Now you've done it," said Amanda.

"Ooooh, this sounds juicy," said David. "Tell me."

"No," said Amanda.

"Don't you feel sorry for me?" said David in an annoying tone. "Just tell me." That made her mad. The kid was using his misfortune to get people to do things for him. What a creepy little jerk.

"Get out of here," said Amphora.

"I don't think you want to talk to me like that," said David. "My mother is suing the school, and you just got Thrillkill in a whole lot more trouble."

"Scram," said Amanda.

"You're going to be sorry," said David.

"You have some nerve—" said Amphora.

Amanda put a hand on her arm and shook her head. This was not the time to beat up on the poor kid, even if he was still obnoxious.

"You look fat," said David, causing Amphora to charge him. He was too fast for her and made it out into the hall before she could catch him.

"Twerp," she said, returning to Amanda.

"Yes, he is," said Amanda. "But let's ignore him. Tell me more about Wink Wiffle."

"Well," said Amphora, "the other thing I found out was that there were some notes on his computer, but they're encrypted. However, you can tell the date first created and the date last modified. Get this: the date last modified was the day before the orientation, and the date created was a couple of weeks before that. So this is a job he was doing for only a couple of weeks before he died."

"Interesting," said Amanda. "I wonder who that informant was who tipped him off about the bee thefts. And what do they have to do with the key?"

"Right," said Amphora. "My key." She seemed to think that because she'd found it, it was hers, like "The Amphora Kapoor Endowment for the Mystery Key" or something. "But what were you talking about when you said that explained that, and what does Eustace have to do with it?" She stopped and smiled in that way she did when she was daydreaming. "He's cute, isn't he?"

Amanda wondered if Amphora knew that Eustace wanted to be a detective. She hesitated to broach the subject. If she didn't know, she'd get all upset that Amanda did.

"He is cute," said Amanda, "but—"

"You want him for yourself," said Amphora.

"I do not!" yelled Amanda. "Would you please listen? When we went into Crocodile's flat we found a sheet of paper with some addresses on it. They turned out to be farms. I'll bet you these places had apiaries. Either bees were stolen from them or delivered to them. We need to check."

"That makes sense," said Amphora. "Crocodile had a list of places that involved bees. Perhaps the bee thieves could be found that way."

"Yes," said Amanda. "Although that's another case. Still, it helps us paint a picture of Wink's movements."

"I heard Mrs. Wiffle didn't know what her husband was doing right before he died."

"Yes. She told Thrillkill—this was a few weeks ago—that he had been away from the house a lot, but that was normal for him. He'd been staying in hotels, but he used a fake name and paid in cash so it will be hard to figure out where he went. This information might help us, though. Maybe he knew where these farms were and stayed near them."

"Yes," said Amphora. "Say, do you suppose the key belongs on one of those farms, or maybe to a safe in one of those hotel rooms?"

"Could be," said Amanda. "We should tell Thrillkill."

When the girls told Thrillkill about the leads they'd come up with, the headmaster was ecstatic. Fortunately he didn't ask how Amanda got the information from Crocodile's flat. Perhaps he already had it and just assumed that she'd seen it somehow. At least she'd managed to dodge that bullet. Also fortunately, the information allowed them to move forward with two tasks on Amanda's list: the key and Wink's murder.

"I think I'm on a roll," said Amphora. "I'm going to do a little more nosing around." She grinned. "Maybe I'll invite Eustace to come with me."

"He's working," said Amanda. "Don't disturb him."

"Oh, I won't," said Amphora cryptically.

"I don't believe you," said Amanda. Her roommate was up to something. You could always tell.

"Too bad for you," said Amphora. "See you."

She flounced out of the room. Amanda just knew she was going to get someone in trouble—if not Eustace, then the new cook or Harry Sheriff, or—

Harry Sheriff. What was going on with that guy? He was becoming obnoxious. She wondered if you could be expelled for harassing other students. Probably not. If that were the case David Wiffle would have been gone long ago. Too bad.

Then she heard voices out in the hall.

"Shut up," she heard Amphora say.

"You shut up," said Simon.

Oh, brother. They were at it again. Good thing Ivy wasn't around.

Then suddenly Simon tore into the room so fast he almost fell over.

"What?" she said.

"I just saw the most amazing thing," he said. "A rainbow just shot out of Scapulus's computer."

14

LEPRECHAUNS

The hacker had struck again! But why a bubble, then a gold coin, and then a rainbow? What was he trying to say? Wait a minute: a rainbow. Amanda had seen several rainbows recently, and one of them was wrong. Could there be a connection?

"Slow down and tell me everything," she said.

"Well," said Simon, "I was spying on Scapulus—" She grimaced. She hated the idea of him doing that. "He was working on Professor Redleaf's computer and this little rainbow came shooting out. He jumped."

"Did he see you?"

"'Course not. I'm a good spy."

Good spy, good kisser. Where did Simon learn this stuff anyway?

"What did he do?" she said, trying not to think of that amazing kiss.

"He frowned," said Simon. He would have made a great witness in court. He never volunteered information beyond what he'd been asked. His reticence drove Amanda crazy.

"And then what?"

"Nothing," said Simon. "He just sat there thinking."

That must have been exciting. Like watching grass grow. "How long did you watch?"

"Couple minutes, I guess."

"It's the hacker," she said.

"Yup. Weird guy. Or maybe it's a woman. I mean rainbows, come on."

"You're a sexist, you know that?" she said. She hoped the hacker really was a guy. It would serve Simon right for making assumptions.

"Am not," he said. "I'm using 'he' as a generic pronoun."

"Right," said Amanda, not believing a word. "We have to find this hacker."

"You mean do something Scapulus isn't?" Simon looked skeptical. "He's the best cyberinvestigator there is."

"That's exactly what I mean," she said.

"How?"

"I don't know. I need to think about it. But I'll come up with something."

She had to anyway. Professor Redleaf's computer was on her task list.

"Hey, Simon," she said, remembering something that wasn't on the list. "What do you think of this zombie thing?"

"Funny you should ask," he said. "Clive and I are going into town to see if we can find one. Want to come?"

"I wish I could." She really did. Anything would be better than dealing with the hacker or facing Holmes. "I've got to work on Thrillkill's list."

"Oh, come on," he said. "It'll be fun."

"Sorry. Can't."

"Suit yourself." He got a weird look on his face. "Want me to kiss you again?"

She did, but there was no way she was going to admit it. Anyway, it wasn't a good idea. Everyone would find out and—ugh. It was bad enough with Harry Sheriff making remarks. She didn't need the whole school hassling her.

"No thanks. Have a good time."

Amanda's phone rang again. She was starting to feel like a human call center.

"Miss Lester," said Mr. Onion on the other end of the line. "A word please."

"Sure," she said. *Join the club.*

"In the matter of Ms. Wiffle's lawsuit, I'm going to need to depose you. Shall we say next week?"

Why not? She had nothing else to do. Not. "Next week."

"Very well, then. I will send you some questions so you can prepare. Just tell the truth."

"I will."

"Check your mail in a few minutes."

"Will do." Unless some other crisis arose. There were only about ten of them right now.

This hacker thing was getting weirder and weirder. It seemed that whoever was invading Professor Redleaf's computer had learned to manipulate matter remotely. But that wasn't possible, was it? It was if there were a control system involved, like they did with the Hubble telescope or satellites, but that was all set up ahead of time, on purpose, and everything fit together exactly the way it needed to. You couldn't just take control and make the devices dance the jig or something, could you?

But this wasn't a mere dance. This was *changing* matter, not moving it. It was turning a screen into a liquid, then back to a solid again, creating objects or phenomena out of something completely unlike them and animating them. It went way beyond 3D printing. It was like alchemy. No, not *like* alchemy. It *was* alchemy.

But alchemy was impossible. You couldn't turn base metals into gold. You could make such things seem to happen by using light—holograms, 3D graphics, and the like—but you couldn't make them happen for real. So what Amanda and Simon had seen couldn't actually be happening.

Whether or not these things were actually occurring, however, the real issue was finding the hacker. He or she was a troll, pure and simple. Right now the phenomena were annoying, but they might become dangerous, and that was the real worry. Professor Redleaf had certainly thought so. The look on her face that day in front of the class was serious. She wasn't a frivolous person. If she was scared, she'd had good reason to be.

The hacker's agenda seemed apparent: disrupt Legatum's operations. Any number of criminals could have managed that one way or another, but Amanda was just about sure that Moriarty was involved. He and Thrillkill were engaged in a personal vendetta, for one thing. For another, his family's battle with the detectives went back more than a hundred years. It had to be him, and he had to have hired someone to help.

What was the type of logic involved in her conclusion—abductive reasoning? Professor Ducey had taught them that with abductive logic, you are looking not only for a logical conclusion, but the *best* logical conclusion. Moriarty was it.

She wondered if Holmes felt the same way. She wished she could ask him. For all she knew he was so far ahead of her on this that she was wasting her time. Why shouldn't she ask him though? The task was on her list. He had no right to withhold information. They were meeting about the film anyway. She'd do it. If he refused to say, she'd sic Thrillkill on him. She didn't have time for games and either did the school.

As she made her way to the dining room for their meeting, Amanda ran into Ivy and Nigel. She noticed that Ivy had gotten her coppery hair cut and it was really bouncy. When she walked it bobbed up and down like a spring.

"What's going on?" said Ivy.

"OMG, so many things," said Amanda, and proceeded to bring her up to speed.

"It's leprechauns," Ivy said when she'd finished.

"What's leprechauns?" said Amanda.

"The rainbows. The gold coins."

"Why do you say that?" She hoped Ivy wasn't going off the deep end. She was starting to sound like Editta.

"You know how leprechauns are said to hide their gold at the ends of rainbows so no one will find them?" said Ivy.

"Yes, of course."

"And you know why, don't you?"

"Why?" She had no idea. There weren't any leprechauns in L.A. Not too many rainbows either.

"Because a rainbow's location is relative to the viewer. It's not absolute. That means you can never actually find it or the pots of gold."

"Wow," said Amanda. "That's really clever." But it still didn't mean that leprechauns were involved. They were as mythical as zombies.

"Yes," said Ivy. "But don't you see? That's what the hacker is doing."

"I don't follow you," said Amanda, leading her friend to the beverage table. She selected two cups and began to make tea.

"He's hiding his gold under rainbows," said Ivy. "Oh, thanks. I could use a cuppa."

"I still don't understand."

"Think about it," said Ivy. "His location is as elusive as that of a rainbow. Is that Earl Grey?" She sniffed the air.

Amanda surveyed the various teas. "Yes. Would you like something else?"

"And he's creating rainbows." Ivy lowered her voice as she changed the subject. "PG Tips is better, thanks. Don't you think so?"

"I like both flavors," said Amanda, exchanging the Earl Grey for PG Tips. Funny how she'd become a big tea drinker. She'd never done that back in L.A. "I didn't say he was creating rainbows. I don't know that."

"No, you didn't, but don't you see that that's what he's doing?"

"You don't mean to tell me that he's the one making those weird rainbows outside," said Amanda.

"I certainly do," said Ivy.

"You're kidding."

"No, I'm not. This guy has got something special going on, and he's making it as difficult to find as a pot of gold at the end of the rainbow."

"But how can he do something in the sky?" said Amanda.

"I don't know," said Ivy. "But my theory is that he isn't just a hacker in cyberspace. He's a matter hacker too."

Amanda thought for a moment. Based on what she'd seen, Ivy's explanation made sense. Except that it was impossible. Unless alchemy wasn't impossible. Well, not alchemy exactly, but manipulating matter remotely.

"Ivy, you'd better be serious about this," said Amanda. "It sounds crazy."

"I didn't see the things you saw," said Ivy. "I have to take your word for it. But I absolutely believe that you saw what you told me you did. Which means it was real. And you know what Sherlock Holmes always said—oh, sorry."

"It's okay," said Amanda. "You can say it. 'Once you eliminate the impossible, whatever remains, no matter how improbable, must be the truth.'"

"Well," said Ivy, "there you are."

"Come on," said Amanda. "We have to tell Scapulus."

"No," said Holmes when Ivy had presented her explanation for the mysterious phenomena. "That's impossible."

"I hate to do this," said Ivy, "but your ancestor—"

"That again?" said Holmes. "I wish I could have known him just so I could strangle him for that."

"Scapulus!" said Amanda. She'd never heard him talk that way before, but more than that, since when did he have a beef with Sherlock?

"It sounds good, but it doesn't always work," said Holmes. "It's too blithe."

"Blithe?" said Ivy. "That's a word you don't hear every day."

"Blithe, facile, whatever. The man wasn't flawless. You know that."

Actually, Holmes *had* said something like that before. He didn't have blind faith in his great-great-whatever. Amanda liked that about him. She liked everything about him, come to think of it. She wished she could tell him just how much.

"What's your explanation then?" she said.

"I don't have one yet," said Holmes. "I'm being as systematic as I can, though. This stuff takes a while."

Could he be right? Maybe Ivy had jumped to conclusions. Her theory was pretty romantic but short on logic.

"That's fair," said Amanda. She didn't feel like arguing. Either did Ivy, apparently, because she said she was off to finish up her audio observing seminar for Professor Sidebotham, and after finishing her tea with a gulp she left the room with Nigel in tow.

"I hope you're not listening to her," said Holmes when Ivy had gone.

"She's very smart," said Amanda.

"Agreed. However, she's starting to sound like your friend Editta."

What did he know about Editta? The whole of last term she'd kept to herself and so had he, for the most part.

"And you," said Amanda, "sound like Simon."

"Good," he said. "Simon is intelligent."

"That's his criterion for liking people too," said Amanda.

"I didn't say—"

"It's all right. It's nothing to be ashamed about. A little narrow, maybe, but—"

Holmes looked annoyed. "Not everyone is touchy feely."

"What's that supposed to mean?"

He seemed to be regretting his words because he started to backpedal.

"I'm sorry. I'm just tense. There's so much riding on all this."

True, but was he using the chaos as an excuse for being tetchy? She knew exactly what he was referring to: Nick. And she was sitting there not doing a thing to help. She wanted to stop his suffering but she knew she couldn't. Not until she found Nick and got some closure.

"Did you finish your interview?" she said.

"With Professor Pole? Yes."

"Any thoughts?"

"He sounds a lot like Professor Mukherjee. You?"

"I'm working on an angle." She wasn't ready to tell him about her suspicions having to do with the Realists. He'd probably pooh-pooh those too.

"All right," he said, letting her be. "Let's reconvene tomorrow. Maybe we'll have some ideas by then."

"There's a lead on the key," she said, hoping to inject something positive into the conversation.

"Oh, good."

She searched his face, but he didn't seem about to ask for detail. He was too depressed to care, and it was her fault.

15

ENTER INSPECTOR LESTRADE

The next morning at ten o'clock sharp, Despina called from the guard gate. Lovely. Amanda was in the middle of working on the "Sand" script for Darius Plover and now she'd lost her train of thought.

"Darling, we're here," said Despina. "Jeffrey, say hello to Amanda."

"Hello, Amanda," said Jeffrey into Despina's phone. "Mother says—"

"Darling, the guard won't let us in," said Despina, interrupting. "I don't understand."

"You have to clear it through the headmaster," said Amanda, realizing that *she* should have done that.

"But the last time I saw Gaston he said we were welcome any time," said Despina.

Amanda sighed. Even if he had said such a thing, Thrillkill was so distracted these days it wasn't surprising he'd missed putting the Lesters on the visitors list.

"Hang on," said Amanda. "I'll speak to him."

"This is an outrage," said Jeffrey. "Scotland Yard should have a blanket authorization. I can't imagine—"

Amanda ended the call and phoned Thrillkill.

"What?" he barked.

"Oh, sorry, Professor," she said. "I've got you at a bad time."

"It's always a bad time," said Thrillkill. The last time she'd seen him this grumpy was weeks before. Not that he didn't have good reason to be. In fact she was surprised that he had *not* been grumpy with all the terrible things going on. Still if he were to deny the Lesters permission to enter the school, that would be a perfect excuse for her not to see them—except that Despina would insist on her coming out instead.

"I, uh, it's just that my cousins Despina and Hill and their son from Scotland Yard are at the guard gate and they can't get in."

"Did you say their son works at Scotland Yard?" said Thrillkill.

"Yes. He's a detective inspector."

"What's his name?" said Thrillkill.

"Jeffrey Lestrade," said Amanda.

"Inspector Lestrade?" said Thrillkill. "Another one?"

"Yes, sir."

"You tell Merlin to let them in at once," said Thrillkill. "I'm going to have to reprimand him."

Great. Now she'd got the guard in trouble. Actually, she hadn't. Despina had. Or maybe it was both of them. In any case, he didn't deserve it. He was just doing his job.

She phoned Merlin at the gate and told him what Thrillkill had said. The next thing she knew, the three relatives were sitting at Amanda and Holmes's table in the dining room with steaming cups of tea, although Despina's was more like a tea-flavored milkshake. Jeffrey was a trim, bald man of about thirty with dull blue eyes. His face was such a perfect oval that Amanda wanted to stick it in an egg cup and crack it with a spoon.

"The very idea," said Jeffrey. "I thought famous detectives were supposed to be respected here."

Amanda did not want to point out that Jeffrey was not a famous detective, even if his ancestor was.

"He's correct, dear," said Despina. "The school isn't going downhill, is it? Because if it is I'll have to consider withdrawing my support."

"Now, Despina," said Hill. "I'm sure it just slipped Gaston's mind."

"That's no excuse," she said. "This school needs to run like clockwork. I'm going to have to look into this."

Amanda wanted to melt into her shoes. Not only was Despina in rare form, but it seemed that Jeffrey was a lot like his ancestor, just as she'd feared. She didn't need this.

Then she saw Holmes. Oh no! He was coming over.

"Hullo, Despina, Hill," said Holmes when he'd reached "their" table. "What a pleasure it is to see you."

"Scapulus, darling!" Despina stood up and threw her arms around the boy, practically suffocating him. "Jeffrey, look who's here. Scapulus Holmes."

Jeffrey rose stiffly and shook Holmes's hand. "Holmes."

"Lestrade," said Holmes.

"Well, isn't this just jolly?" said Despina. "My favorite people all together in one place—"

"Mr. Holmes," interrupted Jeffrey. "I have a bone to pick with you." Holmes looked surprised, which made sense since he'd never met Jeffrey before. "Your ancestor, Sherlock Holmes, did something to my ancestor, Inspector Lestrade, that I've never forgiven him for. It seems that—"

"Now, darling," said Despina. "We're having such a pleasant day. There's no need to bring this up now."

"No, I want to hear," said Holmes.

"It was simply unconscionable," said Jeffrey.

Suddenly Hill got up, took Jeffrey roughly by the arm, and whispered something in his ear. Looking dutifully chastised, Jeffrey turned to Holmes and said, "My apologies. It seems I was misinformed. There's no dispute after all."

Amanda broke into mental guffaws. Good for Hill. At least *he* had some sense. Unfortunately it seemed that Jeffrey did not.

"Now, Scapulus," said Despina, barging ahead. "I hope you're taking good care of Amanda here."

Could Despina say anything that didn't involve sticking her foot in her mouth? Amanda and Holmes looked at each other in horror. Obviously Despina didn't know about Amanda's feelings for Nick and Holmes's feelings about those feelings, which was just as well, even if her ignorance caused her to say gauche things once in a while.

Holmes was the first to regain his composure. He sidled over to Amanda, put his arm around her stiffly, and said, "Of course I am. She's the most wonderful girl on earth. I would never let anything happen to her."

Amanda was trapped. She had no choice but to play along. She turned her face to him and looked at him lovingly. "He's wonderful to me," she said. "I couldn't ask for a better boyfriend."

She felt Holmes jump. He gave her shoulder a painful squeeze and said, "Unfortunately I must be going. I'm so glad to have met you, Inspector. See you soon, Despina, Hill." Then he let go of Amanda and scooted out of the room in a sort of power walk.

"Lovely boy," said Despina.

"For a Holmes," said Jeffrey.

"Darling, you shouldn't say such things," said Despina. "Remember what I told you? Accentuate the positive. Don't let that awful Blixus Moriarty get you down."

Amanda had the distinct feeling that Jeffrey's "mood" had nothing to do with Blixus and everything to do with his unpleasant personality, but she wasn't about to say anything.

"Anyhoo," said Despina, "I wanted to tell you about the archaeological tour of Cumbria we're starting today."

Now that was interesting. Not that Amanda wanted to inflict her relatives on Ivy, but since Ivy's father was an archaeologist, she thought they might have an enjoyable conversation on the topic. Ivy liked the Lesters anyway. Amanda phoned her.

When she heard that the group was about to embark on an archaeological tour, Ivy became incredibly excited and was sitting with them in the dining room about forty seconds later.

"Oh, hello, Nigel," said Despina after making the introductions. Nigel looked up at the large woman and let out a soft whine. Jeffrey looked at the dog distastefully but kept his trap shut. "Ivy, I hear your father is an archaeologist."

"Yes," said Ivy. "He teaches at Bournemouth University. He often takes students on digs."

"And has he made any momentous discoveries?" said Despina.

"Actually he has," said Ivy. "He found a peat bog mummy."

"A mummy," gasped Jeffrey. "That's terrible."

"Why terrible?" said Ivy.

"They're so, so unpleasant," said Jeffrey.

"Not at all," said Ivy. "Some of them are perfectly preserved. You can tell a lot about their societies and them as individuals. It's quite fascinating."

"Where did your father find this mummy?" said Hill.

"On an island off the coast of Scotland. It's called Isle Bethere."

"Do tell," said Despina. "We must go there. Hill, make a reservation."

Hill looked like he'd been ambushed, which he had. "I'm not sure it's that simple, dear."

"Nonsense," said Jeffrey. "It's macabre. Mother, I won't have you rooting around among nasty old bones. You could catch something."

Amanda was starting to wonder if Jeffrey was related to David Wiffle. They seemed so much alike. She thought she'd do a little test.

"Cousin Jeffrey," she said. "If you had to bend the law to bring Blixus Moriarty to justice, would you?"

Everyone sat up. Despina looked horrified. Hill seemed cautiously apprehensive, and Ivy was smiling, seemingly because she knew exactly what Amanda was doing.

"Darling, I think that's rather a personal question," said Despina. "I can give you the answer, however."

"Be quiet, Mother," said Jeffrey. Despina looked as if someone had shot an arrow through her heart. "It is an impertinent question but I will answer it because we are family." He stood up and looked down at her sternly. "I would never, ever break the law, even if it meant I could put Blixus Moriarty back in prison where he belongs."

"Really?" said Amanda. "That's quite fascinating."

"Nothing fascinating about it," said Jeffrey. "Morality is absolute. You do not make excuses, grant exceptions, or alter it in any way. I'm surprised you would even ask such a question."

Ivy was stifling a laugh. Despina looked satisfied, and Hill seemed to be cringing. It was obvious where everyone stood on this question.

"Thank you, Jeffrey," said Amanda. "That's very enlightening."

Yup. He was exactly like David Wiffle.

147

16

AMPHORA'S HIDDEN TALENT

After Despina, Hill, and Jeffrey had left (at last!), Amanda remembered that it was almost time for Professor Kindseth's 3D printing seminar and asked Ivy to meet her at the common room first. And oh no, Simon and Clive had gone into town to look for zombies. They were going to miss the class.

She took out her phone and pressed Simon's icon. It took him a while to pick up.

"You wouldn't believe what's going on down here," he said.

"What?" she said. "Is something wrong, *Simon*?" She could see Ivy enter the room and emphasized Simon's name so her friend would know what was going on.

"Nope, not wrong," he said. "Hilarious."

"He says nothing's wrong," said Amanda, putting her hand over the phone.

"Oh, good," said Ivy, letting out a breath.

"What do you mean hilarious?" said Amanda turning back to the phone. "Do you realize Professor Kindseth's 3D printing seminar is going to start at noon?"

"Blast," said Simon. "I forgot." His voice got softer as he turned away. "Hey, Clive, we've gotta go."

"Now?" Amanda could hear Clive say in the background.

"Yup," said Simon. "Too bad too, because this is quite entertaining."

"What are you talking about?" said Amanda.

Simon's voice got louder again. "Amphora is here and she's directing traffic."

Yeah, right. "What?" said Amanda. She was getting annoyed with him and they hadn't been on the phone for thirty seconds.

"What's going on?" said Ivy. She looked worried.

"Simon says Amphora is directing traffic in Windermere," said Amanda.

"What?" said Ivy. "Has she been hit by a car?"

"She's pretty good at it too," said Simon.

"Have you lost your mind?" said Amanda. She leaned over to Ivy and said, "Amphora's fine." Ivy squeezed Amanda's hand.

"Only when I kissed you," said Simon.

"Man, that was something," said Clive in the background.

"It was not!" yelled Amanda. Would he give it a rest already?

"Simon kissed you?" said Ivy.

"You can hear him?" said Amanda.

"Of course," said Ivy. "When did he kiss you? Did it hurt?"

"You know you wanted it," said Simon. "And I heard that, Ivy. I think *you* should be fined for that."

"No way, Simon," said Ivy. She leaned over to Amanda and said again, "Simon kissed you? Tell me more!"

Amanda whispered, "Yes, but it was a joke," then turned back to the phone. "Look," she said, "I called you as a favor. Don't be a jerk or next time I'll let you miss the class."

"Sorry," said Simon. "That wasn't nice of me. I'll give Ivy a pound."

"See that you do," said Amanda.

"I wasn't lying, Amanda. Amphora's right there in the middle of the street directing traffic."

Hm. It sounded true. "How did that happen?" said Amanda, trying to imagine what that would look like. Cars whirling around

Amphora, people screaming at her to get out of the way, pedestrians caught in the middle of the street, collisions left and right.

Ivy laughed. "They'd better get her out of there ASAP," she said.

"Hang on," said Simon. "We're going to have to do the unthinkable or we'll be late. I'm hailing a taxi."

"You're not," said Amanda. Simon was not philosophically opposed to taxis. Only financially.

"Sorry, what were you saying?" said Simon.

"Can you put Clive on?" said Amanda.

"Don't you want to talk to me?" said Simon.

"Not if you're going to hail cabs in my ear I don't," said Amanda.

"Wait, here it is," said Simon. His voice got quieter. "We're just getting in." *Clunk, thup.* "Legatum Continuatum up on the hill." Then louder. "Sorry. I was just telling the driver where to go. So as I was saying, we ran into Amphora here in town. It seems that she was looking for zombies too."

"Did you guys see any?" said Amanda.

"That we did. Well, she did."

"I don't understand." She wished he'd get on with it already.

"I'm trying to explain," said Simon. "So she sees this zombie and tries to follow him but she loses him in a crowd of tourists, right? She gets really frustrated, and then she sees Harry Sheriff with this girl—"

"Harry Sheriff?" said Amanda. Was Harry actually helping the school during the summer or was he just hanging around trawling for girls? That was all he ever seemed to do. "What did the girl look like?"

"I don't like him," said Ivy, frowning.

"Me either," said Amanda. "He's always grinning at me. And winking."

"Why?" said Ivy.

"No idea," said Amanda.

"I didn't see her," said Simon. "Anyway, so she tries to get a good look because she has this thing about the guy—"

"Harry? Not the zombie."

150

"Of course Harry," said Simon. "So she starts following him and this girl and they're kissing all over the place—not as good as me, of course—"

"Is Simon a good kisser?" said Ivy. Amanda ignored her.

"And then she sees a car break down in the middle of an intersection and it's an old lady and she's afraid to get out of the car, so Amphora calls the police but the traffic is getting all messed up so she starts directing it. Meanwhile, the woman is still in the car and the police haven't arrived, but now that Amphora has it under control the traffic is moving smoothly. You should see."

"Show me," said Amanda. That wasn't what she pictured at all. No offense to Amphora.

"I'm not there anymore," said Simon.

"Oh, right," said Amanda. "I don't suppose you took any snaps."

"But I did," said Simon. "I forgot. When I hang up I'll send you some." He seemed to have moved away from the mic. Probably trying to talk and send the pictures at the same time.

"Don't worry about it," said Amanda. "You can show me later. That is funny though."

"I'll say," yelled Clive in the background. "I thought she was going to be hit by a car at one point, but this guy just pulled up and made a kissing mouth at her and drove off. Then Eustace came with his tram—"

"She didn't do anything weird, did she?" said Amanda. She could envision Amphora being distracted and getting herself killed. When she had a crush on a guy, which was all the time, she was very absent-minded.

"To Eustace?" said Simon. His voice was so loud he almost broke her eardrums. "Nah, she was too busy. He just waved and she just waved and that was it. Hey, we're here. See you in a few."

The call ended. Ivy burst into raucous laughter.

"I never heard anything so ridiculous," she said. "Amphora directing traffic? I'll bet she was furious." She was doubled over holding her stomach.

"Why?" said Amanda. "She likes being important."

"Traffic cop is not considered important, especially by detectives," Ivy managed to squeeze out. She was laughing so hard snot was coming out of her nose.

"Ivy!" said Amanda. "You sound like a snob."

"You know I'm not a snob. But she is. Oh, this is so gross."

"I see your point," said Amanda. "Here, have a tissue." She felt in her bag and pulled out a crumpled one. It seemed clean, so she handed it to Ivy, who promptly dropped it.

"What point?" said Amphora, entering the dining room, shocking them half to death. "What's so funny?"

"I thought you were in Windermere," said Amanda. Ivy snuffled. She was still laughing—and other things.

"I was," said Amphora breathlessly. "I saw this zombie but he got away from me. He was absolutely terrifying."

"What happened?" said Ivy.

"Nothing *happened*," said Amphora. "It was the way he looked. All wild-eyed and ghoulish—kind of like an extreme version of Professor Hoxby." She held her hands around her head as if to simulate messed up hair.

Amanda and Ivy just about burst. The pathology teacher *was* awfully purple, and just a bit scary looking. Nice man, though, although rumor had it that he slept in a coffin.

"I don't suppose you got a picture," said Amanda.

"Oh, sorry," said Amphora. "Why didn't I think of that?"

"Could you draw him?" said Ivy.

"I think so," said Amphora.

"We're going to the 3D printing seminar right now," said Amanda. "Do you want to come?"

"Is Simon going to be there?" Amanda couldn't believe she was going to be so petty. If she kept avoiding Simon, she'd miss half of what Legatum had to offer. More.

"Yes," said Ivy cheerfully.

"Then I'd rather work on my drawing," said Amphora.

"Oh, come on," said Amanda. "This is useful stuff."

"No, thanks," said Amphora. "Zombies are more important."

"Suit yourself," said Amanda. It was her life. If she wanted to fritter it away it was her business.

On the way to the seminar Amanda got an idea. She stopped walking so abruptly that a kid behind her almost ran into her. Fortunately it wasn't Harry. "Do you suppose zombies killed Crocodile?"

"What?" said Ivy incredulously. She and Nigel came to a rather more gentle stop.

"Eustace and I saw one in Ulverston. Near Crocodile's flat."

"You're losing it, Amanda. There are no such things as zombies."

"Of course I don't really think they're zombies. But what if they're a gang of some kind?"

Ivy thought about that. "Seems an odd way for a gang to look, although of course I haven't seen them."

"It might be a thing around here," said Amanda. England was a much stranger place than L.A. It had all that history, for one thing, and all those little villages. How did she know what weird people might be lurking about?

"A thing?"

"Not a thing?" said Amanda. "I don't know. It's just that they seem to be everywhere and no one can tell us anything about them. Maybe it's a cult."

"Could be," said Ivy. "Probably not a murderous one though."
"Let's hope you're right."

17

GORDON, I COULD KISS YOU

The 3D printing seminar was awesome. Professor Kindseth showed them how to make a skateboard wheel, a slider game, and five different types of keys, including one that looked just like Wink Wiffle's and another he claimed was a skeleton key that would open all the doors in 17th century houses, which of course were much more common in the UK than Los Angeles. Fortunately David hadn't been there or he might have got upset about the lockbox key, which probably would have started a whole new round of sulking. Not that he wasn't entitled.

Amanda was still wondering about the whole bee theft thing Crocodile had been involved in and trying to figure out whether it had had anything to do with Wink's death—or Crocodile's. Was it possible that Wink had learned something he shouldn't have? Maybe it was time to do some more snooping around. Come to think of it, it might be a good idea to build a timeline and see if they could figure out where Wink and Crocodile had been at any given time.

Of course there was still that obscure sheet of numbers she and Eustace had found in Crocodile's flat. She wasn't able to make heads or tails of it, but maybe the other kids could. She decided to call an impromptu meeting in the common room, minus Holmes. Ever since the whole "He must be such a good boyfriend" incident with Despina, Amanda had been avoiding him even more than usual. Of course they were still making the film together, so she couldn't escape him altogether.

The meeting comprised Amanda, Ivy and Nigel, Simon, Clive, Amphora, and Gordon. The whole time Amanda kept getting texts and pictures from Despina, who seemed to think she wanted a minute-by-minute travelogue. She was tempted to block her cousin, but she was afraid Despina would have a fit.

The first thing the "committee" did was review the task list.

"What's this 'Speak to David Wiffle' thing?" said Gordon, knocking his knees together. Amanda wanted to grab them and hold them still.

"Thrillkill wanted to talk to David about what happened," she said.

"He's already done that," said Gordon.

"Oh?" said Ivy.

"David wouldn't tell me much, but he was pretty grumpy about it," said Gordon. "He yelled at me." He knocked faster.

"He wasn't expelled, was he?" said Amphora. "Hey, could you stop that thing with your knees? It's making the sofa shake."

Amanda was grateful that Amphora had said something. Let her be the target of Gordon's fussing.

"Of course not," said Gordon, stopping the knocking. Amphora could be intimidating. That was probably why he didn't mouth off to her. "Wiffles don't get expelled."

Oh, right. No matter what they do because they're so important. Amanda glanced at Amphora but couldn't read her face.

"Anyway you can cross it off," said Gordon.

"Why aren't zombies on the list?" said Amphora.

"Thrillkill doesn't know about them," said Amanda. "Besides, we're not even sure they're a thing."

"They are," said Amphora, shoving her drawing in front of the group. It was skillfully done.

"Yikes," said Clive. "That's one scary dude."

"I'll say," said Simon. "Way worse than what I've seen."

"Tell me," said Ivy.

"Rotten-looking, sores all over its face, oily hair hanging down in strings, discolored mouth, sunken eyes, just terrible," said Amanda. "Ew, is that slime?"

"The perfect zombie," said Clive. What was it with boys and zombies anyway? Zombies, ghouls, vampires, werewolves, superheroes. Sure, they were okay for a while, but then they got boring. They were always the same. That was one reason Amanda had never wanted to make a horror movie. And yet, Clive had touched a nerve. The *perfect* zombie. Maybe these creatures were actually different.

"Wait a minute—what did you say?" she said.

"I said the perfect zombie."

"Hm," said Amanda. "Maybe a little too perfect."

"What do you mean?" said Ivy.

"I think these are more than ordinary zombies."

"Ordinary zombies?" said Amphora. "What's an ordinary zombie?"

"I think these aren't zombies and they're not homeless people," said Amanda. "They look different from both—like they have a disease, maybe. Something weird is going on and we're going to get to the bottom of it."

"Do you think this has anything to do with the rainbows?" said Clive.

"The broken rainbows?" said Amanda. "Who knows? Maybe we'd better back up and review everything. I'm starting to get all mixed up."

Amanda and Simon filled the others in on everything that had been happening since they'd returned to campus. Amanda even mentioned Manny, Jackie, and Mr. Onion, as well as Celerie Wiffle and Andalusia Sweetgum.

"Wow," said Clive. "I had no idea all this was going on."

"You forgot something," said Simon.

"No, I didn't," said Amanda, glaring at him. He'd better not say anything about that kiss. Apparently Ivy was thinking the same thing because she chuckled.

"What?" said Amphora.

"Nothing," said Amanda. "Simon is mistaken. Now, what I think we should do is this: go down the list in order. It's the only way to keep things from getting all tangled up."

"They're already tangled up," said Amphora.

"Yes, but worse," said Amanda.

"Okay," said Amphora. "Where is Blixus?"

Of course the whereabouts of Blixus, Editta, and the roommates had to be the most difficult of the questions. The local police had found the white van the Moriartys had been driving at the quarry, but it had been devoid of clues and led them nowhere. Same with the boat, The Falls, they'd sailed up from London. Jeffrey Lestrade had been looking all over the city and had come up empty. It seemed that the trail had gone cold.

Wait a minute, thought Amanda. Jeffrey Lestrade. The man was an idiot, but wasn't he supposed to be on the Moriartys' trail? What was he doing in the Lake District? He didn't have time for archaeology tours. Something was up.

"Blixus is here," said Amanda. Everyone stared at her.

"What, at Legatum?" said Amphora. Amanda could see that she was getting scared again. She wondered if meditation might help. Amphora couldn't go through life being afraid of her own shadow. She'd certainly never be a detective if she didn't do something about her phobias.

"I don't think so," said Amanda. "But he's close by."

"What makes you say that?" said Clive.

"Inspector Lestrade."

"Your ancestor?" said Simon.

"No, the new one."

"There's a new one?" said Gordon.

"My cousin Jeffrey," sighed Amanda. "He's a fool. But here's the thing. He's looking for Blixus, and he's in Windermere. He knows something. Otherwise he'd still be in London."

"Nice work," said Simon. "I'll bet you're right. That's an excellent clue." He seemed excited. Well, as excited as he ever got.

"Of course Cumbria is a big place," she said. It was: 2600-ish square miles, the third-largest county in England.

"Yes, but it's better than chasing all over Europe," said Ivy.

"I wonder how long he's going to be here, though," said Amanda.

"Can't say," said Simon. "We have to move fast. What else do we know?"

"Crocodile!" said Amanda. She was on a roll. The ideas were flooding her brain now. Maybe the 3D printing seminar had primed it.

"What about him?" said Simon.

"He was working for Blixus."

"So perhaps Blixus is in Ulverston near Crocodile's flat," said Clive.

"Crocodile has been dead for a while," said Amanda. "But Blixus might have been there at some point, yes."

"What was this Crocodile working on?" said Amphora.

"Bee thefts," said Amanda.

"Excuse me?" It did sound weird out of context. If you didn't see the words written out, you might have thought she'd said "berefts" or "B thefts" or "beef thefts" or something like that.

"He was the head of a bee theft ring," said Amanda. "You know, apiaries."

159

"What's an apiary?" said Amphora. "Nothing to do with gorillas?"

"No, it's a bee house," said Clive.

"Oh, you mean a hive," said Amphora.

"Not exactly," said Gordon, grabbing a scrap of paper from his pocket and looking around for a writing implement. Spotting a pen on the floor, he picked it up and made a quick sketch. "It's man-made. It looks like a chest of drawers. They cultivate bees that way."

"Yick," said Amphora, half-looking at the drawing. "I wouldn't want bee thefts in my bureau."

Now there was an image—Amphora going to open a drawer and buzzing bees flying out. Amanda couldn't decide if it was funny or horrific. Probably funny as long as they didn't sting.

"That's as may be," said Simon, not rising to the bait for once. "However, it seems likely that Blixus had something to do with these bee thefts."

"And I have a list of addresses of farms with bees," said Amanda.

"What?" said Gordon, whipping his head around to look at her. She wondered what he'd been thinking about. Probably glitter explosions. "Way to go. Give me a high five."

Amanda thought he looked like a caricature behaving that way. "I thought only Americans did that," she said.

"You're American," said Gordon.

"But you aren't," said Amanda.

"Just do it already," said Simon.

Gordon slapped Amanda's hand and grinned. It was obviously a guy thing.

"So, these addresses," said Ivy.

"I've made a map," said Amanda, turning her tablet around so everyone could see it. "They're kind of all over the place, but they're all in the Midlands."

"I wonder if that's because Crocodile was located here or he moved here for the project," said Ivy.

Simon giggled. "Project," he said. "It sounds like school or something."

"All right, gig, caper, antic, I don't know," said Ivy.

"We also know that Crocodile had the phone number of a truck rental place in Birmingham," said Amanda. "I mean lorries. We say trucks."

"We know what trucks are," said Simon.

"Fine," said Amanda. How was she supposed to know what American English they did or didn't know? Amphora hadn't known what a cookie was. To be fair, of course, Amanda hadn't realized that English people called cookies biscuits. But now she knew. She knew lots of English English, like "bonnet" for the hood of a car and "torch" for flashlight. "But this sounds to me like Crocodile was renting trucks to transport the bees," she said, trying to yank her brain back to the subject at hand.

"I don't see what this has to do with Editta, and David's roommates," said Gordon.

"We're getting there," said Simon.

"So Crocodile was doing business all over the Midlands, and especially in Cumbria," said Amanda. "Blixus knew this. In fact, he probably put him up to it, right?"

Everyone nodded.

"Blixus gets out of prison," said Amanda, "and what does he do?"

"Makes crystals," said Gordon.

"Yes, but what else?" said Amanda.

"Causes trouble," said Gordon.

"To be sure," said Amanda. "But he also checks on his bee theft business." The man may have been evil, but he had to make money somehow. Gordon would have to learn about business if he wanted to be a detective. Come to think of it, why didn't Legatum offer a business class? If things ever settled down, she'd suggest it to Thrillkill.

"Oh, right," said Gordon.

"So he goes to see Crocodile," said Clive.

161

"Bingo," said Amanda. "And that was recently. He's only been out of prison a short time."

"So either Crocodile was already dead when he got there," said Simon—

"Or he was alive and Blixus killed him," said Amphora.

"Or… he was alive and someone else killed him after Blixus left," said Gordon.

"Yes!" said Amanda. "Good going, Gordon."

Gordon looked chuffed. Amanda wondered if David ever complimented him. She doubted it.

"My money is on Blixus," said Clive.

"Mine too," said Amanda, "but we have to prove it."

"Let's say he did kill Crocodile," said Simon. "Why?"

"Dispute over money?" said Ivy.

"Crocodile wasn't doing his job properly?" said Amphora.

"Blixus got stung and he blamed Crocodile," said Gordon. Everyone looked at him. Clive seemed especially skeptical. "Why not? It could happen."

"Maybe," said Simon. "Sounds a little over the top though."

"People flip for all kinds of reasons," said Gordon, causing a general discomfort among the group. Amanda was sure she wasn't the only one to think of David. She wondered what Gordon knew about him that they didn't. Not that she cared all that much. For a detective, she wasn't especially nosy about people's private lives. There was too much important stuff to worry about. She hoped Professor Sidebotham wouldn't start asking them to pry into each other's personal business just so she could test them on what they knew.

"What if Blixus went out to these farms to inspect Crocodile's work?" she said.

"So what?" said Simon.

"Hang on. I'm not finished."

"Sorry."

162

Amanda started mumbling as she sorted out the facts. "Blixus goes to the farms with Crocodile. But he doesn't kill him there because the body was found in Crocodile's flat, and it didn't seem to have been moved. So maybe Blixus goes out there and when they get back to Crocodile's flat they argue. Or maybe Crocodile refused to take him. Or maybe Crocodile admitted that there was a problem, so Blixus killed him."

"It would have to be a pretty bad problem," said Amphora. "If he killed Crocodile, who would fix it?"

"Maybe he was going to bring in someone else," said Ivy.

"Good point," said Amanda. "Let me think. Blixus, Crocodile, bees. Obviously something went wrong or Crocodile would still be alive. You don't suppose one of the farmers whose bees were stolen killed Crocodile, do you?"

"It's possible," said Clive. "Maybe it wasn't Blixus at all."

"We need to track down these farms," said Amanda, consulting her map. "Talk to the farmers."

"Stake them out," said Gordon. Everyone looked at him. It was a wonderful idea. Amanda felt proud. It had to be her little group's influence. Wait, was that arrogant?

"Gordon, I could kiss you," she said.

"Hey," said Simon.

"Fine. You kiss him, Simon. Don't you see? We can set up cameras and watch the farms."

"Brilliant, Amanda," said Ivy.

"Fab," said Amphora.

"Not bad," said Clive.

"I want to do it," said Gordon. Yup. He really was coming along. All he'd needed this whole time was a little encouragement. Amanda wondered how he'd fallen in with David in the first place.

"So it's settled then," she said. Everyone nodded. "Then what about these numbers? Anyone know what they mean?

She showed them the picture she'd taken of the sheet of numbers in Crocodile's accordion folder.

"Not Fibonacci," said Simon. Amanda gave him a look. "What? I said it isn't Fibonacci."

"What's Fibonacci?" said Gordon.

"It's a sequence of numbers in maths," said Simon. "It's connected with the golden ratio."

"Golden ratio?" said Amanda.

"I'll explain later," said Simon.

"Read them to me," said Ivy. Amanda did. Ivy listened carefully. "It's an inventory."

"What?" said Amphora. "How do you know?"

"I probably would have figured it out anyway, but hanging around with Editta taught me a lot about accounting," said Ivy. "It's an inventory. Probably of bees and the money that was paid for them."

Simon ran over to Ivy, grabbed her, and kissed her on the lips. She looked pleased. "See?" he said. "Equal opportunity kisser." Amanda gave him a little kick.

18

PENRITH

As great as Gordon's idea was, actually getting to the farms and setting up the cameras was another matter. Amanda didn't have time to worry about it, though, because she had to meet Holmes and make some progress with Thrillkill's film.

When she arrived at their table he was already sitting there, fidgeting. The little session with Despina probably hadn't done him any good either.

"So, we've finished the interviews," Amanda said. It wasn't much of an opening but it might get him talking.

"Yes," said Holmes. "I did the last of the Neutrals this morning. Professor Kindseth."

"That sounds weird: Punitori, Realists, Neutrals."

"A little melodramatic, I'd say," he said rather acidly. He was definitely in a bad mood.

"Yes." She wondered if Professor Pickle had come up with the names before he'd gone to prison. He was the school's language expert, after all.

"You think so too?" Holmes finally met her eyes, then looked away.

"Sure," she said. "Why not?"

"I thought you wanted lots of drama. That's what you told me last time."

"I said drama, not melodrama." That sounded harsh. She didn't mean it that way.

"I see." He was humoring her, and she didn't like it.

"You don't have to get all snippy."

"I'm not being snippy," said Holmes.

"You seem to think that just because I want to make the villains more complex I'm being melodramatic," she said.

"What villains?"

Amanda started. What was she talking about? The villains were in Darius Plover's film, not this one.

"Sorry," she said. "I was confused."

"Okay, no problem." Despite his words, Holmes didn't look forgiving. "So now that we know the positions, what are we going to do with them?"

"I don't know," she said. "It isn't anyone's fault."

"Who said it was anyone's fault?"

"You did."

"I did not."

"Didn't you say that I should have known better?"

Holmes gave her a long look. "I did no such thing."

"Oh, right. Sorry." What was she thinking?

"Do you want to reschedule?" he said.

"No, not at all. Let me think a second." She stared off into the distance. There wasn't much to look at. The walls were still bare. Since the earthquake, the paintings had been removed and stashed in the basements so they wouldn't hurt anyone if they fell.

"Okay, I've got it," she said after a few minutes, during which time Holmes had got them each a cup of tea. "We need to reunify the teachers and save the school. But we can't be didactic. They'd just tune out."

"Agreed. No preaching."

"We can use a carrot or a stick, or both," she said.

"Right," said Holmes. "Scare them straight, inspire them to come together, or a little of each."

"Exactly," she said. "But it would be easy to alienate them either way, wouldn't it?"

"I think so," said Holmes. "They're not in a very conciliatory mood. Except the Neutrals."

"So we have to soften them up."

"Sounds like a good idea. How?" He seemed to be relaxing a bit.

"You're going to think I'm crazy, but just hear me out." He nodded, but knowing him as she did she had absolutely no confidence that he'd sit still for what she was about to say. "We should make a musical."

"What?" said Holmes, spilling his tea all over the table.

"I told you, please just hear me out," she said, grabbing a napkin.

"Fine. Whatever." Her taking charge of his mess seemed to irritate him. "You don't have to do that. I've got it." He mopped up the tea with his own napkin.

"Music goes straight to the nervous system," she said. "There's no barrier between the message and us. It's visceral."

"Yes," he said hesitantly.

"There are happy musicals and sad musicals. The music is written to reflect the mood."

"Uh huh. And?"

"We want to bring the teachers together and save the school, right?"

"Of course."

"So we give them inspiration. An uplifting story set to music. We give them," she hesitated for effect, "The Detective's Musical."

Holmes looked stunned, and not in a good way. "I don't see how that's going to work."

"Have you seen any musicals?" she said.

"I've seen 'Glee.' Once."

She wasn't surprised, but she was disappointed. Everyone should at least see "West Side Story" and "Camelot." Suddenly she wondered what Holmes would think of the movies she'd made, like "Lunchpail," her best, and "Mynah Bird," a close second. Of course they weren't musicals, but she was immensely proud of them. The way he'd been acting lately, he probably wouldn't give them a chance, but then what difference did it make? He was obviously determined not to like her anymore and there was nothing she could do about it. She'd have to do the best she could with whatever he was willing to give.

"Good enough." *Not.* "Don't you feel inspired when you watch it?"

"That's just feel-good stuff, Amanda. A drug."

She didn't see it that way but she wasn't going to argue. "In a way, sure. But underneath the feelings are messages. Subliminal."

"Now you're talking about advertisers' tricks?" said Holmes.

Patience, patience. "Not exactly. Not so crass as that."

"I should hope not," he said. He was being a bit high and mighty for her taste. She hoped he'd get over it soon. Maybe if she showed him how effective her way would be.

"Look, I'll come up with a synopsis and you'll see. How about that?"

"If you say so."

"Tomorrow same time?"

"Whatever you say."

"Look, Scapulus, you know I know what I'm doing."

"You used to," he said, looking toward the door. "Hey, Amphora," he called, catching sight of Amanda's roommate in the hall. Amanda could see them both perk up as they walked out together.

Amanda was not a happy camper. What was that "You *used* to know what you were doing"? Holmes couldn't really mean that. He was just hurt. How she wished she could find Nick, resolve their issues, and end this tension. She'd have to try harder.

She was about to go to her room to work on the synopsis for the musical when Simon entered the dining room and sat down facing her.

"Weird stuff happening," he said.

There was always weird stuff going on at Legatum. It was getting to the point where weird was normal and you didn't even have to use the word anymore. "What weird stuff?"

"More zombie sightings."

"In Windermere?"

"Nope. Penrith."

"Penrith?" It seemed that the zombies were expanding their territory. "Despina and Hill just went there to look at stone circles. I wonder if they'll see them. Oh, brother. I should have gone with them. That's a long way away."

"Twenty miles or more, I'd say," said Simon.

"So they're spreading," she said.

"Sounds like it."

"Did anyone get pictures?"

"I haven't seen any."

Everyone was aware of the zombies, but no one was getting a good look at them, or even snapping a picture from far away that they could enlarge. It was as if these so-called zombies were really supernatural. Not that she believed that for a second.

"We have so much to do, I don't see how we're going to be able to keep up with this," said Amanda. "I wonder if I should ask Despina to keep a lookout. Ugh. What a terrible idea."

"I agree that we're busy," said Simon. "But twenty miles isn't that far. We could get Eustace to take us. It wouldn't take long. That way you wouldn't have to get Despina all excited."

"I think he's working," said Amanda.

"Too hilly for bikes and skateboards. Too far to walk."

Amanda contemplated the options for a moment. "How about Fern?"

"Ivy's sister?" said Simon.

"She might be able to take us."

"In what?" said Simon.

"It's summer," said Amanda. "She's got a car."

"Whoa," said Simon. "Good thinking. I could kiss you." He looked into her eyes, then down at her mouth.

"Don't you dare."

A few minutes later they were standing in the hall outside the dining room. When Fern had heard what they wanted to do she'd got so excited she'd stepped on her own skirt and torn it. She'd had to run back and change or they'd have departed immediately.

On the way to the car they zoomed past Professor Stegelmeyer so fast they almost knocked him down.

"Hey," he yelled after them. "Construction debris. Watch it."

"Sorry, Professor," yelled Amanda.

Then they ran into Drusilla Canoodle.

"Oh, Miss Lester," the dean of admissions and head of administration called out. "A letter has come for you."

Amanda came to a screeching halt. "A letter? On paper?"

"Yes. It's on my desk. From Her Majesty's Prison in Manchester."

This was weird. What did Doodle want with her? She excused herself, ran to Ms. Canoodle's office, and grabbed the letter. With shaking hands she tore it open, ripping the note inside as well as the envelope, just as she'd done with the letter from the school telling her she'd been admitted. She didn't open letters often and was obviously not good at it. The paper contained only three words: "Where's my guitar?"

That was fast. It hadn't been more than a couple of days since she and Mr. Onion had seen Manny Companion, and here he was pestering her about the guitar already. Either he was dead serious or some kind of troll. But did he really have the information she wanted?

Even if he did, she didn't see how she was going to get the guitar past Warden Doodle. Of course there was also the small matter of coming up with a guitar in the first place, but she was sure she could borrow one somewhere. There had to be a few kicking around the school.

Unfortunately there wasn't time to worry about guitars. Amanda raced back to the front entrance where Simon, Ivy, Nigel, and Fern were waiting, and they got into Fern's Fiesta. Amanda hadn't spent much time around Ivy's sister but she could spot her a mile off because she had the same copper hair as Ivy. Although she was seventeen, she was very tiny—barely taller than Ivy, but just as pretty. Both girls had sparkling green eyes, although Ivy usually hid hers behind sunglasses. Fern was specializing in textual analysis, and when Professor Pickle had gone to jail she'd nearly fallen to pieces. He had been her advisor and mentor and she hadn't known what to do without him.

When they'd got rolling Fern said, "Where do you think these zombies are coming from? Nigel, please don't get nose marks on the window."

"He can't help it," said Ivy.

"Well, here," she said, holding out a tissue. "At least wipe them off." Amanda took it and cleaned off the marks, but she soon realized that the exercise was futile. As soon as she cleaned one mark, Nigel would just smear on another.

"Hard to say," said Simon. "They might just be homeless people."

"Amphora sure didn't think so," said Amanda. "And don't say it."

"I wasn't going to say anything," said Simon. "My guess is still that there's a film shoot."

"All over the place?" said Ivy.

"It does happen," said Amanda. "But you'd think we'd know about it. At home they always put up these yellow and black signs to direct the crew where to go. There has to be an indication somewhere. Besides, we would have heard the gossip. Film production is always a moneymaker for the locals. People would be talking."

"I hadn't thought of that," said Ivy.

Yup. Legatum should offer business classes.

When they arrived at Penrith they decided to reconnoiter for a few minutes, then start asking people if they'd seen anything strange. They were hoping they'd find zombies right away, which would mean they wouldn't have to draw attention to themselves. However after ten or fifteen minutes they'd seen nothing but the usual small town activity, so they split up, with Simon and Ivy taking one shop and Fern and Amanda another.

"Uh, hello," said Amanda to the clerk at the newsagent's.

"Hullo," said the spotty young man. He reminded Amanda of the guy who worked at the ice cream store back home in Calabasas—the one who wouldn't let her start a tab when she was hungry and had no money with her.

She hesitated. She didn't want to just come out with, "Seen any zombies lately?" What should she say?

"We're ghost hunters," said Fern before she could decide. Amanda was shocked. Fern had done almost exactly what she thought was a bad idea.

"Do tell," said the kid. "Aren't yew a little young for that?" He spoke in a faint Scottish brogue. Amanda thought he was easier to understand than Professor McTavish, and way clearer than Mr. Onion.

"We're prodigies," said Fern, causing the kid to eye her suspiciously. "We've heard that there are a lot of haunted places around here."

"We don't want no prodigies around here," he said.

"We're licensed," said Fern, pulling out her British Museum membership card. She waved it in front of his face, then quickly stuck it back in her bag.

"Ten quid," he said.

Amanda and Fern looked at each other. Was he asking for a bribe?

"Five," said Fern almost before he'd finished.

The kid didn't flinch. "Eight."

"Six."

"Six and fifty." They were in a rhythm now. Amanda wondered how long it would go on.

"Deal," said Fern, ending the exchange.

"Pay in advance," said the kid.

Shaking her head, Fern dug in her purse and gave the kid six pounds and fifty pence. "This had better be good," she said.

He leaned forward conspiratorially. "Myrddin's Wand."

"Myrddin's Wand?" said Amanda. "What's that?"

"Myrddin is Merlin," said Fern. "Merlin's wand? What about it?"

"It's a wee village four miles from here," said the kid. "Stone circles. Haunted."

"What kind of haunted?" said Fern.

"Ah, that's for yew to find out, innit," said the kid.

"Coordinates?" said Fern.

"Here," said the kid, tearing out a page from a copy of *Creepy Cumbria* magazine and scribbling on it. "There's a bit of a village there. No gift shops, though."

"We're not interested in gift shops," said Fern.

"Well, there ain't none."

"Any zombies?" said Amanda, throwing caution to the wind. The kid already thought they were weird.

"Who's askin'?"

Fern eyed the boy. "I am Morgan le Fey, and this is Rapunzel Silverstein."

"You from London?" he said eyeing her suspiciously. Then he looked at Amanda. "You're one of them Americans."

"No, I'm from Dorset," said Fern. "My cousin is Canadian."

"Hm," said the kid. "Tell you what. You buy me a pizza and I'll tell you about zombies."

Amanda was getting so impatient she wanted to scream. Now they were supposed to run off and find this jerk a pizza? What if none of his information paid off? She let out a huge sigh.

Fern, however, seemed unperturbed and said, "Where can we get pizza?"

The kid nodded toward the street. "Block down. Saccamano's. Best pizza in Cumbria."

"Hold that thought," said Fern, grabbing Amanda and dashing out of the shop.

"What an idiot," said Amanda.

"Yes, but he's got to know something. If there's anything weird going on around here the locals will know." But will they tell? People in small towns could be secretive, or so Amanda had heard. She'd never actually lived in one, unless you counted Windermere, but that was different. She didn't actually know anyone there except Eustace.

On the way to Saccamano's, they ran into Simon and Ivy.

"Got it," said Simon proudly.

"Zombies?" said Amanda.

"Yes," said Ivy. "A man in the chemist's told us that they've been seen around Myrddin's Wand. There's a stone circle there."

"Myrddin's Wand?" said Amanda. "That's what we heard too. You're sure he was talking about zombies, though. Not ghosts?"

"Zombies," said Ivy.

"So we don't have to get pizza," said Amanda with relief.

"Pizza?" said Simon. "I could go for some pizza. Here's a place right here."

Amanda looked at Fern. "I don't think we have to worry about Mr. Six and a Half Quid anymore," said Fern. "Their story confirms what he said. Let's eat and get out of here."

~~◊◊◊~~

When they arrived at Myrddin's Wand, which was a small Iron Age formation of six stones, they saw three more rainbows.

"This is getting really weird," said Amanda. "He's here too?" The hacker was definitely getting around. His ubiquity was unsettling.

"They're all messed up again," said Simon.

"What are you talking about?" said Fern.

"We think someone is messing around with rainbows," said Amanda.

"Define 'messing around,'" said Fern.

The kids described what they had seen and presented their theories about a super hacker who could manipulate matter.

"Pish tosh," said Fern. "That's impossible."

"Look at those rainbows," said Simon, pointing up and squinting. "So are they."

Fern peered up at the sky. "Hm, the colors do seem to be out of order. But I'm sure there's a scientific explanation."

"Nope," said Simon. "We checked."

"Atmospheric conditions?" said Fern.

"What, like none ever seen before?" said Simon.

"Well, there is global warming now," said Fern.

"Not if I can help it," said Simon.

"What—the tilt thing again?" said Amanda. "Come on, Simon."

"They laughed at Galileo too," he said.

"I don't think you're exactly Galileo." Good thing, too, considering what happened to him. The father of modern science had been investigated by the Inquisition and spent a large part of his life under house arrest.

"What's this about a tilt?" said Fern.

"Oh, Simon thinks he can fix global warming by altering the tilt of the earth," said Ivy.

"Really?" said Fern. She looked Simon up and down, then smiled. "What an interesting idea. You're not making these rainbows then, are you?"

Amanda was absolutely sure that Fern was teasing, but her expression was so serious it was disconcerting. She must be quite an actor.

"Nope, not me," said Simon. He lowered his voice, although no one was around. "It's the hacker."

"What hacker?" said Fern.

"You've really had your head in that text stuff, haven't you?" said Ivy.

"Of course," said Fern. "That's why I'm at Legatum for the summer instead of surfing in California." She giggled. There was no way Fern would go near a surfboard. The only way you'd get her onto one would be if it had Shakespeare's plays inscribed on it. "I'm working on those letters in the sparkling feather case—the one where that man left a glittery feather at each crime scene. Well, I say man, but I'm not a hundred percent sure. Only ninety-nine."

"You surf?" said Simon.

"She doesn't," said Ivy.

"Oh, having me on, then," said Simon.

"That she's good at," said Ivy proudly.

"This hacker," said Fern. "You're not implying—"

"We are," said Ivy. "We think he—she—is manipulating matter."

"No," said Fern. "That isn't possible."

"But Simon changing the tilt of the earth is?" said Ivy.

Fern winked, but of course Ivy couldn't see it.

"Say, what's that?" said Amanda, looking toward the tiny village of Myrddin's Wand.

"I don't see anything," said Fern.

"No, it is him," said Amanda. "It's my cousin Jeffrey. He just went into that church. Despina and Hill must be in there. Come on."

19

THROUGH THE SARCOPHAGUS

Why Amanda suddenly wanted to see her cousins she couldn't fathom. Perhaps it was simply the excitement of recognizing familiar faces in a strange place. Forgetting how annoying they could be (even though she loved them, or at least Despina and Hill), she ran toward the tiny village church with the others following.

As the group entered the dark space, the front door creaked. Inside, the church looked disused. The wood was old and split and the place smelled musty. It took a moment for Amanda's eyes to adjust to the darkness, and when they did she was surprised. Jeffrey was nowhere to be seen.

"Where did he go?" she said.

"Maybe he's in the back," said Fern.

The group crept toward the rear of the church. The old building was deathly silent and their footsteps echoed. Thick dust obscured the wood of the pews, but Amanda could see initials carved in them here and there. Perhaps the place had once been popular. Now it seemed a relic.

"Why are we being so quiet?" she whispered, then sneezed, an act that seemed to give the others permission to do so as well. Within seconds everyone was sneezing, even Nigel.

"We don't want to alert the zombies," said Ivy, foraging in her bag for a tissue. *Achoo.*

"Oh for heaven's sake," said Amanda in her regular voice. "There aren't really any zombies." *Sneeze.*

At the back of the church was a closed green door that seemed to have been painted more recently than the one at the front. Perhaps someone was using the back room.

"You open it, Simon," said Amanda. *Sneeze.*

"Be careful," said Ivy. *Snuffle.* "Here, Amanda, take a tissue." She held out a pack of the things. Amanda took two.

Simon grabbed the handle, gave it a good yank, and pushed the door wide open. Then he sneezed—twice.

"Oh, yuck, Simon," said Ivy. "I can hear what you're doing. Please take one of these."

She held out the tissue pack. Simon eyed it suspiciously.

"Simon!" she said.

"Oh, all right," he said. "Give it here."

Ivy passed the pack to him and he pulled, causing a handful of tissues to fall onto the floor.

"Drat," he said, reaching down to retrieve the misbehaving tissues. He looked around, seemed to decide that there was nowhere to throw them, and stuffed them in his pocket. Then he took two more out of the pack and passed it back to Ivy.

"I don't see what the problem is," she said. "They're just tissues."

"It's a guy thing," said Amanda.

She stuck her head through the doorway. There in front of them was an ancient stone sarcophagus with its top moved aside. The way the cover was balanced on the walls made Amanda nervous. The thing must weigh tons. If it fell there was no way they could put it back, even with all of them lifting.

"You don't think he went in there?" said Fern.

"What is it?" said Ivy.

"An old sarcophagus—open," said Simon.

Amanda tiptoed toward the crypt, climbed up on the base, and peered in. Simon heaved himself up on top of the structure and looked down.

"What do you see?" said Fern.

"Stairs," said Amanda.

"Stairs?" said Fern. "In a sarcophagus?"

"I don't think it's really a sarcophagus," said Amanda. "No one is buried in here."

"Well what is it then?" said Fern.

"Let's find out," said Simon.

"Ivy, do you hear anything?" said Amanda as the group prepared to climb down into the space below the sarcophagus.

"Not a thing," said Ivy.

"Me either. That's weird. If Jeffrey went down there, he couldn't have got far."

"You don't suppose he's fallen and hit his head, do you?" said Fern.

"If so, we'd better find him fast," said Amanda. She shined her light into the cavity. "Hm, nothing much to see. Simon, do you see anything? I'm going to text Despina. She probably knows what's going on."

Simon perched himself on the edge of the opening and leaned in as far as he could without falling.

"Nope," he said. "Just stairs."

"I'm surprised that Wink Wiffle was so creative," said Ivy out of nowhere.

"What brought that on?" said Amanda.

"I was just thinking," said Ivy. "He painted all those pictures. From what you tell me he was very talented. David isn't like that."

"No," said Amanda. "Obviously he doesn't take after his father. Or his mother, for that matter. She's a designer." *And a lunatic.*

"Well, what happened to him?" said Ivy.

"Twenty p," said Simon.

"What?" said Ivy tilting her head in Simon's direction. "I wasn't arguing."

"You said something nasty about someone," said Simon.

"I don't think that qualifies," said Ivy. "I was just observing. Anyway, David isn't part of the deal."

"We'd make a fortune if he were," said Amanda.

"Would you guys stop talking about stuff I don't know about?" said Fern. She looked at the opening anxiously. She was obviously keen to see what lay beyond.

"Oh, sorry," said Ivy. "We're talking about David Wiffle."

"That little kid?" said Fern. "Everyone knows about him. He's infamous." She peered into the darkness below. "I don't see anything down there."

"Yes, I'm afraid so," said Ivy. "Poor David."

"We're not all like our parents," said Amanda. "I'm not." *Not at all, and thank goodness.* She made her way to the other side of the sarcophagus and accidentally bumped the cover. Fortunately it didn't budge or it might have fallen. "Ow."

"I am," said Simon. He joined Amanda on the far side of the sarcophagus and pushed on the top. It didn't move. He pushed harder. Still nothing. Then he gave it all he had. Still nothing.

"Why are you doing that, Simon?" said Fern.

"Just checking."

"And what would you do if it fell off?" she said.

"Run," he said.

"I thought your parents were dentists," said Amanda.

"You're getting me confused with Hermione Granger," said Simon. "My parents are scientists. My dad is a physicist and my mum is an astronomer."

"So that's why you're trying to see how much that cover weighs," said Fern. "You're obviously like them."

"Pretty much," said Simon. "My brother too. I'm not just trying to see how much it weighs. I want to figure out the amount of force required to move it."

"How old is your brother?" said Fern. "Why do you want to know that?"

"Eight," said Simon. "He's really into dinosaurs." Amanda tried to picture a smaller version of Simon. Those poor parents. "I want to know how many people it would take to move the cover. I don't see how Jeffrey could have done that alone."

"So he goes on digs, then?" said Fern.

"Jeffrey? I have no idea."

"Not Jeffrey," said Fern. "Your brother."

"Oh, right. He'd like to," said Simon. "So would I."

"We go on digs," said Ivy. "You should come with us sometime." She seemed to have forgotten her irritation with him. Simon was like that. One minute he made you mad and the next you were buds again.

"You do?" said Amanda, testing the cover herself. If Simon couldn't move it she didn't see how she could, but she felt compelled to push anyway. Amphora would have worried. She'd think Simon had loosened it and all you'd have to do was blow on it. "I thought your dad was a professor."

"He is," said Fern. "Archaeology. But he has to do research too. Sometimes we get to go."

"Did you go on that peat bog mummy dig?" said Amanda.

"What peat bog mummy dig?" said Simon, looking up from his experiments.

"Oh, my dad found a peat bog mummy on an island off Scotland," said Ivy nonchalantly. She seemed to know exactly what

Simon would think of her family's adventures and was looking forward to teasing him.

"And you got to go?" said Simon. He seemed disappointed that he hadn't been invited.

"No, missed that one. But I did go on one where we found some Roman coins."

"You're kidding," said Simon, losing all interest in the sarcophagus cover. He walked around to where Ivy and Fern were standing and looked down on the two shorties. Amanda thought that if he was trying to intimidate them into giving up secrets he had another think coming. "Any pictures?"

"Not on my phone," said Ivy. "And no, we're not kidding, are we, Fern?"

"No," said Fern. "The coins were amazing. Of course we had to give them to the British Museum. I have some photos back in my room."

"I want to go next time," said Simon. "And can I see them?"

"It might be during school," said Ivy.

"I'll cross that bridge when I come to it," said Simon. "Do you think your dad would mind?"

"Not if you're responsible and serious," said Ivy.

"Am I ever anything else?" said Simon. Ivy coughed. "What? I'm the picture of gravity."

Ivy, Fern, and Amanda burst out laughing. "No one has ever photographed gravity," said Fern.

"Very droll," said Simon. "So what do you say, Fern? Can I see the pictures?"

"If you behave yourself," Fern said with a twinkle in her eye.

"Say," said Ivy, "speaking of gravity, do you think the hacker could affect that?"

"Gravity?" said Simon. "You're talking about fundamental laws of the universe. That's impossible."

"I hope so," said Fern. "Can you imagine?"

Amanda was getting antsy. She wanted to see what was down there and she was actually worried about Jeffrey. She already didn't like the guy, but wherever he was Despina and Hill were likely to be with him, and although they were undoubtedly fine, something was nagging at her. Not that she believed in zombies. But she did sense danger and she needed to find out what was happening.

"I'll go first," she said, after she'd sent off a text. "Fern, how do you feel about taking up the rear?"

"Fine," said Fern.

Amanda climbed through the opening, dangled her legs, and carefully placed her feet on the top step. She shined her light down the stairs. She couldn't see the bottom. Whatever was down there was way underground.

"This might be a little tricky," said Ivy, attempting to get herself and Nigel through the sarcophagus and onto the stairs.

"Hang onto me," said Simon, maneuvering her carefully.

Amanda looked up at them. Ivy was tentatively placing her foot on the top step while Simon held her. Most of Nigel, and Fern's nose, could be seen above them.

"Got it?" said Fern.

"Yes," said Ivy. "Come on, Nigel."

Wagging his tail, Nigel jumped into the sarcophagus. Ivy grabbed his lead with the non-Simon hand, then stepped down one more stair.

"Here I come," said Fern. "Ouch."

"What?" said Ivy.

"I banged my knee."

"Well, watch it," said Ivy. "If you hurt yourself it will be very difficult to get you out of here."

"You should talk," said Fern.

184

"I think you should fine Fern 20p, Amanda," said Simon.

"Oh, for heaven's sake, Simon," said Amanda. "Would you give it a rest?" She stepped down gingerly. The steps were slippery. One mistake and she could die. She was starting to worry about Ivy.

"Everybody ready?" said Fern.

"Ready," said the others together.

"Can you see anything, Amanda?" said Fern.

"Only stairs," said Amanda. "This is kind of like when—" She stopped herself. She was going to say, "when Nick and I found the secret room at Legatum." The last thing she wanted to do was think about him, though, and both Simon and Ivy knew it.

"Like what?" said Fern.

"Nothing," said Amanda. "It isn't like anything."

It seemed to take forever for the group to reach the bottom of the stairs. They were so steep that you had to be incredibly careful. The only one who didn't seem bothered was Nigel, who scampered down quickly, allowing Simon to look after Ivy. Amanda didn't see how Nigel could have guided Ivy down the steps anyway. They weren't deep enough for him to stand on comfortably.

Ahead of them lay a narrow stone tunnel that resembled the ones under Legatum. This one was rougher, though, and there was graffiti on the walls.

"That's terrible," said Amanda, eyeing the desecration. "Who would do such a thing?"

"Idiots," said Simon. "What does that say?"

"It's hard to read," said Fern. "It looks like it says 'wretch society.'"

"Wretch society?" said Amanda. "What does that mean? You're sure it isn't wrench society?"

"Beats me," said Simon.

"I'm pretty sure it's wretch," said Fern.

"Hm, not sure I can get a signal down here," said Amanda. "I'll see if I can search." She thumbed her phone, which made the light move all over the tunnel like some kind of strobe. She remembered a school dance she'd been to once where there had been a light like that. Of course no one had asked her to dance back in her one-man-band days. Legatum didn't have dances. Too frivolous, she supposed. Probably a good thing considering the state of her love life. "Nope, no wretch or wrench society."

"Let's keep going," said Simon. The group started to move again, slowly. "Anyone hear anything?" Everyone said no. "Got your listening devices?"

"Forgot it," said Amanda.

"What listening devices?" said Fern.

"I think we're going to have to write you a first-years primer or something," said Ivy. She explained how last term Simon had made them some simple hearing aids that magnified distant voices.

"You eavesdrop on people?" said Fern, aghast.

"Have to," said Simon. "Times are desperate."

Fern sighed. "I suppose they are. It's just so uncivilized."

"I hate to break this to you," said Simon, "but being a detective involves a lot of things that are uncivilized."

Everyone stopped. They all knew it was true, but the way Simon had said it was so blunt that it seemed to hit them in the gut. At least that was how Amanda saw the situation.

"Wait. What was that?" She thought she'd heard something and shone her light down the tunnel again.

"I didn't hear anything," said Simon.

"No, there was definitely something," said Ivy.

"Do you think it was Jeffrey?" said Fern, lowering her voice.

"I don't know," said Amanda. "I'm getting the creeps, though. There's something weird about this place."

"There's a draft," said Ivy.

Amanda held still and tried to sense the air. Ivy was right. The air was moving. "Yes, that could be it. Where is it coming from, though? We're too far from the sarcophagus, and that's sheltered anyway."

"There must be an opening close by," said Simon.

Suddenly Amanda saw a tiny flash of light up ahead. "What was that?"

"You mean that light?" said Simon.

"I saw it too," said Fern.

"It looked like something glinting," said Amanda. "Let's see if we can find it."

The group crept along the tunnel slowly. The light came and went as they moved position. Sometimes it was as bright as looking into the sun and at other times it winked out completely.

"It might be Jeffrey," said Amanda. "Maybe Despina and Hill went on ahead and he caught up with them. Look—there are footprints." The tunnel floor was rocky, uneven, and dusty, but a few partial prints were just visible. "That looks like a boot. It could be him. Maybe we can track him."

Simon peered down at the prints. "They do look fresh," he said. "Oh, look at that. Metal." He made his way toward the shining thing he'd seen, then bent down to inspect it. "There's a crack in the ceiling. The sun was reflecting off this."

"Let's see what it is," said Amanda, joining him. "Say, that's a gold coin." She reached out to pick it up.

"Better use gloves," Simon said.

"You don't think—"

"Better to be safe."

"I guess you're right." She reached in her bag and retrieved her gloves. They felt a bit tight. Cool air always made them shrink.

"What, you think there might have been a crime committed here?" said Ivy. "Why?"

"No reason," said Simon. "Just being careful."

"Does it say anything?" said Fern.

"I think so," said Amanda, putting her gloves on. She picked up the coin and looked at it carefully. "I can't make it out though."

"Let me see," said Simon, leaning over Amanda's hand.

"Don't touch it," said Amanda.

"I'm not," he said. "Nope. I can't tell what it is either. Maybe if we make a rubbing or take a picture and blow it up."

"We can do that when we get back," said Amanda.

"No, I see what it says," said Fern. "It isn't letters. It's a picture."

"What?" said everyone.

"A leprechaun."

20

IN THE TUNNELS

The sun was no longer shining on the leprechaun coin. The crack in the tunnel ceiling was so narrow that the light could penetrate for a mere instant each day, if the sun was even visible. The moment had passed.

"Why would someone bring a toy coin down here?" said Fern. "It isn't a chocolate one, is it?" She took Amanda's hand and peered at the discovery in her palm.

"No," said Amanda. If anyone knew chocolate coins, she did. She'd once been a chocoholic. This wasn't one. She could feel the metal. "It's real." She took out an evidence bag and dropped it in.

"But it isn't real gold?" said Fern.

"Looks like it," said Simon. "We'll test it."

"Do you think we're making too much of all this?" said Ivy. "The whole thing could just be a big party—people dressed up as zombies, having one on over the locals." She had a point. Maybe they were making a big deal out of nothing.

"It could," said Amanda, labeling the bag. "If that's the case we'll feel stupid."

"Or it could be a huge conspiracy," said Simon, teasing. "Maybe the government has been covering it all up for years."

"If you want to go back, Simon, you can wait at the car, or hitchhike," said Amanda, putting the evidence bag in her pocket. She was afraid that if she stowed it in her pack, her skateboard would bump against it and damage it.

"You guys are so melodramatic," said Simon. "The zombies probably aren't even a thing."

"Maybe not," said Amanda, "but I want to know what Jeffrey Lestrade is doing here when he's supposed to be looking for the Moriartys in London."

"Fair enough," said Simon.

"How far do you suppose the tunnel goes?" said Ivy, listening in various directions.

"Probably not far," said Fern. "Although it's obviously old. I'd venture a guess that the same people who made the stone circle dug it."

"That old?" said Amanda, inspecting the walls. The tunnel didn't look fresh, that was for sure. Beyond that she had no idea how to gauge its age. "What are we talking—Iron Age?"

"Yes," said Ivy. "Definitely Neolithic."

"Wow," said Amanda. "They were amazing engineers." She'd always thought of cavemen as little more advanced than animals. Not that she'd actually bothered to research them.

"A lot of people don't realize how sophisticated ancient people were," said Ivy. "They could be extremely shrewd."

"Not shrewd enough to make leprechaun coins," said Amanda. That she was sure they couldn't do.

"Definitely not," said Ivy, grinning.

"You know," said Amanda. "You could make another trove of secrets down here. Hey, you don't suppose the monks did that, do you? Maybe we'll find something."

"What monks?" said Simon.

"The ones who built that church."

"What makes you think monks built it?" said Simon.

Uh oh. He was about to deliver a lecture. She could just feel it. "Isn't England full of monks?" He gave her a look. "What do I know? I'm American. Who then?"

"The local lords. Thegns. They built parish churches like this one. One way of becoming a thegn was to erect a church, especially one with a tower. Build a church, be a big shot."

"So if I were to build a church around here, I'd get a title?" said Amanda.

"That's not how it works, Lady Lester," said Simon.

"I'm not interested in that stuff anyway," said Amanda. "I don't like politics." Especially since her dad had lost the election for District Attorney of Los Angeles. It had been an ugly campaign and it had changed him. "But I'm sure that whoever built the church had to know about the tunnel." She still liked the idea of monks. They were so much more mysterious than thegns. "So it's probably used for religious purposes."

"At one time it might have been a bomb shelter," said Simon. "It's possible that the sarcophagus was adapted during the Second World War and you couldn't enter from there before then. Did you know that many children were sent to the countryside for safety? Operation Pied Piper evacuated millions of people."

"So the Germans didn't bomb the countryside?" said Amanda. She didn't know much about military strategy. Okay, she didn't know anything about it.

"A bit early on, but not later. Some people built Anderson shelters, which in many cases were nothing more than fortified garden sheds. Some of them were slightly underground, but nothing like this. This tunnel would have been highly coveted because secure locations were scarce and everyone had to make do."

"Is there anything you don't know, Simon?" said Amanda.

"Not really."

"Ha," said Ivy. "We'll see about that."

The girls giggled.

"Yes, you will," said Simon, completely seriously.

When the group had continued down the tunnel a ways, Amanda, who was in front, stopped abruptly.

"Uh oh," she said. "Fork." She was looking at nearly identical entrances to two tributaries. You had to pick one or the other or turn around. "What do you think?"

"Footprints?" said Ivy.

"Gone," said Amanda.

"Let me take a look," said Simon.

It was true. The footprints they'd seen near the bottom of the stairs had become fainter and fainter, and now they were nowhere to be seen.

"Can you hear anything?" said Fern.

Everyone stood stock-still and listened.

"I can't hear a thing," said Ivy.

"Ears still clean?" said Amanda.

Over the last few weeks, Ivy had had occasional trouble hearing, which had scared her half to death. It turned out that she'd had wax in her ears, and when Dr. Wing had cleaned them out she could hear better than ever.

"No worries," said Ivy.

"So which way do we go?" said Amanda. "Wait a minute. Which way are we facing?"

"North," said Simon, checking his phone.

"Away from the stones?" said Amanda.

"Yes. So if we take the left fork, we'll parallel the river." He was referring to the River Eden, which ran north and south. "The right fork heads toward the Pennines."

"The backbone of England?" said Amanda.

"Correcto," said Simon. Amanda flinched. The word sounded like "Detecto," which was an imaginary planet Nick had come up with.

"I think the zombies are more likely to stay near the river," said Ivy. "More towns."

"If they're deliberately trying to frighten people, that would make sense," said Fern.

"Okay," said Amanda. "Left fork it is."

The group moved forward. When they had entered the left tunnel, which looked exactly like the one they'd come from, and covered a hundred yards or so, Amanda stopped again. "The light is uneven in here."

"I noticed that," said Simon. "I think there are more cracks in the ceiling. They must be minuscule, though. I can't actually see them."

"We must be close to the surface," said Fern.

"I'd say six to ten feet," said Simon. Not exactly Uamh nan-Claigg ionn."

Amanda was startled to hear him mention the cave where Thrillkill had contracted his fear of icicles. Something had happened to him, Wink Wiffle, and Blixus Moriarty up there, and she still didn't know what it was. She had to find out. Whatever it was seemed to be governing events.

"Do you see how there are piles of dirt around here?" said Simon.

"Yes," said Fern. "What do you suppose they're for?"

"I think they're natural." Simon bent down and felt one of the piles, testing the dirt by rubbing it between his fingers. "I wish Clive were here. He'd know."

"Can you get reception?" said Amanda.

"Actually, yes," said Simon. "I'll give him a try."

Simon touched his phone a couple of times and he was talking to Clive.

"Sorry, man," said Simon. "It was spur of the moment. Next time for sure. Let me turn on the streaming like we did at the factory and you can see."

Simon was referring to the time he and Amanda had traveled to the ruins of the Moriartys' sugar factory to look for more of the mysterious living crystals they'd discovered at Legatum. They'd taken Clive along virtually, streaming live video to him as they poked around.

"Here, look at my hand," said Simon. "What do you make of this dirt? Really? Closer? Sure. Uh huh. Okay, got it. Thanks."

"What did he say?" said Amanda when Simon had closed the connection.

"It's loam," said Simon. "We're underneath a farm."

"A farm?" said Amanda. "Wait a minute. What are the coordinates?" She thumbed her phone. "This sounds really familiar. I want to check something."

She looked at the picture she and Eustace had taken of the locations Crocodile had written down. She was right: they were underneath one of the farms on the criminal's list!

"We have to get up there," she said. "This farm is one of the ones with bee thefts."

"Bee thefts?" said Fern.

"Long story," said Amanda. "I'll tell you as we go."

21
ANGRY BEES

The explorers found no signs of Jeffrey Lestrade or zombies during the next few minutes, but they did find an opening to the surface.

Fortunately someone had constructed a sort of ramp that made it easy to climb up and out, and when they followed it they found themselves in a field surrounded by haystacks and a huge number of holes. About two hundred yards to the east lay a farmhouse.

"Ha," said Simon. "Here's irony for you. We're looking for needles in haystacks and here they are right in front of us."

"Do you think you could find a needle in a haystack with a magnet?" said Amanda.

"More likely an x-ray machine," said Simon. "Even if the magnet were to detect the needle, which it could only do if it was really powerful, the straw is too dense for it to pull it out."

"But what are all these holes?" said Fern, surveying the landscape.

"What holes?" said Ivy.

"The property looks like Swiss cheese," said Amanda. It was crazy. The place looked as if it were inhabited by giant gophers. "Someone has been doing a lot of digging around here. Let's check it out."

"I think they've been digging a well," said Simon, looking off to the northeast. "There's a tower over there. It seems deserted, though."

The kids clomped through what used to be a field. Nigel was so happy to have all that space around him that he rolled over on his back and wriggled in the dirt.

"Nigel, don't do that," said Ivy. "Now I'm going to have to give you a bath."

The dog stood up, shook himself, and looked around with his tongue lolling out happily.

"I'll help you," said Simon. "I think I saw a metal tub at Legatum we can use."

"You'll be sorry," said Ivy. "And wet. He's a handful."

"Not at all," said Simon. He really loved that dog. He was always making little contraptions for him. He circled the metal tower that soared high above a large hole. It looked a bit like a crane. "Just as I thought. It's a well."

"Maybe they couldn't find the water so they had to keep digging in other places," said Fern when Simon had returned from his circuit. The kids explored the holes for a few minutes, and then she said, "Nope. I was wrong. These are excavations. Someone has set up grids here. And—"

Suddenly the field around them filled with rainbows, all of them broken like the ones they'd seen before, growing stronger and weaker, then stronger again, like a signal that couldn't seem to establish itself. The shape of them flickered, filling in and winking out in random shapes like some kind of mutant electrical storm.

"Get down," yelled Amanda. "Ouch!" She felt a spark of electricity run through her body.

"Amanda, a rainbow just came out of your phone," yelled Fern.

"OMG, yours too," said Amanda. "Are you hurt?"

She saw that Simon was standing up holding his phone out in front of him. Rainbows were shooting out of it in every direction and he was shaking.

"Drop it, Simon!" she screamed. "You too, Fern. Ivy, throw your phone away." She ran to Simon, grabbed his phone out of his hand, and threw it as far as she could. He fell to the ground. "Simon!"

"What's wrong, what's wrong!" yelled Ivy. "Nigel!"

Nigel was literally chasing rainbows. As soon as he saw motion he'd lunge. Then when he saw something move elsewhere, he'd lunge in that direction. The poor dog was running himself ragged. Then, when he saw that Simon was down, he came over and started to lick Simon's face.

"Mfglb," said Simon.

"Simon, are you all right?" said Amanda, looking at him anxiously. "I was just about to give you CPR."

Simon opened his eyes and grinned. "You want to kiss me again, don't you?"

"Simon Binkle, you are impossible," said Amanda.

"Hey, the rainbows are gone," he said.

Sure enough, the sky was blue once again, with not a rainbow in sight.

"What in the world was that?" said Fern anxiously.

"I'm afraid it was the hacker," said Amanda.

"This has gone too far," said Fern. "No one and nothing is safe."

"We know," said Amanda. "That's why Scapulus has been working so hard to stop him, but he hasn't gotten anywhere."

"Scapulus Holmes?" said Fern. "The genius?"

Amanda sighed. That was exactly what Holmes was—a genius. When she'd originally met him she thought he was a know-it-all. Now she admired him more than she could say.

"Yes. That Scapulus Holmes."

"And this hacker is smarter than he is?" said Fern.

"Apparently," said Simon.

"Do you suppose it's safe to touch the phones?" she said.

"Let's take a look," said Amanda, trying to see where the phones had fallen. She found hers first. "It looks all right. What do you think, Simon? OMG, what's this?" It was another leprechaun coin. "Crazy rainbows, leprechaun gold, what's going on here? You don't suppose the hacker is *making* the gold, do you?"

"Alchemy?" said Simon. "You can't be serious."

A sensation came over Amanda that was so strong her heart started to race. She wished Holmes were there so fiercely that the emotion almost knocked her down. Why was she feeling this way, and what about the idea of turning base metals into gold would prompt it? He'd sneer at the very notion. Not that Holmes was a sneerer. Only when he was trying to pretend to be a bad boy did he even come close, and that wasn't really him.

Now Nick could sneer. Boy, could he. She wondered what he'd make of all this nuttiness, then remembered that he might actually have something to do with it. Ugh.

She turned her attention to more immediate matters. "The phones, Simon?"

"Oh, right," said Simon. "Let me take a look."

He walked over to where Amanda's phone was lying and picked it up matter-of-factly.

"Look out!" she said. "You could be electrocuted."

"Don't think so," he said. He tried switching the phone on. "It's dead."

"Are you sure?" said Amanda.

He tried turning the thing on and off. Nothing happened.

"Yup," he said. "It shorted out or something."

"How about the others?"

He repeated the process with the same results. "Kaput," he said. "Sorry. Now you won't be able to hear back from Despina."

Amanda realized she'd sent her text more than half an hour before and had heard nothing, despite the fact that the connectivity in the tunnel was surprisingly good. Of course maybe at Despina's location it wasn't. Normally the woman was so quick to respond it was frightening so this was unusual, but there was probably a benign explanation.

"She wasn't answering anyway," said Amanda. "We'll just have to limp along without the phones. I'm not sure how we're going to get back through the tunnel again, though. We'll be in almost complete darkness. Do you think Nigel could guide us, Ivy?"

"Probably," said Ivy. "His vision in the dark is as good as ours during the day. Better."

"Good," said Amanda. Nigel had been a lifesaver more times than she could count. They were so lucky to have him. "But to get back to the hacker, it's one thing to deform a solid but quite another to create something out of nothing. Don't you think, Simon?"

"You'd need much more energy to create something, and anyway there's always the law of conservation of energy."

"Refresh my memory," said Ivy.

Simon loved explaining things, although Amanda was sure he wouldn't use the word "love." He'd just say that he was doing whatever was necessary. "Energy can be neither created nor destroyed but can change form. So actually, if the hacker is making these coins—and I strongly doubt that—he's converting something into them. I have no idea what."

"What kind of training would you need to do something like this?" said Ivy.

"You'd have to be my dad, or at the very least a chemical engineer," said Simon. "And no, it isn't him. He'd never do anything like this, although he'd be very interested to see these effects. Very interested indeed." No doubt Simon's dad was a big explainer too. That was probably where he'd got the habit, although he might have picked it up from his mother. Or both of them. Amanda wondered what dinnertime at the Binkle house was like, with all of them trying to explain at once. They probably never got to eat anything, which might help explain why Simon was so skinny.

"Do you think he could help us?" said Ivy.

"He might," said Simon. "I can ask him."

"Good," said Ivy. "So about these excavations, what do you think is going on?"

"Someone found something here," said Fern.

"The coins?" said Ivy.

"Maybe," said Amanda, "but let's think about this a moment." There was a lot to consider. She needed to go through the facts systematically. "The tunnel leads to the farm. We found a coin in the tunnel. Is the source of the coins the farm, the tunnel, or the church?"

"Dunno," said Simon. "But the only place that's been dug up is the farm."

"Is it possible," said Amanda, "that the rainbows and the coins are related? That wherever you find one you find the other?"

"Maybe," said Simon. "If that were true, then wherever these broken rainbows appear, there might also be coins. Maybe even at Legatum."

"So maybe this farmer, or whoever dug all these holes, saw some broken rainbows and dug underneath them," said Ivy.

"Except he wouldn't have set up the grids," said Fern. "An expert would have had to do that. That's for ancient artifacts, so you can track their locations and document everything."

"Good point," said Ivy. "Then what are the holes for? Can you guys look in them and see anything?"

Simon, Fern, and Amanda spent several minutes looking as far into the holes as they could, but they couldn't see anything other than dirt.

"Okay," said Ivy, when they'd huddled together again. "No zombies, no artifacts other than these leprechaun coins, no sign of Inspector Lestrade or Amanda's cousins, and a bunch of crazy rainbows in the air and shooting out of our phones. What does all that add up to?"

"I don't know," said Amanda, "but it's getting late. I think we should think about going back." The others agreed, although Simon put up a bit of resistance first.

As they made their way back to the tunnel they passed the haystacks again. One of them was absolutely swarming with bees.

"Ick," said Amanda. "I don't like bees. But wait a minute. This is one of the farms on Crocodile's list. Since there are bees here it must be a place that received them. I wish my camera were working."

"I'm allergic to bees," said Ivy. "I can't get near them."

"Better be careful," said Fern. "If you get stung we're in big trouble."

"That's right," said Ivy. "I don't have my epinephrine with me."

This was the first Amanda had heard of Ivy being allergic to bees. That was worrisome, especially if she didn't have her medicine. She tried to put herself between Ivy and the bees, even though that wasn't much protection.

"Why do you suppose they're not swarming around the other haystacks?" she said.

"Look," said Simon. "There's a nest."

He pointed to a pile of straw and mud on the ground. It seemed that some of the straw had got loose and the bees had built a home there.

"And look," said Amanda. "That's where the straw came from. There's a thing sticking out of the haystack." A corner of something was indeed protruding from the structure. She drew closer to get a good look, keeping Ivy behind her. It looked like a bit of a metal box.

"Don't touch it," said Fern.

"I'm not allergic," said Amanda. "Let me just—yuck. It's all sticky."

The box was slick with honey, and now Amanda had the stuff all over her fingers. She looked at her hand, then stuck her index finger in her mouth.

"OMG, this is amazing," she said. "You have to try this."

"Are you sure it's safe?" said Fern.

"It's honey," said Amanda. "Here, take a dollop."

Amanda scooped a glob of honey up with her other hand and slid some onto Fern's fingers. Then she did the same for the others, but not Nigel.

"Sorry, Nigel," she said. "I'm not sure if it's okay for dogs to eat honey. But I want to see what this thing is. Let me just pull it out."

She placed her sticky hands on either side of the box and yanked. The thing was in there tight but she was able to pull it out by wiggling. It was indeed a metal box, with a lock that looked just like it might fit Wink Wiffle's key.

Amanda stared at the box. It was impossible. There was no way Wink Wiffle would have come to this farm in the middle of nowhere, stashed the thing in a haystack of all places, and swallowed the key. The whole idea was absurd.

"It's a lockbox," said Simon, examining it carefully.

"No kidding," said Amanda. "You're right. You do know everything."

"Don't make me fine you, Amanda," said Ivy.

"Sorry," said Amanda. "You don't suppose—"

"I think it's a coincidence," said Ivy.

"Who puts a lockbox in a haystack?" said Fern. She had a point. The hay was so dense that it must have taken a lot of strength to get it in there. Wink must have been exceptionally strong.

"Let's think about it," said Simon. "Wink was watching Crocodile Pleth. Crocodile Pleth was involved in bee thefts. This farm was on his list. Mr. Wiffle could have followed him here. Maybe he had to leave in a hurry so he stuck the box in the haystack."

"But what's in the lockbox?" said Amanda looking at it hard, as if that would reveal the nature of the contents. "Do you think it's evidence having to do with the bee thefts?"

"Could be," said Simon. "Unfortunately we can't open it without the key."

"A key," said Amanda. "We don't know that our key is the one."

"I'll bet it is," said Ivy. "You have a picture of it—oh, sorry. Forgot. The phone is dead. That's too bad. We could make an impression with some mud and compare the shape of the lock with the picture of the key."

"We'll have to take the box back with us," said Simon.

"Too bad it's too big to fit in an evidence bag," said Amanda. "It's a mess." She shook it. "Not heavy, though. It feels like there are papers in it. I can hear them rustling. You could be right about the evidence, Simon. Probably some kind of documents. OMG, look out!"

Something with the bees was changing. Instead of going about their business as they'd been doing, they began to buzz louder and louder and fly around wildly. Before the kids knew it, the bees were chasing them.

"Run!" yelled Amanda, dropping the box.

She and Fern took off as fast as their legs would go. They made a beeline for the house, where there might be someone who'd let them in and close the door behind them. When they got there, bees still chasing them, they pounded on the door but no one came. With the bees in hot pursuit, there was nothing to do but try the door. To Amanda's surprise it was open, and they entered the house just as the bees arrived. Fortunately they were able to shut the door before any of the bees could follow.

As they stood there shaking, the two girls looked at each other in horror.

"Ivy!" yelled Fern. "They'll sting her!"

"OMG!" yelled Amanda.

"We have to call 999," said Fern.

The two of them called out but no one answered. They ran around like angry bees trying to find a landline and finally came across a phone in the kitchen. Unfortunately it was dead.

And then they discovered the body.

22

GORDON BRAMBLE TO THE RESCUE

The body was lying in a pool of dried blood in the bathroom. It had obviously been there for some time.

"OMG, it smells terrible in here," said Fern.

"Cover your nose," said Amanda, who was holding her sleeve over her face.

The girls had been looking for some epinephrine when they'd found the corpse. If Ivy had indeed been stung, she'd have a very short window of time in which to be treated. If they couldn't find some medicine she could die! Unfortunately there didn't seem to be any in the house, but they did find baking soda and antihistamine cream.

"Angry bees, no phone, no epinephrine, one dead body," Amanda screamed.

"Who's that?" said Fern, looking out the window.

"Who's who?" said Amanda.

"There's a boy with Ivy and Simon, and by the way, Ivy's lying on the ground. Oh no!"

"We have to go out there," said Amanda. "He might be killing them." She peered out the window. "Oh, wait. It's Gordon."

Bees were still swarming around the house but the two girls had no choice. Screaming and waving their arms they ran back to where

Ivy, and yes, Gordon, who was covered with bees an inch thick, were standing, or in Ivy's case, lying on the ground choking and puffing up.

Ivy looked terrible. She'd been completely immobilized by the bee venom. Her face was purple, her eyes were swollen shut, and she was gasping for air. Simon was running back toward the road, presumably to get help. Nigel was barking at the top of his lungs.

Amanda screamed, "Ivy, don't you dare die!" She went for the baking soda and cream, then saw that there was something thick and brown on the sting on Ivy's arm. It looked like mud.

"Ew, what is that?" she said. Then she noticed that Gordon, in his bee blanket, was talking on the phone.

"Yes, that's right. Those are the coordinates," Gordon said, eyeing Amanda and Fern. "Two minutes? Brilliant. Ta." He ended the call. There was no way he could put the phone in his pocket, so he tossed it to Amanda, who hadn't a hope of catching it. It fell onto the dirt. "The ambulance will be here soon. I pulled out the stinger and made a poultice for her. Simon went for help."

Amanda looked down at Ivy. She was swelling up like Violet Beauregarde in "Willy Wonka and the Chocolate Factory," but she did indeed have a poultice on her arm. It was the brown, muddy thing. "Ivy!" she screamed. "Hang on. The ambulance is coming. What are you doing here, Gordon? Those bees are going to kill you."

"No they won't," said Gordon. "I grew up on a farm. I know bees."

"You're kidding," said Amanda. She wondered what else Gordon hadn't told them. "Thank you!"

"It's no big deal," said Gordon. "They're really quite nice, bees."

"Gordon, you're a hero," said Fern. "I can't thank you enough. If you ever need anything, just ask. Anything."

Amanda could hear the ambulance approaching. It would be there in seconds.

"I already know what I want," said Gordon tactlessly. Amanda hoped his request wouldn't involve her having to be around David Wiffle. "I want to join your group."

Amanda let out a little gasp. Gordon wasn't nearly as obnoxious as he used to be, but she wasn't sure she wanted him around all the time. After all he had once been David's close friend, and what did that say about him?

"You do realize that we don't like David, don't you?" she said.

"I know," he said. "Either do I."

"But he was your best friend."

"I was a child then. I'm not anymore."

"Oh, I see. All right then," said Amanda. "You're one of us now, whatever that means."

"I want to sit at your table at meals." Amanda thought for a moment, then nodded okay. She really did owe him. If he got out of line, she'd have to nudge him back in. Putting up with him seemed a small price to pay for Ivy's life.

The ambulance pulled up and two technicians got out. Simon got out of the back and ran to Ivy. Apparently he'd flagged them down and they'd let him ride with them. They gave Ivy a shot and loaded her into the vehicle. Within a few seconds the swelling had reversed itself and she stopped choking.

"We're taking her to Penrith Community," said one of the technicians, a muscular young man with an appallingly ugly face.

"Is that really necessary?" said Fern. "She's fine now. I'm her sister. We've been through this before."

"Let me check her vital signs again," said the fellow. Using the stethoscope around his neck, he listened to Ivy's heart, then felt her pulse. "Age?"

"She's nearly thirteen," said Fern.

"No, I mean you," said the guy.

"I'm seventeen."

"Good, sign here," he said, and shoved a clipboard in front of Fern's face. "Release form. Just do this and you can take her."

Fern read the form carefully, then took the blue Boot's pen the guy was holding out and signed it.

"Drop off?"

Amanda whispered to Simon, "How does he know Alexei?"

"I beg your pardon," said Fern.

"We can drop you all off if you like," said the guy. "Where to?"

"I left my car by the stone circle," said Fern.

"Easy peasey," said the technician. "Hop in."

Amanda was surprised at how little time it took to get from the farm to Fern's Fiesta. What had required forty minutes or more to do on foot took about two minutes by car, including getting out of the ambulance.

When everyone was safely buckled in, the technician stuck his head into the driver's side window, looked into Fern's eyes, held out a card, and said, "Here's my number. Call me anytime." Then he winked.

Fern looked as though she was the one who had been stung. Her face turned bright red and she seemed unbelievably embarrassed. She took the card gently and examined it. "Thank you, er, Salty," she said hesitantly. The guy flashed a shy grin, then turned around, said, "Let's go" to his very tall partner, and drove away.

"OMG, have you ever seen anyone so good looking?" said Fern when he'd gone. "I think I'm in love. Salty Pinchbeck. That has such a lovely ring to it."

Amanda and Simon, who were sitting in the back seat, looked at each other at the exact same moment. Simon stifled a giggle while Amanda suddenly found something fascinating to look at outside the window. Gordon, who was now beeless and sitting to the left of Simon, shrugged. Fern started the motor, broke into a lively rendition of "Oh My Man, I Love Him So," and headed back toward Legatum. Her voice was so good she could have been the next Adele.

"We need to report the dead body," said Amanda when she and Simon had stopped laughing.

"What dead body?" exclaimed the other three in unison.

"Not another one," said Ivy.

"'Fraid so," said Amanda. "I think it's the farmer."

"Murdered?" said Simon, pumping his knee.

"Yes," said Amanda. "Shot, I think. Simon, you're making me bounce." It was almost the same thing that had happened earlier with Gordon and Amphora in the common room. Did this bouncing thing have something to do with the Y chromosome?

"Oh, sorry." Simon pressed his knees together. "You didn't check?"

"We were a little busy," said Amanda. "You don't have to shrink yourself. I was just getting a little sick is all."

"Got gingersnaps?" said Simon.

"Always," said Amanda, and extracted one from her bag. "Hm, last one. Oh well." She bit into the cookie. It was stale.

"Just the one?" said Gordon.

"Gingersnap?" said Amanda. She wished she had something to wash it down with.

"Body," said Gordon patiently.

"Oh right. Yes, just the one. Although, OMG, Fern, we didn't look everywhere, did we?" For all they knew, there were dead bodies all over the house. Maybe that was where the so-called wretch society met and someone had massacred them.

"No, we didn't," said Fern. "The police will have to search."

"Don't tell Thrillkill how sloppy we were," said Amanda.

"We sort of had other things on our minds," said Fern.

"How dead was he?" said Gordon.

"He's been dead for a while," said Amanda.

"Smelly?" said Gordon.

"Yes."

"And I missed it?" He seemed incredibly disappointed. Maybe that was one of the reasons he and David Wiffle weren't getting along so well these days. David definitely did not like dead and smelly.

"Sorry, Gordon," said Amanda. "There will be others. What are you doing out here anyway? Say, you didn't happen to see my relatives, did you?"

"That fat woman and her dumpy husband? No."

Gordon certainly wasn't diplomatic. He was observant, however. His description of Despina and Hill was accurate, if not kind.

"Too bad. We think they might be lost. Well, not lost exactly. Something is weird though."

"Just because you haven't heard from them for a while doesn't mean they're lost," said Simon. "Maybe they don't have reception."

"Possibly," said Amanda. Simon might be correct, but Despina wouldn't let a little thing like a lack of cell reception bother her. She'd send a carrier pigeon if she had to. Something wasn't right. "How did you get out here anyway?"

"Eustace," said Gordon matter-of-factly.

"Eustace!" said Simon and Amanda. Gordon was full of surprises.

"I thought he was working," said Amanda. Eustace was always working during the summer. There were lots of tourists in Windermere then and they wanted to see the sights.

"I didn't know you knew him," said Simon.

"Who's Eustace?" said Fern.

"Tell you later," said Ivy.

"So Eustace dropped you off out here?" said Amanda. "Why would he do that?"

"I made a deal with him," said Gordon.

"A deal?" What could Gordon possibly have to offer? Was he rich? How much money did farmers make, anyway?

"Yes. I told him I'd help him become a detective in exchange for transportation."

"You what?" said Simon.

"Oh, brother," said Amanda. "This is wild." Gordon help someone become a detective? *Gordon?* He was a mediocre student at best. She hoped he hadn't sold Eustace a bill of goods.

"Was he going to pick you up too?"

"Oops. I was supposed to meet him. I'd better text him."

"You mean he's waiting for you in Penrith?" Amanda could see Eustace sitting there for hours waiting. He was an easygoing guy but he wouldn't be happy about that. Gordon had a lot to learn.

"He might be," said Gordon. "Actually, that might not be a bad thing, though."

"Keeping someone waiting forever isn't a bad thing?" said Ivy.

"He might see something," said Gordon mysteriously.

"Yes, he'll see Penrith," said Ivy. She laughed at her own joke. Amanda had to admit it was pretty funny.

"No. Other things," said Gordon.

"Like what?" said Amanda. Pizza?

"Zombies," said Gordon.

"What about zombies?" said Ivy.

"I quite like zombies," said Gordon.

"Who doesn't?" said Simon.

"I heard there were zombies around Penrith and I wanted to see them," said Gordon.

"Same as us," said Simon.

"Ssssh," said Amanda. Even if he had saved Ivy's life, she wasn't sure she wanted to share all their findings with Gordon.

"So I got Eustace to take me, and that was when I saw it."

"Would you get on with it already?" said Amanda. "What did you see?"

"I saw a rainbow come out of a hole," said Gordon.

210

23

THE LOCKBOX

The kids might not have seen a zombie in Penrith, but things were getting verrrry interesting all the same. Secret tunnels, a strange church, gold leprechaun coins, crazy rainbows, a lockbox, killer bees, a dead farmer, wretch societies, romance for Fern, Gordon full of surprises, and now another rainbow, although this one was coming out of the ground. Amanda desperately hoped that these discoveries would help her cross some of Thrillkill's tasks off her list. Certainly finding the lockbox, if indeed it was Wink's, would contribute. She wasn't sure about the rest, especially the rainbow.

When they returned to the school, Amanda, Simon, Ivy, Fern, and Gordon, who had texted Eustace to say he was riding back with the others, reported the dead body and the local police were dispatched to examine it. Thrillkill was overjoyed at what he called "a break in Wink's case." He went to get the notorious key, attempted to clean the honey off the box, and stuck it in the lock. It turned! They had indeed found the answer. Crowding around Thrillkill's desk, the kids watched as he lifted the lid with gloved hands.

The lockbox, which had gotten a bit sticky on the inside as well as the outside, contained a pile of letters and a small silver coin in a little bag. Thrillkill changed his gloves, which were thick with honey, and picked up the coin. It looked ancient. It lacked writing, but as worn as it was it was possible to make out an image of a man with a crown on his head. Thrillkill whistled, dropped the coin into an evidence bag, and labeled it.

Then he turned his attention to the letters, and that was when the group got the shock of their lives. They were love letters from Mavis Jamm (Mavis Moriarty before she married Blixus) to Wink Wiffle! Thrillkill shook his head and buried his face in his hands.

"OMG," said Amanda. "Mavis with Mr. Wiffle? This doesn't make sense."

"It was a long time ago," said Thrillkill. "Look at the postmark."

Sure enough, the letters were fifteen years old.

"Interesting," said Simon.

"I'd say it's a little more than that," said Ivy.

"I wonder if David knows," said Gordon.

Amanda and Ivy gasped. "This isn't good," said Amanda. "He's been through enough already. To think that his dad was once involved with that woman…"

"This explains the ring we found in Mavis's room," said Thrillkill. Everyone had been aghast when David had identified the ring in the criminal's jewelry box as belonging to his father. "I think she's been nursing a grudge all this time. Look at this letter." He read aloud, "'I can't believe you'd leave me. You said you loved me, and now you go and do this, all over nothing. Please, Wink. I love you. Don't go.'"

Amanda almost couldn't listen. The idea of Thrillkill saying mushy things like that, even if the words were someone else's, was embarrassing. He didn't seem bothered though.

"Hoo boy," said Simon. "That clinches it, doesn't it?"

"It certainly adds weight to our theory that Mavis killed Wink," said Thrillkill, waving the letter around.

"Are there any letters from Mr. Wiffle to Mavis in there?" said Fern.

Thrillkill riffled through the pile. "Apparently not. Hard to say whether he never answered or she has them. Had them."

"Too bad," said Fern. "They would be helpful."

No one said anything for a moment. They all seemed to be in shock. Then Gordon spoke.

"David can't know about this."

"I'm afraid it's going to have to come out," said Thrillkill.

"How about Mrs. Wiffle?" said Amanda. Celerie was a volatile woman. She'd go ballistic.

"Yes, the indomitable Mrs. Wiffle," said Thrillkill. He sighed. "The lawsuit. This is going to make things much worse—unless, of course, she already knows."

"Do you think so?" said Amanda.

"Maybe David does," said Simon.

"Uh uh," said Gordon. "No way."

"I'm going to have to tell him," said Thrillkill. "I'm just not sure whether to tell him or his mother first."

"So what's this coin?" said Gordon, suddenly losing interest in his ex-friend and eyeing the piece of silver. Amanda had visions of him as a pirate with his ill-gotten doubloons. "Do you think it's real?"

"I'm not an expert," said Thrillkill. "We'll have to have it evaluated. Obviously Wink thought it was important or he wouldn't have hidden it."

Gordon peered at the coin. "It's a king," he said.

"Let me see that," said Simon, taking the evidence bag out of Gordon's hand.

"Simon!" said Ivy. "I heard that."

"Oh, sorry," said Simon, but he didn't give up the bag. He examined the coin closely. "I think you're right. He's wearing a crown. Either that or his cowlick is worse than mine."

Everyone laughed.

"I wonder," said Amanda, and stopped.

"Go on," said Simon.

"Say this coin is valuable—very valuable. Where did Mr. Wiffle get it? We know he was watching Crocodile, and we know that Crocodile was associated with that farm. We also know that someone had been excavating at the farm. Do you think they were looking for more of these coins?"

Simon grabbed Amanda and planted a big kiss on her mouth. What was with him anyway?

"Would you stop it already?" she said. The kiss did feel nice. She wondered... No. Don't think about you-know-who.

"Don't you see?" said Simon. "You've cracked it."

"It does sound like a good working theory," said Thrillkill. "If Miss Lester is correct, then this coin is indeed valuable. Otherwise whoever dug up the farm wouldn't have gone to the trouble."

"Unless they were looking for leprechaun coins," said Ivy.

"Leprechaun coins?" said Thrillkill.

"Uh, another long story," said Amanda. "We'll tell you in a minute."

"Do we think Crocodile knew about the coin?" said Ivy.

"He must have," said Simon. "If he went to the farm he would have seen the digging and wondered what it was. He may have even stolen some—aha! I'll bet he killed the farmer for the artifacts."

"Or the other way around," said Ivy. "Perhaps Crocodile stole artifacts and the farmer killed him to get them back."

"Let me make sure I've got this straight," said Amanda. The chain of events was hard to follow. Stories were always like that until you figured out the flow. "Mr. Wiffle watches Crocodile and finds out about the bee thefts. Then he goes to one of the farms on Crocodile's list and finds a coin. He also sees the excavation so he knows it's important, although maybe he gets it evaluated and that's how he knows. Hm, that implies that the coin *is* valuable. I can see why he'd put it in the lockbox but I'm not sure why he'd stick the box in a haystack."

"Do you think Crocodile found out about the lockbox and Mr. Wiffle put it there to protect it?" said Fern.

"Wait a minute," said Simon. "You don't suppose Crocodile found out about the letters and was blackmailing Mr. Wiffle, do you?

Or Mavis? What would Blixus do if he found out about them? Do you think he already knows?"

"We have lots of questions to answer," said Thrillkill. "For now, Miss Lester, you may cross the key off your list. Excellent work. Mr. Bramble, do not breathe a word of this to David Wiffle, you got that?"

"Yes, sir," said Gordon. Amanda didn't think he would talk. The boys didn't seem to be sharing confidences anymore.

"That goes for all of you, of course," said Thrillkill. "Now, the police are looking into the murder of the farmer and we should know something soon. I will text you when I hear. You may go. Except for you, Miss Halpin." He indicated Fern. "I want to know about these leprechaun coins."

"Thank you, sir," said the kids, and left Thrillkill's office to reconnoiter, except for Fern, who stayed to talk to the headmaster, and Gordon, who went off to look for more rainbows.

When Amanda, Simon, and Ivy had ensconced themselves in the dining room with steaming cups of tea, Clive came running in all aflutter. He was as pale as a zombie.

"Something terrible has happened," he said, looking from one to the other. "My acoustic levitator is gone!"

"You didn't leave it somewhere?" said Ivy.

"Are you kidding?" said Clive. "I'd never do that. It's too valuable."

"It's not the maids again?" said Amanda. The maids had turned out to be responsible for the *Bible* having been misplaced. That was the last thing they needed to happen again.

"Why would they take it?" said Clive. He was absolutely despondent. "They've seen it a thousand times and never touched it."

215

"Someone stole it then," said Simon, slurping. The tea dribbled onto his shirt. He rubbed the spot as if that would make it go away.

"You don't think David—" said Ivy.

"That's exactly what I think," said Clive.

"Oh dear," said Ivy. "This isn't good. He's such a mess. What could he be planning?"

"We need to find him and ask him," said Amanda, blowing on her tea. She didn't want to end up like Simon.

"If he took it, he isn't going to admit it," said Clive.

"Then we'll force him," said Simon.

"I don't think that's a good idea," said Clive. "We need to go to Thrillkill."

Suddenly Gordon ran into the room and said, "Too late. David's gone. He's run away."

24

ALL EYES ON DAVID WIFFLE

The dining room had suddenly become the scene of astonishing announcements. First Clive had run in and delivered the shocking news that his levitator was gone, and then Gordon had topped him, all within the space of three minutes. What was next?

"How do you know David's run away?" Simon said.

"He left a note," said Gordon. "In his room."

David wasn't the type to bluff. Whatever his faults, making empty threats wasn't among them. If he'd left a note, he'd actually followed through.

"He can't have been gone long," said Amanda. "Surely Thrillkill can find him and bring him back."

"I don't think so," said Gordon. "He's completely disappeared."

"When was the last time anyone saw him?" said Ivy.

"Can't say," said Gordon. "I haven't seen him all day. Have you?" The kids shook their heads.

"What does the note say?" said Amanda.

He pulled out his phone. He'd taken a picture of the missive. "'My dad was a great detective. You're trying to ruin his memory. I'll bet you planted that stuff there. Don't say those things about him. And don't try to find me.'"

"What in the world?" said Fern, who had joined them after her talk with Thrillkill.

"How could he have found out so fast?" said Amanda. They'd only just delivered the letters to Thrillkill. Surely the headmaster hadn't told David already. Perhaps the boy had overheard. People were always overhearing things at Legatum. Of course that was how she uncovered a lot of important secrets, so she couldn't exactly complain.

"Found out what?" said Clive. "Oh no! He's taken my acoustic levitator wherever he's gone. This is not good."

"Where would David go?" said Amanda. "Home?"

"To Cornwall?" said Clive. "I could ask my parents to spy on his house." Clive lived in Cornwall too.

Simon shook his head. "I don't think he'd go there."

"Why not?" said Clive.

"Too obvious. He doesn't want to be found."

"Good point," said Ivy.

"I've got a terrible feeling," said Amanda. Everyone looked at her. "If he knows about the letters, he may have gone after Mavis." David was just dumb enough to do something like that. Act first, think later.

"I have a worse thought," said Ivy. She wrinkled her forehead. "He might not need to find her. If Blixus knows about Mavis and Wink, he might want to take his anger out on David. He'll find *him*."

"Wouldn't he have done that already?" said Amanda. Blixus had had ample chance to take his wrath out on David at the quarry. He hadn't done so.

"Yes, he would," said Simon, "which is why I don't think he knows about Mavis and Wink. Or at least he didn't. He's never shown any interest in David. Of course he might now."

"Why?" said Amanda. "Just because we found out—" How could Blixus possibly have heard what had just occurred in Thrillkill's office? Oh, right. Simon meant that David heard and he'd tell Blixus. What an awful thought.

"I have news," said Holmes, entering the room. He seemed to be in a good mood. "Professor Thrillkill wants me to tell you that the farmer in Penrith died *after* Crocodile was murdered. What does that mean?"

"Well, that settles that," said Simon. "Then who did kill him?"

"A zombie?" said Clive.

"It's possible," said Simon. "We don't know who or what these zombies represent. Remember that graffiti we saw in the tunnel—the one that said 'wretch society'? What if the zombies belong to this society or whatever it is? If they're a gang or some kind of crime syndicate, they might want the same things Blixus does."

"Like valuable coins," said Ivy.

"And secret hiding places," said Amanda.

"What are you people talking about?" said Holmes.

"It's a long story," said Simon. "We'll fill you in later."

"Do you think the zombies got my cousin Jeffrey?" said Amanda. Now she really was sounding ridiculous. Whenever they did find out who these strange people were, they were all going to be embarrassed. Zombies indeed.

"What zombies?" said Holmes, losing his patience.

"Why would Wink get involved with Mavis?" said Ivy suddenly.

"Wink Wiffle was involved with Mavis Moriarty?" said Holmes.

"She's hot," said Simon.

"Yeah, but she's evil," said Gordon.

"Was *he* hot?" said Ivy. Everyone stopped talking. The idea of David's father being attractive didn't seem to have occurred to them. Mavis must have seen something in him, though. Amanda wondered what it was.

"Wink hot?" said Simon.

"Don't ask me," said Ivy.

"Nah," said Gordon. "He looked a lot like David."

Was David nice looking? Amanda had never thought about it. His personality was so terrible that she wouldn't have noticed even if he had been.

"It does seem unlikely, doesn't it?" she said. "I mean the two of them being involved. I thought Wink was supposed to be a good guy."

"You don't think she had something on him, do you?" said Clive.

"I think that woman is capable of anything," said Holmes.

"But what about Wink?" said Gordon. "You're right. Everything we know about him says that he was a hero."

"Everything *David* knows about him, you mean," said Simon.

"Welllll," said Gordon. "I suppose."

"I think we've done all we can do on this stuff for now," said Amanda. "We don't know where to look for David. We don't know where to look for Blixus, or Editta, or Mavis, or—"

Suddenly Ivy froze. "Ssh," she said. Amanda was glad her friend had interrupted her. She was just about to say "Nick," and that would not have been good, especially with Holmes there. Ivy held up her hand, listened for a moment, then leaned forward and said in a very low voice, "Big trouble. I can hear Professor Snaffle talking out in the hall. Someone's got into the secrets trove."

The news that the secrets trove had been breached almost failed to move the kids, who were so overwhelmed with the school's other problems that they could barely process it. They sat in stunned silence for at least a minute and then Amanda said, "David."

"You think David did this?" said Holmes.

"It had to be him," she said. "He finds out about his dad and Mavis and freaks out again but this time he goes after the secrets trove rather than the *Bible*, and runs off. It's obvious."

"I think we should find out more before we jump to conclusions," said Ivy. "We don't even know what happened."

"I don't care," said Amanda. "I still think it was David."

"You're not being fair to him," said Gordon.

"Oh really?" said Amanda. "Explain how we should trust him at this point." She'd bent over backwards to give David the benefit of the doubt, but just because he was grieving didn't mean he was innocent. Besides, she'd had just about enough of him.

Gordon sat there for a moment with his chin in his hands and then said, "I can't."

"Told ya," said Amanda unkindly.

"He is kind of insane," said Ivy. "But we really should find out what happened."

"Fine," said Amanda. "If you want to go into the trove, I'll go with you." She was sure she'd find strands of pale red hair in there.

"All right," said Ivy. "I'm game. For what it's worth, though, I don't think David did it."

"Why?" said Amanda.

"He follows rules," said Ivy.

"Not anymore," said Amanda.

"That's his personality," said Gordon. "The *Bible* was an exception."

Suddenly there was a loud crash. It seemed to have come from outside. There were no windows in the dining room so the kids got up and ran into the Holmes House common room next door. Outside the shining plate glass windows in the summer evening light, a riot of rainbows was making a huge crackling sound and blinking on and off.

"It's him," said Holmes. "This has got to stop, and it's got to stop now."

25

STINKY LOCKS

If the trove had truly been breached, it wasn't just the detectives' secrets that were at risk, it was the entire school. Once you were inside the Legatum gates, you could go pretty much anywhere. The detectives believed in securing the perimeter but letting the students roam the grounds. Such freedom was conducive to learning.

Amanda, Ivy, and Nigel entered the basements through the door near the dining room and made their way to the tunnels. Apparently the décor gremlins had been hard at work underneath the school because the property department, as Amanda liked to think of it, had been rearranged. Now instead of laying out furniture and other items as entire rooms, the gremlins had grouped everything according to function: furniture for sitting on was all together, such as couches, Queen Anne chairs, and kitchen stools. Likewise all wall fixtures, including paintings, candelabras, and safes for valuables had been collected in rooms dedicated to them. Amanda thought this a more sensible arrangement than the previous scheme and mentally applauded Alexei and Noel for the improvement.

The last time they'd been in the trove they'd found exposed drawers, but that was because of the earthquake and its aftershocks. Now thousands of drawers were open all over the place, not just in areas that had been damaged. The girls and Nigel walked from one clearing to another, through this tunnel and that, and found breaches everywhere.

"Funny," said Amanda. "The locks look untouched. What would a breached lock look like?"

"Not like anything if the person opened them the way I did," said Ivy.

"So how are these locks different from any other lock?" said Amanda.

"Good question," said Ivy. "You'd think the teachers would have used a more sophisticated technology. Let's check one of the ones I opened last term."

"Where were those?" said Amanda.

"I think they were in the section the teachers call the Bridge of Sighs," said Ivy. "I can't imagine why they call it that. There's no water in here."

"Who can fathom the mind of a Legatum detective?" said Amanda. "I think I know where that is. You go past Anne Hathaway's Cottage, then around the Bodlean, and turn left at Portia's Porch."

"It should be Portia's Pooch," Ivy giggled.

"Hear that Nigel?" said Amanda. "How's my favorite pooch?" She bent down and tousled the hair on the dog's back. He swung his head around in pleasure, then sneezed.

The girls made their way to the familiar spot. As they were wending their way Ivy said, "Do you smell something?"

"Don't think so," said Amanda. "Like what?"

Nigel sneezed again. "It's kind of sickening," said Ivy. "It's bothering Nigel. I can't say I like it either."

Amanda stopped and sniffed. "I can't smell it. What do you suppose it is?"

"Something the earthquake released?"

It was possible. The earthquake had created the crystals they'd found the previous term, thrown up dust, liberated spores and gases from their hiding places, and more. They'd probably feel the effects for years.

"I hope it isn't dangerous," said Amanda. "Amphora would be running out of here screaming by now. She'd think it was radon. By the way, speaking of dangerous, what do you make of this Mavis and Wink thing?"

"I was certainly surprised," said Ivy.

"I think we all were." And bothered. The idea of Wink and Mavis together was mindboggling. Amanda still couldn't get her head around it. "Ivy, I want to ask you something, and please don't criticize me." Ever since they'd discovered the letters, she'd been worrying. She couldn't stand it anymore. She had to know.

"All right. Not a problem."

"Do you see a parallel between Wink and Mavis and me and Nick?"

"What?" said Ivy. "You can't be serious."

"A couple made up of a criminal and a detective."

"Oh, I see what you mean," said Ivy. "I suppose it's not unheard of."

"What do you mean it's not unheard of?" said Amanda. She didn't know if that meant she was unexceptional or a curiosity. Most likely it meant she had extremely poor judgment. "Isn't it terrible?"

"It depends," said Ivy. "Emotions are complicated."

"But wouldn't it compromise the detective?"

"You'd think so," said Ivy. "It might compromise the criminal though."

"Cause them to go straight, you mean?" said Amanda. If such a thing ever happened it must be extremely rare. It certainly hadn't done that for Mavis. Wouldn't that be something, though—Blixus Moriarty's wife going straight. She'd love to see that. Although what that would do to Nick—

"Perhaps," said Ivy. "Or maybe they'd both quit and just live their lives some other way."

Amanda couldn't believe her ears. The thought of her and Nick riding off into the sunset was laughable. "You don't think Wink was planning to quit the detectives, do you?"

"I have no idea," said Ivy. "I wonder what David would have made of that. No, actually I don't. I know exactly what he'd think. He'd go bananas."

"Do you think Wink was doing just that and David found out?" said Amanda. "Maybe that's why he went so crazy and destroyed the *Bible.*"

"I think we need more information," said Ivy. "For all we know, Wink was once a criminal."

"No," said Amanda. "Never." Thrillkill would never have let David into the school if that were the case. Even more to the point, he never would have hung around with Wink.

"Stranger things have happened," said Ivy.

"I'm dying to know what happened at that cave," said Amanda.

"Me too," said Ivy. "I have a feeling we'll find out someday." She stopped and felt the walls of the tunnel. "Here. This is where I got into the drawers."

"Here's a closed one," said Amanda, reaching out and testing a compartment. "Good and tight. Want to try this one?"

"Sure," said Ivy.

Amanda guided her friend to the compartment in question and watched as Ivy extracted a lock-picking kit and inserted a pick into the lock on the right. She manipulated the pick, listening carefully, until she had opened it. The whole thing took about thirty seconds.

"That's amazing," said Amanda. She couldn't imagine what Ivy had done but it was certainly effective. Her friend was developing quite the expertise. She'd helped Amanda get past the electronic lock at the sugar factory just by listening to the noises the keypad made. Between her and Eustace, they could probably break into anything. "Where did you get the picks?"

"Fern," said Ivy. "I'm not sure if she got them for Professor Snool's class or what."

"But he teaches the weapons class," said Amanda. She hadn't taken it yet. You had to be a second-year student.

"Yes. Picks aren't exactly weapons. Kind of anti-weapons, I guess. Anyway, you try."

"What am I supposed to do?" said Amanda.

"You want to move the pins. They should be all lined up so there's no obstruction. You can hear when they get into the right position."

Amanda took the pick from Ivy and stuck it into the lock, then moved it around. "I can feel something," she said, "but I can't hear a thing."

Ivy moved her head close to the lock. "I can hear it," she said. "There, no, oops, no, back, no, almost, no, oh dear."

"Ivy, I can't hear one thing except your voice," said Amanda. She pulled the pick out of the lock.

"Hm," said Ivy. "Maybe I can hear things you can't."

"Ya think? No wonder you can open these locks so easily."

"Are we saying that the thief has exceptional hearing?"

"They must," said Amanda. "Except I don't see how they could have gotten into so many drawers in so little time."

"I don't either," said Ivy. "Something doesn't add up."

"I'll tell you one thing. I don't smell anything here."

"Me either. And Nigel has stopped sneezing."

"Great," said Amanda. "A picky thief who opens certain drawers and not others. Ivy, you don't think they know what's inside and are targeting only the ones they want?"

"I don't see how," said Ivy. "The only way that would be possible would be if they had the metadata or if it was one of the teachers."

"One of the teachers steal the secrets?" said Amanda. The idea was unthinkable. Unless, of course, one of them was a mole. "Who would do such a thing?"

"I don't know," said Ivy. "The teachers are divided into factions now. Maybe this is their way of fighting."

Amanda didn't like that suggestion at all. If the teachers were so far gone that they were resorting to dirty tricks, her film would never convince them to stay together.

"That's terrible. They're destroying everything Legatum has. First the *Bible*—"

"Which had nothing to do with the teachers," said Ivy.

"As far as we know," said Amanda.

"What are you saying? That David was in cahoots with one of the factions and that's why he destroyed it?"

"I don't know. I'm just trying to think outside the box. OMG, Ivy, do you really think David did this?"

"You mean he's flipped and gone bad? Or are you saying that he was always in cahoots with someone and all that goody-goody stuff was just an act?"

"I don't know. The whole thing is crazy."

"What's crazy?" said a voice.

Amanda whirled around. It was Professor Kindseth. He was standing on his own two feet, no longer using the crutches he'd had to rely on since his injury in the earthquake. Although he was ostensibly one of the neutral teachers, she didn't want to tell him of her suspicions. As great a guy as he was, you never knew who you could trust at Legatum.

"Hello, Professor," she said.

"Amanda, Ivy," said Professor Kindseth. "What a mess, eh?"

"I'll say," said Ivy. "I just don't see how they could have picked all these locks so quickly."

Professor Kindseth surveyed the situation and shook his head. "Well, now that the cat is out of the bag let me show you something. We have to go back past the Porch, the Cottage, and the Bodlean. Er, not in that order."

The girls and Nigel followed Professor Kindseth back the way they'd come. As soon as they got close to Anne Hathaway's Cottage, Nigel started to sneeze.

"It's that smell again," said Ivy.

"Yes," said Professor Kindseth. "It would be."

"I don't understand," said Amanda.

Professor Kindseth pointed to the mechanisms on the compartments. "The newer section of the trove works differently from the older one. In this area, the locks are controlled by odors."

Odor-controlled locks! Then why did the drawers have keyholes? Amanda couldn't process what she had just heard. She looked at the locks again. They seemed just the same as the one Ivy had just opened.

"Are you saying that the thief got into the compartments by releasing a scent?" said Ivy.

"It does look that way," said Professor Kindseth.

"I can smell it," she said. "So can Nigel. He's allergic to it."

"Isn't it extremely difficult to duplicate a scent exactly?" said Amanda, her brain beginning to function properly again.

"Monumentally," said the teacher. "Which is why we never expected anything like this. The chances of someone duplicating the formula are infinitesimal."

Amanda thought for a moment. Suddenly something clicked. "Not if you have access to the world's most powerful hacker."

"Ooooh, good point," said Ivy.

"You think whoever hacked Professor Redleaf's computer did this?" said the teacher.

"I do," said Amanda. "The same guy—or girl—who's making those crazy rainbows."

Professor Kindseth stroked his chin for a moment. "You can't hack the trove electronically," he said. "There's no computing equipment in here. I'm not sure the formula is even stored in digital form." He lowered his voice. "To tell you the truth, I think it's in one of these compartments. In code."

It would be, wouldn't it, thought Amanda. The formula for the scent that opened the locks had to be one of the teachers' most important secrets. The trove was the logical place for it.

"So you'd have to know the code to break in and get the code," said Ivy.

"Something like that," said Professor Kindseth.

"That doesn't make sense," said Amanda.

"Professor," said Ivy, "does this mean that only the areas with odor-controlled locks were breached?"

"I don't know," he said. "It's possible. If you permeated the area with the right smell, you could open them all at once. But in the older parts, you'd need to pick each lock separately. Or have the keys."

"Why are there keyholes if there aren't any keys?" said Amanda.

"To fool people," said Professor Kindseth. "There are teachers who don't even know that."

"So why are you telling us?" said Amanda.

"It doesn't matter now, does it?" he said.

26

A THIRD WAY

The idea that you could open all the locks in a large area of the trove at one fell swoop seemed crazy. Not for the first time Amanda wondered what the teachers were thinking. Were they so cocky that they thought nothing could ever happen? If they had been before, they certainly weren't anymore. The Moriartys had planted moles in their midst, conducted illegal operations under their noses, hacked them (maybe), and foiled one of their most critical security measures. Maybe whatever was in the *Bible* wasn't worth going after at all. It seemed that the teachers' tricks were out of date. Of course she'd never say that to them.

But Ivy would. "Professor Kindseth, why would the school use the same combination for all the locks?"

"Ever heard of OpenID?" he said.

"The open source authentication system that lets you use one password to enter lots of sites," said Amanda. She'd been learning a lot about computing from Holmes.

"Indeed," he said. "We thought the odor would be like that, especially since we designed it to be absolutely unique."

"You designed it yourselves?" said Ivy.

"Actually, Professor Pargeter and Professor Stegelmeyer came up with it together," he said. "As you know, they're our best chemists."

It would probably be a good idea to keep Amphora from finding out about that. Professor Pargeter was a toxicologist. Amphora would think the scent was poisonous.

"But the thief can't use the secrets, can he?" said Amanda. The secrets were in code. You'd have to be able to break it to read them.

"All right," said Professor Kindseth. "You didn't hear this from me." The girls nodded. "You can't make sense of any of this without the metadata," he whispered.

"That's what we thought," said Amanda. Ever since the kids had found out about the trove, they'd suspected there had to be something that made sense of all those snippets—an index, maybe. Of course what it was and where it was located they had no idea.

"I suppose you don't have to be a genius to figure that out," said Professor Kindseth.

"They didn't get the metadata too?" said Ivy.

"Nope," said Professor Kindseth. "Thank goodness. And don't ask me where it is. I don't know and I wouldn't tell you if I did."

"I'll bet it's in that cave in Scotland," said Ivy, voicing exactly what Amanda was thinking.

"What, Thrillkill's cave?" said Professor Kindseth. "I doubt it."

"Why?" said Amanda.

"Not secure and too obvious," said the teacher.

"Good point," said Ivy. "So what now?"

"I don't know," said Professor Kindseth, "but I suspect whatever we do will be drastic. We'll have to secure the trove first, of course."

Drastic. What did that mean? The teachers might do anything, from destroying the trove to moving it lock, stock, and barrel. And then what?

"You do know how they got in, don't you?" said Ivy.

"No, not yet."

"We do," she said. "You should speak to Clive Ng."

"Clive Ng helped them break in?" said Professor Kindseth. He looked stung.

"Of course not," said Amanda. There was no way that Clive would ever work for the Moriartys. What you saw with him was what you got. If he ever went rogue, she'd hang up her magnifying glass. It would mean she didn't have the judgment to be a detective. Of course it was possible she didn't. She'd believed in Nick and look how he'd turned out. "It's just that—you need to talk to him as soon as possible."

"I'm afraid to even ask this," said Ivy. "If the thief were able to read the secrets, what would happen to us?"

"That's a valid question," said Professor Kindseth. "It depends who you ask. The Realists would have additional ammunition for their argument that we should close the school and go on to other things. The Punitori would vow to find the *Bible* and the secrets. At least that would put us and whoever took them on a level playing field."

"What do you think?" said Ivy.

"Me? I don't like either option," said the teacher. "I guess I'd have to hope that there's a third way. I'm just not sure what it would be."

When the girls had returned to the common room, Amanda elbowed Ivy and said, "Did you hear what Professor Kindseth said? He thinks there's a third way."

"For the teachers?" said Ivy.

"Yes," said Amanda. "Do you realize what this means?"

"It sounds sensible," said Ivy, tousling Nigel's fur. "Perhaps Professor Kindseth and the other neutral teachers can convince the others."

"Maybe," said Amanda. "But it's also an opportunity for *us*. We can come up with that third way and save the school. What do you think?"

"I think that's a fantastic idea," said Ivy. "How can I help?"

Amanda grinned like the Cheshire cat. She was feeling especially chuffed. "How would you like to compose some music for the film Scapulus and I are making?"

After the teachers had conducted an initial survey of the damage to the trove, Headmaster Thrillkill announced that they were going to recreate the secrets as soon as possible. This news elicited outbursts from the Realists, who said it was too late and the trove should be destroyed, while the Punitori claimed that they should be put in charge and Thrillkill should step aside. They and only they could remedy the situation. Although everyone knew their stated objective—to recover the *Bible* and resume operations—no one outside their group seemed to know how they planned to accomplish it.

Amanda was beginning to think that all the teachers were wrong. All except Professor Kindseth, that is. There *was* a third way and she was going to find it. She'd present it in cinematic form and revel in being called a genius.

Of course to get Holmes to go along with her ideas would take some doing. She couldn't in good conscience try to be his girlfriend again just to influence him. That would be immoral as well as hurtful. It would also probably backfire. She would have to confide in him, though, because he was her partner in the endeavor, although maybe she could do it in such a subtle way that he wouldn't realize she was pulling the strings.

As if. Scapulus Holmes might not have been so good at relationships, but he was awfully smart. Truth be told, he was the smartest person she'd ever known—even smarter than Professor Ducey or Professor Sidebotham or Simon. He'd see right through her.

No, the only way to proceed was to tell him the truth. Of course she'd have to come up with the answer first.

How could she bring together people with opposing views? Perhaps she should start by profiling the groups. Actors always ask, "What's my motivation?" so they can understand where their characters are coming from. Amanda had approached many non-cinematic problems the same way. So why did one group want to give up and the other fight?

When she looked at the lists of which teachers belonged to which group, she could see that the names were predictable. Professor Buck absolutely had to be a Punitor and Professor McTavish a Realist. Why? Professor Buck, the profiling teacher, was a pretty feisty guy. Professor McTavish, who taught police procedure, tended to be systematic and rule-bound, almost like David Wiffle, but nicer and more competent. Was it true that the Punitori were like soldiers and the Realists peaceniks? From her experience in Professor Sidebotham's classes, Amanda doubted that the observation teacher was a dove even though she was a Realist. The woman was like a steel girder, she was so tough. And Professor Ducey, a Punitor, was so nice and easygoing. No, that couldn't be it.

If the differences didn't have to do with the teachers' proclivities toward war and peace, what else could they be attributed to? She looked at her list of groups again. Maybe she'd see something she'd overlooked.

Realists. They believe the *Bible* is the undying symbol of Legatum and they can't go on without it. The members are:

Browning. Sketching.
Mukherjee. Legal issues.
Hoxby. Dead bodies.
McTavish. Police procedure.
Pickle (still in prison). Textual analysis.

Pole. Fires and explosions.
Scribbish. Evidence.
Sidebotham. Observation.

Punitori. They believe in finding the thieves, recovering the *Bible*, and resuming operations. The members are:

Also. History of detectives.
Feeney. Criminals and their methods.
Snool. Weapons.
Pargeter. Toxicology.
Buck. Profiling.
Stegelmeyer. Crime lab.
Ducey. Logic.
Peaksribbon. Self-defense.

Neutrals. They refuse to take sides.

Thrillkill. Headmaster.
Snaffle. Secrets.
Kindseth. Photography.
Tumble. Disguise.

She examined the list of Realists. These were the people who wanted to throw up their hands—or did they? If they were advocating ending the school, what was next for them? Perhaps Professor Sidebotham would retire. She was certainly old enough. Professor Pickle was still in jail, but he'd be out soon. Of course he could concentrate on his pickle business full time if he wanted to. But the others were in the primes of their careers. What would they do?

As far as the Punitori were concerned, they refused to give up on the idea of Legatum. They clung to the school fiercely and would keep it going no matter what. It was an admirable stand except for one thing: what would happen if they never got the *Bible* back? What would they do then? If they felt the *Bible* was necessary to the school, they believed the same thing the Realists did: that the *Bible* was essential and there was no Legatum without it. They just used that conclusion in different ways.

She'd been looking at the list all wrong. The Realists, who were willing to cut their losses and move on, were the resilient ones. They'd take whatever came and make it work. But for all their militancy, the Punitori were more fragile. They assumed they'd get their way. They had no backup plan. They simply refused to consider that they might need one.

Wow. The thought of Professor Buck being fragile was mind-boggling. Something must be going on underneath the facades of the teachers who subscribed to the Punitori philosophies. Was it possible that they were tough on the outside but their insides were made of jelly? Amanda couldn't believe it. Professors Feeney, Snool, Pargeter, and Buck were downright scary. They had to be as indestructible as gravity.

Truth be told, the Punitori *needed* the other teachers. Even though it looked as though they were the leaders, they would be at sea without Professors Mukherjee, Browning, and Thrillkill. The problem was that no one seemed to realize it. No one except her, that is.

She knew what she had to do. Now she just had to come up with a way to do it.

The next morning at breakfast Clive announced that the acoustic levitator had magically reappeared in his closet. "It's not damaged or anything," he said.

"When did you find it?" said Simon, buttering his toast. It looked like he was going to use an entire stick of the stuff.

"This morning after my shower," said Clive, picking at his eggs. "I came back to my room and there it was." He seemed so relieved that his entire body had changed shape. Amanda hadn't realized how angular he'd been looking since the theft. He'd obviously been even more worried than he'd let on.

She took a bite of English muffin. "David didn't take it after all. Unless he's back. Is he?"

"Don't think so," said Simon, contemplating his toast. He slathered on more butter. "I think we would have heard."

"Someone at Legatum took it then," said Amanda. "Who's new around here?"

"You're not suggesting the new cook—" said Clive.

"I certainly hope not," said Amanda, grabbing a crumpet. "We've had enough trouble with cooks already. I really would like to feel that there are good cooks in the world."

"Nice pun," said Simon, smiling. He looked good that way. He should do it more often, she thought.

There was no butter left so she took a bite of dry crumpet. It wasn't bad. The new cook knew what he was doing. "What? Oh, I didn't realize what I was saying. You don't think Gordon—"

"No," said Simon. "He's changed."

"I agree," said Amanda. "Clive, are you absolutely sure it was gone?"

Clive hung his head. "I'm not going crazy. It was there, then it was gone, then it was back." He pushed his eggs from one side of his plate to the other.

"Hang on," said Simon, looking around for more butter. "You know how we got out of the gates in the trove?"

"Using the acoustic levitator," said Clive. "Sure."

"And you know how the trove has been breached?"

"OMG," said Amanda. "Someone took the levitator to get into the trove!"

"Bingo." Simon took a bite of his toast. He chewed for a moment and then stopped to pass judgment. His concoction must have been okay because he took another bite, this time larger. Amanda didn't see how he could even taste the bread with all that butter, but maybe that was the point.

"Someone at Legatum."

"Looks like it," said Simon. "Clive, is there any evidence that would lead us to the thief? Fingerprints?"

"Not a one," said Clive. "I checked."

"Substances?" said Amanda.

"No," said Clive. "The levitator's been wiped clean."

"Nuts," said Simon. "How about marks on your carpet?"

"I forgot about that," said Clive. "Let's go check."

The two boys ran off to the dorm to see if the thief had left footprints or fibers or any other clues in Clive's room. Although Amanda had a million things to do, she was somewhat stuck until her phone was working again. Unfortunately that meant she had to talk to Holmes. He had taken the broken phones from her, Simon, Fern, and Ivy and said he hoped to have them working in a few hours.

When she found him, he was in the cyberforensics classroom as usual. "I got it to work," he said. "It's a bit unreliable though."

"What do you mean?" said Amanda.

"It cuts in and out. Also sometimes the screen turns rainbow colors."

"Is it dangerous?"

"I don't think so. You should back up all your data though."

"Okay. Thanks, Scapulus."

He got that pained look again. "Amanda, be careful."

"With the phone, you mean?" she said.

"With everything. I don't for a moment believe there are zombies out there, but dangerous things are happening and you tend to be a bit bold sometimes."

"I'm a detective," she said. "I have to be."

"What good is being a detective if you're dead?"

That threw her for a loop. If a descendant of Sherlock Holmes was advising caution, things must be really bad. His family history was rife with risk-taking. Jumping into dangerous situations was second nature to him.

"Just try, please," he said. "I think this thing with Mavis and Wink is going to lead to unimaginable chaos. It's just a hunch, but it's a strong one."

"Why?"

"Detectives and criminals fraternizing never turns out well." It was one of the worst things ever to come out of his mouth. He wasn't talking about Wink Wiffle and Mavis Moriarty. He was talking about Amanda and Nick.

"I can take care of myself," she said, and flounced out of the room.

Now that her phone was working, Amanda was really starting to worry about Despina and Hill. Not only had she texted them ages ago and heard nothing, but Despina had promised to keep in touch and had even started to do so. Now, however, she had gone completely quiet. This behavior was so unlike her that Amanda thought the zombies might have got her. How silly was that? Zombies indeed. On the other hand, there had been murders in the area, and someone might still be looking for valuable artifacts. If Despina had got hold of one, or ended up in someone's way, they might even have killed her!

She texted Despina again, and this time she texted Hill as well. She didn't have a number for Jeffrey or she would have tried him too.

Funny how once Jeffrey had entered the church they hadn't seen him again. Had he made it to the farm too? Surely if he had he would have reported the murder. On the other hand, he might not have gone to the house at all. But he would have been curious about the holes, and the kids would have caught up with him then. He hadn't been that far ahead of them.

Perhaps he'd turned the other way at the fork. Yes, that was what must have happened. Amanda wondered where the other tunnel led. Maybe they should go back and try it. She'd see if Fern could take them again, maybe the next day.

Why did Holmes have to be so difficult anyway? He used to smile all the time, act so laid back. Now he could be downright snide. Sure he was worried, and a lot of responsibility lay on his shoulders. That was true of all of them, but no one else was sniping—not unless you counted David Wiffle, of course, but in his case the behavior was understandable.

Did she still love Holmes? She wasn't sure. Maybe what she thought she'd felt had been an illusion—a late night talk, a few shared intimacies, some laughs. Perhaps they had simply experienced a moment she'd mistaken for something deeper. It hadn't lasted beyond a day. That wasn't love.

Simon thought it was though. He thought they were good together and she should try harder. But he was crazy. What did Simon Binkle know about love? Sure, he liked to kiss people—especially her, it seemed—but so what?

Funnily enough, Holmes did know about love. He may have been logical, systematic, and unbelievably smart, but he was sensitive— sometimes a little too sensitive. Amanda wondered if he'd ever had a girlfriend before. They hadn't touched on the subject. She hoped he hadn't. She didn't like the thought of him looking into another girl's eyes the way he had hers. She wanted to be his first, although he wasn't strictly hers, was he?

Despite what Simon had said, he *was* her first. Nick was never her boyfriend. They'd been close, of course, but he'd never tried to kiss her, which come to think of it puzzled her. If Nick had cultivated their relationship to get inside information about Legatum, why hadn't he? Wouldn't that have brought them closer together, made her more likely to divulge confidences? There wasn't a shy bone in Nick Muffet's body so what had stopped him? Did he find her that repulsive?

If Simon were inside her head right now he'd say Nick *had* been her boyfriend. Otherwise why would she be thinking about kissing him? Was Simon right? Wouldn't she have known if they were boyfriend and girlfriend? Of course she would. Simon was nuts.

She was all mixed up. Holmes, Nick, what did it matter? There were so many problems facing Legatum that she didn't have time for idle speculation. Plus there was Darius's film to work on. Yikes! She'd forgotten all about Darius. She'd better get to her writing.

She climbed up to her room, booted her computer, and opened the folder containing the "Sand" project. But before she could go further, Ivy and Nigel ran into the room.

"Oh boy," said Ivy. "Just when we thought things couldn't get any worse."

"What is it?" said Amanda.

"Celerie Wiffle is in Thrillkill's office," said Ivy. "She's furious about Mavis and she's blaming Thrillkill for making the letters public. She and Editta's mum have organized a parents' revolt."

27

REVOLTING PARENTS

Great. Just what they needed: a mob of angry parents. Amanda pictured Frankenstein's monster and villagers carrying torches. She hoped the parents wouldn't go as crazy as that.

Celerie Wiffle was turning out to be as big a thorn in Legatum's side as her son. Yes, a lot of bad things had happened to her, but she should be taking constructive action, not distracting Thrillkill from looking for David, Editta, and Wink's murderer. Of course no one knew why Wink had kept Mavis's letters, so Celerie's hysteria was somewhat understandable. Surely he couldn't still have loved her. Ugh. What a disgusting thought. That really would have pushed David over the edge.

As if the disappearances and the murder weren't bad enough, some of the parents were now getting wind of the fact that the *Bible* was gone. Although most of them hadn't known of its existence in the first place, they had plenty to say about Thrillkill's negligence in allowing it to disappear. Many of them were threatening to withdraw their financial support from the school, and a number of them had begun the process of withdrawing their children. The situation was a disaster.

Amanda and Ivy decided to go to Thrillkill's office and see what was happening. When they arrived, there were about ten parents spilling out of the headmaster's door and they were furious.

"Did you hear that?" said Amanda.

"You mean the part about charging Thrillkill with being an accessory to kidnapping?" said Ivy.

"That and the lynching threat," said Amanda.

"This is super serious," said Ivy. "If the Realists don't destroy the school, the parents will."

Then something even worse than a mob of rioting parents with virtual pitchforks occurred. Lila Lester came clicking down the hall in her high heels, pushed her way past the onlookers, and forced her way into Thrillkill's office, stopping for half a second to acknowledge her daughter and her daughter's best friend. Her hair was freshly dyed and her nails polished to a high gloss. She looked radiant.

"Amanda, Ivy, come with me," said Lila.

"Mom, what are you doing here?" said Amanda.

"Fixing things," said Lila. "Come on."

"I don't think—"

Lila snapped her fingers, motioned toward Thrillkill's office, and gave Amanda a withering look, which fortunately Ivy couldn't see. Amanda let out a huge sigh, took Ivy by the hand, and followed Lila.

When they entered Thrillkill's office they found more angry parents screaming and pounding on the desk. Lila stepped forward, turned that look on each of them, and said, "Shut up." The room went silent. "Now you all listen to me.

"Gaston, fellow parents, I have written something I want you to read. Here are copies of my guide to predicting criminal behavior." She passed a few copies of a book with a red cover to the parents and gave one to Thrillkill. "I've updated it to include UK institutions and locations so you'll find everything you could possibly need. With my tips you should be able to find those awful Moriartys post-haste and return the situation to normal. Except for your husband's death, Ms. Wiffle, for which I am very sorry."

"Who are you?" said Celerie Wiffle. "What do you know about my husband?"

"I'm Lila Lester and I know that the Moriartys killed him. Now I want you to understand that things will be all right in the end. If we can just get through this rough period—"

"I've never heard such rubbish in all my life," said Andalusia Sweetgum. "You don't recover kidnapped children by reading a book."

A look of astonishment came over Lila's face. "Of course you do if it's mine," she said. "If you'd read any of my books you'd know I'm an expert."

The parents looked at each other as if to say, "Who let her out of the asylum?"

"I can see that you good people are skeptical," said Lila. "Let me assure you that Scotland Yard has a copy of my book and they're on the Moriartys' trail as we speak."

"You're loony," said a woman in a green Chanel suit.

"Certifiable," said a man in a tan corduroy jacket.

"Ha!" said Lila. "You skeptics always want proof. Very well. Take a look at this."

She threw a newspaper clipping onto Thrillkill's desk. The headline read, "Acclaimed Novelist Helps Police Solve Cases." It was from the *Calabasas Rancho* and had run on page 12. There was no date.

"Mom," said Amanda.

"Now, darling, I know I forgot to tell you about the article, but you can read it when we're finished here," said Lila.

"That wasn't what—" said Amanda.

"Mrs. Lester," said Thrillkill. "I appreciate your concern and your enthusiasm. Thank you for the books and the article. I must tell you, however, that the staff and administration at Legatum have come up with a plan to find the missing children and bring Wink Wiffle's murderer to justice. I was just trying to explain—"

"Nonsense," said Lila. "You don't need a plan. It's all here in my book."

"Mom, would you just let him talk?" said Amanda.

"He doesn't need to, dear," said Lila, holding up a copy of the book. "It's in here."

Ivy was giggling but Lila didn't notice. She stopped at once, however, when Mrs. Wiffle said, "I don't know who you are or what your problem is, but if you don't get out of here at once I will extend my lawsuit against this school to include you. Good day, madam."

"You have no idea who you're talking to," said Lila.

"Yes I do," said Celerie. "An escapee from Bedlam. Now if you don't get out of this office in two seconds I'll throw you out myself."

Lila smiled at Celerie and stood her ground. This behavior so enraged Wink's widow that she lunged for the author and pulled her bottle-blonde hair. Lila screamed and bashed Celerie with her extremely large designer purse, which managed to sideswipe several of the other parents before it made contact. This unfortunate move led to a general mayhem in which people were falling on top of each other, punching each other's chins, and vowing to get one or the other of Thrillkill, Lila, Blixus Moriarty, and the entire Legatum staff. By the time everyone had stopped flailing, brushed themselves off, and retrieved missing shoes, earrings, and wallets, there were so many threats of lawsuits and other punishments flying around that the place looked like a soccer stadium after a Manchester United game. Fortunately, during all the chaos Thrillkill had managed to contact Professors Buck, Snool, and Peaksribbon, who had arrived too late to break up the fight but were now standing guard in case something else happened, and the group was eyeing them warily.

"I want you to know," said Lila when the noise had died down, "that I do have a guide to conflict resolution available for all who would like to read it. Unfortunately I don't have copies with me. However, if you'll just write your mailing address on this—"

While Lila was speaking, Andalusia Sweetgum pulled a doll out of her purse, absently grabbed a few pins from who-knew-where, and began to stick them into the effigy. As she did so she muttered under her breath. Then, suddenly, she stopped in mid thrust, looked down at the figure, and said, "Not *you*." She'd been sticking pins into a monkey doll. She threw the monkey aside angrily and felt inside her purse. After a moment her hand emerged clutching an effigy of a woman with blonde hair. This gesture did not faze Lila in the least, but rather inspired her to ooh and ah and ask Ms. Sweetgum if she could interview her for a book she was thinking of writing. If the three teachers hadn't been there, Ms. Sweetgum would have stuck a pin directly into her.

As the parents were dispersing, Lila took Amanda aside and said, "That Wiffle woman is crazy. No wonder her son is such a mess."

"She's grieving, Mom," said Amanda.

"I know, but she doesn't have to take it out on me. Now darling, I want you to keep me informed. I know my guide will help. I'd go out and find those crooks myself but I have a deadline. I'm sure it won't take the school long to track down Blixus Moriarty if they pay special attention to pages 89 through 103. Do point that out to them, won't you?"

Amanda sighed. There was no point arguing with her mother. She was sure Thrillkill would do what he liked anyway.

"Yes, Mom. I will," she said as if she really meant it. "I'm sure they feel lucky to have your help."

"Indeed they should," said Lila. "Oh, while I have you, I just wanted to tell you that I've started dating."

This news practically knocked Amanda on her butt. She couldn't picture her parents with other people and didn't want to. "Oh?" she managed to squeak out.

"You'll like him," said Lila. "His name is Banting Waltz. He's taken the position your father vacated when he decided to drop out. He's never lost a case. He's a good man."

Amanda wasn't so sure that just because her mother's new boyfriend had never lost a case he was a good man. In fact, chances were that he was quite the opposite, however she'd try to keep an open mind. Still, the thought of her mother dating was weird. She wondered if her dad was too.

"Sounds great, Mom," she said. *Choke.* "I can't wait to meet him."

"Oh, you will, darling," said Lila. "And before I forget, here's a copy of my new book. You're going to love it."

28

THE SILVER COIN

Amanda wasn't sure what might come out of the parents' meeting, if you could call it that, but so many other things were happening that she didn't have time to speculate. For one thing, Professor Also had stopped by the common room and told them that the silver coin had been assessed, and it was a doozy.

The numismatist had declared it the rarest thing he'd ever seen. Subject to more testing, he had pronounced the coin a relic from the age of Camelot, most probably depicting King Arthur himself. This news had sent Thrillkill and the teachers into such a tizzy that they'd forgot they were feuding and rushed off to examine the artifact every which way.

Professor Also was so excited she could hardly speak. "The thing is—the thing is," she said, "normally—well, never—we don't—well, I don't, and I know the school doesn't—except one time when Professor Pickle vouched for the art history expert—well, it wasn't exactly art history, more current art. Well, not even that. It wasn't art—crafts really. Anyway, we don't accept these assessments at face value, or book value, or whatever it's called, I forget, could it be par value? That doesn't sound right. Of course we're skeptical. We're detectives. But Fashly Terrapin is the foremost expert—oh, yes, we were lucky to get him—he's the top numismatist in the world, except for that fellow in Shanghai. At any rate, he said this is definitely—well, probably—no, absolutely—a coin from King Arthur's time, can you imagine?"

This outpouring was so unlike Professor Also that Amanda thought one of the other teachers might be wearing a Winifred Also mask and playing a practical joke. Once she and her friends realized it really was the History of Detectives teacher and she was serious, they started jumping all over the room. They were so exuberant that poor Nigel freaked out and hid in a corner.

"But this is amazing," said Amanda. "King Arthur? I thought he was just a myth."

"Lots of people do," said Professor Also. "Apparently they're wrong. Although again, we do need to wait for the final judgment."

"Don't you see what this means?" said Ivy. "This is why Mr. Wiffle hid the coin in the haystack. He knew how valuable it was."

"And it may have been the reason he was killed," said Professor Scribbish, who had been walking by and heard the fuss.

"And Crocodile and the farmer," said Simon.

"Of course Mavis Moriarty may have killed Wink for other reasons," said Professor Also.

"Those letters were awfully emotional," said Amanda. Wink's heart must have been made of stone for them not to move him. She wondered what he was really like. He didn't seem to have much in common with his son, that was for sure. With him away from home so often, Celerie must have exerted the larger influence over the boy and he'd ended up like her.

"I feel sorry for her," said Amphora, who had come to see what the to-do was about. She'd been off somewhere doing who knew what and this was the first time Amanda had seen her in ages.

"Sorry for Mavis Moriarty?" said Simon. "A cold-blooded killer?"

"Watch it, Simon," said Ivy.

"I'm just saying."

"See that you keep it to that," said Ivy.

"I know she's a terrible person," said Amphora. "But she's human. Criminals fall in love too."

Amanda hoped she wasn't referring to her and Nick. Of course she wasn't. Nick didn't love her and Amphora knew it.

"Oh, brother," said Simon.

"Love isn't simple, you know," said Amphora. "You can end up loving the wrong person."

Simon looked straight at Amphora. "Or *knowing* the wrong person."

"Twenty p," said Ivy. "Hand it over, Simon."

He took out a couple of coins and shoved them into Ivy's hand.

"And don't push," she said. Simon gave Amanda a look that said, "What's with her?" Amanda shrugged. "I heard that, Simon."

How Ivy could hear a look Amanda didn't know, but it seemed that you couldn't get anything past her, regardless of what medium you chose. Amanda imagined that Simon was thinking the same thing and trying to come up with a new and astonishing way to fool her. She gave him a fifty-fifty chance.

"I'm sure we'll sort out who murdered whom for what reason," said Professor Scribbish, who didn't seem to notice that the kids were fining each other. Or maybe he did and approved. In any case he didn't say anything.

"Doesn't the coin have to be turned over to the government?" said Ivy.

"That it does," said Professor Scribbish. "Historical artifacts like this one belong to the people. They can't be held by a private person or entity. UNESCO treaty and UK laws."

"Why didn't Mr. Wiffle turn the coin in then?" said Clive.

"Good question," said Professor Also. "The fact that he didn't might have had something to do with his murder as well."

"I don't understand," said Amanda. "Why can't a person keep something they found?" There wasn't much to find in L.A., unless you counted fossils, and those you could keep—as far as she knew.

"Cultural treasures," said Simon. "No one can own them."

"But people try to, right?"

"Correcto," said Simon. "Which makes me wonder who else might be after this coin. Come to think of it, where did Mr. Wiffle get it?"

"From the holes at the farm, I'd say," said Amanda. Which implied that there were more of the little treasures. Were they still down there?

"Possibly," said Simon. "Except why was the farmer digging in the first place? I'll bet he found that coin accidentally and then went looking for more."

"You're not saying Mr. Wiffle stole it from him, are you?" said Amanda. David wouldn't like that at all, although he'd never find out unless he came back. He'd have to, of course. How would he survive by himself? Thinking about what he might be facing out there in the wild, she felt afraid for him. As upset as she'd been with her parents over the years, she'd never considered running away. How would she take care of herself?

"Probably not," said Professor Scribbish. "But Crocodile might have."

"Oooooooh," said everyone in the room.

"Of course," said Amanda. "Crocodile stole the coin from the farmer, Wink was watching him and found out about it, Wink got hold of it—how did Wink get hold of it?"

"That we don't know," said Professor Also. "But I like your theory as far as it goes."

"What happens to someone who has a coin like this and doesn't turn it in?" said Amanda.

"It's considered a criminal act," said Ivy. "You can go to prison for seven years."

"Wow. I had no idea." She wondered if her father had prosecuted an artifact thief before he'd quit the Crown Prosecution Service. It must be weird for someone like that to be in prison with all those hardened criminals. "Hello, I stole an old coin." What would the other prisoners think of that?

"How do you suppose Crocodile found out about the coins?" said Amphora.

"We don't know that he did," said Professor Also.

"But he knew the farm, obviously," said Amanda, still trying to picture her father cross-examining archaeologists. Perhaps Ivy's father had testified. Or maybe she was just getting carried away. "And if he came when the farmer was digging, he would have realized something was up. He probably knew about the tunnel too."

"And Mr. Wiffle," said Ivy. "They all had to know about it. Do you think one of them dropped the leprechaun coins?"

"What about the leprechaun coins, Professor?" said Simon.

Professor Also brushed her curly bangs out of her eyes. "Mr. Terrapin hasn't a clue about those," she said. "He's never seen anything like them."

"I'd love to be Guinevere," said Amphora when the teachers had left the common room.

"Don't say it, Simon," said Ivy.

"I wasn't going to say anything," said Simon. "Actually, that's wrong. I was going to say that Amphora would make a beautiful queen."

Amphora looked at Simon as if he had just turned into a walrus. "Why, that's the nicest thing you've ever said, Simon Binkle."

"I want credit for that," said Simon. "It should cancel out some of my fines."

"What, you're making preventative comments now?" said Ivy. "Twenty p."

"I am not," said Simon. "I really mean it. She would be extraordinary."

"Better watch it, Simon," said Amphora. "We'll think you've flipped your lid. We'll have to send you to a mental hospital."

"I haven't flipped anything," said Simon. "Can't a guy give a girl a compliment?"

"Not when it's you," said Ivy.

Amanda tried to picture Simon with a girlfriend. She couldn't. Even though he could occasionally say something nice, the thought of him being nice enough to a girl to win her over was ludicrous. She thought Ivy had been a bit harsh actually saying it, though.

"I think you should fine yourself for that one, Ivy," she said.

"Oh, all right," said Ivy. "I give myself 20p. Satisfied?"

"That was most generous of you, Ivy," said Amphora. "You didn't need to do that."

"Let's just get back to the coins, shall we?" said Ivy, taking 20p from one pocket and sticking it in another. "Professor Also says we should accept the verdict of this turtle guy."

"Terrapin," said Simon.

"Right," said Ivy. "But as you may know, there are other places believed to be Camelot. Perhaps this isn't it at all. Perhaps the coin was moved from somewhere else."

"Or forged," said Clive.

"Professor Also seems to think it's genuine," said Ivy.

"Bah," said Simon. "There never was such a place. It's a fake."

"If it's a fake, a lot of people have lost their lives over a worthless piece of metal," said Amphora.

"Wouldn't be the first time," said Simon.

"Do you think the zombies did it?" said Clive. He was really obsessed with those zombies. Every time a question of culpability arose he suggested them. He might actually be right for all they knew.

"If they're as stupid as they look," said Simon.

"Do you think they're the ones who broke into the secrets trove?" said Clive.

Now that was a scary thought. Zombies in the tunnels beneath the school. Amanda was astonished that Amphora didn't scream at the prospect.

"That doesn't sound right," said Simon. "Unless they're just the muscle and Blixus put them up to it."

Finally a theory Amanda could get behind. "I think you're onto something, Simon," she said. "The zombies are Blixus's associates. He has to stay in hiding but they don't. He tells them what to do and they do it."

"So you think Blixus is responsible for the trove and the murder?" said Simon.

"Yes," said Amanda. "In which case, he's not done with the farm. If he thinks there are more coins there, he'll come back. Or he'll send the zombies back to look."

"So if we watch the farm we'll figure out where he is?" said Ivy.

"Sort of. We'll have to follow the zombies to find him. Er, unless they never go to him in person. Maybe they work by text or something."

Zombies texting. She'd have to remember that if she ever decided to make a horror movie after all. She'd always resisted doing that, but she'd never been around real live zombies before. The idea was starting to look promising.

"If that's the case, we have to capture one of them and get Scapulus to hack his phone," said Ivy. "Then we can figure out where Blixus is."

"Capture a zombie?" said Clive. "You can't capture a zombie. They'll eat your brain." He burst into laughter.

"Don't zombies have something to do with voodoo?" said Ivy.

"You're not suggesting that Mrs. Sweetgum has anything to do with this?" said Amanda.

"Oooh, I hadn't thought of that," said Ivy.

"You girls are nuts," said Simon shaking his head. "There's no such thing as zombies, and voodoo doesn't work."

"Maybe not," said Amanda, watching his cowlick bounce, "but some people think they're real. Or want to give the appearance that they are."

"Rubbish," said Simon. "It's a coincidence."

"I'm with you on this one, Simon," said Ivy. "It's an interesting idea, but that's all it is."

"Say, you don't think the zombies got David, do you?" said Amanda.

"Now that is a very real possibility," said Simon. "Whoever they are, we need to go after them."

29

AT THE ZOO

Amanda thought a trip back to Penrith would be helpful. In addition to hunting for zombies, they could take the other tunnel fork and see where it led. However, Simon and Clive had other ideas.

"We want to go to the zoo," said Clive. "We heard there's a huge rainbow cluster there."

"Any zombies?" said Amanda.

"I don't think so," said Clive.

"Which is more important, the zombies or the rainbows?" At this point, she couldn't tell. It seemed that the hacker could do just about anything, including harm them, but if the zombies had got Despina, Hill, and Jeffrey, that might be worse.

"We can do both," said Clive. "Zombies don't move very fast."

"They aren't real zombies," said Simon, sighing.

"Oh, right," said Clive. "I guess I'm getting a little carried away. I do think we should investigate these rainbows though. They're supposed to be different from anything else we've seen."

"How is that?" said Ivy.

"Much denser," said Clive. "More energy."

Perhaps the hacker was becoming more advanced. Or targeting the zoo for some reason. Or both.

"Is there something about the zoo that would contribute to that?" said Amanda.

"What, like monkey pee?" said Amphora.

"Very funny," said Simon. "The answer is we don't know. Not monkey pee, though."

"Maybe the methane from the animals," said Amphora.

"Now you're thinking like a scientist," said Simon. Amphora stuck her tongue out at him. This time Ivy didn't seem to notice. "Except why not on sheep farms then? Or pig farms. Now *they* are going to give off a lot of methane."

"Do we know that there aren't rainbow clusters on sheep or pig farms?" said Amanda.

"No, we don't," said Ivy. "I heard that, Amphora."

"Shut up," said Amphora.

"Do bees give off methane?" said Amanda.

"I'm sure they do," said Simon. "Not very much though." Amanda tried to picture a bee big enough to give off the same amount of methane as a large mammal. It wasn't a comforting image. "At any rate, I don't see how a quick trip to the zoo could hurt. I'm game. Who else wants to go?"

"Me," said Clive.

"Me too," said Amanda, who couldn't really spare the time but wanted to go anyway.

"Not me," said Ivy. "Thanks anyway."

"Amphora?" said Simon. On the heels of that compliment about being queenly, the invitation seemed like an absolute love letter, but Amanda didn't believe it would have any effect. Simon and Amphora would get together the day elephant-sized bees roamed the earth.

Amphora thought for a moment and said mysteriously, "Sorry. Things to do."

"Okay, that's it then," said Simon.

"What about Gordon?" said Amanda. "We promised him he could be a part of our group."

"Oh, all right," said Simon. "I'll text him."

But like Amphora, Gordon had a different agenda and declined. That left Simon, Clive, and Amanda, who grabbed their skateboards and tooled down to the zoo. The place was known for its wild boar and wolf exhibits, and even if they didn't find rainbows it would be fun.

When they got there, there wasn't a rainbow in the sky. "Are you sure there are supposed to be rainbows here?" said Amanda.

"That's what I heard," said Clive, peering all around.

"From who?" said Amanda.

"I got a local weather alert."

"We'll wait," said Simon.

"Let's check it out," said Amanda, looking at the various signs. They appeared to be smack in the middle of the zoo because arrows were pointing in all directions: birds and monkeys off to the left, large animals and reptiles to the right, the marine section and insects straight ahead. "We may as well see the animals. What are your favorites?"

"Emus," said Clive.

"Really?" said Amanda. "Why?"

"They're just so impossible," said Clive. "They shouldn't exist but they do."

"How about you, Simon?" said Amanda.

"Boars," said Simon.

"How come?" said Clive.

"They're indigenous to the UK," said Simon. "I don't like the idea of taking animals out of their natural habitat."

"Me either," said Amanda. "I like wolves. I most definitely do not like monkeys." Ever since that nasty monkey had peed on her on the train to London during her first term at Legatum she'd grown to detest the creatures. She hoped never to see one again. "Let's start with Clive's emus, which, oh dear, have been moved far away from their natural habitat in Australia."

"I'm not going to boycott them," said Simon. "Let's go."

The kids had just started toward the bird section when suddenly the sky crackled and a huge broken rainbow appeared. It was so bright and shimmery that it seemed alive. The end appeared to be very close to them, which made no sense because normally you can only see rainbows in the distance. This one defied the laws of optics.

"Come on," said Simon. "Let's see if we can find the end."

The group made off toward the spot the rainbow seemed to be coming from. They'd gone just a few yards when the entire sky lit up with rainbows in every direction—big ones, small ones, curved ones, straight ones, all with the colors in different orders. The air was filled with the hum of electricity. And then each rainbow gradually changed color, shimmering in the light, until they were all purple. Zoo visitors began to panic and scattered this way and that, except for the children, who tried to run toward the rainbows. Animals were snorting, barking, screeching, wailing, honking, tooting, and skittering. Zookeepers ran to and fro, some throwing blankets over animals' eyes so they couldn't see the rainbows. To say that the scene had devolved into complete chaos would not be an overstatement.

"Let's keep going," said Amanda, grabbing both boys' hands and continuing on toward the supposed end of the first rainbow.

"Take pictures," said Clive, reaching for his phone.

"Yes," said Amanda, retrieving hers and shooting video as they ran. It was going to come out awfully bumpy.

"What's that?" said Simon.

"OMG," said Amanda, eyeing something shiny in the dirt some hundred yards away from them. "Is that gold?"

Now they could see the end of the first rainbow and there was indeed gold underneath it. However, before they could reach the spot they saw men removing the gold on wheeled carts.

"Follow them!" yelled Simon, stepping on his skateboard.

The other two grabbed their boards from their backpacks and took off, but by the time they reached the end of the rainbow, or at least where the end *had* been, because the whole thing was gone, the men had disappeared and the sky had cleared. There wasn't a rainbow in sight.

"Which way did they go?" said Simon.

"I think that way," said Clive, pointing off to the left.

"No, it was the other way," said Amanda, pointing right.

"I thought they went *that* way," said Simon, pointing straight ahead.

"Let's split up," said Amanda, and wheeled to the right. Behind her she heard the boys zoom off.

It wasn't easy to skateboard around the zoo. There were so many obstacles, like visitors, for one thing, that Amanda wouldn't normally have attempted it. It wasn't allowed anyway. But the opportunity was too important to ignore, so she dodged this way and that. In the end, though, she gave up, grabbed her board, and ran. Unfortunately the men with the gold were nowhere to be seen. They seemed to have gone the way of the rainbows, vanishing into thin air.

She texted Simon and Clive but they didn't answer. Probably still looking, or maybe they'd even found the mysterious gold men. She wasn't sure what to do, so she decided to return to the last place they'd been together and wait.

People were beginning to calm down, but an awful lot of them seemed to be leaving now so it was slow going getting back to the entrance. When Amanda got there the place was so clogged that she was pushed this way and that and had to fight her way to the edge of the walkway. From that vantage point she scouted for Simon and Clive, but all she could see was bobbing heads and strollers. The hubbub was loud but at least the animal cries had ceased.

She texted both boys again and told them where she was but got no answer. The people continued to stream by her but she recognized none of them. Then after about twenty minutes she heard Simon's voice coming out of the crowd.

"Amanda," he called. "Is that you?"

"Simon! Where are you?"

"In the middle of all these people. Is Clive with you?"

"No. I've been alone here forever. Didn't you get my texts?"

"Oh, sorry. I was trying to find those guys, and then I could barely make my way back."

First Simon's head and then his skinny body emerged from the mass of people. He sidestepped a young woman with two tiny boys in tow and stood disheveled in front of Amanda.

"Did you find them?" she said.

"Nope. You?"

"No. Maybe Clive did. He didn't answer me either but he must be on his way back. Unless he found them, of course. Ooh, do you think he did?"

"Dunno. If he did, he might be a while."

"You don't think they're dangerous, do you?" She was still searching the crowd. No Clive.

"Don't see how. They're just workmen collecting something." He scanned the crowd. She didn't know why she bothered to look. Simon could see so much better. He was way taller than she was.

"Gold, Simon," said Amanda. "They're collecting gold." For a moment she thought she saw their missing friend, but no. It was some very tall little kid with his parents.

"Optical illusion," said Simon. "You sound like Editta." He was blocking her view. She moved to the right.

"I suppose you're right," she said. "Except for the leprechaun coins." Was that Clive? Here he—oops, no. It was a girl with short hair. Nuts.

"Don't tell me you think those guys were collecting leprechauns' treasure at the end of the rainbow?" said Simon. "Come on."

"No, of course not. That would be ridiculous. So what are they anyway?" Why was that boy staring at her? No, wait, he was looking at something behind her.

"The leprechaun coins? Party favors."

"They're real gold, Simon."

"Billionaire party favors? I don't know. Just forget about them. They're not anything."

261

"You don't think the hacker could be making them, do you?" Was that him? Nope. Fooled again.

"How's he going to do that?" said Simon, blocking her view again.

"I don't know. Turning rainbow energy into a solid?"

"Can't be done," said Simon. "Not without nuclear power or something."

"Okay. You know best. Say, where's Clive already?"

"Do you remember the time we got separated at Euston Station and you couldn't find me? And then you had me paged?"

"Yes. That was Scapulus's idea," said Amanda. "You're saying we should page Clive?"

"Yes. If we can get to the information kiosk over there." He pointed toward a small blue booth. It reminded Amanda of the Tardis in "Dr. Who."

"It's thinning out a bit," she said. "I think we can make it."

"Maybe one of us should go and one stay here in case he comes back," he said.

"Okay. I'll wait here."

Within about two minutes Amanda could hear the loudspeaker blare, "Mr. Clive Ng, please come to information kiosk. Mr. Clive Ng." Obviously Simon had made it there.

She sat and waited, and in about thirty seconds Simon reappeared, examining his phone.

"No answer," he said. "You?"

She checked her phone. "Nope. You'd think he would have heard that, though. It was really loud."

"Yes," said Simon. "He should be texting us any second."

But he didn't. They must have sat there for another twenty minutes. Amanda was getting more and more panicky. It was obvious that something bad had happened to Clive. Had the rainbows been a come on to get them to the zoo? What did the hacker want with Clive?

Then Simon's phone finally rang. He listened for a moment and turned to Amanda. "It's Clive. Hey, man, where are you?" He held the

262

phone to his ear, looked at Amanda, and moved the phone so they both could hear. There was a bunch of squawking coming out of the speaker.

"Clive?" said Amanda.

More squawking, and then the phone went dead. Simon dialed back but got no answer.

"Did he say anything?"

"No. This isn't good," said Simon. "We have to figure out where he is and go get him."

He phoned Holmes and asked if he could hack Clive's GPS. Holmes tried, but he called back and said that Clive's phone must be off. Simon and Amanda thought the squawking might have come from the bird section of the zoo and went off to check, but Clive wasn't there.

"We're going to have to tell Thrillkill," said Amanda. "He has better resources than we do."

"Agreed," said Simon. "Let's phone him and head back."

30

THERE'S SOMETHING
ABOUT MAVIS

By the time Simon and Amanda returned to the school, they had concluded that Clive had been kidnapped. That brought to eight the number of people missing: Clive, David, Editta, Philip, Gavin, Despina, Hill, and Jeffrey. Of course there were also the three Moriartys, but they weren't exactly missing, just gone. Add to those the three murders—Wink, Crocodile, and the farmer—and the situation was appalling. Amanda wondered when Thrillkill was going to notify Clive's family and what he would say. She hoped Clive's parents wouldn't join the revolt too, or worse, start their own lawsuit.

It turned out that Green and Bullard Ng were upset, of course, but they kept their cool and expressed complete confidence in the headmaster. They knew their son and were sure he'd find a way out of whatever jam he was in. Amanda didn't exactly breathe a sigh of relief, but she was glad that Clive's family wasn't creating yet another crisis.

Everyone was beginning to think that Blixus was behind all the crimes, if crimes they were. His grudge against the detectives in general and Thrillkill in particular was just too strong for him not to be. In addition, the man was so greedy that if there was a way to profit from the discovery of Camelot, he'd find it. Of course if he'd become so powerful that he could manipulate matter, the detectives might not have a chance against him. Amanda didn't want to think about the awful things he might do. She got the fleeting idea that Simon might even join up with him just for his help fixing the earth's tilt, but she knew that was crazy.

She went to her room and opened the video she'd shot at the zoo. If she hadn't seen the rainbows with her own eyes she'd never have believed they could behave that way. The entire sky was filled with color and movement, the sound a riot. If she hadn't known all that glory had been created by a dangerous hacker she'd have thought it beautiful.

She should show the video to Holmes. It might provide important clues in his search for the hacker. She didn't feel like talking to him, but she was going to have to meet him about the film anyway. She texted him.

"Was going to text U," he said. "Can we meet?"

"Y," she sent back, and the next thing she knew she was sitting at their spot in the dining room drinking tea.

"I tried hacking Clive's phone," he said. "No luck. I'll keep at it."

"Thanks, Scapulus. Maybe you can show us how to do that next term—if there is one."

"Happy to," he said. "And if we have anything to say about it there will be. We're going to fix all this, Amanda. I know it."

"On that note, I have something to show you," she said, and produced the video from the zoo. Holmes stared at it and asked her to play it over about a dozen times. Watching him watching it made her think of Nick and his *Explosions!* game. The rainbows were like explosions. Could Nick be the one creating them?

Holmes looked up and said, "Incredible. It's like a light show against the sky, but it's more than that. See the way the rainbows are hitting those trees? They're actually moving the leaves. They're dangerous."

"Are they laser beams?" she said.

"I don't know. They have elements in common with them, but lasers are coherent, which means they're narrow. Hang on a second." He thumbed his phone. "Hm, not necessarily. There's a Gaussian beam laser that spreads light out. See?" He showed her a diagram depicting a conical laser beam.

"Oh, that looks like it could be it, except that he's bending the beams. Or she is. They're arced."

"Yes, which means that this light isn't any kind of laser we know of. I'll tell you what I'm going to do. I'll model these in 3D. That might help explain what's going on."

Amanda thought Holmes's idea was brilliant. She was good at 3D stuff. Should she offer to help? Finding the hacker was so important, but it would mean spending more time with him. He might even be offended.

As Amanda was pondering her dilemma Amphora wandered in. Holmes cheered up and said, "Hey, would you look at this?"

Amphora drew close to Holmes and watched as he played the video a couple of times. She seemed to be reveling in being near him. Was she flirting? Of course she was. She flirted with everyone. Amanda wished she'd give him some space.

"Come sit here," she said, patting the chair next to her.

"I'm fine," said Amphora.

That set Amanda off. "Scapulus," she said, "would you like me to help you model the explosions?"

Holmes looked up. "You, help me with the animation?"

"Of course. You know I know how to do that stuff."

"Yes, you do," he said enthusiastically. "That would be great. Thanks."

Amphora huffed, moved over to the chair Amanda had indicated, and sat down.

"I'm good at designing," she said. "I'm very aesthetic."

Holmes gave her a look and said, "That you are."

This flirting between the two of them sent Amanda into paroxysms of jealousy. She knew she shouldn't feel that way—she had no claim on Holmes—but she wanted to scream.

"Scapulus," she said. "I have an idea for *our* film."

Amphora looked daggers at her and said, "Hm. You're just at the idea stage, are you?"

Amanda ignored her. "Would you like to hear it?"

"Yes, of course," he said. "You have good ideas, Amanda."

The compliment so enraged Amphora that she huffed again and said, "I have ideas. Would you like to hear them?"

Amanda almost laughed out loud. Amphora was digging her own grave. What could she possibly suggest about the film that Holmes would want to hear?

Amphora sat back and said smugly, "I think you should scare the teachers half to death."

Holmes looked like he was thinking over the idea and then said, "Why?"

"They're tough," said Amphora. "You have to hit them in the gut or they won't listen."

"I don't think so," said Amanda, mentally weighing her own theory. If there were holes in it, Amphora would skewer her.

"Why not?" said Amphora. "You've seen how Professor Buck and Professor Sidebotham are."

Amanda couldn't help herself. "Professor Buck and Professor Sidebotham are completely different from each other," she blurted out.

"Well, of course," said Amphora, "one is a man and the other is a woman."

"Not that," said Amanda, growing impatient. "Professor Sidebotham is resilient. Professor Buck isn't."

"What are you talking about?" said Amphora. "Professor Buck is one of the toughest teachers here."

"On the outside," said Amanda. "Not on the inside."

"What, you think Professor Buck is a big teddy bear? Get real, Amanda."

"No, I don't think he's a teddy bear. I think he's a scared little boy."

"That's quite a theory," said Holmes. He seemed fascinated. Amanda was glad. She was winning the argument and getting one over on Amphora at the same time. "Care to elaborate?"

"Bah," said Amphora. "Stuff and nonsense."

She got up from the table, batted her eyelashes at Holmes, and sashayed out of the room. Amanda wanted to gag. She was glad to see the back of her.

"Tell me more," said Holmes. His liquid eyes were wide with interest.

Amanda did her best to ignore his charms and explained her thinking about the Realists being resilient and the Punitori fragile. Holmes sat back and thought for a very long time, staring off into the distance. Finally he took a last gulp of his tea and said, "Brava, Amanda. I think you're right."

"You do?"

"I do. That's why I—" He gave her a longing look.

"That's why you what?"

"Nothing. Sorry. I do want to tell you, though, that I've been thinking about that musical idea of yours and I think you're right. It sounds crazy, but I think we could pull it off. Music speaks directly to the emotions. Thrillkill might not see it at first, but I think we can convince him with a little demonstration. My only concern is whether we have the time to write all those songs."

"I wouldn't worry about that," said Amanda, not even trying to suppress her grin. Holmes was full of surprises. No wonder she adored him. "I've got it covered."

The next thing that happened was the teachers announcing that they had learned more about Mavis Moriarty's background. Everyone was so interested that Thrillkill called the entire school together and squeezed everyone into the Holmes House common room, which was farther away from the construction than the others and less dusty. All the teachers and many students attended, despite its being summer. Quite a few students were pitching in, trying to help the school out of its difficulties.

"As you know," said Thrillkill, standing in front of the group, many of whom were sitting on the floor for lack of space, "Mavis Moriarty was born Mavis Jamm. This much we know. Until now, however, that's almost all we've known about her. We examined her arrest record: nothing until this past April, which we all know about. School records, traffic tickets, social media, all clean. We've interviewed her former neighbors. They had nothing to say except for mentioning two of her old boyfriends, neither of whom seems to be Wink Wiffle or anyone connected with us or Blixus Moriarty. We tracked down her family. Of course they refused to speak to us.

"Finally, however, we found someone who was willing to talk—a waitress who once worked with Mavis. You can thank Professor Scribbish for persuading her."

Figures, thought Amanda. The dishy professor could melt just about any woman.

"You won't find this surprising, but when she was working at the restaurant, Mavis killed someone. Our former cook, the late Mrs. Dump, witnessed the murder and blackmailed Mavis. That was what she was holding over her, and that was why Mavis ended up cooking all the meals. It was part of their deal. Apparently Mrs. Dump helped her dispose of the body in return for hush money."

Actually Amanda was surprised. She knew Mavis was capable of murder, but for some reason it was hard to picture her working as a waitress. She wasn't sure why. When she'd first met the woman, she'd

269

been an assistant in a kitchen. Now that she knew Mavis was Nick's mother, though, those jobs seemed so pedestrian. A criminal with Mavis's abilities should have been something else—a nightclub owner or a cat burglar, perhaps.

"Professor," said Holmes. "Why did she kill the person? Who was it?"

"We don't know, Mr. Holmes," said Thrillkill.

"So she was already a criminal at that point?" said Ivy. "Was she dating Blixus, or married to him?"

"She wasn't married to him, no," said Thrillkill. "Actually, this was just before she started dating Wink."

"Did Wink have anything to do with the murder?" said Amanda. Another possible blow David didn't need.

"We don't know," said Thrillkill. "We certainly hope not."

"Was she dating Wink and Blixus at the same time?" said Amphora.

Now that was an interesting thought—one Amanda could relate to. If that had been the case, she wondered how Mavis had managed her emotions—assuming she actually had any. But of course she did. The letters demonstrated that. So how had she juggled two lovers at the same time? Under other circumstances it might have been illuminating to discuss the topic with her. Wait—what was she thinking? This was Mavis Moriarty, for heaven's sake. Who cared what she thought about anything? Amanda turned her attention back to the conversation.

"We don't believe so," said Thrillkill. "Not if you go by those letters, anyway."

"Did she know Blixus then?" said Simon.

"We don't know," said Thrillkill.

"Does Blixus know she was dating Wink?" said Fern.

They'd touched on the question before, and it was a scary thought. Blixus was not the type of guy to understand his wife dating anyone else, let alone a detective, and especially one he knew, although he may not have known Wink at the time. Amanda wondered if Nick was the jealous type. He certainly didn't seem to be.

"That we don't know either," said Thrillkill.

"What does this news mean for the investigation?" said Simon.

"Obviously we have to dig deeper," said Thrillkill. "We do know that Mavis was desperate. First she lost the man she loved. And second, she had been blackmailed for many years."

"How did she make enough money to pay the cook?" said Simon. "Waitresses don't make much."

"We don't know that either," said Thrillkill. "However, my guess is that once she became involved with Blixus, she had access to plenty of money. He probably didn't know about the blackmail. He wouldn't have stood for it."

"So she was stealing from her own husband?" said Fern.

"It's likely," said Thrillkill.

"Does this mean she's in danger?" said Amanda. She'd never contemplated that possibility before. How weird it was to think of Mavis as an underdog.

"Only if he finds out," said Thrillkill. "It seems that he hasn't, and now that Mrs. Dump is dead he probably won't. Mavis won't be stealing from him anymore."

"What do you think he'd do if he found out about her and Wiffle?" said Amphora.

"We don't know that he doesn't already know," said Thrillkill.

"Do you think he was the one who killed Wink?" said Amphora. "Out of jealousy?"

"We don't think so," said Thrillkill. "Our money is still on Mavis." That made sense. It would have been difficult for Blixus to get past Legatum's security. Since Mavis was already living at the school, she didn't have to worry about that.

"Do you think Blixus knows about the King Arthur coins, Professor?" said Simon.

"We do think so, yes, Mr. Binkle. We can't prove it at the moment, but we suspect he does know about them."

"He's here," said Simon. "He has to be. Zombie henchmen or no zombie henchmen, he's close by. I'd say he's in Penrith, and if we find him we'll find Clive and the others."

"And the hacker, Mr. Binkle?" said Thrillkill. "What's your theory about him or her?"

"Blixus," said Simon. "Or, I'm sorry to say this, Amanda, Nick."

Simon had finally given voice to something Amanda had been fearing for days. She hadn't wanted to admit it but the hacker had to be Nick. Blixus was brilliant but he didn't have the expertise. Mavis certainly didn't. She was sure of that now. There was still the outside chance that Blixus had hired someone, but why do that when you have your own computer genius in the family?

Nick had hid a lot from Amanda, and everyone else. Now it occurred to her that even his mistakes might have been staged, that he'd given incorrect answers in his classes and bolstered them with invalid arguments to make it seem that he wasn't that smart. But if you considered his genes he had to be. And he certainly had the motivation.

Oh, how she wished it weren't so. If only Nick had kept that picture she'd found in his room last term—the one of her—because he cared about her. But she knew in her heart why he'd done it, and kept the video of their time discovering the secret room too. They were trophies, trophies of his conquests and successes in fooling the gullible little American girl.

She wanted to pull Holmes aside and tell him that she'd made a terrible mistake, that she'd finally come to terms with the whole Nick thing and it was over forever. She would—she'd do that, throw herself on his mercy and tell him that she'd never leave him again.

As the group dispersed, she rose and made her way to where Holmes was sitting. She was about to call out to him when Amphora sat down beside him, linked her arm through his, and started to speak in a voice too soft for Amanda to hear. Amanda stopped, lowered her gaze, and headed for the door. The last thing she saw before she left the room was Simon looking at her with pity in his eyes.

31

CHASING RAINBOWS

For all the disasters occurring around Amanda, at least something was going right. Holmes actually liked her idea for the film, so she met with Ivy and described the kind of music she wanted.

"The film will be short, so three songs should be enough," she said. "One to set things up, one to develop the idea, and one to bring everyone together."

Ivy spoke some notes into her tablet. "What style do you want?"

"Broadway," said Amanda without hesitation.

"I can do that," said Ivy just as quickly. "So in the first song we show that everything is a mess." She doo-doo-dooed a quick melody. It was perfect. "In the second song, we bring in some history so they can see they've faced this kind of thing before, just in a slightly different way." She tried a few notes. Amanda thought they were spot on. The girl was a genius. "Then in the last song, we urge them to stick together because that's what always works. We want lots of energy. Is that right?"

"Yes, that's it," said Amanda. Ivy was so smart. Anything you told her she grasped immediately.

"That's a tall order."

"I know, but we can do it. We'll work on the words together."

"Got it. Anything new on Clive?"

"Nothing," said Amanda. She couldn't believe someone had got him. After everything that had happened over the last few months, they should have been more careful. *He* should have been more careful. Not that she was blaming him.

"I hope he's holding up okay," said Ivy.

"He's a resourceful guy," said Amanda. "He's got lots of tricks up his sleeve."

"Look," said Ivy. "About Scapulus—"

Amanda knew what she was going to say and didn't want to hear it. "Don't say it. If she wants him she can have him."

"I'm afraid she does want him," Ivy said sadly. "I'm not sure if he wants her, though."

"It doesn't matter. It's too late."

"You never know. Don't give up. He picked you for a reason."

Yes, like Nick picked me for a reason.

"I know a hopeless situation when I see one, Ivy. Anyway, I have to go see him now. We're going to work on this 3D modeling thing."

Holmes had set up in the cyberforensics classroom, so Amanda joined him there. Using the video of the rainbows she had made, they worked till the wee hours to create an algorithm that would simulate the rainbow riot. The next day they'd create a cybervirus to disrupt it and test it out.

"I've been doing some research," Holmes said. "Apparently scientists have recently discovered something called Airy pulses. They follow a curved trajectory. And get this: they can also ionize the surrounding air molecules and create curved plasma filaments. After this group of scientists discovered Airy pulses, some others found a way to bend light and wait for it—they're working on optical tweezers, which can move objects!"

"Science fiction comes true," said Amanda, wondering if all this messing with light was such a good thing. It hadn't been so great for the crystals they'd discovered. "Do you think that's what the hacker is doing?"

"It's possible. He might be even more advanced than the people I've been reading about."

"But why would they care about Professor Redleaf?"

"Why indeed?"

The cyberforensics teacher had been so mysterious. Now though, it was becoming critical that they know what was really going on behind her strange persona. The time for secrecy was over.

"Scapulus, can you tell me more about her? Professor Redleaf, I mean? Maybe there's something about her we can use."

Holmes sighed. "She was such a private person. I hate to go digging into her life."

"We wouldn't if it weren't important," said Amanda.

"I know." He'd guarded the woman's secrets so carefully. Now Amanda could see that he was accepting that he couldn't protect her anymore. She understood how he felt. Another reason to hate the Moriartys—if indeed the hacker was associated with them. "Of course there are all these rumors about where she was born. They're not true."

"You mean the ones about her being from the Congo or the Amazon rainforest or something?"

"Yes. I think those came about because she was so mysterious. People felt compelled to invent some glamorous past for her. She was actually born in East London."

"Aha." The truth comes to light at last. Amanda wondered how the other students would feel if they knew. They'd invested a huge amount of energy in the myth of Professor Redleaf.

"She came from a disadvantaged background. Her parents were Jamaican immigrants. Her mother died when she was a baby. Her father raised her until she was about our age. Then he died too."

"Oh dear."

"After that she bounced around in foster care. In one of the homes she met a kid who was a computing genius. Girl name of Pupsy Miracle. She was fascinated by what the girl could do and asked her to teach her. She had a natural talent for computing and the two of them cooked up all sorts of projects together."

It was hard to picture Professor Redleaf having a BFF. She was so self-contained. "What happened to the girl?" said Amanda.

"She works for MI-6," said Holmes. "That's all I know. Anyway, somehow Professor Redleaf managed to get a scholarship to Oxford. Don't ask me how. She went there, got a first in computer science, and ended up here. I don't know how that happened either."

"You said she was a family friend."

"Yes," said Holmes. "She met my mum at university. My mum is a botanist, but somehow their paths crossed and they became good friends. Come to think of it, maybe that's how the rumor started that she was from the Amazon. My mum takes these trips all over the world to study plants. She spends a lot of time there. I think Okimma—I mean Professor Redleaf—went with her a few times."

Amanda hadn't realized what an interesting mother Holmes had. She'd known that his dad, Olimus Holmes, was a private detective. He hadn't talked much about Pastiche Holmes though. Of course there hadn't been much time in which to do it.

"It must have been weird being in her class when you knew her so well."

"Kind of, yes," he said. "I'll tell you something, Amanda. That hacker targeted her. I'll get him if it's the last thing I do."

If the hacker *was* Nick, that gave Holmes a third reason to find him and put him away, besides the damage he was causing. The first, of course, was that he was a Moriarty, and the Holmes-Moriarty vendetta went back a century. Next there was the fact that Nick was his rival in love, or so he believed. And now Professor Redleaf. Amanda did not want to be there when the two boys met again. It would be terrible.

"What about her would cause the hacker to target her?" said Amanda.

"I've been trying to figure that out," said Holmes. "Perhaps it's simply the challenge of getting to someone of her stature."

"Could there be a personal reason?" said Amanda.

"I don't know. Her private life wasn't all that interesting. At least not that I know of."

"Perhaps it was more interesting than you think."

"That's always a possibility. However, I think our task for now is to finish this modeling and find a way to disrupt the hacker's creations."

They spent the next few hours developing a model of the rainbows. Holmes had been able to turn Amanda's video into a set of equations. She had helped him spot errors and inconsistencies in the animation. By the time they'd parted it was late, but they were pretty sure they'd nailed it.

When Amanda saw Holmes the next morning it was obvious he'd been up all night. His eyes were red and his clothes rumpled—a rarity for him—but he was typing away as fast as ever.

"How's it going?" she said.

"Almost there. I just have to finish this virus and I'll be ready to try it out." He was working and talking at the same time. She hoped he wouldn't make a mistake.

"What can I do?"

"Will you check the animation again? Then we'll try out the virus on the computer, and if it works we'll be ready for the real thing. We'll have to find the rainbows though. Have you heard any news, or seen anything?"

"I don't know yet but—"

Suddenly there was a huge crash. Amanda and Holmes looked out the window and saw purple rainbows filling the sky.

"Guess that's taken care of, then," she said. "How does the virus work, anyway?"

"First it breaks the pattern of the rainbows," said Holmes. "Then it sends a signal from the rainbows back to the hacker's computer. We stop the effects, then we jam him. If it works, of course. Oh, hullo, Amphora."

Amphora, who had just opened the door, took one look at Holmes and Amanda together, marched over to them, and sat right on the desk next to Holmes. "Hi," she said in a simpering tone. "You didn't text me back, Scapulus."

"Oh, sorry," he said. "I was up all night working on this algorithm."

"I see," said Amphora. "Well, we can do that thing later."

"Yes, later," he said. "Apologies."

"What are you doing, Amanda?" she said. "I thought you and Ivy were writing songs for your film."

"We are," said Amanda. "Scapulus and I are just finishing up this 3D thing. We're going to test it in a few minutes."

"I'll watch," said Amphora, moving closer to Holmes. She laid her hand over his. It looked ridiculous with him still trying to type.

Amanda was horrified. Her friend had become brazen. In front of *her*, Holmes's former girlfriend! Amphora gave her a smug smile. Well, if that didn't beat all. Then Amphora whispered in Holmes's ear and he turned and smiled at her in a way that was so warm he seemed to radiate heat. He wasn't just smiling, he was beaming. He not only didn't mind her attention, he welcomed it.

That was it. They were together and she was not wanted there. Amanda picked herself up, said goodbye, and left the room. As she walked out the door she could hear Holmes saying, "I'll text you when I'm ready."

32

HOLMES VS. HACKER, ROUND ONE

Amanda couldn't stop thinking about Holmes and Amphora. There were a million boys in the world Amphora could have chosen, but she'd gone for him. What had Amanda ever done to her to deserve that? She'd helped her friend when she'd found the living crystal, defended her when her crush on Rupert Thwack had backfired, fought the Moriartys alongside her, and been there every time she'd wanted to talk, even at 3:00 in the morning.

It was true that Amphora had had her problems. Her inferiority complex was as big as Soho. She was falling further and further behind the other students, many of whom had already developed their detective's mystiques and begun to excel in their specialties. And she had paid Ivy way more in fines than Simon had. Was she also so envious of her best friend's successes that she felt the need to take her boyfriend?

Actually, Amanda wasn't surprised. Amphora had always been irritable. From the first day they'd met that had been obvious. She was also a social climber and a flirt. But there was so much to do at Legatum—such important work—that Amanda thought she'd have changed by now, just from the exposure, if not from the responsibility. Apparently she was wrong. Just because Legatum had changed

Amanda's attitude didn't mean it had had the same effect on everyone else.

What saddened her the most, though, was Holmes. How could he go from her to Amphora, from someone who loved him to a girl who did nothing but collect trophies? Was he that blind? For a guy who seemed to know everything, he certainly hadn't observed very carefully or he'd have realized how completely wrong Amphora was for him. Could he really be happy with a girl who was so frivolous and mean-spirited?

Oh well. It wasn't Amanda's concern any longer. She had more important things to worry about: friends to save, teachers to unite, a school that needed her. What difference did it make if Holmes ruined his life? He'd just have to figure that one out himself.

When they met on the east deck a little while later, Amanda was glad that Amphora hadn't come. Her silly distractions would have posed significant danger to them. Who knew how the hacker would react when they executed the algorithm? He might alter his tactics on the fly. They'd need every ounce of speed and concentration to counter him or her.

Sure enough, the rainbows were still coming and going outside the school. Holmes punched a few keys—the last one with a flourish—and watched to see what would happen. Within a few seconds the rainbows began to flash and writhe as if in pain. No longer were they graceful arches of Tyrian and Han purple, Palatinate, heliotrope, and purpura. Now they blinked on and off in what could only be described as a Möbius strip of lavender so weak that it looked almost white.

"It's working!" said Amanda.

"Yes, it seems so," said Holmes.

They watched as the rainbows seemed to lose energy. They were defeating the hacker! People started to come outside to watch, and cheered as each rainbow weakened. Then suddenly there came a huge crack and the entire sky flashed purple. One by one the rainbows reversed themselves, gaining in strength, hue, and shape, until they had become even more saturated and defined than before. The static they put out was so loud that some of the onlookers ran inside to preserve their hearing. Amphora, who had finally joined the group, ran screaming, complaining that her whole body was tingling.

"Let me try something," said Holmes. "Obviously he's got the message, but I think I can match him."

He pressed a few keys, squinted, and pressed some more. The rainbows started to weaken again, this time faster than before. Some of them winked out altogether. Everyone cheered.

Then there was another loud crack and the rainbows grew back again. This time there were hundreds covering the sky as far as the eye could see. Professor Tumble, who couldn't hear as well as the others, kept saying, "My, my. Isn't that beautiful?" Professor Sidebotham was taking notes, and Professor Kindseth was shooting video. Headmaster Thrillkill was shaking his head, and Fern kept saying she wished Salty were there.

"Scapulus, can you do anything?" said Amanda.

"I'm trying," he said. "Nothing seems to be working."

"Are they off your map?"

"Yes, I'm trying to expand it. He's blocking me."

"What can you do?" she said.

"I need to stop targeting the rainbows and concentrate all the energy on the signal to his computer," said Holmes.

"Is that a problem?" she said.

"It won't be in a second. Just let me—" He fiddled a bit and then watched to see what the effect of his tinkering would be. Suddenly the entire sky opened up and a huge purple bolt pierced the ground, creating a trail of smoke.

"OMG," said Amanda. "This is dangerous. We have to go in."

"One more second," said Holmes.

Then, as if all the lightning in the world had gathered in one place, a gigantic purple arc hit Holmes in the chest. Amanda screamed as he turned every color of the rainbow, then fell to the ground, the colors still washing over him until finally he glowed purple and then slowly returned to normal.

"Fern, get Salty here *now!*" Amanda yelled.

Fern jabbed her fingers into her phone and screamed for someone to get Dr. Wing. Amanda rushed up and started to compress Holmes's chest while Fern checked for vital signs.

"He's alive," she said. "His pulse is thready though."

Tears were running down Amanda's face as she pumped Holmes's chest. No thoughts went through her head. She was one with her hands, and they were all that mattered.

Then they heard a siren and all at once Salty and the other paramedic were there. The tall guy took over from Amanda, and Salty gave Holmes oxygen. Then they put him in the ambulance and drove off. As they pulled away Fern jumped into the back. Then they were gone.

Amanda faced the rainbow-filled sky and howled. "How could you do this, Nick?" she screamed without thinking. Everyone who was still standing around outside stared at her. Thrillkill came over, put his arm around her shoulder, and walked her back into the common room.

"He'll be all right," he said.

"No, he won't," she said. "Even if he recovers he'll never be the same. He's such a good person and Nick is ruining his life."

"We don't know that it's Nick," said Thrillkill.

"Of course it is. Don't you see? He's doing it to get back at me." She was shaking so hard she could barely get the words out.

Thrillkill took Amanda by the shoulders and looked into her eyes. As hard as he was holding her and trying to keep her still, she was still moving all over the place.

"Amanda Lester, I don't ever want to hear you talk like that again. The Moriartys are evil. What they do or don't think of you, me, or your cousin Despina has nothing to do with anything. We're not that important, and you should thank your lucky stars we aren't."

"With all due respect, Professor, we are. You with your cave thing and me with Nick. He was aiming for me from Day One. You know that."

"I don't know any such thing. You've read your history. You know what the Moriartys are like. Evil is their family culture. They don't know any other way."

"I thought he did," said Amanda. "He seemed like he had so much potential. He was so creative and fun, and he tried to help me. He did help me."

"Then how can you think he did this?" said Thrillkill.

"Because I was wrong."

Amanda insisted on going to the hospital to see Holmes. On the way there all she could think about was how bad she felt about the way she'd treated him. The injury was her fault and she'd do anything to make it up to him. Perhaps she should give up filmmaking and sever her ties with Darius Plover. That way she could give Legatum and Holmes her full attention. Not that anything she could do would ever be enough of course. She'd feel guilty the rest of her life.

When she arrived at Holmes's room he was unconscious and hooked up to all the usual things you see in ICU rooms: oxygen, tubes, sensors. Thank goodness he was no longer purple.

She sat by his bedside and took his hand. It was cold, so she pulled his blanket around him in the hope of warming him up. Then she drew close and whispered in his ear.

"Scapulus," she said. "It's Amanda. I'm so sorry. Please forgive me. This was all my fault."

She couldn't tell if he'd heard her. He didn't move—not even a twitch.

She caressed his face gently. "I love you," she whispered. Then she heard the door open with a bang as Amphora entered and saw her.

"What are you doing here?" she said, planting her hands on her hips. "You don't want Scapulus, so why don't you leave him alone? He's mine now."

"I came to see how he is," said Amanda.

"You shouldn't have. This is all your fault."

"I didn't make the rainbows."

"Your boyfriend did."

Amanda started to protest, but she knew Amphora was right. What could she say? She let go of Holmes's hand, glanced at the vital signs monitor to reassure herself that he was stable, and left without looking back.

As Amanda skated back to the school she thought about everything that had occurred in the last couple of weeks. Why hadn't she fought to keep Holmes? So what if she still had issues with Nick? Holmes was the one she wanted. What an idiot she'd been letting him go. Now he might die. Even if he lived, and even if he broke up with Amphora, it was too late. It *was* her fault that Nick had almost killed him. He'd never forgive her for that.

She'd been so selfish. She was just like her mother—completely self-centered and tone deaf. And that was the most frightening thought of all.

When she returned to Legatum, Simon shanghaied her in the hall.

"Were you just at the hospital?" he said.

"Yes."

"How was he?"

"Unconscious but stable."

"Are you sure?" said Simon.

"Well, his numbers were okay. Pulse, blood pressure, that kind of thing."

"Amanda," said Simon, very seriously, "I hate to tell you this, but I don't think he was unconscious at all. He's disappeared. Thrillkill thinks he's gone vigilante."

33
METADATA IN DANGER

There was no way Holmes could have gone after the hacker. When Amanda had seen him at the hospital he'd been unconscious. You don't just emerge from a coma, get up, and go. Perhaps he'd awakened and gone for a walk around the ward. He'd been in no shape to do anything more.

If by some miracle he *had* been well enough to leave, how would he know where to go? If he wanted Nick, or Blixus, he'd have to find them. Surely he hadn't run off just to ask around. But if he'd known where they were he would have told Thrillkill at least, and he hadn't.

What if he thought he was well enough but wasn't and collapsed on the way to wherever he was going? Amanda had to find him at once. If he was lying in a ditch somewhere, or worse, had been hit by a car—the idea was too much to bear. But where should she look?

What if Holmes hadn't left at all, though? What if someone had taken him? She found the number for the hospital front desk and phoned, but the stuttering information clerk told her he'd seen no one matching Moriarty's description. Just to make sure she described Mavis and Nick, but the man hadn't seen them either. That was something, anyway.

Where would Nick have gone? Amanda was sure the Moriartys had remained in the area, but Holmes didn't know that. He might think they were in London, close to the ruins of the sugar factory. Why he'd think that she didn't know, but criminals always return to the scenes of their crimes so he might have reasoned that way.

If Holmes had gone to London it would be difficult to find him. He'd have taken a train but it would have already departed. She'd never catch up. She'd have to try though. There was no other alternative.

Of course she should try to contact him first. She sent off a text: "Scapulus, where are you?" Then she tried phoning but he didn't answer. She also tried to IM but he didn't answer that either. Finally she emailed him, with the same result. Perhaps he'd answer in time. He might be walking or speaking with someone. As soon as he'd settled down she'd hear from him.

The thing to do was hack his phone and find out what his GPS coordinates were. She still didn't know how to do that, but the teachers probably did. She went to Thrillkill and asked who would be best to consult.

"They all know how to do that," he said. "But I'll do it for you. Let me try."

He turned to his computer and started pressing keys. After a moment he said, "Got him. He's in Windermere, at the train station. Let's go."

Amanda followed the headmaster to his car and got in. He was still driving the Citroen that had been in the school's garage during the explosion spring term. It had needed some bodywork, but he'd got that done and the car looked as good as new—er, as good as the ten-year-old car that it was. He fired up the engine and tore out of there like a rocket ship.

When they arrived at the station, Amanda jumped out of the car and ran inside before Thrillkill had even stopped. She looked around frantically but Holmes was nowhere to be seen. The place was small, and she was able to inspect the premises in a flash. No Holmes.

"Scapulus!" she screamed over and over.

Thrillkill joined her. "Holmes!" he yelled.

Nothing.

They spread out and looked beyond the station. They ran into the trees, down the track, everywhere, but Holmes wasn't there. Thrillkill took out his phone and tried to test Holmes's mobile again. This time he got nothing.

"He must be on the train to Oxenholme," said Amanda. "With his phone off."

"Come on," said Thrillkill, and they ran back to the car and raced toward Oxenholme, but Holmes wasn't there either.

"He must already be on a train to London," said Amanda.

"I'll call the railroad," said Thrillkill. "They can check."

But that strategy yielded nothing either. It was as if Holmes had vanished into thin air. Amanda was beside herself.

"They must have got him, sir," she said. "He was probably about to get on the train when they took him."

"They can't have got far," said Thrillkill. "I'll call the local police and have them put out an alert. We're going to find him *and* Blixus. You'll see."

Thrillkill phoned the Penrith police station and explained what had happened. Then he and Amanda made their way back to Legatum.

When they returned to the school, Gordon was all in a dither.

"Amanda, come with me," he said, stepping around as if there were bees in his pants.

"What's going on?" she said.

"I want you to hear something. It's important."

He led her to the teachers' lounge and told her to listen carefully but stay out of sight. "I think this has something to do with the metadata," he said. "I think I might have found it."

"Do you think he knows about the decoy vault?" Professor Snaffle was saying.

"Does it matter?" said Professor Scribbish. "There's nothing in it."

"I know, but if he's found it he might find the church too," said Professor Snaffle. "I think we should move it."

"Excellent idea," said Professor Hoxby. "The old rules no longer apply."

"And the vault at Penrith?" said Professor Snaffle.

Gordon turned to Amanda and said, "I saw that building. A girl was breaking into it. Before I saw you at the farm."

"What?" said Amanda. "Why didn't you say something? Do you think that building was the vault they're talking about?"

"Yes. It makes perfect sense. It was outside of Penrith and it was all locked up tight. It looked like someone had gone to a lot of trouble to hide it. I have to tell them."

"Agreed. If you're wrong, what can it hurt?"

Gordon coughed and knocked on the doorjamb leading to the teachers' lounge.

"Who is it?" said Professor Snaffle.

"It's Gordon Bramble," said Gordon. "I'm a student."

"We know who you are, Mr. Bramble," said Professor Snaffle. "What is it?"

"Uh, I have something important to tell you, and I'm here with Amanda Lester."

"Well, come in and make it snappy then," said Professor Snaffle.

Gordon opened the door and entered the lounge with Amanda on his heels. Six teachers were sitting round a table: Professors Snaffle, Scribbish, Stegelmeyer, Hoxby, Also, and Pole.

"Uh, sorry to disturb you, but I wanted to report something I saw. Near Penrith."

That got the teachers' attention. They sat up straight and looked at each other apprehensively.

"Well, what did you see?" said Professor Snaffle. Her salt and pepper hair looked wilder than usual, which was saying something. The kids sometimes called her Medusa after the mythical Gorgon, whose head was full of snakes.

Gordon hesitated. Professor Snaffle could be very intimidating. "There was this little building."

"A little building. So what?"

"Uh, I think a crime was committed there."

"What crime? Where was this building?"

"Um, I don't know the name of the road. It was outside of town. No, wait a minute." He looked up as if trying to remember. If he hadn't been as observant as he should be the teachers would give him grief. "It was called Snortle Road. The place looked like a bomb shelter. It was built into a hill, like a barrow."

The teachers looked at each other guiltily. Obviously Gordon had hit a nerve.

"And what about this bomb shelter in the barrow?" said Professor Snaffle cautiously.

"I saw a girl trying to break into it. Well, she did break into it."

"You what?" said Professor Snaffle almost viciously. Gordon didn't flinch.

"Yes. I'd gone to Penrith. If you must know, I went to look for zombies."

"Ah, yes, the famous zombies we've all been hearing about," said Professor Snaffle dismissively. "Was this girl a zombie?"

"Oh no," said Gordon. "She was beautiful. She had long blonde hair and looked like a queen."

"Did you recognize her?" said Professor Scribbish.

"No," said Gordon. "I never saw her before."

Uh oh. Was it possible? "Wait a minute," said Amanda. "She wasn't wearing turquoise shorts and a red T-shirt was she?"

"I think she might have been," said Gordon. "I remember she was colorful." He did that looking up thing again. Professor Sidebotham would have been proud of him. "Yes, she was. If I had to take a pop quiz, I'd definitely say she was wearing red and blue. Or was it green?"

"I saw her with Harry Sheriff in Windermere the other day," said Amanda. "They were kissing."

"Lucky guy," said Gordon, breaking into a smile. "Er, I mean, oh never mind."

"Did you speak to this girl, Miss Lester?" said Professor Snaffle. "Or Mr. Sheriff?"

"Not then," said Amanda. "Harry did make a rude remark later. He keeps grinning and winking at me."

"Yes, I imagine he would do," said Professor Snaffle.

Amanda glanced at Gordon. What was that supposed to mean?

"Mr. Bramble," said Professor Scribbish. "What did you do when you saw this girl trying to break in?"

"I tried to stop her," said Gordon.

"Yes? And what happened?" The teacher was having to coax every little morsel out of him. Gordon may have been a good observer but he was terrible at describing things.

A sheepish expression passed over Gordon's face. "Uh, she coshed me, sir."

"She hit you on the head?" said Professor Scribbish. He seemed outraged and disappointed at the same time.

"Yes, sir."

"And then what happened?"

"I was out for a few seconds, and by the time I came to she was gone."

"Did you see the nurse after that, Mr. Bramble?" said Professor Hoxby.

"No, sir."

"Whyever not?" said the dead bodies teacher.

"I was fine, sir. Really I was. It was nothing."

"When someone knocks you out it isn't nothing, Mr. Bramble," said Professor Hoxby. "Now I want you to go to the nurse this instant. No dilly-dallying. Off you go." He shooed Gordon out the door.

"Yes, sir," said Gordon.

"Miss Lester, will you please stay for a moment," said Professor Snaffle. "I have some additional questions for you."

Gordon scrambled off and Amanda braced herself. She didn't know Professor Snaffle and the secretive woman made her uncomfortable.

"Now then," said Professor Snaffle, "I want to hear more about this blonde girl. Did you notice her shoes?"

Her shoes? Amanda had been so startled to see Harry kissing the girl that she wasn't sure she'd seen them. She tried to conjure up the scene in her mind. Red T-shirt for sure. Bright turquoise shorts, check. Shoes? Wait a minute. They were bright white Amanda remembered the color combination and thought Amphora might be interested in it. Amphora. Some friend she'd turned out to be.

"They were white, Professor," she said.

"Good. And what style were they?"

Amanda thought again. There was a lot of white, not just a sliver. They had to have been sneakers.

"I'm pretty sure they were sneakers, ma'am," she said.

"Excellent. Now I want to tell you something. We found some unidentified footprints in the secrets trove. As you know, we've been maintaining a database of all the teachers', students', and staff's shoe prints, although not visitors'. The prints in the trove did not appear in the database. Mr. Sheriff's did, although of course we're not surprised to find students' footprints on campus. Of course this evidence is all circumstantial, but I'm now wondering if this blonde girl had something to do with the breach.

"Thank you for your help, Miss Lester," the teacher continued. She seemed pleased. "Do you have any additional observations that may be of use to us?"

293

"Wasn't there a smell in the trove?" said Amanda.

"Yes, indeed there was," said Professor Snaffle. "It opened most of the locks, which was quite a feat. Our formula is quite unusual. There's almost no chance it can be duplicated. What is your point, Miss Lester?"

"I didn't get close enough to the girl to smell her, but I did catch a whiff of something on Harry," said Amanda. "I think it was the same as the scent in the trove."

Professor Snaffle clapped her hands so suddenly and loudly that Amanda jumped. "Chris, we need to check the decoy at once," she said.

"Absolutely, Saliva," said Professor Scribbish. "I'm on it." He bounded out of the room and almost knocked Amanda down. "Sorry, Miss Lester," he said as he ran down the hall.

"Well done, Miss Lester," said Professor Snaffle. "You and Mr. Bramble have done good work today. We won't forget this. Now off you go."

"Thank you, ma'am," said Amanda, and ran to tell her friends what had happened.

When the kids met in the common room Ivy said, "Do you think Blixus has got the metadata? If he found that decoy vault he might have discovered the real hiding place. Did you say it was a church?"

"It sounded like that," said Amanda. "I don't know which one though."

"You don't think it's the one with the sarcophagus?" said Simon.

"I don't know," said Amanda. "They didn't specify."

"If Blixus has the secrets and the metadata and the *Bible*, we're in huge trouble," said Ivy. "That would mean the end of the detectives. Even the Punitori couldn't survive that."

Amanda didn't even want to contemplate what life would be like if all that happened. The idea of the detectives falling apart after more than a hundred years was too terrible to imagine. What Nick would be like then—well, that would bring closure at last, wouldn't it?

"We don't know that he has any of those things," said Simon. "This blonde girl, whoever she is, may not have anything to do with him."

"We should confront Harry," said Amanda.

"Don't you think the teachers are already doing that?"

"Yes, I suppose they are. He could be in a lot of trouble. I'd be happy to see that happen. He's been acting so weird to me."

"He is kind of smarmy," said Ivy.

"What are we going to do if this is the end?" said Amanda. "I suppose I'll go back to my filmmaking."

Suddenly the idea of making movies didn't seem so appealing. Being a detective had got into her blood. Those Lestrade genes were more powerful than she'd realized. The thought of that was still scary, especially after meeting Jeffrey. The prospect of turning out like him was frightening.

"It isn't the end," said Simon.

"But if it is."

"I'll cross that bridge when I come to it," he said.

"I know what I'd do," said Ivy.

"What's that?" said Amanda.

"I'd start my own school."

"That's the spirit!" said Amanda. "Count me in." Thank goodness for Ivy. She was always so positive. It was that hidden treasures thing of hers again. There was always a silver lining if you looked hard enough.

"Me too," said Simon.

Amanda tried to imagine them as replacements for Thrillkill, Also, and Sidebotham. She burst out laughing.

A little while later, Professor Scribbish returned from Penrith. He had found two sets of fingerprints at the decoy vault. One of them matched nothing in the fingerprint database. The other belonged to Nick Muffet.

34

BREAKING UP IS HARD TO DO

When the teachers discovered that Nick Muffet had been inside the decoy vault they went ballistic. They couldn't figure out how he had learned of its existence. They were now certain that the Moriartys were behind the theft of the school's secrets. They'd have to act fast to guard the metadata, unless it was already too late, or their secrets would be useless. And if the Moriartys had the *Bible*—they didn't want to think about that.

While the teachers were having fits, something else was happening. Professor Redleaf's computer was going crazy, deforming and reforming itself and shooting rainbows all over the place. The teachers debated whether to destroy it or hang onto it on the off chance that they might be able to neutralize the hacker with it. With Holmes gone they had no idea how to do that. Professor Pole was trying to recreate Holmes's algorithm without success, and the other teachers' skills weren't advanced enough to tackle the problem.

As if these developments weren't disturbing enough, Amanda got bad news from her mother. Her father had gone to live in Tibet and wasn't coming back. He hadn't even called to say goodbye. He just texted Lila and took off. Amanda was so upset at her father's disregard that she burst into tears and couldn't hold up her end of the conversation.

After she'd finished the call a thought popped into her head. What if her mother were to marry this Banting Waltz she was seeing?

Would he try to be her father? With Herb gone she didn't really have one anymore, but she didn't want some stranger stepping in. She briefly considered running off to Tibet to find her father, but rejected the idea when she realized he wouldn't want to see her. Now she had two choices: make peace with this new man or reject him.

Maybe she should find out something about him. She knew he had taken her father's job and that he had, as her mother described it, "never lost a case." But what kind of person was he? Would they get along? Was he related to any detectives? Was he truly the good guy her mother thought he was?

She had no time, but she could at least squeeze in a quick search. She punched "banting waltz" into her phone. As the results were displaying, Professor Scribbish came by and said, "Miss Lester, I—what is that? Banting Waltz? Why are you looking him up?"

"My mother is dating him," she said.

Professor Scribbish frowned. "It isn't serious, is it?"

"I don't know. Why?"

The teacher sat down next to Amanda and looked into her eyes. "I'm afraid he is not a good person," he said.

Uh oh. She'd been afraid of this. "What do you mean?"

"Miss Lester, that man is a crook. You don't want your mother seeing him."

"How is he a crook, sir?" she said, hoping against hope that maybe he was just a kleptomaniac or something small like that.

"He's dishonest, for one thing," said Professor Scribbish. "He tampers with juries. He gets the police to plant evidence—the bad ones. We all know they exist. I won't pretend otherwise."

"Yes, sir. Unfortunately."

"We also think he's on the take," said the teacher. "He'll accept a bribe from just about anyone."

This was not the kind of thing Amanda wanted to hear. She had enough to worry about. What was she supposed to do?

"Are you absolutely sure about this, Professor?"

"I'm afraid so. You can ask the other teachers, but they'll tell you the same thing. You need to warn your mother."

There was no way Lila would want to hear news like this from anyone, especially her daughter. Amanda knew exactly what would happen if she tried to say something. Her mother would have a fit and end up closer to the interloper than she might have been otherwise. She was very stubborn.

"I can't," she said. "You don't know my mother."

"I know more than you think I do," he said. "If you can't speak to her, at least let's monitor the fellow. How does that sound?"

What could she say? There wasn't much more she could do.

"Fine. If you—"

Just then there was a huge commotion in the hall. Amanda and the teacher ran out of the common room just in time to see Professor Snool pushing a cart piled high with slingshots, blowguns, darts, and boomerangs toward the parking lot. Following him was Professor Stegelmeyer wheeling a trolley filled with glassware and lab supplies, and coming around the corner to join them was Professor Peaksribbon carrying a bunch of martial arts equipment. Bits were falling off carts and out of their hands and soon the hallway was littered with broken glass, karate belts, and nunchucks.

"What's going on?" called Professor Scribbish.

"Come on, Chris," said Professor Stegelmeyer. "It's time you joined us. We're leaving."

"What?" said Professor Scribbish, rushing over and surveying the collection. "You can't do that. This equipment belongs to all of us. Look here, the electron microscope? You can't have that."

"You don't want it," said Professor Stegelmeyer, grabbing hold of the microscope and pulling it away. "You Realists want to throw your hands up and let the Moriartys have everything. Remember?"

"You're twisting our position," said Professor Scribbish, eyeing the lower shelf. "We aren't done fighting them. Aw, come on, Richard. The DNA sequencing stuff?"

"You need the *Bible* and the secrets to do it. You know that."

"But we don't. That's where you misunderstand us."

"You want to close the school and go on to other things."

"Yes," said Professor Scribbish. "But we never said what those other things were." He opened a box and peered inside.

"Care to enlighten me then?" said Professor Stegelmeyer.

"I don't think so," said Professor Scribbish. "You'll deliberately misunderstand. I'm sorry to see you go, Richard, but I think you're right. We can't work together anymore."

"Very well," said Professor Stegelmeyer, shutting the box before Professor Scribbish had even got his fingers out. "It's a shame you're not tougher, but it's best that we've found out now. Goodbye, Chris."

"Professor, don't go!" said Amanda.

"Ah, Miss Lester," said Professor Stegelmeyer. "You were really starting to come along. Your lab work has improved tremendously. You and Mr. Binkle make quite a team." Amanda and Simon had never been lab partners, but they had spent a lot of time together in the lab working on their own. That was probably what he meant. "I'm sorry your crime-fighting lives have been cut short."

"But they haven't," said Amanda. "We're not giving up."

"Well, then," said Professor Stegelmeyer. "When I get settled I'll let you know where I am. Perhaps there will be a way for us to continue working together."

"No!" she yelled. "Don't go!"

"I'm sorry," he said, and shuffled down the hall, glasswork tinkling.

"We have to stop them," she said to Professor Scribbish.

"No," he said. "Let them go. It's too late."

"But it isn't," she said. "My film—"

"It was an interesting idea Thrillkill had, but it won't work. We need to move on."

For the second time that day Amanda burst into tears. "This is terrible," she said, snuffling. "I don't want it to be this way."

"Sometimes we just have to accept things as they are and start over," said Professor Scribbish kindly.

She knew that. Nick had taught her that lesson. She'd never been able to do it though. She was starting to collect baggage and she didn't like it.

"What will they do?" she said.

"I don't know. It seems that they're looking for a new location."

"Where?"

"I heard something about an island, but who can say?" he said. "Oh, look. There's Honoria Pargeter digging up her poison plants." He pointed out the common room window.

"Out of my way, Scribbish," came a voice. Professor Feeney was trundling a library book truck down the hall. It was piled high with thick volumes. As she passed where they were standing, a couple of them fell off. "Oh, nuts," she said. "Miss Lester, would you get those for me?"

Amanda scurried to pick up the books: *The Criminal Mind over the Centuries: A Comparison of Twenty-first Century Murderers and Their Predecessors* and *The Bad Bairn: Are Criminal Children Born or Made?* Seeing the second title, Amanda started blubbering so hard that she got the book all wet. All she could think of was Nick.

"Oh, never mind," said Professor Feeney. "Give them here."

She snatched the books away from Amanda and put them back on the truck.

"You don't have to be so irritable with her," said Professor Scribbish. "She was just trying to help. This is upsetting for her. It's upsetting for all of us."

"You should have thought of that before," snarled Professor Feeney. She was so mad Amanda could almost see smoke coming out of her ears. "If you Realists had been sensible, we could have pulled this all together ages ago. It's your fault Moriarty has made so much headway."

"How can you say that?" said Amanda, no longer snuffling. "It's nobody's fault. Don't blame the Realists. They've been trying to help as much as you have."

"You have no idea what you're talking about," said Professor Feeney.

"Don't speak to her like that," said Professor Also, appearing from nowhere. She was carrying her snow globe with the Hobbit house inside. The snow was swirling around like a real blizzard. "She's a child."

"Not so much," said Professor Feeney. "We don't take children here. You know that."

"I'm not a child," said Amanda. "I'm a detective."

"You are a student," said Professor Feeney, glaring at her. "You are neither a detective nor a child."

"Stop it, Seashell," said Professor Also. "Isn't it enough that we're leaving? You don't have to be nasty to the students. Miss Lester has more than proven her worth. Give her some credit."

"Worth schmirth," said Professor Feeney. "This is serious business, not playtime. You students have caused more trouble than can ever be compensated for. That Wiffle boy—"

"That Wiffle boy lost his father," said Professor Also. Amanda was glad to see that she still had some compassion. "He didn't know what he was doing when he destroyed the *Bible*."

"Death is no excuse," said Professor Feeney. Amanda gasped. The woman had no sympathy at all. "His father was weak too."

"Wink was not weak," said Professor Scribbish.

"Oh really?" said Professor Feeney. "Involved with Mavis Moriarty? What a fool. He should have checked her out."

"I feel sorry for you, Seashell," said Professor Scribbish shaking his head. "You have no heart."

"Detectives don't need hearts, Chris," she said. "Hearts get in the way. Now if you'll pardon me."

Was that true? If so, Amanda would never make a good detective. She had so much heart that she wouldn't have been surprised to learn that she had two of them.

Professor Feeney pushed her book truck down the hall and disappeared through the south door. As she exited, Professor Peaksribbon reentered the hallway.

"Miss Lester," he said, "I want you to know how sorry I am about the way things have turned out. I wish I could stay and be your teacher."

"Why don't you, Professor?" said Amanda.

"I can't. It's all got too late, you see." He looked very sad.

"Why does everyone keep saying that?" said Amanda.

"It's detective stuff," said Professor Also. "There's a lot you don't know."

"Then tell me," said Amanda.

"There's no time," said Professor Also. "And it doesn't matter now anyway."

"Please don't go," said Amanda.

Professor Also smiled at her sadly. "I'll tell you what," she said. "Take my snow globe. Keep it safe. Perhaps it will bring you good luck."

"But you don't believe in luck, Professor," said Amanda.

"I know, dear," said the teacher. "I know."

35

NOW YOU TELL ME

After the Punitori had left Legatum, Amanda concluded that much of what had occurred was her fault. She'd been completely wrapped up in herself, obsessing over Nick, worrying about Holmes, wringing her hands over her parents' foibles. It was time to look outward again. She had responsibilities to other people. No more indulging in her own problems, desires, and fears, and definitely no more boyfriends. Love just caused trouble.

Obviously the most important task now was to find her missing friends and relatives. She was pretty sure they were all nearby, somewhere in the Penrith area. A trip back there was in order. She, Ivy, Simon, and Fern would have to go. Perhaps Eustace could join them. She preferred not to invite Amphora, but she wasn't sure she could get away with that. Her roommate would want to save her boyfriend, after all, and also Editta. How she felt about Clive, Amanda didn't know. She was sure Amphora had no interest in Despina and Hillary Lester and Jeffrey Lestrade, but who cared?

Soon after the exodus Thrillkill delivered news: the Penrith police had found Blixus Moriarty's fingerprints in the farmer's house. While that didn't prove he had killed the treasure hunter, it did show that he'd been there. They'd also ascertained that Blixus had been the one to kill Crocodile. *That* information strengthened their conclusion that Blixus did know about the King Arthur coins and had come after them. If there were more, they were probably in his possession.

With this new information in hand, Amanda, Ivy, and Simon decided to flesh out their timeline. Because so much had occurred in the last few days, they wanted to make sure they had everything straight in their minds. Amanda wrote everything out. First, the older stuff:

1. Wink is murdered.
2. *The Detective's Bible* disappears, although no one knows about it until later.
3. The pink sugar conspiracy is uncovered and the factory in London is destroyed.
4. The Moriartys go to jail.

All of those things had happened during spring term. She could never get used to the fact that spring term ran from January to April. That seemed more like winter to her. Anyway, these events were still causing ripples.

Then, during summer term (which should really be spring term):

1. Professor Redleaf discovers the hacker.
2. The crystals are found.
3. Wink's body is discovered.
4. The Moriartys escape from Strangeways.
5. David finds the *Bible*.
6. David's roommates run away with the *Bible*.
7. Nick shows up alive.
8. Legatum fights the Moriartys and the roommates at the quarry.
9. David destroys the *Bible*.
10. Editta runs off with the Moriartys.
11. Philip and Gavin disappear.
12. The teachers split into factions.

Wow. A lot of important things had happened during April, May, and June. No wonder her task list was so long.

Then, during the summer:

1. Crocodile is murdered. He might have been murdered during spring term though.
2. The farmer is murdered.
3. Harry is seen with a mysterious blonde girl.
4. Zombies are seen in the area.
5. Professor Redleaf's computer screen does weird things.
6. Rainbows start appearing around Legatum.
7. Despina, Hill, and Jeffrey disappear.
8. The tunnels are found.
9. The leprechaun coins are found.
10. Ivy is stung. Gordon saves her.
11. The lockbox and Mavis's letters are found.
12. The King Arthur coin is found.
13. David runs away.
14. The secrets trove is breached.
15. The purple rainbow riot occurs at the zoo.
16. Clive is kidnapped.
17. Holmes blocks the hacker, but not for long
18. Holmes is injured, then disappears.
19. The decoy vault is breached. Nick's fingerprints are found.
20. The Punitori leave Legatum.

"And that's just the highlights," she said. "Or should I say lowlights?"

"Can you read it out to me again?" said Ivy.

"Sure," said Amanda, and did as Ivy asked.

"I wonder if we can hone the list," said Ivy tapping her fingers on her knee. "I don't think the part about my being stung is significant."

"Of course it is," said Amanda. "It was very serious."

"I know," said Ivy, "but it isn't germane. Why don't we ignore it?"

She had a point. Ivy's rescue was hugely important but it had nothing to do with any mysteries. The incident had merely been a case of collateral damage.

"For now," said Amanda, eliminating the item from the timeline. "Don't forget that your crisis was also Gordon's coming out party."

"Of course not," said Ivy. "Who would have thought? Maybe we should get him here now."

Amanda punched a text into her phone. "Done."

"Did you ever think we'd want Gordon around?" said Ivy.

"I still don't want him around," said Simon.

"Simon!" said both girls, laughing.

"Naw, he's all right I guess," said Simon. "He did save you." He said it as if it were no big deal. Amanda wasn't sure if he was baiting them or just being Simon.

"Simon!" she said again.

"Just joking," he said. "Ivy's indispensable."

"You just like me for my dog," said Ivy, grinning.

"I sure do," said Simon, grabbing a fistful of dog. Nigel turned around and licked his hand.

"But getting back to the timeline," said Ivy, "I have to say that I don't think the zombies are relevant."

"You don't think they're Blixus's henchmen?" said Amanda.

"No," said Ivy. "They don't figure into anything that's actually happened. I think they're a distraction."

Amanda wasn't sure she agreed but she was willing to entertain the idea. If Ivy was right, Despina et al's disappearance might be chalked up to nothing more than adventure.

"All right," she said. "We'll ignore them too. But then how did Blixus do all this without help?"

"Oh, he had help," said Ivy. She hesitated.

"You can say it," said Amanda. "I've heard it all before."

"Very well then," said Ivy. "I'm sure Nick helped him with some of this. Mavis too. And who knows how Editta might have participated. If she's gaga over Nick, she'd probably do anything to please him and his parents."

"Sadly I think you're right," said Simon, still petting Nigel. The dog was loving it. He turned over on his back so Simon could stroke his chest.

"What about this blonde girl, though?" said Ivy.

"I have no idea who she is," said Amanda. She'd racked her brain and had come up with nothing. It seemed that no one else could figure her out either.

"You don't think Harry is working for them too?" said Ivy.

"I wouldn't put it past him," said Simon.

"Why, just because he's a Lothario?" said Amanda. The older boy was frivolous but that didn't make him a criminal. Although there was something evil about the way he kept winking at her. He really enjoyed making her uncomfortable.

"Now there's a five-pound word," said Simon.

"Okay, fine. Casanova, Romeo, stud. Better?"

"Aren't we literary?" said Simon.

"I'm going to fine you," said Ivy.

"I don't play this game with Amanda," said Simon. "Only Amphora."

"Says you," said Ivy, giggling.

"Who's a Lothario?" said Gordon, responding in person to Amanda's invitation. He sat down next to Amanda and looked at her list.

"Harry Sheriff," said Amanda.

"That guy?" said Gordon with obvious distaste. "Don't get me started."

"What do you mean?" said Amanda.

"He sure gets around," said Gordon.

"Like what?" said Amanda. Gordon hesitated. He seemed to want to backpedal. Amanda gave him a look. "Well?"

"One day I heard him in the tunnels with a girl."

"What do you mean 'a girl'?" said Amanda. Harry being with a girl was hardly anything new.

"I didn't see her, but I could hear them," said Gordon. "She was all like 'oooh' and 'aaah.'"

"You mean they were making out?" said Ivy.

"That too, but no, I think he was trying to impress her by giving her a tour or something."

Amanda and Simon sat up. Ivy froze. "GORDON!" said the girls together.

"You heard this and you didn't report it?" said Ivy.

"I thought it was one of the students," said Gordon. "They're allowed to be there. Oh no—you don't think it was that blonde girl?"

"YES!" said Amanda. "It had to be her. Don't you see what this means? She was seen in Penrith breaking into the decoy vault with Nick. She's working for Blixus and she's been hanging around with Harry. She's probably using him to get our secrets. We have to go to Thrillkill right now."

"You mean—" said Gordon.

"Yes," said Amanda. "We mean just what you think we mean."

"Yikes, I'm sorry," he said. "I had no idea. Then I suppose he was doing something bad that other time I saw him in the tunnels too."

"What other time?" said Amanda. She was getting unbelievably antsy. She wished Gordon would be more forthcoming. He was a terrible communicator.

"The day you and Simon went to the factory to look for the crystals. You know when you took that boat—"

"You were there that day? Aaaaaaaagh!" screamed Amanda. This was not good news. If he meant what she thought he meant— "No wonder he's been grinning at me. He saw me naked! Wait a minute. You didn't see me, did you, Gordon?"

"I wish," he said a bit absently. "I was too far back."

"Oh, right," said Ivy. "The time Simon came back for your clothes."

"I took the wet ones off," said Amanda. "After jumping in the lake. OMG, I'm so mortified."

"You shouldn't be," said Simon. "You have a nice body."

"Simon Binkle, you didn't peek?" yelled Amanda.

"'Course not," said Simon. "But I've got eyes, haven't I?"

Amanda screamed and kicked her feet and carried on for a full minute until at last she realized there were more important things to attend to.

"Come on, let's go," she said, then muttered, "Harry Sheriff indeed." She grabbed Ivy and raced out of the room wishing that for his next trick Simon would come up with a memory eraser.

36

BACK TO THE TUNNELS

The weather had turned cold. Rain was coming down in buckets, the first time that had happened since the end of last term. In Thrillkill's office, water was streaming down the windows and it was impossible to see outside. The four kids sat around the headmaster's desk hoping he wouldn't explode.

"You realize you should have come to me at once, Mr. Bramble," said Thrillkill in a strained voice.

"I know, sir," said Gordon. "I'm ever so sorry. You can expel me if you want."

"I'm sure you are," said Thrillkill. "However before you bite your fingernails off, I'm not going to punish you. We are beyond that now."

"Yes, sir," said Gordon. "Thank you, sir."

"However, I'm not finished with you," said Thrillkill.

"No, sir," said Gordon. "Of course not."

"We are going to find Blixus Moriarty today," said Thrillkill.

"Yes, sir," said Gordon.

"For heaven's sake," said Thrillkill, "stop saying 'Yes, sir.'" Gordon clamped his lips together to stop himself from speaking. "Now, we are going to Penrith and we are going into those tunnels. We will bring Mr. Sheriff with us, since he seems to know more about what's been going on than we do."

"Excuse me, sir," said Gordon, "but do you think that's a good idea?"

Amanda couldn't believe this was the same Gordon who had recently been so unsure of himself that he needed to hide behind David Wiffle. Creating those glitter explosions in Professor Pole's class had transformed him completely—perhaps too completely. Now he seemed overconfident.

"I do," said Thrillkill, doing that peering over his glasses thing. "If it turns out that Mr. Sheriff has been in cahoots with the Moriartys he will be arrested. If he has been an unsuspecting accomplice he will be expelled. He's old enough to know better. However there will be an investigation. No steps will be taken without proof."

Gordon opened his mouth, seemed to think better of whatever he was going to say, and shut it again.

"I very much suspect that the Moriartys and our missing students are ensconced somewhere in those tunnels," said Thrillkill. "Possibly your relatives too, Amanda."

"Sir," said Simon. "Why do you suppose Inspector Lestrade didn't call for backup?"

"I have no idea," said Thrillkill. "We don't even know that he's with Blixus, although where else would he be?"

"You don't think anyone is dead, sir?" said Gordon.

"How should I know?" thundered Thrillkill. "I don't even know my own name right now. What with lawsuits, kidnappings, runaways, rainbow monsters, defecting teachers, and whatnot, I am slightly too busy to speculate at the moment. Now, grab your gear and meet me at my car in ten minutes. I will notify your sister, Miss Halpin, and get her to drive a second car. Unfortunately, there isn't room for six people and a dog in my Citroen. I don't care how wet it is out there, you be there. Got that?"

Each of the kids nodded.

"Good. Now off you go."

Thrillkill was a demon on wheels. The car careened over narrow roads and around corners, throwing up so much mud that the hedges on either side looked like cliffs. Amanda felt as though she were sitting in an electric blender, she was bouncing around so much. Fortunately she had brought her usual supply of gingersnaps and managed to pop one or two into her mouth on the way.

In his usual fashion Harry tried to wriggle out of everything, failing to assume any responsibility whatsoever. He played completely dumb, acting as if he had no idea who the blonde girl was or what was going on. His act bordered on insolence, which made Amanda so mad that she lost control and screamed at him.

"You think you're so great just because you have this Brad Pitt thing going on," she yelled. "Get a clue. There's a lot more to life than looking pretty. And yeah, I know you saw me naked. So what? You want to see more?"

She reached down to the ribbing of her sweater and started to lift it up, but Simon, who was sitting in the back between her and Harry, stopped her. "Don't give him the satisfaction," he said.

"I don't care. I've got nothing to be ashamed of."

"It's actually quite a nice body," said Harry.

"Shut up!" yelled Amanda.

"Be quiet, you two," said Thrillkill. "Mr. Sheriff, your behavior is disgraceful. I see that Legatum has completely failed you. It's quite a shame, too, because you seemed to have so much potential when you entered. I suppose it's our fault. Nevertheless, pending our investigation, you will not be returning."

"Who cares?" said Harry. "There won't be a Legatum anyway."

"There will," said Thrillkill.

"What, you and old Tumble?" said Harry. "Making dresses together?"

Now he'd stepped in it. Amanda couldn't believe he'd talk to the headmaster that way.

"Shut up, Harry," said Ivy, who was sharing the tiny front seat with Nigel. "You're such a stereotype."

"Speaking of stereotypes, who's your girlfriend?" said Amanda.

"How's that criminal boyfriend of yours?" Harry said.

This dig made Amanda so mad that she lunged at him and tried to grab him around the neck. Harry was much stronger, though, and blocked her easily. Then he started laughing. And that made Simon mad.

"Nigel, sic!" he yelled to the dog.

"Simon, no!" screamed Ivy.

She grabbed Nigel but he was too strong for her. The retriever went for Harry's leg and dug his teeth into it. Harry yelped and tried to pull Nigel off, to no effect. Then he raised his hand as if to hit the dog, and Simon punched him in the face. Harry was so stunned that he pulled back and buried his nose in his hands. Amanda wondered how the handsome Harry Sheriff would look with a purple clown nose.

Thrillkill stopped the car. "That's it," he said. "I don't care what or who you know. You're finished, Mr. Sheriff. Mr. Binkle, take these cuffs—" he reached into the glove box and removed a pair of handcuffs—"and secure his hands behind his back. Miss Lester, please phone Professor Kindseth and get him to collect Mr. Sheriff. We'll wait until he arrives."

"Nigel, come," said Ivy. The dog bounced back into the front seat and laid his head on Ivy's lap.

"You're a loser," said Simon, pulling Harry's hands behind his back. The older boy struggled, but Simon motioned toward Nigel with his chin. "Don't even think it."

"You're a geek," said Harry.

"Why thank you," said Simon.

"I hate dogs," said Harry.

"Figures," said Amanda.

Soon Professor Kindseth showed up in his white sedan. The rain was still coming down hard and the road had turned to slime. When the teacher got out of his car, mud splattered all over his trousers and soaked his shoes. Amanda had thought he was too nice to play bad cop, but he seemed to have no compunction about shoving Harry into his car, making sure he got plenty of goo all over him first. Simon was obviously surprised as well because he gave Amanda a look that said, "What the—" The weirdest thing about the incident was that Harry didn't even fight. He just went silent and let the photography teacher take him back to Legatum, where who knew what would happen to him.

When Harry was gone, Thrillkill started the motor but the car wouldn't move. They were stuck in the mud. The headmaster stepped on the accelerator repeatedly but nothing happened.

"How about reverse?" said Simon.

Thrillkill changed gears and tried again. They were still stuck.

"We need some traction," said Simon. "Have you got any boards or straw? We could put them under the wheels."

"I have evidence kits," said Thrillkill. "And of course maps and tools."

"Hm," said Simon, "I wonder if Fern has anything."

He phoned Fern, who was parked nearby with Gordon.

"Evidence kits," she said. "A couple of books—will those do?"

"They might," said Simon, "but they'll be ruined. Anything else?"

"Our clothes," said Amanda.

"I think we've had enough nudity for today, Miss Lester," said Thrillkill. "I suppose we ought to see if some leaves from those plants over there will work. Mr. Binkle, care to join me?"

Thrillkill and Simon grabbed plastic bags, waded over to a hedge that was growing by the side of the road, and started to pull. The rain coated their glasses and soaked through their clothes. The fedora Simon wore so often went limp and he removed it. The one good thing about all that water was that it finally made his cowlick lie flat.

When the two detectives had filled a bunch of plastic bags, they came back to the car and scattered leaves near the two front tires. By this time they were completely soaked, and when they got back into the car they couldn't help getting Amanda, Ivy, and Nigel all wet too.

"No dry clothes this time, I'm afraid," said Simon.

"Oh well," said Amanda. "If we find Blixus it will be worth getting sick."

Thrillkill started the motor, put the car into first gear, and gently stepped on the accelerator. The Citroen inched forward a teensy bit and then fell back into the rut.

"It's working, kind of," said Simon.

"Let's try that again," said Thrillkill.

He accelerated again, slowly. The car crawled forward as before, then gave up again.

"Get Fern on the phone, will you?" said Thrillkill to no one in particular.

Amanda took out her phone and pressed Fern's icon. Fern picked up before the first ring.

"You want a push?" she said.

"Yes, please," said Amanda.

"Okay. Here I come."

But Fern didn't come. Her ignition had got so wet her car wouldn't start.

"Oh, bother," she said through the still open line. "I'm stuck too."

"Great," said Thrillkill. "Try Kindseth, would you?"

Amanda ended the call with Fern and phoned Professor Kindseth.

"I just left you," said the teacher. "What's happening?"

"We're both stuck because of the rain."

"Well doesn't that beat all," said Professor Kindseth. "I guess old Harry and I are in for a little delay then. I'm coming."

It took the photography teacher twenty minutes to drive back to where the others were waiting. In Thrillkill's car no one said a word. Amanda thought the teacher would pull in behind the Citroen and give it a nudge, but instead he parked next to Fern. Within a few seconds the door opened and Professor Kindseth got out. Then Harry emerged, still cuffed, and trudged over behind Professor Thrillkill's car. Professor Kindseth uncuffed Harry's hands, threw a net over him, and said, "Push. Don't even think about trying to escape. Gaston, Simon, Gordon, be ready to rush him if he even thinks about running. You too, Amanda."

Amanda and Ivy burst into laughter. Professor Kindseth was awesome. He had obviously made a full recovery from his earthquake injuries and was as energetic and resourceful as ever.

Of course the logical thing would be for someone to help Harry, but that didn't happen. The poor guy was stuck trying to push the Citroen out of the mud by himself. He pushed and pushed, and each time the car slipped back. Finally Professor Kindseth said, "If you don't get this car out of the mud right now I'm going to shave your head." That seemed to make Harry work harder, and within about fifteen seconds the car was out of the mud hole.

Fern's car still wouldn't start, though, so now the group faced a difficult choice: squeeze into Thrillkill's car or get Professor Kindseth to take them to the farm. Despite the fact that everyone volunteered to turn themselves into sardines, Thrillkill wouldn't hear of them all crammed into his car. Harry would come with them after all, as would Professor Kindseth. Harry was cuffed behind his back again, and Fern and Gordon joined him and the teacher. They would call the automobile club regarding Fern's ignition later.

Now that he was out of the mud, Thrillkill resumed the drive and the bumping around. Within minutes both cars had arrived at the farm.

"You say the tunnels diverged back a ways?" said Thrillkill, when they'd all congregated at the opening.

"Yes, Professor," said Simon. "We took the left fork after that and ended up here."

"And you didn't hear or see any signs of life?" said Thrillkill.

"Other than the leprechaun coins, no," said Simon.

"I think we should split up," said Thrillkill. "Fern, you and Gordon will come with me. We'll continue on to the left from here. Ken, you, Amanda, Simon, Ivy, and Harry will head back to the fork and take the right-hand tunnel. The phones work down there, do they not?"

"Sometimes," said Amanda.

"Very well, then," said Thrillkill. "We will keep an open video line to each other. Questions?" The kids glanced from one to the other, then back to Thrillkill. Harry looked like he was going to say something but didn't. "Let's get started."

No sooner had Thrillkill uttered those words than a huge purple rainbow appeared above the farm. There was something about it that made it look angry. The shade of purple could only be described as aggressive, and the light that came out of it was spiky. Amanda thought it looked like it was having a fit. Nigel barked at it. He didn't like it either.

"We're in the right place," said Professor Kindseth. "The hacker must be down there too."

Thrillkill, Fern, and Gordon went first. The slope that led into the tunnels was like a river of mud and they worked hard to keep their balance. Amanda watched as they disappeared into the tunnel that faced north. Then she, Professor Kindseth, Simon, Ivy, Nigel, and Harry followed and headed toward the fork. They were all such messes that they barely recognized each other.

A stream of mud was running down the tunnel. Simon made a game out of straddling it. Amanda wondered if Professor Kindseth was going to force Harry to walk in it, but he didn't. It didn't last that long anyway. Within about fifty yards it was gone.

"Where's Moriarty?" said Professor Kindseth.

"Are you talking to me?" said Harry, not looking at him.

"Yes, you."

"How should I know?" said Harry insolently.

"Because your girlfriend is working for him," said the teacher.

"Taffeta?" said Harry. "That's ridiculous."

"So her name is Taffeta, is it?" said Simon. He was examining the ground as he walked. Amanda thought of poor Clive and his rocks.

"What's it to you?" said Harry.

"What's her last name?" said Simon.

"Get stuffed," said Harry.

"Her footprints are here," said Simon.

"What?" said Harry. "How can you tell? There are millions of prints."

"I recognize the tread," said Simon snapping a picture. "So the two of you have been in here before."

"I never was—" said Harry, then caught himself.

"You never were what?" said Simon.

"Get lost," said Harry.

"But we are lost," said Simon.

"No we're not," said Amanda.

"Shhh," said Simon.

"What is with you, man?" said Harry. "Don't you geeks have hormones?"

"Sure," said Simon. "We just don't let them get us into relationships with criminals."

Halfway through the statement he seemed to realize what he was saying, and with the last two words he trailed off. Harry wasn't the only one who had fallen for a criminal and Simon knew it. Harry turned around and gave him a snotty smile. He knew it too.

But Amanda didn't have a chance to be upset. She saw something glinting and ran ahead to see what it was. Another leprechaun coin.

"What's that?" said Harry, trying to get a look. Amanda didn't like him being close to her and moved away.

"Oh, I think you know," said Simon.

"I don't know anything," said Harry.

"Now you're telling the truth."

"Shut up."

"As you wish," said Simon. He really was able to keep his cool with the guy. Amanda wished she could do that.

They toddled along in silence for a while, and finally they arrived at the fork. The tunnel they had taken from the farm went off to the south, toward the crypt. The other opening veered northeast. Professor Kindseth looked into his phone and said, "We've arrived at the fork, Gaston."

"Good." Thrillkill's face appeared on the screen. We're just plodding along. Nothing to report yet."

"We're going to enter the other tunnel now," said Professor Kindseth.

"We found another leprechaun coin," said Ivy.

"Any hint as to what it is?" said Thrillkill.

"No," said Ivy. "More of the same."

"Very well," said Thrillkill. "Let's keep at it."

Amanda's group entered the unexplored tunnel. Before they had walked twenty yards, Amanda saw a flash of rainbow. It looked like one of the broken ones, with the purple in the middle. "Look!" she said.

"Approach with caution," said Professor Kindseth.

Amanda turned off her light just in case the Moriartys were up ahead, then crept forward slowly. The rainbow was still flashing. She could see it now. Something was there at the side of the tunnel. It was round and black but the top was shining. As she drew near she got one good look before the rainbow winked out. There in front of her was a pot of gold.

37

LIKE A MYTH COME TRUE

Amanda thought she was hallucinating. Surely she wasn't looking at an honest-to-goodness pot of leprechaun's gold! The thing had to be someone's idea of a prank.

"Professor," she yelled. "Come see this."

She turned her light back on and illuminated the treasure. In a moment the others had caught up to her.

"What is it?" said Ivy.

"You're not going to believe it," said Amanda, eyeing the coins inside the pot. "It looks like the pot of gold at the end of the rainbow. Of course it can't really be."

"Do you think it's safe to touch?" said Ivy. "I want to feel it."

"Hang on," said Professor Kindseth. He took a vial of something out of his pocket and sprinkled a drop of liquid on top of the gold. Nothing happened. "All right, Miss Halpin. Go ahead."

Amanda guided Ivy toward the pot. The tiny detective reached in and felt carefully, turning the coins over.

"Oh my goodness," she said. "They're the same as the ones we found. A whole potful of them."

"Looks like it," said Simon. "If we hadn't had those coins assayed, I'd say they were a hoax." He picked one up and bit it.

"The whole thing is unreal," said Amanda, recoiling. Just because they were real gold didn't mean they were sanitary.

"Taffeta's footprints are here," said Simon, throwing the coin back in the pot.

"I wonder what she has to do with this," said Ivy. "Do you think she could be the hacker?"

Harry huffed.

"What?" said Amanda. "Too stupid?"

"Something like that," said Harry.

Professor Kindseth spoke into his phone. "Gaston, we've found something."

"What's—" Thrillkill spoke the one word and the connection went dead.

Professor Kindseth kept trying to reconnect but he couldn't get anything to happen. "It looks like we're out of range," he said. "I'll try again in a few minutes."

"I'll take some samples, shall I?" said Simon.

"Please do that, Mr. Binkle," said the teacher. "Let's continue on."

Simon took an evidence kit out of his backpack and proceeded to collect specimens. While he was doing that the others moved on down the tunnel. Within about five minutes, they saw another rainbow, and when they got close they found yet another pot of gold.

"This is a little spooky," said Amanda. "It's like a myth come true."

"It's no such thing," said Simon, catching up with them. He was jingling ever so slightly.

"Then what is it?" said Ivy.

"The hacker," said Simon.

"You don't mean he's doing real alchemy?" said Ivy.

"No, not at all. There's quartz here. Gold is often found with quartz."

"What's that got to do with the rainbows?" said Amanda.

Simon examined the rock on both sides of the tunnel. He pulled out a magnifier and brought his face right up to it. He seemed to take forever.

"Well?" said Ivy. "Don't keep us in suspense."

Suddenly a rainbow flashed through the cavern and struck Simon in the head. He oofed and fell to the ground. Harry laughed.

"Simon!" screamed Amanda.

"What happened?" said Ivy.

"The rainbow hit him!" said Amanda. She bent down and was just about to check for vital signs when Simon put his hand to his head.

"Ouch."

"Are you okay?" said Amanda. "Shut up, Harry. You'll be next."

"Don't think so," said Harry. "They only hit geeks."

"I'm not sure," said Simon. "I feel like someone coshed me."

"That rainbow hit you," said Amanda. "Can you stand up? You know something about these rainbows, Harry?"

"I know as much as you do," said the older boy.

"I don't believe you," said Ivy. "You know exactly what's going on here."

"Nuh uh," said Harry.

"He doesn't know anything," said Simon, getting to his feet. "He's just a pretty face."

"I'm not going to fine you for that one," said Ivy, giggling.

"So what *is* going on?" said Amanda. She wondered if she should try to help Simon. Maybe he had a concussion, like Clive back at the quarry.

"Oh, right," said Simon, rubbing the spot where the rainbow had hit him. "I don't have a concussion so you can stop worrying, Amanda." How did he know? He must have been developing hyper senses like Ivy's. "What's happening is this: gold and quartz both put out electrical signals. Like any electrical signals, they can be detected."

"So he's doing some kind of electrical prospecting?" said Amanda.

"Yes," said Simon. "That's exactly it. He's boosting the signal from the gold and the quartz using the rainbows. When the rainbows detect the signals they turn purple."

"You're kidding," said Harry. "I never heard anything so dumb."

Simon looked straight at him and said, "I never *saw* anything so dumb." Ivy and Amanda stifled giggles.

"So the purple rainbows indicate the presence of gold?" said Ivy.

"Yep," said Simon. "And the fact that it's rainbow quartz—it resonates with the rainbows. It's a sort of symbiotic relationship, like the crystals with their parasites."

"Well, I'll be," said Professor Kindseth.

"But where does the gold come from in the first place?" said Ivy.

"I'd venture a guess that it's already here," said Simon. "In raw form, that is. And I'd also guess that once it's detected and mined, someone is making it into these coins."

"But why?" said Amanda. The whole thing seemed so strange she couldn't begin to speculate on what was going on. No way were there real leprechauns any more than there were real zombies. But there might be delusional people who thought they were imaginary creatures. She'd read about that in one of her mother's psychology magazines.

"That I don't know," said Simon. "Blixus has very advanced technical capabilities, but why he'd use them for something as frivolous as this I can't say."

"Wait a minute," said Amanda. "The zombies."

"What about them?" said Ivy. "Oh, I know. You think the zombies are making these coins? Then they must be working for Blixus."

"No, that's absurd," said Simon. "Say, did we ever establish how old these coins are?"

"I don't think so," said Amanda. She didn't remember anyone saying, which was odd. Surely they'd asked Mr. Terrapin to find out. "Why?"

"You don't suppose—" said Simon.

"No," said Amanda. "That's nuts."

"What are you talking about?" said Professor Kindseth.

"Simon is wondering if the coins were created by King Arthur," said Amanda.

"I know it sounds ridiculous," said Simon, "especially given that King Arthur was a Briton and these coins are associated with the Irish." He seemed to have forgotten his skepticism regarding the king's existence.

"Not necessarily," said Ivy. "Geoffrey of Monmouth portrayed Arthur as head of an empire that included not only Britain, but also Ireland, Iceland, Norway, and Gaul. He might have been right."

How did Ivy know these things, thought Amanda. She'd never even heard of Geoffrey of Monmouth.

"Even so," said Professor Kindseth, "it does seem like a far-fetched idea."

"You people are crazy," said Harry. "I'll bet it isn't even real gold."

"Oh, it is," said Simon. "We've had it tested."

"Do tell," said Harry. "How much you think it's worth?"

"Couldn't say," said Simon. "Why don't you do the math, though? Oh, that's right: you don't know how."

Harry lunged at him, but Simon dodged him and he fell. He turned around, stared daggers at Simon, and said, "You pathetic little wanker."

Simon just laughed and said, "Nerds rule."

"Get up, Harry," said Professor Kindseth. "And I don't want to see you attack anyone again."

Harry mumbled under his breath as he got to his feet.

"That's right, I am a short little weasel," said Professor Kindseth. "But at least I'm making something of myself. You should try it sometime."

Amanda didn't like all this fighting. It was getting too personal. They had enough problems without descending into rancor. "Come on, guys," she said. "Let's keep going. I have a feeling we're starting to get somewhere."

They continued down the tunnel for a bit and then Ivy said, "Sssh. I hear something."

Everyone stood stock-still. Amanda peered around to see if she could detect whatever Ivy had heard. Suddenly Nigel took off, racing down the tunnel until he was nearly out of sight. "Nigel!" Ivy stage whispered to him. Simon took off after the dog, his footsteps thumping as he ran. Then Amanda heard, "Oh, brother."

"What is it?" yelled Ivy.

"A mouse," said Simon.

"He didn't kill it, did he?" said Ivy.

"No," said Simon. "It climbed up the side of the tunnel. It's looking at me."

Amanda and the others picked their way down to where Simon and Nigel were standing. Nigel was eyeing the mouse as if he were starving. The poor mouse was shaking, but there was only one way down, and that was directly in the path of Nigel's mouth.

"He's so cute," said Amanda.

"Stinking vermin," said Harry.

"Glad to see you're constantly coming up with new names for yourself," said Simon.

"That's enough, you two," said Professor Kindseth.

"Come on, Nigel," said Ivy. "Let's go. Now." The dog looked up at her with his big brown eyes. "I can feel that, Nigel, but it isn't going to work. Leave the mouse alone and come with me."

Nigel looked as if someone had snatched his dinner away, which in a way Ivy had. He slunk away from the mouse and took his place by her side again. She reached down and petted him.

"You heard the mouse?" said Amanda.

"So it seems," said Ivy. "Wait a minute. I hear something coming from down the tunnel."

"What does it sound like?" said Amanda, who couldn't hear it.

"Dishes clanking," said Ivy.

"Really?" said Simon. He craned his neck. "Maybe it's some hobos or something."

"Maybe it's Blixus," said Amanda.

"What are we going to do when we find him?" said Ivy.

"I'll talk to him," said Amanda matter-of-factly.

"You'll talk to him?" said Harry. "*That's* your plan? The guy will kill you."

"Shut up, Harry," said Amanda.

"Actually, we haven't discussed this," said Simon. "What *are* we going to do?"

"Ha!" said Harry. "I'm right."

"I know what I'm doing," said Amanda.

"You'd better," said Editta out of nowhere. "He's not going to like this at all."

38

PRISONERS!

Amanda gasped at the sound of Editta's voice. Professor Kindseth dropped his phone. Simon tripped over his own feet. Harry laughed.

"I knew it was you," said Ivy. "I know your walk, Editta."

"You shouldn't be down here," said Editta, stepping into their light. She was rather unwashed but her brown eyes were sparkling. Amanda had never seen that look in her eye before. What had Nick done to her?

"Either should you," said Amanda. "You shouldn't have run off like that. Your mother is going crazy."

"I'm sorry about that," said Editta. "I'd ask you to let her know I'm okay, but I don't think you're going to be seeing her again."

"She's suing the school," said Ivy.

"Can't be helped," said Editta. "Who cares anyway?"

"He isn't worth it," said Amanda.

"Oh, yes he is," said Editta. "You'll never have him though." She looked positively arrogant. This wasn't the Editta they knew.

"Did you hear what I just said? I said he isn't worth it. I don't want him."

"What's going on out there?" came Blixus's voice. Emerging from the shadows, the master criminal caught sight of the Legatum group and said, "You? You should have known better." He was holding some silver coins. He stood back and surveyed the visitors while he tossed the coins from one hand to the other.

"That's what I said," said Editta.

"I see you have more of the King Arthur coins," said Amanda.

"You know about them?" said Blixus.

"Wink saved one for us," said Ivy.

"He did not," came a voice. It was David. He looked a bit the worse for wear himself. His clothes and hair were grimy, his cornflower blue eyes dull. "He wouldn't steal."

"Oh, so that's what happened, is it?" said Simon.

"David," said Amanda. "Your mum is worried sick about you." No response. "David, did you hear what I said?"

"You said my dad stole that coin." He was barely looking at her.

"I did not," said Ivy. "I said he had one. Are you telling me he stole the coin from Crocodile?"

"I told you," said David. "My did wouldn't steal. Why is everyone saying these things about him?"

"Shut up, kid," said Blixus. "Your dad had no honor. I wish I had killed him myself."

Amanda wondered if he was talking about the fact that David's father had once been involved with Mavis. It did sound as though Blixus wasn't the one who had killed Wink though.

"Nick, come here," yelled Blixus to the tunnel behind him. Bring Taffeta and the boys."

This was the moment Amanda had been dreading. She had sought Nick ever since the battle at the quarry, wanting, needing to resolve their unfinished business. Now that she had found him she felt the urge to turn and run. She couldn't face him in front of all those people. She wasn't even sure she could face him alone.

But there he was, looking positively wild: bruises from the crystal fight still visible, thick dark hair longer than ever, the light in his eyes intense. The air around him was electric and she could feel it licking her skin. When he caught sight of her he started, then relaxed into a defiant half-smile.

Behind Nick was the girl, Taffeta, radiant and self-assured, glowing as if supernatural. When Harry saw her he broke into a huge grin, but it faded when she failed to acknowledge him. Serves him right, thought Amanda. She'd been using him as much as he'd used her. They deserved each other.

Following Taffeta were Philip Puppybreath and Gavin Niven, David's roommates who had stolen the *Detective's Bible*, looking sullen and smug. David didn't even glance at them.

"Bring them here," said Blixus. "I wouldn't try anything if I were you, kiddies." He pulled some fully charged crystals out of his pocket. "We all have them. One wrong move and we'll blast you out of this cavern."

Amanda had wondered before whether the Moriartys had taken any crystals from the quarry. At the time she hadn't thought so, but apparently she'd been wrong.

"David, where's the *Bible*?" Amanda called out.

"How should I know?" said the Wiffle boy.

"It's not here?" said Ivy.

"I threw it in the pit," said David. "You know that. Boy, you're stupid."

"So Blixus doesn't have it?" said Amanda. It didn't sound like he did. Maybe the book hadn't fallen into the wrong hands after all.

"Why do you waste your time with him?" said Blixus. "He doesn't know what's going on." Or maybe the criminal did have it and David wasn't aware of the situation. Amanda wondered whether Editta knew. "Stop dragging your feet and move."

Amanda glanced at Nick. His eyes were full of fury. This wasn't the time to speak to him.

The Moriartys, Taffeta, and the roommates prodded the Legatum group down the tunnel into a set of connecting caverns. These had been set up as a sort of camp with sleeping bags, cooking equipment, and even a lab bench of sorts. Someone had piled boulders all around the edges, and throughout the rooms were shining pots of gold. So this was where the Moriartys had been all this time—underground collecting gold. But where was the gold coming from and how had they known about it?

When the visitors entered the living area, Mavis was doing something at the lab bench. This struck Amanda as strange, as she had never seen Mavis display any sort of technical abilities, but then again the Moriartys relied on such skills. Just because Amanda hadn't seen the woman do technical things didn't mean she couldn't. Could that mean she was the hacker after all?

Mavis looked up and laughed. She had a beautiful smile. So what, thought Amanda. Looks had nothing to do with being a decent person.

"You again," said Mavis maliciously. "Ever the lost cause. You just can't keep away from my son, can you, Amanda?"

The remark stung. "Just can't keep away from Wink Wiffle, can you?" said Amanda. Simon gave her a look that said, "That wasn't a good idea."

Blixus turned around with an expression of such rage that Amanda thought he was going to kill someone then and there. Mavis stared at Amanda for a moment, then lunged at her. Ivy screamed and Nigel went for Mavis's throat. Mavis released Amanda and tried to fend him off. Blixus ran into the fray and raised his hand against the dog, who let Mavis go and attacked him instead. "Nigel, no!" yelled Ivy, and the dog let go. "Come back here." Nigel crept over to his mistress and growled, keeping an eye on Mavis and Blixus.

"Why did you do that?" said Simon in a whisper. "You should have let him kill them."

"How can you say such a thing?" said Ivy, whispering back. "That would make me a murderer."

"That would make you a self-defender," said Simon.

"I will be phoning animal services about that miserable cur," said Mavis. "Then again, I don't need to. None of you will be around much longer."

"We'll see about that," said Professor Kindseth.

"And you," she said, turning to him. "How's *Charlotte* these days?"

Amanda and Simon looked at each other. Ivy sucked in her breath. Charlotte was the mysterious recipient of the love letters the kids had found last term—the letters signed "Ken." They'd wondered if Ken was Professor Kindseth. Now they knew. But who was Charlotte?

"What was that about Wink?" said Blixus, looking at his wife.

"I didn't say anything about Wink," said Mavis.

"The Lestrade girl. She said something about the two of you. What was that?"

Mavis looked at Amanda like she was going to kill her.

"They were in love," said Amanda. Simon nudged her and shook his head.

"No they weren't!" yelled David. "The letters are forgeries."

"What do you mean 'in love'?" said Blixus. "What letters?"

"They used to date," said Amanda. "He kept her letters. We found them."

"Shut up!" yelled David.

Mavis glanced David, then looked at Nigel as if evaluating whether to go for Amanda again.

"Never," said Blixus. "You're a fantasist. Just what I'd expect from a Lestrade."

"No, I'm not," said Amanda. Simon practically shoved her this time. "It was a long time ago—before you knew her."

"Oh?" said Blixus. "And when was this?"

"Fifteen years ago," said Amanda, watching his reaction. He was looking quizzical. "But Wink dumped her."

"He did not," said David. "My dad wouldn't do that. He'd never be involved with someone like her."

"Tell me more about these letters," said Blixus like an attack dog being prodded out of a nap.

"There are no letters," said Mavis. "As you said, she's a fantasist."

"Then why is Wiffle here talking about letters?" said Blixus.

"They were in Wink's lockbox," said Amanda. "With the coin."

"What coin?" said Blixus. He sure seemed to be asking a lot of questions. Maybe he didn't have any more moles at Legatum. He certainly wasn't privy to their latest discoveries.

"The King Arthur coin."

"Wink had a King Arthur coin?" said Blixus. He seemed genuinely surprised. "Where did he get it?"

"It doesn't matter," said Amanda. "He kept the letters and we found them. They were love letters from her to him." She looked at Mavis.

"What's she talking about?" Blixus said to his wife.

"They weren't letters," said Mavis. "Just a few notes, if that."

"So it's true?" said Blixus. He was starting to look like a volcano about to erupt.

"Not really," said Mavis. "We didn't date. We just knew each other."

"What do you mean 'knew each other'?" He was raising his fist. Amanda noticed that it was his left hand. Nick was left-handed too.

"We went out a few times."

Amanda glanced at Nick. He was looking horrified.

"In my book that's dating," said Blixus. "Did you love him?"

"Of course not," said Mavis.

"She did—passionately," said Amanda. She stole another glance at Nick. He was staring daggers at her.

"She did not!" screamed David. "Not *my* dad."

"Mavis loves no one passionately but me," said Blixus, lowering the fist. "Obviously Wink was having ego problems so he forged these letters to make himself feel better."

"Yes," said Mavis. "That's just what he did."

"Then why did she have his ring?" said Amanda. At this point Simon was beside himself. He kept poking her so much that she hissed "Stop it" at him. Nick looked like he was about to charge her.

"What ring?" said Blixus. "What are you talking about?"

"Wink's wedding ring. We found it in her jewelry box after he was murdered."

"That's ridiculous," said Blixus. "She must have seen a ring lying around and stolen it."

"It was engraved," said Amanda. "From his wife, Celerie."

Blixus turned his head slowly and looked at Mavis. "What were you doing with Wink's ring?"

"All right, fine," said Mavis. "I took it. I loved him. He dumped me. I killed him. Mr. Tunnel helped me. I'm proud of what I did. One less annoying detective in the world."

Veins stood out all over Blixus's neck and his face went bright red. He looked like some sort of Halloween character. "You what?" he bellowed. He made the fist again, pulled back his arm, and hit Mavis in the face.

"No!" screamed Nick, grabbing for his father.

"Get off me," said Blixus, and kicked Nick in the shins. Nick yelped and fell to the ground.

"Nick!" yelled Taffeta, running to the boy. Amanda felt a pang of jealousy.

"You stupid cow," said Blixus. "I didn't authorize you to kill him."

"Since when do I need *your* permission?" spat Mavis.

Suddenly Editta stepped up and said to Mavis, "You never should have done that without asking him. He's your lord and master."

"Are you insane?" said Mavis, now going for Editta. "What century are you living in, voodoo girl?"

Nigel was growling and Amanda was shaking with just about every emotion she'd ever felt and David and Editta and Ivy were screaming and Harry was egging them all on like a rabid boxing fan and Simon and Professor Kindseth were throwing themselves at Blixus and the roommates were running around in circles and all of a sudden there was a bang. Everyone stopped moving except Mavis, who fell to the ground. Her chest was covered with blood and Taffeta was standing there with a smoking gun.

"Mum!" Nick screamed, and ran to Mavis. He knelt down and began compressing her chest.

Blixus shoved him off, said, "This is your fault," looked down at Mavis, and kicked her.

Taffeta turned and ran down the tunnel with the roommates following.

Professor Kindseth started after her but Blixus stopped him. "Let her go," he said. "She's useless anyway."

Amanda couldn't believe Moriarty wasn't pursuing his wife's murderer, for at this point it was murder. Mavis was dead.

Blixus turned to his son and said, "You brought that Taffeta girl around. You should have known what she was like. This is on your head."

The Legatum group was aghast. Even Harry seemed to find Blixus's behavior inexplicable. His wife had just been murdered by some teenager in front of his eyes and he was blaming *Nick*?

"Where did she get the gun?" said Blixus.

"How should I know?" said Nick.

"Get out of my sight," said Blixus. "Go get the others and put everyone in the brig."

Blixus rummaged around and found some thick rope and plastic ties. "Editta," he said, and the girl joined him. "Here." He threw her the plastic ties. "Make it snappy."

Editta bound the captives' hands while Blixus roped them together. Ivy pleaded with her, but Editta wouldn't listen. Simon just gave her a dirty look.

The main living area opened into the small space Blixus had referred to as the brig, and the criminals pushed Amanda and her group into it just as Nick returned with two more captives: Clive and Holmes. Their hands had been bound as well. The criminals and Editta—not David, for whatever reason—shoved them into the space, tied them to the other prisoners, and rolled some boulders into the "door" to keep them there, using ramps to get the rocks to the higher levels. Then they moved heavy pots of gold in front of the boulders, and *then* Amanda heard them erecting an electric fence. She, Ivy, Nigel, Simon, Professor Kindseth, Harry, Clive, and Holmes were prisoners in the tunnels.

39

SO THAT'S HOW HE GOT THE COINS

Amanda was overjoyed to see the two boys, even if they were Blixus's prisoners, even if her feelings for Holmes were complicated, and even if Nick had bound the two of them together like Siamese twins. No doubt he'd done that on purpose.

"Scapulus! Clive! Are you all right?" She wanted to hug them but she couldn't move.

"More or less," said Clive.

"We're okay," said Holmes.

"What happened to you?" said Simon, trying to turn around and look at Clive, who was behind him. "You disappeared from the zoo."

"I was kidnapped," said Clive. He seemed tired. "Taffeta and some of her friends chloroformed me and dragged me into a zookeeper's van. When I woke up I saw these mynah birds in the back. At first I didn't realize they were birds. I thought I was hearing the bad guys talking."

"What did they say?" said Ivy.

"They were talking all about gold and bees and King Arthur," said Clive. "It was wild."

"Ha," said Harry. "I'd like to have seen that."

"What's he doing here?" said Clive.

"Long story," said Amanda, Ivy, and Simon together.

"What did they want with you?" said Amanda.

"My acoustic levitator," said Clive. "Taffeta wants me to make more of them. She saw *him*," he pointed to Harry, "use it to open the trove. He's the one who took it."

Those who could see him looked daggers at Harry. Ivy signaled her disapproval by blowing a raspberry. Nigel pricked up his ears. It would have been funny under other circumstances.

"You breached the trove?" Ivy said.

"It was no big deal," said Harry. "Bunch of old scraps."

"Old scraps!" said Professor Kindseth. "Why, I ought to throw you in a tank full of sharks. Do you realize what you've done?"

"What?" said Harry sullenly.

"You've just about ruined us!" said the teacher.

"It was worth it," said Harry. "That girl is awesome."

Simon wriggled around so he could see Harry. He seemed to be assessing whether he could reach him. Then he moved back, shook his head, and said, "You're a loser."

"What about the acoustic levitator?" said Amanda. "Clive, you haven't—you didn't—"

"Not yet," said Clive. "They've been feuding among themselves. I've had a reprieve."

"What happened to you, Scapulus?" said Simon.

"After the rainbow hit me?" said Holmes. He seemed all charged up. "It's strange. It packed quite a wallop at first, but I recovered quickly. I'm not sure why."

"Thank goodness," said Ivy.

"When I was in hospital…" he gave Amanda an uncomfortable look—what she could see of it anyway. She couldn't stand thinking about what had gone on there. Now she knew that he'd heard her say she loved him. She wished she'd kept her mouth shut. "I realized I had to do something. I couldn't let that hacker get the better of us, so I went looking for him. Or her."

"You mean you still don't know who it is?" said Simon.

"Unfortunately no," said Holmes. "I thought he might be in London, so I went to the train station and they grabbed me."

"We followed you there," said Amanda. "Thrillkill hacked your phone. By the time we got there you were gone."

"I forgot to turn blocking on," said Holmes. "I guess for once that was a good thing."

There was a pause.

"Mavis is dead," said Simon.

"We heard the bang," said Clive. "We were wondering what was going on."

Simon explained what had happened. Even though Holmes was no fan of Nick's, he expressed sorrow at the loss of the boy's mother and his father's treatment of him.

"That man is heartless," said Ivy.

"He's a sociopath," said Professor Kindseth.

"We did witness Mavis's confession, though," said Simon. "Now we know for sure that she killed Wink."

"So does David," said Amanda.

"Poor David," said Ivy.

"Poor Editta," said Amanda. "She's been brainwashed."

"Not so much," said Simon. "She was always like this."

"Simon!" said the girls.

"She's always been nuts," he said. "You know that."

Amanda sighed. "This is no time to argue about Editta. We have to get out of here."

"What do you suggest?" said Harry.

Everyone looked at him. No one cared what he thought, even though the question made sense.

"We have to get free," said Amanda. "These ropes are awfully tight. But if we can get our hands loose, we should be able to undo them. I like your toothpaste, Simon."

"Oh, brother," said Simon. "Not that again."

"No, you smell good," she said.

"You guys are all wet," said Clive, looking around as best he could. "And muddy."

"It's raining really hard," said Amanda.

"I have an idea," said Ivy. "Nigel, come here." Fortunately no one had thought to bind the dog. He bounded over to Ivy and wagged his tail. "Bite," said Ivy, attempting to shove a roped arm into the dog's face. Nigel moved his mouth close to the rope and started to chomp at it.

"You're nuts," said Harry. "He can't bite through all these ropes."

"He doesn't have to, yoyo," said Simon. "One will do. How did you ever get into Legatum anyway?"

"Once I'm free, I can back up to one of you and you can undo my wrists," said Ivy.

"Good thinking," said Clive. "I want to be your lab partner next time."

"If there is a next time," said Amanda.

"There will be," said Professor Kindseth.

While Nigel was working on the rope Simon said, "What's going on with all these coins?"

"Which ones?" said Holmes. "The gold or the silver?"

"The gold ones," said Harry.

"Shut up," said the others together.

"What about the King Arthur coins?" said Amanda. Obviously Blixus had them. He'd been tossing them about. She wondered how many there were.

"The farmer discovered them," said Holmes. "He was digging a well. He wanted to sell them but didn't know how. He got drunk at the pub and started asking people how to do it. Apparently Crocodile heard him and stole them. The farmer didn't report the theft because he discovered that it's illegal to keep historical artifacts."

"But we didn't find any coins in Crocodile's flat," said Amanda.

"No," said Holmes. "Blixus stole them."

"Then how did Wink end up with one?" said Ivy.

"Wiffle saw the coins through Crocodile's window. He broke in and managed to steal one of them while Crocodile was out. He was probably going to use it as evidence."

"But you can't use stolen evidence in court," said Amanda. Wink would know that. Was she missing something?

"No," said Holmes. "I don't know what Wink was thinking when he did that. But somehow he found out about the farm and went out there, and that was when he hid the lockbox in the haystack."

"No doubt Blixus killed Crocodile to get the coins then," said Simon.

"Yes," said Holmes. "When he got out of Strangeways he went to see Crocodile about the bee thefts. He was the one who put him up to them, of course. He looked through the window, overheard Crocodile talking to himself about the coins, and decided he wanted them. Boy, did he want them. You wouldn't believe."

"What do you mean?" said Simon.

"That man is crazy," said Holmes. "He figured he had found Camelot. He wants to set up his own round table, build a castle, and become the new Arthur."

This didn't sound like the Blixus Amanda knew. He was a technician, as logical as they came. That kind of talk was more up Editta's alley. "You have got to be kidding. He thinks he's King Arthur?"

"Or will be soon," said Clive. "It's unbelievable."

"Of course he killed Crocodile and took the coins," said Simon. "

"Yes," said Holmes. "He found the farm and the tunnels, killed the farmer, and set up down here. What a lunatic. We heard him call Mavis Guinevere."

"That's insane," said Amanda. If it weren't so personal the story would make a great film. Come to think of it, Blixus would make an amazing cinema villain.

"What about the gold coins then?" said Simon.

"I'm not sure about those," said Holmes. "Clive, do you know?"

"No," said Clive. "They're still a mystery."

"Does he have the *Bible*?" said Professor Kindseth.

"I don't know," said Holmes.

"Can't tell," said Clive. "He's so obsessed with King Arthur, that's all he talks about."

"What were Philip and Gavin doing here?" said Simon.

"Don't know that either," said Clive. "They seem to be tight with Taffeta."

Harry started to say something, but Simon's half of a dirty look stopped him.

"And you don't know who the hacker is?" said Amanda.

"No," said Holmes. "I—"

Suddenly a light appeared in the middle of the cavern. As they watched, it sparkled like the rainbows and became a hologram. A young boy with long dark hair was sitting behind a laptop, sneering at them. He looked about eleven.

"I do," he said.

40

HOLMES VS. MORIARTY

The mysterious boy in the hologram looked straight at Holmes and said, "Holmesy! How's it hanging?"

"Who are you?" said Holmes.

"You know perfectly well who I am," he said. "We've been chatting for weeks now."

"You're the hacker?" said Amanda. "You're just a kid."

"I think you'll find that my son is much more than just a kid," yelled Blixus from behind the boulders.

"Your *son!*" gasped Amanda. "I forgot he had another son," she said low so Blixus couldn't hear. But the boy did.

"Hugh Moriarty at your service," he said. "You must be that buffoon Lestrade."

"She's not a buffoon," said Holmes. Amanda was surprised, and pleased, that he'd defend her.

"What's this?" said Hugh. "Do I detect a love interest for Holmesy here?"

"He's as bad as his father," Ivy whispered.

"Oh, much worse," said Hugh, who had obviously heard. "My father is a pansy. Speaking of my father, Dad? Come and get this dog. He's going to bite through the ropes."

Amanda's heart sank. If Blixus hurt Nigel she'd be devastated. And what that would do to Ivy she didn't want to contemplate. Of course they'd have to figure out another way to get free, but that was the least of it.

"Doesn't matter," said Blixus through the boulders. "They can't get out."

"No, of course not," said Hugh. "If they try I'll just zap them with one of my rainbows."

"You," said Amanda. "You've been making all the rainbows."

"But of course," said Hugh. "Aren't they beautiful?"

Amanda wondered if a little psychology might work on this arrogant boy. "Not especially," she said. "I could do much better."

"Don't try that with me," said Hugh. "I'm not my brother. Oh, did you know, Holmesy, that your girlfriend there can wrap my brother around her little finger? He's weak. I'm not. And by the way, Harry, take note. Never get involved with a scheming woman. I'm surprised you'd let yourself be taken in like that."

Harry snorted. "I wasn't taken in, bozo. I used her, then threw her away. You'll understand when you're older."

"You're a git," said Hugh snidely.

"Your rainbows suck," said Clive.

"Oh really, rock boy?" said Hugh, boring his eyes into Clive's. "I suppose you think they're just rainbows then."

"I don't know what that means," said Clive.

"No, you wouldn't, would you, pea brain," said Hugh, and the hologram winked out.

"Blixus's other son," said Ivy. "I forgot about him too."

"What a creep," said Harry.

"Look who's talking," said Amanda.

"Shut up, *Lestrade*," said Harry.

"How's Nigel coming with that rope?" whispered Holmes.

"Almost there," said Ivy quietly. "Hurry up, Nigel. And…he's through." Nigel pulled the rope with his teeth. "Good, Nigel. Now I can turn around. Professor, can you undo this plastic thing?"

344

"Delighted, Miss Halpin," said Professor Kindseth in a low voice. Ivy moved her back to his back and the teacher worked at the tie with his fingers. "Slippery thing. This will take a minute."

"Where do you suppose he is?" whispered Simon.

"You mean Hugh?" said Amanda as softly as she could. "No idea."

"I suspect he's with relatives," said Holmes, making circles with his head. That wasn't a bad idea. Amanda could feel her neck and shoulders getting stiff too. "He may be a genius but he's too young to live alone. I'm guessing he's in London somewhere."

"Is there a way to trace that hologram back to the source?" said Simon.

"There has to be," said Holmes. "And I can do it if I can get to a phone. Anyone have one? They took ours."

"I have one," said Simon. "It's in my back pocket."

"I'll undo your hands, Simon," said Ivy. "I'm free now."

Ivy freed Simon's hands, then moved on to the others. Simon took his phone out of his pocket and gave it to Holmes.

"I wonder when he's coming back," said Holmes. "I need the signal in order for this to work."

"Can you make him come back?" said Amanda.

"Actually, I think I can," said Holmes, pressing the screen and sliding his hand over it.

"That's impossible," said Simon.

"Not necessarily," said Holmes. "If Blixus has a connection to Hugh, I can bounce my signal off him and get there. Or Nick. His phone should work too. All I need to do is find a hole in those boulders and get a line of sight."

"I wish I had my acoustic levitator right now," said Clive.

"We'll find a chink in the boulders," said Holmes.

"Wait a minute," said Ivy. "Taffeta."

"What about her?" said Amanda.

"Her perfume," said Ivy. "Or whatever it is. It smells terrible. Nigel will be able to smell it through any cracks. It's still in the air out there. Come on, Nigel."

Ivy moved over to Harry, grabbed a handful of T-shirt, and stuck it in Nigel's nose. Then she walked him over to the wall of boulders and said, "Smell." Nigel snuffled and sniffled and moved all around the wall, standing up on his hind legs, getting back down, searching for the scent. Within thirty seconds he was standing on his hind legs again wagging his tail. He'd found a hole in the wall that was about as high as Amanda's shoulders.

"Brilliant," said Holmes quietly, looking through. "Thanks, Nigel. Now I need to get line of sight to one of the phones out there."

He lowered his head and looked through the hole, then moved around. "See anything?" said Simon.

"I think I might," said Holmes. "Yes. There's a phone lying on the workbench. I don't know whose it is, but as long as it's turned on it shouldn't matter. I've also got a special extra something for him."

He fiddled around with the phone, then placed it in the crack. After about twenty seconds the phone started to hum. The noise got louder and louder and then suddenly the hologram was back, tethered to Holmes's phone.

"Hey!" said Hugh. "What the—"

"Hughie, dahlink," said Amanda. "Back so soon?" Ivy and Simon giggled.

"I see you've discovered one of my little tricks, Holmesy," said Hugh. "You won't be able to control it, though. It's not something you should be fooling around with."

Suddenly a bolt flew out of Holmes's phone and made straight for Hugh.

"Ouch," he said. "What was that?"

Holmes looked triumphant. "Oh, just a little trick of mine. Like it?" He held the phone up as if it were a weapon.

"Is that all you've got?" said Hugh smiling wickedly.

"What's going on in there?" came Blixus's voice.

"Nothing, Daddy," said Hugh, lifting his chin in Blixus's direction. "Go back to Mummy."

"Your mummy is dead," said Amanda.

"Very funny," said Hugh, looking at her as if she were an ant.

"No, she's serious," said Simon. "Taffeta shot her."

"Don't make me laugh," said Hugh. Amanda thought she detected a note of fear in his voice, but it went by so fast she couldn't be sure.

"No, she's really dead," said Clive. "Ask your dad."

"Shut up," said Hugh. "You're tiresome, geology boy."

"Hugh, stop messing around now," said Blixus. "I need your help."

"Turn it off," whispered Amanda.

"But I've only just started," said Holmes.

"Just do it. I've got an idea."

Holmes turned off the phone and the hologram disappeared. "What is it?"

"You can zap Blixus and Nick. They won't be able to use the crystals to hurt us if you keep them busy. Then we can get out of here."

"Good plan," said Holmes, with eyes so warm they made her uncomfortable. "The only problem is that if they're not in front of the hole, I won't be able to hit them."

"Can you carom your beam off the walls?" she said, trying not to think about the way he was looking at her.

"I could if I knew where they were going to be at any given moment," said Holmes. "Oh, I see. You want me to use a heat-seeking beam. Excellent idea. I'll need to do a few calculations, though." He almost looked as if he was going to take her hand. Thankfully he didn't.

He started poking at Simon's phone and mumbling to himself. In a few minutes he looked up and said, "Ready."

"How sure are you that this will work?" said Ivy.

"Pretty sure," said Holmes.

"What if you miss?"

"What can he do to us that he can't already do?"

"Right," said Ivy. "Go on then."

Holmes put the phone to the crack. There was a whiz and a crackle and a moment later Blixus yelled, "Ow. What was that?"

"More," said Amanda.

Holmes grabbed the phone, twiddled something, and replaced it. The whizzing started again.

"Ouch!" yelled Nick. "Oh, it's you, Holmes. Tough guy, are you?"

Holmes zapped him again, the expression on his face frightening. Amanda had never seen him like this before. Why hadn't she understood that he could hate so much—and that it was her fault he did? Here had been this smart, self-assured, happy boy, and she'd turned him into a mess. What was wrong with her? Why was she always ruining everything?

Nick laughed. "So, Lestrade, I hear you think Holmes here is a dork. Or do you? I know you two were canoodling on that ridiculous tram in Windermere. Boy, you just love 'em and leave 'em, don't you?"

Holmes winced. Amanda was about to say something when Nick interrupted her.

"Just as I thought. I can hear the pain seeping through the rock. You gotta watch out for her, Holmes. I'd be careful if I were you too, Binkle, or you'll be next."

Holmes zapped him again, harder, then harder again. The bursts were no longer controlled. It was as if he was letting all his wrath out and it was concentrated on one point: Nick Moriarty. Nick shrieked with each blast. Editta screamed, "Nick!"

There was silence for a moment, and then Nick yelled, "Get away from me, Editta. I don't want you. I never wanted you. I don't care what my dad thinks of you. You're a lunatic."

"But I love you," screamed Editta.

"Get lost."

"You're an idiot, Editta," said David. "Go stick a pin in a doll or something."

"Shut up, David," Editta screamed. "You're just like your father."

"What's that supposed to mean?" said David.

"Shut up, all of you," yelled Blixus. "Someone help me. I've broken my arm."

"Blixus!" yelled Editta. "Here I am."

The friends on the other side of the wall looked at each other. Editta had truly left them behind. What was really weird was that she seemed to be tighter with Blixus than with Nick.

"Lestrade," said Nick. "See what you're missing? You could have had all this if you'd just killed your father."

Amanda was so angry she wanted to walk right through the rock and punch him in the nose.

"What did your parents do to you to make you like this?" she said.

Nick laughed. "You wish you had parents like mine. Come on, Lestrade. You know you love the dark side. Isn't that what you told me?"

"I said no such thing."

"Oh, I don't know about that. I seem to remember you telling me that Professor Moriarty was romantic."

"Shut up."

"Did you really say that?" said Clive.

Amanda was horrified. Nick had taken her words out of context and made her look like a monster in front of her friends. "I didn't know anything then. I'm a different person now."

"You were really like that?" said Harry. "Good for you."

Amanda screamed, "I wasn't! He fooled me. And you're just envious, Harry Sheriff. You wish you could do something really well—anything other than flex your muscles. You're nothing but a spoiled brat. You're not even that good looking."

Simon, Clive, and Professor Kindseth stood there with their mouths open. Ivy screamed for them to shut up, then dissolved into tears. Nigel whined.

Holmes gave Blixus and Nick another whap. This time he turned up the juice even higher and Editta started to scream again. "They're turning colors. Stop it, Scapulus! They can't move. You're killing them!"

But Holmes couldn't—or wouldn't—stop. He let Nick have it over and over again. Each time Nick let out a scream so plaintive that Amanda wanted to drag Holmes away. Finally, in a lull between grunts Nick said, "She's quite a woman, isn't she, Holmes? Worth going to prison for, do you think? If I die, that's exactly what will happen to you."

Holmes faltered, then broke off the signal. Amanda was furious. A moment ago she'd felt sorry for Nick. Now she wanted Holmes to keep going, to prove to Nick that he was wrong. This wasn't her fault, Nick wasn't going to die, and Holmes wasn't going to prison. He shouldn't let Nick get to him like that. Except it was her fault—it was *all* her fault. She'd should have kept herself to herself, remained a one-man band like back in L.A. Relationships just messed everything up.

Suddenly the cavern filled with a tremendous hologram. Hugh's fingers were poised over the keys of his laptop and he was laughing.

"So that's the way you want it, Holmesy? Let's see what you think of this."

He pressed a key and a purple rainbow slowly filled the space, arcs shooting out of it in different colors. The air crackled with electricity. Nigel screamed as a bolt of red hit him in the snout. Green tendrils snaked out and wrapped themselves around Ivy, squeezing her until she could hardly breathe. Yellow, blue, and orange filaments attacked Harry, Clive, Professor Kindseth, and Simon. Then silver light shot out of the rainbow and encircled Amanda, choking her and making it almost impossible for her to see.

Holmes, a riot of flashing colors, was holding his phone and sending bolts of electricity into the hologram. Hugh was obviously feeling something because he kept wincing and at one point he cried out. In between, though, he was laughing his head off as he manipulated the rainbow, which was now pulsing and looked as if it was getting ready to explode.

"Get out of here, Dad," said Hugh. "You don't want to be here for this." Amanda could hear crashes in the next room. "Here's some motivation for you. Zap!"

"Hugh, you're hurting him!" yelled Editta.

"Nonsense," said Hugh. "It's good for him."

There was another crash on the other side of the boulders and Blixus screamed.

"Stop it!" yelled Editta.

"You too, Nicky," said Hugh, and blasted Nick.

"You little prat!" yelled Nick. "What is wrong with you? You almost killed me."

"Grab the gold," yelled Blixus, and Amanda could hear clinking as coins were thrown around. Then the two Moriartys and the two runaways ran out of the camp and down the tunnel, leaving Mavis's body behind.

Now the battle between Holmes and Hugh escalated. Beams flew everywhere, ricocheting off the cavern's walls, ceiling, and floor. The entire cavern started to shake. On the other side of the boulders, first one rock, then another and another fell. What started as a trickle became an avalanche, and the chamber roared.

"It's caving in!" yelled Amanda, but her words were drowned out by the roaring of the rocks falling. In the hologram, Hugh was laughing like a maniac. "Stop it, Hugh! You're going to kill us." She turned to the others. "We'll never get out of here now."

"Good," he laughed. "You're no fun anyway. Goodbye kiddies. Too bad we didn't get to spend more time together."

"Stop it, Hugh!" yelled Professor Kindseth. "We'll make a deal with you."

"A deal?" said Hugh. "What kind of deal?"

"Let us out and we'll give you your own lab. You can have any equipment you need in exchange for a promise never to hurt anyone again."

"You bore me," said Hugh. "I don't need your stupid lab. I've got more money than I could ever want."

"Does this feel good to you?" said Amanda. "Hurting people?"

"Yes," said Hugh. "It feels wonderful. You should try it sometime, Lestrade. Oh no, wait. You already have. You broke poor Holmesy's heart."

Holmes let off a huge yellow bolt, which hit Hugh directly in the forehead. He laughed.

"Can you do that again?" he said. "I've got an itch."

"He's pure evil," said Ivy.

"Worse than Blixus," said Simon.

Holmes let go with a volley of beams that came at Hugh so fast you couldn't tell one from another. In return Hugh sent out angry balls of lightning, which intercepted Holmes's bolts and neutralized them. They went back and forth, back and forth, attacking, blocking, attacking and blocking again, until the room was filled with so much energy Amanda's skin started to buzz. Ivy and Clive had fallen, Nigel was cowering between them, and Simon was woozy. Professor Kindseth was struggling to stand up, and Harry was sitting in a corner looking spaced out. Only Holmes and Amanda were still operating at full capacity.

And then, as Amanda and Holmes watched, a figure entered the hologram, crept up behind Hugh, and hit him over the head with a black figurine. The hologram went dark, but the energy was still there, sparkling. Suddenly a flash of purple broke through the roof of the cavern, filling the space with the light of a perfect rainbow, then blue sky, and the faces of four firemen who had come to the rescue.

The hologram reappeared for a moment and the face of a beautiful dark-haired young girl appeared. She smiled, winked, and said, "No one hurts my brother." Then she and the hologram disappeared and the rescuers' ropes descended.

41

INSIGHT

Nigel was the most tricky of the captives to lift out of the cavern, but the firemen were able to throw down some kind of harness and Simon fixed him up. One by one the others were hoisted to safety and wrapped in blankets. Salty Pinchbeck and his partner were up top with their ambulance, as were several other paramedics with theirs. The group was loaded in and taken to the hospital.

As they rode in the ambulance, Simon turned to Amanda and said, "Who was that girl?"

"I have no idea," she said. "She referred to her brother, but she wasn't anybody's sister that we know of."

"No," said Simon. "And David doesn't have a sister, so she didn't mean him."

"It doesn't make any sense."

Simon laughed. "Maybe she got her signals crossed. Perhaps she was trying to rescue someone else who'd been trapped in a cavern."

"You don't think Hugh has done this to other people, do you?" said Amanda.

"I was joking," said Simon. "But come to think of it, we haven't heard from Thrillkill."

"I hope Hugh didn't get them too," said Amanda. "Let's see if we can raise them."

They both tried to get a video line to the others. The connection was still dead.

"I'm getting worried," said Amanda. "Maybe Blixus got them when he ran away."

"Or Taffeta," said Simon.

"Or Taffeta. Isn't she a piece of work though?"

"Yes," said Simon. "Do you suppose she's related to the Moriartys?"

"They didn't act like it. I have no idea who she is. Do you think Harry knows?"

"I don't think he knows much of anything, but we can try to get it out of him."

Harry did know, as it turned out. They spoke to him in Thrillkill's office, where Professor Mukherjee was detaining him. Despite the fact that the girl had been a student at the Moriartys' Schola Scleratorum, the school for criminals they'd established in the sugar factory, he'd become involved with her anyway. He wasn't bothered about where a girl came from as long as she was hot.

"What do you think will happen to him?" said Amanda afterwards.

"Expelled for sure," said Simon.

"Jail," said Clive.

"Maybe they'll put him in with Manny or Jackie," said Amanda.

"Ha!" said Simon. "That would be some justice anyway."

When Amphora saw Holmes return in one piece, she screamed and threw her arms around him. Amanda couldn't bear to look, so she climbed to the top floor and gazed out the Disguise classroom window. She should speak to him, of course. There was so much to clear up and apologize for, but that could come later, when she'd figured out exactly what to say.

Had things changed as a result of her seeing Nick? She wasn't sure. His life certainly had. Now that Mavis was dead nothing would be the same for him. Blixus was as mean as ever, and now their buffer was gone. Or had Mavis been as awful to her son as Blixus? Amanda realized she had no idea and might never know. But even if she did, it wouldn't affect what she'd say to Holmes. Now that he was with Amphora her hands were tied and she should find a way to forget him too. Great. Now she had two impossible problems to solve.

"We never discovered anything about the *Bible*," said Ivy when they'd all got together again. "Blixus was very cagey about it."

"I don't think he has it," said Clive. "He'd have been lording it over us if he did." He looked almost back to normal, except for a scrape he'd got on his face. Amanda was glad nothing worse had happened to him, like being pecked to death by mynah birds.

"He's not exactly subtle, is he?" said Ivy.

"If he doesn't have it, then where is it?" said Amanda. "It's not in the pit where David threw it. That's been dragged and searched a million times. You don't think Philip and Gavin took it, do you?"

"From the way they looked in those caverns I'm guessing no," said Simon. "They didn't seem too cocky."

That they didn't. They'd had weird expressions on their faces, as if they were afraid of Blixus. They even seemed a bit intimidated by Taffeta. Some tough guys.

"Perhaps Mavis retrieved it and never told Blixus," said Ivy. "Although how could she get it without him seeing?"

"Editta?" said Amanda.

"No way," said Simon. "She'd never jump into that pit."

"Eustace didn't come back and get it, did he?" said Clive.

"Impossible," said Amanda. Or was it? What did she really know about Eustace anyway? He seemed like a good guy, but she'd been fooled before.

"Then it's gone," said Simon. "End of story. Cross it off the list and forget about it."

"The teachers really will split then," said Ivy. "Unless Amanda and Scapulus can work a miracle with their film."

"OMG, the film!" said Amanda. "Is it even worth finishing now?"

"Of course it is," said Simon. "You should never give up hope. Say, let's see how your task list looks now."

Amanda brought up the list and read it off to everyone. She was flabbergasted to see that she had accomplished most of the items on it—with help, of course.

1. Rescue Editta Sweetgum.
1. Find Philip Puppybreath and Gavin Niven.
2. Find out what the key discovered with Wink's body goes to.
3. Find the *Detective's Bible*.
4. Solve Wink Wiffle's murder.
5. Monitor Professor Redleaf's computer.
6. Find attorney and prepare for wrongful death lawsuit.
7. Make film about our options without the *Bible*.
8. Speak to David Wiffle.

"Well, number one's still there," said Clive, craning his neck so he could see Amanda's phone. "We didn't rescue Editta. We did find her, though. Of course now that she's run off, she's missing again."

"The same is true for Philip and Gavin," said Ivy. "Except they didn't run off with Blixus, they ran off with Taffeta."

"Seems we're not doing so well," said Simon, looking at Amanda's screen. "What's next?"

"We found the lockbox," said Amanda. "Cross off number two. Number three, the *Bible*, we've discussed. Should I cross it off?"

"I don't think Thrillkill will be ready to give up," said Simon. "Keep it."

"Okay," said Amanda, adjusting the various items. "But I can cross off number four. We solved Wink's murder."

"And number five," said Clive. "We've more than monitored Professor Redleaf's computer. You can get rid of that."

Amanda edited some more. "Number six. That's done. Mr. Onion has taken on our defense. There's still the preparation to do, though. I'll change it."

She deleted the "Find attorney" part of the task, leaving "prepare for wrongful death lawsuit." Then she looked back at the list. There were only two items left.

"The film. Can't cross that off. It's close, though."

"Thrillkill spoke to David," said Simon. "Cross off number eight."

"Poor David," said Ivy. She was starting to sound like a broken record.

"Pretty good for a few days' work," said Simon. "Except that some things are more messed up than before. The Punitori are leaving and Thrillkill, Fern, and Gordon might be missing."

"We need to go back and look for them," said Ivy. "Do you think the cave-in reached them?"

"Highly unlikely," said Clive.

"Are you sure? I'm really worried."

"Ninety-nine point nine percent," said Clive, sounding like Simon.

"I'm going to hold you to that," said Ivy.

"What about Blixus and Taffeta?" said Amanda.

"No point running after them when we've got detectives missing," said Simon logically. "Finding them has to be our number one priority."

"And Mavis's body?" said Amanda.

"It'll have to stay there," said Clive. "It'll take ages to dig through that rock."

"What about Hugh?" said Amanda.

"When we find Thrillkill we'll make a new list," said Simon.

Mrs. Wiffle and Mrs. Sweetgum would have to be told about their children, of course. The kids supposed one of the teachers could do that, probably Professor Kindseth since he'd actually seen them. Amanda didn't envy him. The task was a live grenade. At least the two women would know that their children were alive and relatively healthy. And if the detectives could find them once, they could find them again, so there was that encouragement for him to deliver. Somehow, though, she didn't think that would calm them down. Both women would explode and probably file a suit against him too.

Suddenly she remembered that she hadn't finished her assignment for Darius Plover. Fortunately she knew exactly what she was going to do with it.

She excused herself, ran to her room, booted up her computer, and stared at the document she'd started, rereading the last few sentences. She was surprised at how easily the words conjured up vivid images in her mind. It was as if they were living things, each one bursting with energy. Each word, each phrase was filled to capacity with potential. They were alive!

And then she realized what she had to do in order to finish her assignment. The villains needed the same kind of energy as those words. They needed to brim with life, burst off the page with creativity and will and purpose. She closed her eyes and let the images and the feelings they stirred wash over her, and she knew. The characters, all of them—good guys, bad guys, and everyone in between—needed what she'd seen in Nick's eyes. But what was it?

She could feel whatever it was, recognize it, but she couldn't name it. If she couldn't name it she couldn't use it. Or could she? What was it about Nick that made him so different from Blixus or Mavis or Holmes? She concentrated, picturing the eyes that held whatever it was, the sky blue irises with their little flecks of black and the dark lashes that framed them, but that didn't help. She thought about the way they sparkled when he was excited, and the way they held so still when he was concentrating, but that didn't help either. She'd seen all of that a thousand times in a thousand different people. It wasn't a big deal.

What had she seen in the tunnels? Why had she felt that connection with him even as he'd said ugly things? Why couldn't she let go? She must be as bad as Editta, falling for someone who wasn't real, cherry-picking the good things and ignoring the bad. Nick was an actor. He was a master of illusion. That was all it was: smoke and mirrors, sleight of hand. Whoop-de-doo. There was nothing really there at all.

And then, just as she was about to give up, another image popped into her head. It was Nick's eyes again, but this time she could more than see whatever it was. She could feel it, and she knew. She knew that she'd been missing what was behind them. It was as if he was lit from within, with a flame so powerful it couldn't be contained. He wasn't avaricious like his father, or power hungry like his brother, or angry like his mother, or single-minded like Holmes. He was driven by something else entirely, but what? She couldn't put her finger on whatever it was, but she knew that it should illuminate Darius's villains as well.

And then it came to her: Nick was at one with everything he did. He was always in the moment, not standing outside himself observing, the way Blixus did, or Hugh, or even Harry Sheriff. Whatever he did he was completely immersed in it—not in an obsessive way, but so that he was deeply, truly present. It might be good, bad, or something else, but it didn't matter, because it was all part of him and he was part of it.

He wasn't a villain at all. He was just Nick, with all his contradictions and complexities and complications. You couldn't sum him up because he was everything at once. No wonder he was so full of life.

Keeping this new insight in mind, Amanda began to work at the "Sand" scenes. Whenever she got stuck she'd think of the way Nick looked when she'd first caught sight of him in the tunnel. It was hard to put her feeling into words, and after flailing about with a thesaurus she finally gave up and let her subconscious take over. When she did she could see images of molten lava, twinkling stars, Japanese lanterns, and luminous sea creatures in her mind's eye. What made them so magnificent? She couldn't tell. They just were.

Then she got an idea. Like an actor preparing for a part, she became each thing. Instead of watching it, she crawled inside it, seeing what it saw, moving the way it moved. And then the words came tumbling out of her, and the characters sparkled, and they were all Nick.

When she had finished she felt so energized that she started to dance around the room. She swayed and jumped and twirled and leapt until she could dance no more. And then she sat down on her bed and stared out into space and it hit her.

Simon was right. She'd never escape Nick. He could become the worst villain on earth and it wouldn't matter. Whatever they shared was indelible, as much a part of her as her brain, or her heart, because it was life.

But if that was the case, what about Holmes? There was no doubt that her relationship with him was over, but her feelings were as strong as ever. How could she love two people at the same time, both of whom were off limits to her? Love was supposed to bring joy, not leave you at a dead end.

And yet for some reason, impossible questions and dead ends weren't important right now. All that mattered was that *she* live in the moment. She copied her work to Darius's cloud server and pinged him. He'd either like what she'd done or he wouldn't. And life would go on.

The kids asked Professor Kindseth to drive them back to the farm so they could look for Thrillkill, Fern, and Gordon, but he declined. "We have to mount a proper rescue," he said.

"We can do this, Professor," said Amanda.

"Not this time. You've been through enough. And we don't need to lose more of you."

Amanda wanted to protest, but it did seem that the teacher had the situation under control, and they had plenty of other tasks demanding their attention. She didn't fight him.

"Despite the, er, delicate situation among the teachers, Professors Buck, Ducey, Feeney, and Snool have agreed to go," said Professor Kindseth. "If anyone can find them, they can."

He was right. They were the toughest teachers at Legatum. She just hoped Blixus or Taffeta hadn't caught up with Thrillkill and her friends.

"What do you think about this King Arthur stuff, sir?" she said. "Is it genuine?"

"The numismatist certainly seemed to think so. We're going to turn the coin over to the British Museum and they'll send their archaeologists to the farm. As I understand, Dr. Halpin is going to consult as well."

"Yes," said Ivy. "Dad told me I could observe."

"If they actually have found Camelot, do you think Blixus would come back?" said Amanda. "He seems to think it's his."

"Yeah, that's nuts, isn't it?" said Simon. "What a git."

"When you think of it, if Blixus is Arthur and Mavis was Guinevere, then Wink was Lancelot," said Clive. Guinevere, of course, was Arthur's faithless wife, who fell in love with Sir Lancelot, a Knight of the Round Table and Arthur's greatest champion. It was said that their love affair brought about the end of Arthur's kingdom. Amanda found the story incredibly sad. She'd watched the movie "Camelot" about ten times.

"Who's Merlin?" said Ivy. Everyone was enthralled with Arthur's wizard. Amanda wasn't sure who was a better one: Merlin, or Gandalf from *The Lord of the Rings*.

"Hugh," said Simon.

"You got that right," said Clive. "The kid is a wizard."

"What about Taffeta?" said Amanda. "Morgan le Fey?" Morgan le Fey was a powerful enchantress. Amanda didn't like her because she was always plotting against Guinevere and Lancelot.

"Pretty good," said Simon. "She's a sorceress, that one."

"You know, now that I think of it, I'm sure I saw her at Schola Sceleratorum when I was there," said Amanda. "I thought she looked familiar."

"Wait a minute. Her name is Taffeta, right?" said Ivy.

"Yes," said Amanda.

"OMG," said Ivy. "I think she's Taffeta Tasmania, the girl who was expelled from Legatum for telling an outsider about the school," said Ivy.

"The one Editta was so worried about?" said Amanda.

"Yes," said Ivy. "The one she said was bad luck. That's ironic. She was right. I wonder where she went."

"Dunno," said Simon, "but she'd better stay clear of Blixus. Taffeta Tasmania. What a name."

Amanda was glad that Simon hadn't mentioned Nick. *He* had been the one to bring Taffeta into the Moriartys' organization, and the girl had turned around and killed his mother. Amanda couldn't imagine what he must be feeling. She could, however, picture what Blixus would do to him, and that horrified her. That the man had blamed Nick and let Taffeta go rather than grieve over the loss of his wife said a lot about him. However, the idea of trying to intervene and save Nick was ludicrous. Even if she could, which was unlikely, he'd just sneer at her.

There was something else to consider, though. Mavis, Nick's mother, had been involved with Wink, a detective. She'd loved him passionately. If Mavis had ended up with Wink, Nick wouldn't have been born. Either would David, or Hugh. Surely Nick had worked that one out. How did he feel about it? If it hadn't been for Wink leaving his mother, he wouldn't exist. Should he be grateful to a detective for his existence? Would he mourn his mother even more, or would he be repulsed by the thought that she had once loved his enemy?

How did David feel about all this? He'd lost his father, been betrayed by his roommates, been abandoned by his best friend, destroyed the school's most important possession, and caused the teachers to split. Who could bear that kind of burden? What would he do now—stay with the family of his father's killer? Or would he and Nick bond over their debt to fortune?

Blixus had been furious with Wink when he found out that Mavis was once involved with him. Since he couldn't take his anger out on a dead man, he'd turned to David. But David was also a symbol of Blixus's victory: Blixus had been the one to win Mavis in the end, not Wink. If Wink had prevailed, David wouldn't exist. So in a way David served as a reminder of Blixus's potency.

The whole thing was so complicated it made Amanda's head spin. Her own life was simple by comparison. Lots of people's parents were divorced. So what if her mother was dating a crook and her father had run off to be a monk? She could handle that. She'd coped with much more and would continue to do so.

As she was breaking her head on these thoughts and the other kids drifted away, Holmes entered the room and sat down next to her. She knew they had to finish the film, but that wasn't what was on his mind.

"Amanda," he said, and stopped. He seemed to be finding it difficult to look at her—again.

"Don't say anything," she said.

"No. I suppose it wouldn't be right. It's just—what you said."

"Ssssh," she said. She looked into his eyes. "I'm sorry."

"You don't need to—" He raised his head and met her eyes. "Just be careful. Promise me you will."

"Of course." She looked down at her hands, then back up at him. "Scapulus—"

He put a finger to her lips and shook his head. Then he rose and walked out of the room.

42

UNHAPPY ENDINGS

Drusilla Canoodle was having a tea break when Amanda ran into her. The dean of admissions said that the rescue team had left and she hoped Headmaster Thrillkill would return soon. In addition to the other issues that were facing him, a parent had just phoned and said she'd been approached by a group of teachers. They were opening a new detective school in Scotland and wanted her daughter to attend.

"Oh no," said Amanda. "They're really doing it."

"I'm afraid so," said the dean. Her phone rang and she answered. "Yes, Mrs. Pomfritter. Thank you for letting me know. No, Legatum Continuatum is not closing its doors. Yes, we will be here in the fall, and forever. Well, yes, you are closer to the new location, but—" She listened for a moment with a worried expression on her face. "If you'll just give us a chance—yes, I'll have him phone you. Goodbye."

"That didn't sound good," said Amanda.

"No. Dreidel Pomfritter's mother said she'd received a high-pressure pitch from the Punitori. That's the second call in twenty minutes. She thinks Scotland is the future and wants to withdraw her son."

"Then it's too late for the film," said Amanda.

"Never say never, Miss Lester," said Dean Canoodle.

Just then Professor Also walked by. "What film? Do you mean the one we talked about?"

Amanda and Drusilla Canoodle exchanged looks. "Yes, Professor. It's almost finished."

"I shall miss that," she said. "I don't suppose you're giving sneak peeks?"

"Of course," said Amanda, glancing at the dean. "Is now a good time?"

"It's the only time," said Professor Also. "I'm afraid I'm on my way out. I won't be returning."

"Come with me," said Amanda, and led the history of detectives teacher to the dining room. On the way they passed Professor Pargeter.

"Honoria, Miss Lester is about to give me a sneak peek of her new film. Would you like to join us?"

Professor Pargeter looked skeptical. "I was just leaving, Winnie. I don't think—"

"Nonsense," said Professor Also. "Two seconds. She's terrific."

"Very well," said Professor Pargeter with no enthusiasm whatsoever, and followed the two down the hall.

They sat down at Amanda and Holmes's table and Amanda started rolling her rough cut. She had managed to patch in the first and third of Ivy's songs but not the second one.

"It's not finished," she said as the teachers watched.

"We can visualize," said Professor Pargeter ungraciously.

As the film played, several people came up to the table and looked to see what was going on, including Professors Peaksribbon and Stegelmeyer. Soon there was a crowd. By the time the film had finished, Professor Also was humming along with the music and Professor Pargeter was sniffling. Everyone clapped and Amanda beamed.

Then Professor Pargeter got up and said, "Well done, Miss Lester. But futile. We're leaving."

"I'm afraid she's right," said Professor Peaksribbon. He seemed so sad. "Nicely done, though."

Everyone filed out of the room and Amanda was left sitting alone. Holmes came in and sat across from her.

"It didn't work," she said, her voice catching.

"We tried," he said, placing his hand on hers. She jumped. She didn't dare reciprocate but she didn't want to ask him to move. "We tried really hard."

"Yes. It was good, wasn't it?" Her hand was shaking. She was sure he could tell.

"It was the best thing I've ever seen, Amanda." He was smiling. *Please don't look at our hands. I can't—I just can't.*

Amanda's phone rang. She was so relieved she wanted to whoop. Holmes removed his hand so she could answer.

It was Mr. Onion. "Guess what," he said. The line was terrible.

"I'm fresh out of guesses," she said, holding up a finger so Holmes wouldn't leave. As long as he didn't get too close, she wanted him to stay. Maybe he would tell her that the film had worked after all, that the teachers had been so moved that they'd changed their minds. That everything would go back to the way it was. "Tell me."

"Doodle is out," said Mr. Onion.

"Excuse me?"

"Doodle—the warden," he said in a louder voice. "He's been transferred. The new warden says it's okay to give Manny a guitar."

Great. Couldn't he have transferred in a week ago? "We don't need him anymore."

"What's that?" the lawyer said. Static crackled through the line.

"Manny. We found Blixus. We don't need him." She was practically yelling. Holmes started to laugh and she broke into a grin. Why couldn't the two of them be like this all the time?

"Where is Blixus then?" said Mr. Onion. She could hardly understand him with all that background noise.

"I, uh, I don't know."

"But you just said you found him."

"We did. He ran away."

"I can't hear you, Amanda. Did you just say he ran away?"

There was a huge burst and Amanda had to move the phone away from her ear. She waited a moment. Holmes shrugged.

"Yes, he ran away," she yelled into the phone.

Suddenly the static was gone. 'Then you do need him," said the lawyer. "Manny. You still need him."

"I guess we do after all. Do you really think he would know, though? Blixus has gone, uh, underground. They might not be in communication."

"It can't hurt to try. Tomorrow at 9:00? I'll pick you up. That enough time to find an instrument?"

"More than enough," she said. "See you then."

"What was all that about?" said Holmes when she'd hung up.

"I'm going to prison," she said. "Again."

After Amanda had phoned Ivy and asked if she could borrow her guitar, she turned to Holmes and said, "There's something I don't understand." She was starting to believe that there was nothing he didn't know—just like his ancestor. But this Holmes was different. He wasn't smug.

"What's that?"

"Why purple?"

"You mean why were the rainbows purple?"

"Yes."

He sat back and thought a moment. "Purple doesn't have its own wavelength. It's a combination of red and blue, short and long wavelengths. It isn't part of the spectrum."

This was interesting. She knew a lot about color and wavelengths from all the film lighting she did. She'd even fiddled around trying to make different shades of purple light. What she didn't understand was why a pure color wouldn't have worked just as well.

"Why does that matter?" she said. "That purple isn't its own color."

"There's a theory that some non-spectral-colored light can be used as a sort of x-ray to detect hidden structures," he said. "Hugh must have discovered that purple light works well to find gold, or quartz, or both. Purple is harder to work with than spectral colors, though. You have to get just the right proportions. That may be why he was experimenting so much."

"I get that. I've always struggled with purple lighting. What about the deformations on Professor Redleaf's screen?"

"I don't know. I've never seen anything like it. He's a genius, that's for sure."

So was he. Holmes could do anything Hugh could and more, and would probably soon have to. Amanda couldn't imagine who or what else could stop him. Unless that girl...

Who was she anyway? Blixus had only the two kids so she wasn't Hugh and Nick's sister. The question was nagging at her. Surely *she* didn't have anything to do with the rainbows or the gold. The gold! Where had those leprechaun coins come from anyway?

"You don't think Hugh was actually creating those leprechaun coins, do you?" she said.

"Let's be clear," said Holmes. "The gold creates the rainbows, which in turn can be used to detect gold. They cannot *create* gold."

"But could he have made the coins some other way?"

"You mean out of the gold ore?"

"Yes."

"It would be very involved. Even if he could find raw nuggets, he'd have to process them, and shaping them into the coins would require precise work, not to mention the right equipment. But you can only retrieve so much that way. Normally you have to do a lot of work to separate the gold ore from the material around it. I can't imagine how he could do all that from his computer."

"Those men at the zoo then—"

"What men at the zoo?"

That's right. He hadn't been there. How would he know?

"When Simon and Clive and I were investigating the rainbows there, we saw gold at the ends of them. Some men were collecting it."

She expected him to look aghast, but he took her words calmly. "Gold at the end of the rainbow. Who knew? Blixus's guys, no doubt."

The idea of Holmes accepting that there could be gold at the end of a rainbow was so incongruous that for a moment, Amanda felt as if she must be dreaming. Wait a minute. The idea of *her* believing that was absurd. Blixus Moriarty had certainly changed her life in ways she never could have imagined. Had her father known what he could do way back in L.A. when he seemed to be having nightmares about the criminal? Why had he left her to deal with him anyway? Perhaps when he'd got over his PTSD he'd change back and come help—assuming Blixus was still at large by then, which she certainly hoped he wouldn't be.

"So Blixus did hire people to help him," she said.

"It seems so." Holmes seemed distracted. She had no idea whether he was thinking about strategies to use against Hugh, his lunch, or a forthcoming tryst with Amphora. She didn't have the right to inquire, though, so she moved the conversation on.

"What now then?"

"He has to be stopped, of course," said Holmes. "I must say, that little girl seems to know more about how to do that than we do." He laughed.

"Who is she?" said Amanda.

"No idea. A cousin maybe? I hope she's not a hacker too. I don't see how we could handle two of them."

"No," she said. "I don't either."

The next morning at 9:00 sharp, Balthazar Onion picked Amanda up in his convertible and the two took off for Manchester. Amanda had never ridden in a car with the top down before and hadn't prepared. Her hair whipped around her face the whole way, getting in her mouth and eyes and tickling her so much that she couldn't stop sneezing. Mr. Onion regaled her with tales of his cases, including the strange affair of a dog that had divorced its owner. How that could have happened was somewhat murky, despite his repeated attempts to explain.

The lawyer was a crazy driver and they arrived at Strangeways before 10:30. The new warden was much more conciliatory than Mr. Doodle. A giant of a man with Somalian features, Mr. Okapi slapped the lawyer on the back, kissed Amanda's hand, and ooohed and aahed over Ivy's Fender guitar, which he insisted on trying out. Of course he had to play "Stairway to Heaven," which Mr. Onion told Amanda later was the standard guitar song despite the fact that it was close to fifty years old. The warden wasn't half-bad on the instrument and seemed reluctant to give it up, but an urgent phone call put an end to his impromptu concert and they once again found themselves facing Manny Companion in the visitors' room.

A guard had delivered the shiny red guitar to Manny, who was practically drooling over the thing. If Amanda hadn't been on the other side of the glass she would have offered him a tissue. Fortunately he didn't get saliva on Ivy's instrument and Amanda relaxed.

Unlike Mr. Okapi, Manny did not play "Stairway to Heaven." He played a blues number Amanda was unfamiliar with, and he was amazing. Until now both she and the lawyer had thought he was just talking big, but the man really had soul. When he played, it was as if you'd entered a portal into another universe. Even Mr. Onion was mesmerized, and the guards in the visitors' room were having a hard time keeping straight faces.

When Manny had finished playing—and it was difficult to get him to do so—Mr. Onion said, "So, how about Blixus then?"

Manny looked like he was in seventh heaven and for the longest time he didn't say a word. Finally Amanda had to nudge him. "Mr. Companion, we had a deal. Where is Blixus Moriarty?"

Manny gave Amanda and Mr. Onion a long, hard look and said, "It isn't him you have to worry about. It's the girl."

"You mean Taffeta Tasmania?" said Amanda.

"Yeah," said Manny. "Her."

Amanda and Mr. Onion looked at each other. Finally Amanda said, "You can tell us about her later. What about Blixus?"

Manny opened his mouth to say something. He had just managed to get the word "He's" out when a prisoner sitting at another visitor's station produced a knife out of nowhere and stabbed him in the heart. Within seconds the guards were on the man, wrestling him to the ground, but there was nothing anyone could do for Manny. He was dead.

Amanda and the woman visiting the murderous prisoner shrieked, Mr. Onion tried to lunge through the glass, and Mr. Okapi and more guards appeared on the scene. They whisked Manny's body away, subdued the killer, and escorted Amanda and Mr. Onion back to the warden's office. Ivy's guitar had fallen to the floor and the impact had damaged a corner. The warden returned the instrument to Amanda and promised that he would pay to replace or repair it, whichever Ivy preferred.

Amanda had now seen two people killed in front of her eyes. Was this what being a detective was about? No wonder the teachers were so weird. She wondered how many murders they'd witnessed. The entire way back to Legatum she didn't say a word and either did Mr. Onion. When they arrived at the guard gate she was finally able to squeeze out a question: "Why did that prisoner kill Manny?" Mr. Onion replied that he didn't know, but the warden would be opening an investigation. He promised to phone her later in the day to see how she was doing, and then he was off.

Amanda's first order of business was to talk to Ivy. She felt terrible about the broken guitar, especially since the sacrifice had failed to deliver the information she'd been promised. Whether that would have happened if Manny hadn't been attacked she didn't know. He had told the truth about his guitar skills. Whether he also would have been forthright about Blixus they'd never know.

As it turned out, Ivy wasn't particularly upset about the guitar. She decided to have it fixed, though, because she liked the sound. She was curious about the killer, however, and about what Manny had—and hadn't—said. Why had he been so concerned about Taffeta? What was it about her that made her more dangerous than Blixus? Wasn't Hugh a greater threat, or did Manny not know about him? It seemed that Amanda had left the prison with more questions than answers.

When she told the others about what had happened, they were off like a shot to see what they could learn about Taffeta. Their first stop was Harry Sheriff, who sneered at them and kept his trap shut until Simon tricked him into revealing that he'd met Taffeta in Windermere when a mugger had stolen her purse. Simon, being who he was, concluded that the theft was staged and that Taffeta had been targeting Harry from the start. He didn't tell Harry that, though, figuring that he would just have gotten defensive and tried to make a show of how attractive he was to women.

There was some talk about trying to get Jackie his meat cookbook, but considering what had happened to Manny, Amanda didn't try very hard. When Mr. Onion called, he told her that the warden had suspended all visits to prisoners until further notice, so there went that idea anyway.

After Amanda had spoken with the lawyer her phone rang again. It was Darius Plover.

"Amanda, super revisions," he said with a smile in his voice. "You're hired."

"Thank you, Darius." She was so relieved. She'd had no idea how he would react to her changes. Wait—Darius Plover liked her writing! Hurray!!

"I have some more scenes for you to do if you're ready."

"Absolutely. Any time." She couldn't wait. Nothing this wonderful had ever happened to her. How she'd fit the work in with her other responsibilities she didn't know, but she'd figure it out.

"Say, what's this I hear about King Arthur?" he said.

Amanda just about dropped the phone. How did he know about the coins?

"I, uh—"

"I think this discovery would make a blockbuster film. I want you to work on it with me. Deal?"

He wanted her to work on a new film with him? She had to be dreaming. "Um, did you say—"

"I did. You and me, kid. How about it?"

"Sure!" she said so loudly she scared herself.

"Excellent," he said. "I'll see you Friday then."

What? Here in England? In person?

"Amanda?"

"Um, yes?"

"Friday okay?"

Of course it was. Sunday at 3:00 in the morning would be okay. Darius Plover was coming to meet her. What did it matter when, even if it was in the middle of Professor Feeney's seminar, which had been cancelled anyway?

"Yes. Friday is wonderful. See you then."

Darius's announcement that he was about to arrive in Windermere was just about the worst news Amanda had ever heard. Actually it was the best news she'd heard. No, wait, everything was in chaos and she might have to run off. It was the worst. No, it was the best. After a few minutes during which she weighed just about every possible outcome, she threw up her hands and decided to split the difference. She'd take whatever came her way.

What came her way next turned out to be outrageous, to say the least. Harry Sheriff was indeed expelled from Legatum, but first he was debriefed. He explained the whole series of events to Professor Kindseth. He had met Taffeta, been completely smitten, and resolved to impress her. He'd wanted to take her into the trove but he couldn't bring her in through the school so he'd had to break her in from the outside. That was why he'd stolen Clive's acoustic levitator—to raise the hinges on the outer gates so he could open them. Taffeta had been mightily impressed with that. No doubt that was why she had kidnapped Clive—so he'd make some of those devices for her, although Harry hadn't known about any of that.

Inside the trove Harry had showed the girl the drawers, and she'd tempted him into committing a whole series of misdeeds, asking leading questions like, "Don't you want to know what's in them?" and "Wouldn't it be fun to try to put this puzzle together?" By that time he was so completely under her spell that he'd have done anything for her. He planted a secret camera in Professor Snaffle's office so he could find out how to open the locks. That hadn't worked, but he had learned about the vault in Penrith and had told Taffeta. At that point he hadn't thought about the risk to the metadata. If Taffeta wanted something he'd give it to her, no matter what the consequences might turn out to be. Of course he hadn't known that the metadata wasn't really in the vault. Presumably Taffeta and Nick had learned that when they'd broken into the barrow, but she hadn't discussed that with Harry.

Harry and Taffeta had returned to the vault to make out and had accidentally discovered that the locks were odor-controlled. It seemed that Taffeta made her own perfume, and just by chance the formula happened to match the one the detectives had come up with. When the locks suddenly clicked the pair had investigated, and the girl had convinced Harry to explore the snippets. That was when they'd taken pictures of the secrets to see if they could decode them. What she'd done with the pictures he didn't know.

As if Harry's actions weren't outrageous enough, instead of being angry with him, a bunch of students had turned him into a hero! Many of the girls, including Amphora, defended him. "He was only trying to help." "How can you be so harsh with him?" "If you kick him out I'm going too." They began to see him as a martyr. At the same time many of the boys admired him for scoring with such a beautiful girl. They wanted to know how he'd met her, how he'd won her over, and whether she had a sister. Amanda, Ivy, Clive, and Simon were so disgusted they could barely stand to be around these kids. Holmes was furious, and his outright refusal to keep his mouth shut led to a number of quarrels with Amphora.

Amid this craziness the remaining Punitori left the campus. They were pleasant enough to the students but they ignored the other teachers, even the Neutrals. Amanda thought their behavior small-minded. She was very fond of Professor Also in particular, and she didn't like seeing her or any of them behave this way.

As the group was heading toward the door to the parking lot, she noticed that Alexei Dropoff was with them.

"Alexei!" she called. Why bother to call him Mr. Dropoff when he was leaving?

"Amanda, dahlink," he said without enthusiasm.

"You're going?"

"I'm afraid so. The rift between myself and Noel has grown too wide. He supports those dreadful Realists. I am more of the mind of these soldiers. And so I shall betake myself to Scotland."

"We're at war with the Moriartys too. Can't you stay and fight with us?"

"I'm afraid not, my love. Noel and I no longer agree, and besides, I'm awfully fond of your Professor Pargeter. I've discovered that I can't live without her."

The poisons teacher? Honoria Pargeter was one of the most cantankerous, ungenerous, nutty teachers on the staff. That was one for the books.

"I'll miss you," she said, trying to hide her surprise.

"Of course. We've always got along." She noticed that he didn't say he'd miss her too.

"Goodbye, Alexei. Good luck."

"Dasvidaniya, dahlink," he said, and then he was gone.

Amanda felt completely drained. She decided to lie down for a while, but as she was heading to her room she ran into Professor Kindseth.

"I'm afraid I have bad news, Amanda," he said. "The rescue team has looked everywhere for Headmaster Thrillkill, Miss Halpin, and Mr. Bramble. They found signs that someone had been living in those northern tunnels but no one was there when they arrived."

This was disconcerting. "Any clues at all?"

"Not yet," he said softly. It seemed that the energy had gone out of him as well. "We're going to have to regroup."

"Have you told Ivy?" she said.

"No. I've only just found out myself."

"Do you have any theories?"

"Not a one." His phone rang. His ringtone was the theme music from "Rear Window." He pulled it out of his pocket. "What's this?"

The two of them looked at the screen and Amanda gasped. There, quite the worse for wear, was the streaming image of Thrillkill, Fern, Gordon, Despina, Hill, and Jeffrey tied up and surrounded by a throng of ghoulish figures. Whether they were male or female was hard to tell, but they looked like they'd been living below ground their whole lives. Scratches marred their green-white skin, unwashed hair fell in repulsive strings, and dark circles ringed their bulbous eyes. They stood menacingly against a granite wall upon which the words "wretch society" had been scrawled in white letters.

"Despina!" Amanda screamed, and the connection failed. The screen went dark. "Professor, get them back!"

"I'm trying," said Professor Kindseth, punching and swiping. "Nothing's happening." He fiddled and fiddled without success. Finally he shook the phone, but the picture was gone for good. "Who were those people?"

Amanda looked up at him. He was so short that she barely had to tilt her head. His lips were white and his eyes were wide. He looked as if he'd seen a ghost.

"I'm not sure," she said. Of course the idea was ridiculous, and yet here was the most solid proof she'd seen. She'd have to say what she was thinking, if only so he'd laugh and dismiss the notion for the insane thing it was and they could get on with solving the problem.

She looked at him again. The color hadn't returned to his face. If anything he was even paler, like the things on the screen. That frightened her. He was never afraid of anything. What did he know that she didn't?

Of course—that was it. Something wasn't adding up big time. Despite all their observations and theories, the kids hadn't been able to figure out the mysteries because they lacked vital information. And who had that information? Who else—the teachers. There was so much they were still holding back. With their layers and layers of secrets and lies, they were much more like onions than the lawyer. Even Professor Kindseth, the nicest of all of them, knew things she couldn't imagine. She was beginning to think she and her friends would never solve anything without that knowledge. It wasn't fair, and it wasn't right to be left out. They'd have to learn the secrets themselves or force the issue with the teachers. And it would have to happen soon, before things deteriorated beyond all possibility of repair.

But first they'd have to rescue Thrillkill and the others, and the only way to do that was to say what she was thinking, even if it wasn't much, and even if it was crazy.

"Professor?" she said. He looked at her numbly. "I might have a clue. Do you want to hear it?" He nodded ever so slightly.

She couldn't understand why she was so nervous. She cleared her throat but it didn't help. She could hardly get the words out.

"Those people we saw?" She waited for him to nod. He didn't. He seemed lost in his own world. "I know this sounds crazy," she said, "but if I didn't know better I'd say they were zombies."

For a moment he said nothing. He looked off into the distance, as if he were thinking about something long ago and far away. And then in the softest voice imaginable he said, "Yes. She is."

DISCUSSION QUESTIONS FOR YOUR READING GROUP

If you were in Headmaster Thrillkill's position—students missing, parents threatening to sue, and Legatum's most important possession destroyed—what would you do?

Should Amanda take Simon's advice and get back together with Holmes? Why?

Do you think Warden Doodle is being fair in not letting Manny have a guitar? Why? Can you play air guitar?

How would you attempt to keep the teachers from splitting up? Do you think the Punitori are being unnecessarily stubborn? Do you agree with any of the factions?

If you had a mynah bird, what would you teach it to say?

What do you think the zombies really are? How about drawing some?

How do you feel about bees? Could you wear a coat of them the way Gordon does?

How do you feel about the way Amanda reacts when she finds out why Harry is grinning at her? How would you react in her situation?

Did you guess who the hacker was? Who did you think it was?

What is your favorite zoo animal? Why?

If you discovered a mysterious sarcophagus wide open, what would you do?

Would you break into Crocodile's flat to investigate? Why?

What would you do if you discovered a mysterious silver coin with a king's face on it?

Who is your favorite Legatum teacher? Why?

Was Amanda right to make the film a musical? Why? What would you do if Thrillkill assigned you to make a film like that?

Where do you think *The Detective's Bible* is?

What do you think of Scapulus Holmes? Would you change him in any way? How and why?

What summer seminars do you think the teachers should offer? (Please let me know so I can work them into the curriculum.)

Is Amanda still too bossy? What do you think she needs to learn about herself and the world?

Would you rather have authentic King Arthur coins or leprechauns' gold? Why?

How would you help David Wiffle if you could? Would you?

Q AND A WITH AUTHOR
PAULA BERINSTEIN

Where did you get the idea for the purple rainbows?

Brainstorming. I make lists of all kinds of potentially interesting phenomena, creatures, events, and so on, and then pick the ones I think will work the best. I chose purple because I thought the color would be very dramatic.

I also liked the idea of a broken rainbow. I thought just reversing the colors would create a rainbow that can't exist, but lo and behold I found out that there are such rainbows! However, to my knowledge, there's no such thing as a rainbow where all the colors are completely out of order.

Of course as Hugh experiments with the rainbows and discovers how well purple works for his purposes, he drops the other colors and focuses completely on purple. Then it's just a matter of getting the right purple and the right amount of energy.

As it turned out, the fact that purple doesn't have its own wavelength was extremely convenient, although I didn't know that when I started outlining the book. There really is a theory that non-spectral-colored light can be used to detect hidden structures. See the article "New Frontiers for Color" at the Color Matters site, http://www.colormatters.com/color-and-science/new-frontiers-for-color. If you can use non-spectral colors to detect hidden things, then why not use purple, which is a non-spectral color, to look for gold and quartz, which give off electrical signals? Hence the purple rainbows.

Why did you include bees in this story?

I asked a friend of mine if there was anything special he'd like to see in my stories, and he said bees and ninjas. I was able to pull off the bees, but obviously there are no ninjas in the story.

Will there be ninjas in another story?

At the moment I have no plans that include ninjas.

Have you ever actually looked for a needle in a haystack?

Not literally, no. Sometimes when I park my car in a huge lot, like at a shopping center, I feel like I'm looking for a needle in a haystack, but no, I never have. I'd like to, though. I'd like to see if I can find it using technology. (My cat swallowed a needle and thread once, and the vet found them using x-rays. Fortunately she was able to remove them and the cat is now fine. Needless to say, I'm very careful when I sew around her now.)

Would Wink really have been able to jam a lockbox in a haystack?

I doubt it. But he was a resourceful guy, so you never know.

Is there really such a thing as an odor-controlled lock?

Yes! Google this article: "A Novel Odor Key Technique for Security Applications Using Electronic Nose System" by Mahmoud Z. Iskandarani.

Why do you exaggerate so much?

Fiction is larger than life. All novelists, playwrights, and screenwriters exaggerate. Shakespeare was a huge exaggerator. Charles Dickens too. Of course you have to do it right or it detracts from the story.

What does Punitori mean?

The punishers. Like that, do you?

Do you think you do it right?

I hope so. Time will tell. A writer can never be sure her readers will receive her work the way she envisions it. I've been astonished at some of the things people have said about my books. One person who shall remain nameless said, "My goodness. You have an astounding amount of dialog in the books." Another said, "Shouldn't the kids be taking English and math?" So you never know.

ABOUT THE AUTHOR

Paula Berinstein is the former producer and host of the popular podcast, The Writing Show (www.writingshow.com). She lives in Los Angeles.

CPSIA information can be obtained at www.ICGtesting.com
Printed in the USA
LVOW10s1808081215

465959LV00025B/1721/P